THE SUNDERED STARS

THE STARBORNE SAGA
BOOK ONE

H.E. BAUMAN

First paperback edition May 2025

Cover design by Mayhem Cover Creations

Indie Edits with Jeanine

ISBN 978-1-965479-02-5 (paperback)

ISBN 978-1-965479-03-2 (hardcover)

ISBN 978-1-965479-01-8 (ebook)

www.hebauman.com

To those who have been told they're broken and unlovable

Content Warning

Thank you for picking up *The Sundered Stars*, the first book in The Starborne Saga. The story includes themes and events that may not be suitable for some readers:

- Fantasy and magical violence, including character deaths and suicide

- Descriptions of blood, injuries, and chronic pain

- Casual alcohol consumption

- Loss of home world/planetary destruction

- War and imperialism

- References to past intimate partner violence (domestic violence)

Please take care of yourself as you read.

Chapter 1

Mo was no stranger to having an energy gun pointed at her head. She could either let this scumbag pull the trigger or wrestle it from him before he found the courage.

His leather gloves creaked as he tightened his grip on the weapon. "Who the fuck are you and what the fuck do you want?"

This was one of the problems with being a bounty hunter. Marks like this—the murderers, outlaws, and criminals of space—never went in the easy way. This target was no different. Gideon Benre had been accused of killing some arms dealer's son on Ibara, a dingy and dark underworld of a planet out in the Zel'dov System. It was the latest in his long line of murder charges according to the report Mo had read.

Those who'd put the bounty on his head would surely get their own type of justice, but who was Mo to judge? Justice was justice, and a payday was a payday.

"I asked who you are, sweetheart," Gideon sneered, his thin lips pulling up and revealing sticky strings of spittle and teeth yellowed by too many years of smoking.

It was a good thing Mo had her helmet on and he couldn't hear her gag. She lifted her hands, but she itched to reach for one of the weapons at her belt—or the magic pulsing in the very center of her being. "Name's none of your business."

Mora Cevi's name was *nobody's* business.

"Just out for a walk," she added when he just stared at her.

Gideon chortled, a hearty belly laugh despite his gangly frame. "Here?" He gestured to the darkening desert around them. The second sun would finish setting in just an hour, maybe less. "In this shithole?"

She hadn't meant to stumble into him. She'd been tracking him across the arid land, going off intel the client and a series of civilians had provided. She'd been so distracted by the way her bones and joints ached that she hadn't realized how close she'd gotten. She was better than that.

"It's as good as going for a walk on the beach, don't you think?" she quipped.

"Bullshit. Who sent you?" he hissed as he took a step forward. He was easily three heads taller than Mo, forcing her to tilt her head back slightly to look up into his narrow, dark brown eyes.

"Nobody."

"Bullshit," he said again.

His stance didn't change. Nothing in the air changed, though it should've by now.

"Cass, where are you?" Mo whispered into her comms. This would be a lot easier if Cass was in position and could just take this man out, especially with the way Mo's body hurt. Damn hyperspace travel really got to her sometimes.

"Well?" His finger tightened on the trigger.

Shit. Mo was going to have to do this the hard way.

"All I know, Gideon"—Mo inched forward—"is that you've pissed off the wrong people if they're sending me to clean up their problems."

Recognition flickered across his face, and color rose to his gaunt white cheeks. "Fuck the Bronze Brotherhood and fuck you," the man snapped. "Stupid whore."

"Yeah, yeah, I've heard worse than that."

Mo slammed into Gideon, the edge of her spaulder jamming into the soft flesh between his chest and underarm. He toppled to the ground, and his gun fell at Mo's feet. She grabbed it with her left hand and pulled the hilt of her sword from her belt with her right. Her thumb found its familiar spot on the trigger, and the blade ignited, casting a cool white glow over the man.

Fuck, that hurt. Mo's already aching body throbbed more. This was a bad night for her to be on the hunt. And where was Cass?

"Now," Mo said, pointing both weapons at Gideon. "It looks like it's time for you to come with me."

"You'd turn me over to the Bronze Brotherhood?" he asked. "They'll kill me."

"It's not my job to give a shit." Mo gestured to the left with the gun. "Ship's that way. Get moving."

Coughing, Gideon slowly rolled onto his side, then pushed to his knees. He glared at her as he stood to his full height.

Mo raised the blaster. He lurched forward, and before Mo could get a shot off, the high-pitched squeal of an energy rifle broke through the air. The man stumbled, clutching his upper arm as he fell to his knees again.

"Fuck!" he shouted.

"Sorry about that," came Cass's light, soothing voice through Mo's helmet.

"You good?" Mo asked.

"Had a little trouble."

"Meaning?"

"I'll meet you by the ship in ten, tops."

Frowning, Mo disengaged her sword and reattached the hilt to her belt. She stooped, grabbed the man's thin arm, and hauled him to his feet. "One bad move and I'll blow your ass to pieces," she said, pressing the blaster into the small of his back. "Or my friend will put a shot right between your eyes. Your choice."

"Better than the Bronze Brotherhood getting to me," Gideon barked, though he remained pliant as Mo cuffed his hands behind him.

"You really don't want to piss me off." Mo nudged him with the gun again. "Start walking."

He trudged forward with slow, heavy steps. Any other day, Mo would've been annoyed. But she was grateful now; her joints protested slightly less at this pace.

The second sun continued its descent as they passed through the desert. Mo's ship, *The Revenant*, sat proud on the horizon, its metallic hull glowing in the last remnants of the sunset. The lights in the cabin were on, a beacon against the darkening night. A lithe shadow sometimes popped into view—Cass.

Cass Farr was Mo's best friend and fellow bounty hunter, a sharpshooter with one of the best shots in the entire Federation. When they were younger, Cass had been scouted by the Federation Space Command to join their elite program, but she'd refused. Cass was one of two people Mo would ever work with. Their trust went beyond that of colleagues, their bond deep and forged by years of pain and sweat and blood.

"Whatever they're paying you, we can triple it," said Gideon.

We? That must've been what slowed Cass down; this man had to have a partner, which meant their payday just got bigger. She couldn't help but smile a little at the thought.

"Let me walk away," he said, "and I'll make it worth your while. More credits than you've ever *seen*."

"I highly doubt that."

"I just need to divest a few—"

"Divest a few what?" Mo asked. "Last I heard, you're a bottom of the barrel murderer who steals what little he does have from other criminals." At least, that was what the single-page report on the man had said that Mo had received from the Syndicate.

"Maybe I am, but you know who the real criminals are? All those senators and councillors sitting on Aerilia, oppressing the people and hiding in their palaces and estates while they send the rest of us to war."

"I'm not at war, and you're a fucking murderer, so you're not exactly innocent," she said, shoving him forward. "Stop wasting my time."

"Surely you know about the recent Ascended attacks," the man said, turning toward Mo. His face was shadowed, but the night vision in her helmet revealed his pinched expression. "Those of us living out here in the outer systems? We're going to need weapons to fight them off. Let me go, and I promise I'll bring all the weapons you could need!"

"I have what I need," Mo snapped, adjusting her grip on the gun. "Walk."

"But do others?" Gideon asked.

"And how are you going to get 'the people' these weapons?" asked Mo. "You murdered someone close to the Bronze Brotherhood, the second largest arms dealing gang in the outer systems. Doubt anyone's welcoming *you* with open arms."

"I could try—"

"Like you tried to run away? From where I'm standing, you've got a terrible success rate."

Gideon must have known what was good for him, because he started moving again. Mo shook her head. He wasn't wrong about the Ascended attacks. The Ascended were a powerful empire, at war with the Cosmic Federation on and off for generations. Things had escalated in the last few decades.

The people of Miduna—Mo and Cass's planet of residence—already had what they needed, and besides, Mo couldn't worry about every other damn planet in the Federation. There were thousands of them, too many to even know by name. Why was this man speaking as if she were leading the charge in protecting the outer systems? That was not her job. In fact, that was far above her pay grade. It was *supposed* to be the Federation's job, not that they were any good at it. Mo already had a job cleaning up the messes people made, and while she was great, she did not want to add the entire Federation to her list of clients.

A few more minutes passed and the distance between Mo and *The Revenant* closed. Cass stepped off the entry ramp, the last rays of sunlight catching on her opalescent armor. Cass's energy rifle poked up from behind her left shoulder, and her hand rested on the pistol at her hip. Her helmet and dark visor hid her expression from Mo, but she knew that stance. Cass was ready to go.

"I've got the second one already in lockup," came Cass's modulated voice.

Gideon stiffened.

"Thought he'd watch your back?" taunted Cass, a clear smile in her voice. "You two make a lousy team."

"Come on," Mo said, shoving Gideon up the entry ramp. "Let's re-unite you with your friend."

"I work alone!" he protested.

"Sure you do."

Their steps echoed on the floor as they entered *The Revenant*. It was a converted small cargo ship, modified after its time serving the Federation Space Command decades earlier. It could operate with a crew of two but accommodate up to four, had two decks, space to sleep and live, and a cargo hold. It was old, but it was Mo's. She'd bought it so she and Cass would always have a place to call their own. They'd spent years fixing it up and upgrading it. They'd outfitted it with two laser canons, new shielding, and a top-tier hyperdrive.

She nudged Gideon up the ramp to the ship's second deck. His co-operation stopped, and Mo half dragged the man through the kitchen and into the command room just outside the cockpit. She'd had the old storage closet converted into a small brig. Some of her ... *colleagues* ... thought it was an odd place to put a prison, but Mo liked to keep her targets close. Leaving them alone in the cargo bay—the farthest part of the ship—always seemed like too much of a risk.

Inside, another man dressed in worn traveling clothes and leather armor similar to Gideon's was hunched over on the floor. Whatever weapons he'd had, Cass had obviously disarmed him. "Sorry, Gideon." He tilted his head up, the tattoos on his pale forehead obscured partially by a large bruise and the knit cap covering his hair and ears. "The other one was like a ghost, I couldn't even—"

Mo shoved Gideon inside the brig. Even that much movement made her joints protest. She couldn't take it anymore. Her armor was getting to be too heavy, too constricting. Mo desperately wanted to take her helmet off, to take all her armor off.

"Shut *up*." Gideon stared daggers at his companion. "Just shut up!" He fixated back on Mo. "Listen, if—"

Mo forced what she knew was her nastiest smile, the smile she'd practiced in the mirror for years. He couldn't see her face, but he'd hear the venom in her voice. "I already told you, Gideon, I'm far worse than the fucking Bronze Brotherhood. Now shut up unless you want me to cut your tongue out. I don't want to listen to your nonsense for the whole flight."

He snapped his jaw shut. Mo slammed the brig door closed, then punched her code into the keypad next to it. The door hissed as the secondary locks engaged. Gideon watched her, but he didn't dare make another sound, so Mo turned on her heel and joined Cass in the cockpit.

As soon as the door sealed behind her, Mo yanked her helmet off, relishing the ship's dry, recycled air as it caressed her skin and settled deep in her lungs. She pushed back the hairs that had escaped her braid and tickled her nose and forehead.

Cass had taken her helmet off too. She'd dyed the tips of her black hair a deep purple in recent weeks, and the color suited her. So did the sleek, angular cut just above her shoulders.

Mo dropped her helmet into the empty crew station behind the captain's chair, then climbed into her position at the helm.

"Ready?" Cass asked from the copilot's seat. Her small, wide nose wrinkled as their marks shouted again about offering the women a better payday.

"This is your last warning!" Mo yelled. "I really don't want to get my ship bloody, but I will." The men hushed, and she rolled her eyes. "Let's just get out of here," she said, flipping several switches on the dashboard in front of her. It lit up, a blend of blinking lights and panels.

Cass engaged her side, and when the system gave them the all clear for takeoff, they kicked the engines on. The ship lurched off the ground, then sped off through the atmosphere. Mo braced herself as they cleared the planet and Cass reached for the hyperdrive button.

"Course charted back to Miduna," Cass said. "Ready?"

Mo nodded. "Do it."

That inevitable pause right before the jump to faster-than-light travel hit. Mo held her breath, and then they were off, hurtling back toward home—and their payday.

Chapter 2

As soon as the lush green landscape of Miduna's capital, Kalyndra, came into view, Mo relaxed back into her seat. They were finally home for a while, at least until they had to go out on another job.

Part of her thought to take a week off and enjoy their recent hard work, but the other part thought better of it. She and Cass needed the credits if they were finally going to get out of the bounty hunting game for good, and they had a long way to go before they could retire. After more than a decade as a bounty hunter and even longer training with the Syndicate, Mo was tired. Leaving one's profession and starting over were never easy, but both Mo and Cass had dreams of a quiet life, one in which they could supplement any financial needs with odd jobs and investments rather than long manhunts.

If Mo was honest with herself, she had no idea what she'd do when she someday had that quiet life. Her life hadn't been quiet for a very, very long time. But that was a problem her future self could sort out.

"Let's get this over with," Mo said, straightening and piloting them down to the surface.

They soared above the city, circling down until reaching a small shipyard on the southwestern side of town. Only a couple of other ships were in port, including a familiar silver and blue ship that gleamed in the late afternoon sun. The high walls of the yard did little to block out the elements.

"Looks like Kynn's back from whatever nasty corner of the galaxy he's been in," Mo said.

Cass smirked. "He does take the worst jobs, doesn't he?"

"Good for us, bad for him." Mo shook her head. "He'll never learn."

"Which is still good for us," Cass quipped.

They finished their final landing preparations and powered *The Revenant* down. Mo couldn't wait to wrap this contract up, come back home to her beloved ship, and crawl into bed. But it'd be a while yet.

She hoisted herself up from the captain's chair, groaning as her joints popped. They were especially stiff. She really needed a damn break, or at least to spend some credits on another few vials of soltherin. It was the only medication that ever helped her. But that stuff was expensive, especially in the outer systems. Healing from a sunshaper would be expensive too. Maybe a good night's sleep would help.

"You good?" Cass asked, eyeing Mo warily. "You're moving like shit."

"Love you too," Mo said with a wry smile.

"I can take them in if you want."

"The walk'll be good for me."

Cass shrugged a slender shoulder. "If you say so."

Both women put their helmets back on. There was a certain comfort in not being seen, even if her suit was sometimes claustrophobic. Besides, the tinted visor made Miduna's glaring sun more bearable and kept people from staring.

Mo opened the cockpit doors. The travel hadn't even taken twelve hours, but both marks were passed out in the brig. She unlocked the cell, and both men groaned as they tried to sit up.

"Out," she ordered. When they barely moved, she added, "Before I make you."

That got them going. Cass took the smaller man; she was a petite woman, a few inches shorter than Mo and a little more than half her weight. She was lithe, agile, and quick. And though Mo was fast, too, her speed was nothing like her best friend's. Cass had some of the best reflexes she'd ever seen—a great quality in a sharpshooter. If anyone was going to be at Mo's back in a fight, it was Cass Farr.

They disembarked from *The Revenant*, only nodding at the attendant dressed in a black and blue uniform. There was a rotation of attendants here, all hired by the Starlight Syndicate, one of the premier bounty hunting guilds in the Federation. It was one of the perks of membership, even if Mo hated all costs associated with the Syndicate.

"Best to get moving," called the attendant. They were Luxinae, one of the founding species of the Federation. Their pale blue skin, white hair, and dark blue geometric tattoos didn't stand out among Miduna's population. All sorts of people called the planet home. "New FSC ships are coming in daily. Rumor has it more are on their way, Vanguards too."

Mo wrinkled her nose. The Federation Space Command? They had a base on the outskirts of Kalyndra already, but why would they be sending more people out? Especially Vanguards, the military's most elite soldiers, people with incredible weapons skills, physical prowess, and even magic.

What were they coming to Miduna for? All things considered, Miduna was a quiet planet. Crime was well-managed, and it wasn't a major political player. It was out of the way and all but forgotten by the Federation despite its wealth of trading posts and commerce. It was better that way. Everything the Federation touched turned to ash. They only cared about themselves.

"Thanks for the heads up," Cass called over her shoulder.

They passed through the tunnel leading from the shipyard out to the streets of Kalyndra. This part of the city wasn't as nice as others, but Mo didn't mind. She and Cass could take care of themselves, and besides, nobody was going to bother them. Their armor meant something, especially around these parts.

Cass led the way with her mark, whose name Mo still didn't know. She didn't care. The Syndicate could sort all this out for them.

The Syndicate's headquarters weren't far from here; they practically owned this section of the capital. Just half the usual number of street vendors were out now, but Mo still made a mental note to stop for dinner on the way back to the ship. Her stomach growled as they passed a stall with grilled meat and fresh flatbread. Even the sidewalks were less busy than usual.

"Told you the Aerilians were out to oppress us," said Gideon. "You heard that attendant, that—"

He snapped his mouth shut as they turned a corner. Up ahead were six Federation soldiers dressed in sterile black armor with the FSC's logo—an indigo and silver shield broken by a sword—emblazoned on the front.

Mo hated them.

But nothing illegal was going on here; bounty hunting was perfectly acceptable in the Federation, a way to fill in the gaps left by the government, especially during wartime. It wasn't unheard of for bounty hunters to even take contracts sanctioned by the government and military on occasion. Traitors, all of them. Well, traitor may have been too strong of a word, but still, Mo would rather die before taking a contract for anyone at the FSC.

She and Cass exchanged a look but kept escorting their prisoners. The soldiers paid them no notice, instead continuing on their way, wherever that was.

They passed more well-worn tan and gray buildings, turning down several streets and more Federation soldiers before Cass stopped in front of a heavily fortified steel door at the bottom of a three-story building. The fortress actually went several stories underneath the city, too, a massive place the Starlight Syndicate worked out of. Though they were on fine terms with the Federation government, sellswords weren't always trusted, and that was actually something Mo could agree with most people on. She trusted Cass, of course, and Kynn Sathir, their longtime friend.

Cass knocked on the door, the knuckles of her armored glove meeting the metal with a heavy crack. A slider opened, revealing a pair of white eyes.

"Oh," came the light voice on the other side.

The slider closed, and a moment later, the door creaked open, revealing the dimly lit interior. Mo and Cass prodded Gideon and his companion inside the dark building. Gideon's muscles trembled under Mo's hand.

"I can't change your mind?" he asked her.

"If you don't want to face the consequences for your actions, stop murdering people," Mo said dryly.

"Ril's in his office," said that soft voice again—Jala, the Ivari enforcer on duty this time of day. White markings covered her pink skin, and she had a new piercing at the long point of her right ear. She towered over Mo, as all Ivari did.

Like Luxinae and Humans, Ivari were one of the founding species of the Federation. So were Sorthians. The four groups made up the vast majority of the Federation's population, though some species from independent worlds and even some Ascended defectors called the Federation home.

Mo and Cass nodded their thanks to Jala, then forced Gideon and his companion to keep walking. Several bounty hunters passed the women and their prisoners, and they all ignored each other. Such was the way among the Syndicate, at least when Cass and Mo were involved. Their impeccable record—and first choice when it came to contracts—meant they weren't the most popular members.

They took the elevator up two floors, then turned right. Another left turn and they arrived at Ril Staga's office doors. Guards flanked each side, younger members of the Syndicate who were still proving their worth. Mo and Cass had been those guards once, but not in many years. They'd been training with the Syndicate since they were just eight years old and had started taking contracts younger than most at just sixteen. Now they had twelve years under their belts. Twelve years too many.

The guard on the right nodded at Mo, then opened the corresponding door as her companion opened the one on the left. Cass and Mo forced their prisoners through the doorway.

Ril Staga's office hadn't changed in years. It was the same large, ornately decorated space it had always been, filled with fine furniture and rich tapestries from around Miduna and other systems. Gifts and prizes he'd received over the years, he claimed. Mo once heard some older members talking about how he'd stolen everything from a gang leader on the opposite side of the planet, and she believed that was entirely plausible.

"The Demon and the Phantom," Ril drawled, standing up from behind his desk with a smile. "Back so soon?"

Mo and Cass had worked hard to earn their reputation, but something uneasy prickled down her spine as Ril said her call sign. *The Demon.* She kept her back straight, grateful for her dark armor that would hide her face from Ril.

"You know we're efficient," Cass said coolly.

For all the gaudiness of his office, Ril Staga kept his personal appearance simple. He always wore a black leather jacket, dark gray pants, and black boots. His only weapons were two blasters, one on each hip. He'd just recently started shaving his head, and he ran a brown hand over his scalp. Like Mo and Cass, he was Human.

"That you are, two of my top performers!" Ril sat back down and reached for the top drawer on his desk. He pulled out a data pad and began tapping on its screen. "This was the job for the Bronze Brotherhood, right?"

"Gideon Benre and his partner we picked up on the way," Mo said.

Gideon tensed, but he kept his mouth shut.

Ril glanced up from the tablet, one thick eyebrow raised. "Partner?"

"I assume you'll work out the details of an increased payment?" she asked. "Unless the Brotherhood would rather not have both."

"I'll ensure you get all the credits you're due," Ril said with a nod.

Of course he would. The Syndicate took a cut from all member-fulfilled contracts. It was how they kept everything running smoothly. *Or how Ril affords everything he wants*, Mo thought as the Syndicate leader set his tablet down, then poured rich red wine into a crystalline goblet.

He used his free hand to push a button at the edge of his desk. The doors swung open, and two more enforcers entered. Mo didn't know their names, either, but they took Gideon and his partner, who complained and protested the entire time.

"You're already past this month's quota, but you two looking for more work?" Ril asked once the doors were closed and the three of them were alone.

Mo already knew they were past their quota. She kept careful records of every mission and every bounty after Ril had tried to stiff them out of a payment once years ago. An honest mistake, he'd said, but Mo didn't trust it.

"Depends on what you've got," Mo said.

Most bounty hunters took jobs directly from Syndicate job boards around the Federation, but Mo and Cass often got top pick, offered up by Ril himself. Technically he could offer the contracts to multiple hunters, but that was discouraged. Rare. "Competition doesn't bring community" was what Ril had always said to them, but Mo didn't see how there *wasn't* competition inherent to their jobs. The best bounty hunters got the best jobs and the most money, simple as that.

"All manner of things."

"We want whatever pays the highest," Mo said. "At least five thousand credits each." If she was going to leave the planet again, it had to be worth it. Her body needed a break, and that would help replenish some of the money they'd been spending on ship repairs, gear, and even Mo's medicine.

Ril's eyebrows raised again. "Five thousand each?" He shook his head.

"There's got to be something," Cass said. "We used to get higher payouts all the time."

"You know how things are," Ril said. "Nobody wants to spend anymore. Not when things are looking down."

After so much turmoil with the Federation-Ascended war going into its third decade, and with unrest around the Federation, people were tightening their purse strings. Mo understood the inclination, but this was how she and Cass made their living. They couldn't fall back down to minuscule payouts. They weren't new recruits.

"So?" Cass shifted her weight and put a hand on her hip. "You've got to have *something*."

"Well ..." Ril pursed his lips. "The FSC is looking for additional security for a group of archaeologists they're escorting to a site outside of Kalyndra."

"What's that shit got to do with us?" Mo asked.

"That *shit* is paying fifteen thousand credits per person, Mora. Isn't that what you wanted?"

"What could they possibly need that much security for?" she asked.

"You know how it goes." He sighed and relaxed back into his chair. "One whiff of Separatist sentiments and they finally leave the Inner Systems to pay us a visit. They want to be extra careful."

"So bullshit politics is why they're going to clog up our streets and ports?" Mo asked.

"As usual," Cass said.

"That, and increased Ascended attacks on the Federation's borders," Ril said, then pushed another small button on his desk.

Mo frowned. She never cared much for politics, especially when it was clear nothing was going to change in the Federation. She heard bits and pieces about the war, but she didn't keep as close an eye on it as she should. Miduna wasn't near the border, but it wasn't in the safety of the Inner Systems either.

"How bad's it getting?" Mo asked.

"An attack on Ender Station yesterday resulted in over three thousand casualties," he said. "Separatists, though? Nothing to worry about here. It's just talk."

That was how it always was. It wasn't like the Separatists had the means to break away from the Federation, and as loathe as Mo was to admit it, doing so in the middle of a war with the Ascended would probably be a mistake. The independent worlds outside of Federation protection were constantly falling to the Ascended's colonization attempts.

Ril's office door slid open. A tall, muscular Human man with dark brown skin strode in, his bronze saber hilt glinting in the low light. Mo would know that saber and his dark green jacket anywhere.

Kynn Sathir, second best bounty hunter on Miduna, second only to Mo and Cass.

"Nice of you to join us, Silencer," Ril drawled. The use of Kynn's call sign was so foreign—and so unnecessary. "I was just telling these two about the contract."

Kynn stopped next to Mo, smiling down at her. "And let me guess, Mo's not ready to take it?"

She glared up at him. He was two heads taller than her. She'd known Kynn almost her entire life, and he'd always had a way of both irritating her and endearing her to him. In fact, Mo hadn't realized how much she'd missed him until he'd walked into that room. They were usually on separate contracts and rarely on Miduna at the same time; Kynn liked to work alone more often than not. He hadn't always been like that, but things changed the older they all got.

Even though they weren't a permanent team, Kynn also knew her just as well as Cass did. If Cass was her sister, Kynn was their older brother: protective, mildly annoying, and beloved to them both, even if he wasn't around as much lately.

"Haven't decided," Mo said, turning back to Ril.

"The Midunian Council has assured me the FSC will be out of our hair soon, once they've completed their assignment." Ril sighed again. "You want the job or not?"

"How many are they looking for?" Mo asked.

"Four or five, but I figure that you three are more than equivalent to that and can negotiate higher pay for you, probably twenty thousand each."

Mo pressed her lips together. Twenty thousand credits each?

Shit, Mo *hated* the Federation and the FSC. They weren't worth a damn thing. And yet they had deep pockets.

"Mo?" Cass murmured. "What're you thinking?"

Shit, Mo *really* hated this. There she'd been, just minutes before, thinking that anyone who took a Federation contract was a traitor. And now here she was, considering taking one herself.

But twenty thousand credits each? That would cover living expenses and ship repairs for nearly an entire year, and they could funnel everything else into savings for retirement. With that kind of boost, they could possibly even quit bounty hunting in the next few years.

And besides, weren't they really going to be helping civilians, not the FSC? Those scholars or professors or whatever deserved to feel safe while they worked.

Kynn raised his eyebrows at her with a silent question, and Cass tilted her head slightly.

Was Mo willing to go back on her promise to never take a contract like this?

"Fine," Mo said to Ril. "We'll take it. What do we need to know?"

Chapter 3

"Watch it, Lyre!"

A fiery shield flared to life in front of Ezra. He relished the heat, the way his magic absorbed the discharge from Jarek's blaster. Sweat poured down Ezra's face and back, soaking into the gym's training mats as he rolled away from the swipe of Kira's blade. He pushed to his feet in one swift move, pivoting to face his team. Ezra smirked. Talon was already down, out of the exercise based on the rules of the game. Just two more ...

"Wipe that smug look off your face, asshole!" called Darius.

"You'll have to do it yourself!" Ezra yelled back.

Darius and Talon laughed—a reaction Ezra often pulled from his team during drills—but neither Jarek nor Kira broke their concentration. Their black Vanguard armor obscured their faces, but it was for their own good. Their own protection.

Ezra hit the trigger on the hilt in his right hand. His energy sword ignited, casting a golden glow across the gym's floor. Ezra smirked again.

He charged.

Kira met his blade with hers, igniting in a clash of blue and yellow sparks. He shoved her away, spinning out of Jarek's range just in time. Ezra collided with Kira again, grabbing her arm with his left hand and yanking. She stumbled and disengaged her sword; the blade shrank away. Ezra tapped her with the butt of his hilt, and she was out.

"Fuck you," Kira said with a laugh, her voice modulated through her helmet. "You better win this one, Jarek!"

Ezra pivoted toward the younger man. Jarek took aim with his blaster.

Ezra charged, ignoring the questioned shouts of his team. Unlike Jarek and Kira, Ezra wasn't in his armor.

He liked to train without it. Liked the risk, the danger in wielding energy weapons without any protection. It helped him feel prepared for anything out on the war front, where so much could go wrong.

His shoulder slammed into Jarek's midsection. Ezra grunted; Vanguard armor may have been lightweight, but it was durable and *hard*. He'd have a bruise, no doubt.

Jarek lost his balance. Ezra swept his legs out from under him, and when Jarek was on his back, Ezra re-engaged his sword. The blade roared to life and reflected off Jarek's visor.

"Alright, alright!" Jarek said, holding his hands up. "I forfeit, Commander. Again."

Ezra's blade disappeared. He attached the hilt to his belt, then helped Jarek back to his feet.

"You don't have to call me that, Jarek," Ezra said. "You know that."

He may have been their leader, but Ezra wasn't a fan of such formal rules. Hierarchy was important on the battlefield, but here, in this gym? They could be more casual.

They weren't the first team to push him on the issue. In fact, this was his fifth team in ten years. There'd been casualties—far too many—and transfers to other programs, as well as retirements by those who just couldn't stand to fight anymore. Ezra didn't begrudge them for it; the Federation Space Command had taken its toll on him over his seventeen years of service.

"Yeah, I know." Jarek pulled off his helmet. His silky black hair was damp against his forehead, largely obscuring the white swirls of tattoos most Sorthians had. His chestnut brown skin glistened with sweat. Flashing a crooked smile, he said, "You know how the higher-ups get."

"And you know I don't give a shit."

"You should," came Darius's deep voice.

Ezra turned. First Sergeant Darius Cane, his second-in-command and the more protocol-conscious of the two of them. They'd known each other for over a decade and had been in the same class of the Vanguard training program, two of the youngest to ever be accepted. In fact, Darius was the only carryover from Ezra's last team; everyone else had gone their separate ways. Ezra had been promoted to commander sergeant first and given charge of their new team, the younger Vanguards gathering around them.

Growing up, Ezra had been an only child and longed for a sibling. Many Vanguard teams ended up bonding deeply, but Ezra had never been able to find his people. Darius *could've* passed for one of Ezra's maternal cousins. They had the same imposing height and broad stature, and they even had the same black hair, though Darius's skin was closer to white than Ezra's tan. And where Darius had brown eyes, Ezra had forest green. But that was where the comparisons stopped. Where Ezra liked to relax, Darius kept things strict. He took the word "professional" too seriously and wasn't interested in anything beyond work.

"Well, the higher-ups aren't here right now," Ezra said, gesturing to the empty gym. "Relax, Darius. No one's gonna find out."

"Maybe not, but we've got to go. Generals called us in."

"All of us, Sergeant?" asked Kira. She put a water bottle to her lips and drank.

"Nope, just me and Commander Lyre." Darius jerked his chin toward the door. "Get cleaned up."

Ezra couldn't help but laugh. "Shouldn't I be the one giving orders around here?"

Darius shrugged. "Just meet me in twenty, alright? Messenger said it was urgent."

Ezra gave him a lazy mock salute, then headed for the showers. His day just got a whole lot longer, he feared.

After a quick shower and change into standard black fatigues, Ezra tended to a few minor aches and pains with his sunshaper magic. Just as he could create shields and intense damage, his fire could heal—useful in his line of work. But where his magic was explosive and dangerous on the battlefield, his healing was more like sitting by a warm, gentle hearth on a winter's night.

With that done, he made his way into the crowded hallway. He headed straight for a while, then turned left. The new arrivals taking up space in the halls moved to the side as Ezra pushed through, most of them watching him with wide eyes.

He got looks like that a lot; it wasn't every day that run-of-the-mill FSC soldiers got to see Ezra Lyre in person. Vanguard Units were the best of the best, assigned to the toughest missions and counter attacks against the Ascended.

As always, Ezra just ignored the attention. Sure, he *was* the best of the best—literally, the Vanguard with the highest marks and strongest record—but that didn't mean people needed to stare.

A few more turns and one ride up an elevator to the base's fourth floor, and Ezra found himself outside Command's glass double doors. Darius was already inside.

Ezra let himself in. Darius didn't move a muscle, always a stickler for proper pretense *especially* when facing any commanding officers. Sure, the Federation Space Command needed hierarchy to function, but Ezra didn't see why Darius was still so rigid about it. Even FSC leaders were just people, as was everyone else on this base.

Three generals sat at the sleek glass table in front of Ezra. They weren't just Aerilia's FSC leaders but *the* leaders of the entire military, experts in their respective fields and powerful to boot. As a Vanguard, Ezra sometimes reported directly to them or advised them on things he saw during missions, but he didn't usually encounter all three at once.

There was General San'ri, an Ivari woman with snow white skin, sage green hair, long pointed ears, and height to rival Ezra's. She was head of Special Operations, which Ezra's team fell under. She sat in the middle of the table.

Next was General Miron, a Human woman far shorter than Ezra. She had russet brown skin and eyes to match. She was the head of Fleet Command, overseeing everything about the FSC's armada, from starfighter squadrons to large-scale operations in space.

Last was General Rithel; he was half Human and half Sorthian, with tan skin and red hair streaked with gray. He was head of Ground Forces Command and notorious for his brutality.

"Commander Sergeant Lyre," said General San'ri. "Nice of you to join us."

"I was just getting cleaned up after training, ma'am," Ezra said as he came to stand beside Darius. When Darius nudged him in the ribs, Ezra added, "Apologies for the delay."

The general gestured toward her two colleagues. "We wanted to update you."

"On what, ma'am?" Ezra asked.

"Your next assignment."

Ezra schooled his features. Now where would they be going? Out to the borders of the Ascended's territory? To a Sorthian outpost that needed protection? An Ivari moon colony?

General San'ri's hand waved over the glass-top table, and a series of holograms flickered to life in front of her. "You're going to Miduna," she said.

"What the fuck is on Miduna?" Ezra asked, and Darius coughed.

Miduna was a small planet in the Edaar System, near the middle of Federation territory. Its capital city, Kalyndra, was a decent-sized trading hub, but otherwise? It was just another planet, like many of the thousands in the Federation that had either been terraformed or colonized to support their growing population. There was nothing special about it.

One corner of the general's mouth quirked up. "Aerilia's university is sending an archaeological team there to study an ancient site they believe may be connected to the Ascended," she said. "We need you to go as security."

They were being assigned to a security detail?

Ezra laughed. "Ma'am?"

"This isn't a joke, Commander Lyre," said General Miron, her eyes narrowing.

"All due respect, ma'am, but it sounds like a joke," Ezra said. "We're Vanguards, not bodyguards and definitely not historians. Is there an Ascended threat against the site or something?"

"None at present," replied General San'ri, "but we've seen a pattern in recent attacks on outer worlds. The Ascended seem to be targeting planets with sites dedicated to the Eternal Ones."

Legend had it that thousands of years earlier, gods called the Eternal Ones had gifted humanoid species with magic and technology. That was long before any of the current power struggles existed, before anyone in the galaxy even had the ability to get off their home worlds. And then the Eternal Ones had disappeared, leaving the mortals to figure out how to use all of the tech and magic appropriately. All they'd used it for was war and expansion.

"And, given the Separatist sympathies on Miduna," General San'ri continued, "the government fears for the archaeologists."

Ezra almost scoffed. The Separatists were a whole lot of talk, nothing more. They were just people disappointed with the way the government ran things from Aerilia. They were no threat to archaeologists who wanted to dig around for old treasures or whatever.

Miduna wasn't even *that* far outside of the Federation Core or Inner Systems. It was several hundred light-years away, but there were planets much closer to the borders of the Federation than that. Ezra should know; he spent a lot of his time fighting off Ascended attacks in those regions. Would the Ascended really try to move as far into Federation territory as Miduna just to attack some site dedicated to the old gods?

Darius pressed his thin lips together.

"Something to say, Sergeant?" asked General San'ri.

"No, ma'am," he said. "I was just wondering if Separatist activity is really that high out there."

"High enough," the general said, a noncommittal answer if Ezra had ever heard one. He fought the urge to roll his eyes.

"What about the intel on the Ascended?" Ezra asked. "How likely is an attack?"

General San'ri pursed her lips.

"I'd like to know what I'm walking into, ma'am," he added.

With war raging on, they needed to be prepared for the Ascended to strike at any moment. But there were still some planets that had a much higher probability of being besieged than others. If Miduna really was a target in the war and not just the location of some pointless treasure hunt, Ezra needed to know. He needed information to do his job to the best of his ability.

Her long, pointed ears pinned back against her head. "Can I trust your team to get this done?"

That didn't exactly give him what he needed, but Ezra just nodded and said, "Yes, ma'am."

"We'll get it done, ma'am," Darius said.

"Careful out there," said the general. "You will be briefed upon your arrival in the Edaar System. Dismissed."

Ezra led the way out of the room and down the hall to the elevator. Only when they were inside did Darius's rigid posture relax.

"Well," Ezra said. "Any thoughts?"

Darius raised one eyebrow. "My *thought* is that it's a mission."

"Right, but isn't it strange that San'ri—" Darius glared at him, so Ezra said, "That the general wouldn't give us any other information?"

"You know we don't always get what we need."

That was part of the job. They did what they were told, when they were told. That was how the FSC operated. Always had, always would.

"Command knows what they're doing," Darius said.

Ezra glanced sidelong at him but didn't push. While Ezra respected General San'ri, he and Darius had different opinions about those in charge, and that was clearly never going to change. Darius even had dreams of someday commanding a base of his own. Ezra wasn't sure he could see himself in that kind of role; he'd never known anything other than being out in the field, and he wasn't sure he wanted to.

CHAPTER 4

Traveling with a bunch of archaeologists was hardly Ezra's idea of a good time, especially when he ran into them in the mess hall. If he had to listen to one more of Professor Oron's stories about past expeditions, Ezra might just throw himself into the airlock to get away from it.

So when they finally dropped out of hyperspace and the pilot came over the loudspeaker announcing their approach to Miduna, Ezra breathed a sigh of relief, the first since he'd learned about their new "mission" several days prior.

He'd spent as much time as possible in his quarters, reading the short briefings Command had prepared for him before his departure. There was nothing in them to suggest there was an imminent threat to Miduna or these scholars, but clearly FSC leadership saw *something* to the mission. And, annoying as the professors may have been, he wouldn't let them down. Dealing with threats both anticipated and unknown was his specialty.

Ezra chugged the last of his coffee, then grabbed his bag and left the mess hall. The rest of the ship buzzed with energy and people, but he didn't see his team anywhere. Their quarters were empty. Maybe they'd already gone down to the launch bay.

Turning right at the next junction, Ezra stopped in front of the elevator that would take him several levels down to find his team. Just as the lift dinged and the doors slid open, a husky voice called out, "Ah, Commander Lyre! Just the Vanguard I was hoping to see."

"Professor Nyssara," Ezra said.

Professor Nyssara was a Sorthian woman and leader of the dig. She waddled up to him and ran her free hand through her salt-and-pepper hair. The other gripped her steel gray suitcase. Thankfully, Professor Oron was nowhere in sight.

"What can I do for you?" Ezra asked, motioning for her to step into the elevator first.

"Are you and your team prepared for our outing?" she asked.

Ezra pushed the button to take them down to the launch bay. "Vanguards are always prepared."

Nyssara chuckled good-naturedly. "I don't know why anyone would say otherwise. Every Vanguard I've had the honor of meeting has been a perfect soldier. So polite, the lot of you."

Ezra gave her a tight-lipped smile. "Just doing our jobs. If you're worried about the upcoming dig, don't be. My team and I will ensure everything goes smoothly."

His team was good. Great, actually. He was the top Vanguard, and his four teammates held four of the next twenty highest spots. They were some of the best.

Even if Command saw something to this Miduna mission, Ezra still couldn't help but wonder if his team's talents were better suited elsewhere. Running this security detail wasn't what they usually did. He rolled his shoulders.

"Have you ever been to Miduna before?" Professor Nyssara asked.

Ezra shook his head.

"Well, what with the remote location and all the whispers of Separatist sympathies in Kalyndra, I expect it'll be different from my last trip out here. You see, when I was much closer to your age, I—"

The lift stopped, revealing the enormous launch bay. The wide doors at the far end were open, protected just by a blue forcefield that kept out the harshness of space. Soldiers in gray uniforms worked at various stations and small transport shuttles scattered around the bay, and several of the archaeologists milled about excitedly. Ezra's team waited near one of the shuttles.

"If you need anything before we leave tomorrow morning, just ask someone at the base in Kalyndra, Professor," Ezra said to Nyssara. "If you'll excuse me."

He left without waiting to hear her stuttered response. Ezra wove his way through personnel and civilians alike until he stopped just short of his team.

"Took you long enough, boss," Talon said. His usually bright smile didn't reach his eyes.

"You all could've told me you were headed down," Ezra said.

Kira started to speak, but Darius set a large hand on her shoulder. "Figured you'd find us when you were ready," he said. "Sorry."

"Nothing to apologize for." Ezra tilted his head toward where a group of professors were congregating. "They all behaving?"

"No complaints," said Darius.

Ezra nodded. "Good." The last thing they needed were civilians who thought they knew better than a Vanguard Unit. But Ezra had been doing this work long enough to encounter all kinds of people, including civilians with huge egos.

His team continued chatting among themselves as they helped load the professors onto the shuttles. Ezra assumed one of the piloting positions, taking both his team and several enlisted soldiers down into Kalyndra. They landed in the shipyard reserved for the FSC base on the northeast side of the capital.

It took nearly a half hour to corral all the professors. Not only were there a dozen professors, but they each had at least one assistant, most of them university students. That put them at just over two dozen people. Two dozen for Ezra and his team to guard. It was only once a squad of soldiers took up the lead and herded the scholars toward the base that Ezra finally relaxed.

The base was smaller than what he was used to. Back on Aerilia, no expense had been spared for the Space Command's setup. That was, after all, their headquarters. But this planet? It was barely half the size of Aerilia. And Aerilia was an entire city on its own, whereas Kalyndra encapsulated just one hundred and fifty square miles. There were neighborhoods on Aerilia bigger than this so-called capital.

"Let's go get our mission brief," Ezra said to his team. "Then I'm taking you all off base to get something to eat." Yes, he needed to feed his people, but he also wanted to scope out Kalyndra and get a sense of the atmosphere for himself.

"Thank fuck," muttered Kira, the newest and youngest of the group. "Why is ship food always the worst?"

"No idea, but I'm starving," said Jarek.

The second they stepped foot inside the base's main building, a young soldier in marbled gray and tan fatigues hurried up to them. "Commander Lyre," she said with a quick salute. "I'm here to escort you to Colonel Thalora's office."

"Lead the way," Ezra said.

Every FSC base Ezra had been to in all his years of service might've had the same aesthetics of gray stone and metal, but there were telling details about each. And this Kalyndran base? Its floors and walls were more worn out than normal, suggesting less upkeep and fewer resources. Why, though? Miduna had some wealthy people and plenty of trade. Taxes should've covered repairs.

After several turns down long corridors—which resulted in plenty of wide-eyed stares from enlisted soldiers who had likely never seen a Vanguard Unit in person—their escort brought them to an elevator. They rode up two floors in silence, which seemed to be as high as the building went. They went down one more long, straight passage and stopped outside a reinforced metal door.

"Colonel Thalora is inside," said their escort. "She should be ready for you, Commander."

Ezra knocked, sending an echo down the mostly empty hallway. A weary voice called out for him to enter, so he pushed inside. The rest of the team followed him into the small conference room that seemed to double as the colonel's office. It was clean and sparsely decorated. A large window overlooked the training yard below.

Painted on the wall behind her was the FSC's shield and motto: *"In duty, we rise. With honor, we fight."* Every time Ezra saw those words, his heart swelled a little.

The long desk that should've been used for a meeting had just one seat behind it. A middle-aged Sorthian woman sat in the single chair, her coily black hair pushed away from her face with an indigo headband. White geometric tattoos peaked out from under her uniform, stark against her umber skin.

"Commander Sergeant Ezra Lyre." The woman seated behind the table didn't move to stand. "Welcome. I'm Colonel Thalora, the base commander here in Kalyndra."

"Ma'am." Ezra gave a quick salute. "This is First Sergeant Darius Kane, Specialists Talon Rive and Jarek Voss, and Private Kira Vael."

"It's nice to meet you all," Thalora replied. "Though I was admittedly surprised when I heard we'd be receiving a group of Vanguards for this little excursion."

"It's our understanding there may be some concerns about Separatist sympathies," Ezra said coolly. "As well as concerns about potential Ascended attacks. Can you tell us more about that and the location we'll be patrolling?"

"Oh, it's all being blown out of proportion if you ask me," said Thalora. She stood, bracing one hand on the glass table and waving the other over a small panel near her hip. A hologram appeared just above the tabletop, revealing a mountainous landscape and forest. Within it were ruins. "This is where you'll be hiking. Apparently the university on Aerilia thinks it's some ancient Ascended worship site?" Thalora shook her head. "It's nearly five klicks in each direction."

Five of them couldn't patrol that much space alone.

Darius shifted and sucked in a breath as if to speak, but the colonel raised her hand.

"We'll be sending an additional platoon with you," she said. "And we've issued a contract to the local branch of the Starlight Syndicate."

"Bounty hunters?" asked Darius. Then he cleared his throat and added, "Ma'am."

"Indeed, bounty hunters." Thalora pressed her full lips together. "It's a remote location, but they'll know it well. They're locals. No disrespect to your unit intended."

Ezra ground his teeth together. Bounty hunters?

He didn't like bounty hunters. Sellswords. How was he supposed to trust someone who was only loyal to the highest bidder?

But they were *supposed* to be professional, at least if they were Syndicate members. The Starlight Syndicate guild spanned the entire Cosmic Federation, with branches on many planets, major and minor. They had a reputation for getting the job done and mostly staying within legal parameters to do so.

"Understood, ma'am," Ezra said. As much as he wanted to argue, he wouldn't. "It won't be an issue." Behind him, his team shifted uneasily.

"I'll send you what information we do have on them," Thalora said. "And I recommend you go into the city tonight to meet them. You should be able to find them at The Aurora, a bar near the Syndicate's headquarters here."

Great. This whole fucking mission was going downhill faster than Ezra had anticipated. His ego could deal with playing bodyguard for a while, but working with bounty hunters? It was more than a bit insulting. How was he supposed to trust them, and how were they all going to work together to get the job done?

Chapter 5

Mo couldn't believe what she'd gotten herself into.

What had she been thinking, taking this contract? She rolled her shoulders as she and Cass headed for The Aurora. The sun had set, but Kalyndra was just coming to life with all the people who preferred the darkness. There were other Starlight Syndicate members, of course, as well as the day laborers, the off-duty city guards, and the merchants who ran the night markets.

And then there were the criminals, but Mo wasn't particularly worried about them. She had her sword hilt attached to her belt, and Cass had opted for two blasters.

"We should've come more heavily armed," Mo said. "To remind the FSC not to fuck with us."

Cass shoulder-checked a short man when he glared at her instead of moving from his spot in damn near the middle of the sidewalk. He shouted a curse, and Mo turned around and flipped him off.

"It'd make the wrong impression," Cass said as they rounded the next corner. "We're supposed to be supporting the Vanguards, remember?"

"That's the problem," Mo muttered.

"You're being too negative," Cass said, then slung her arm around Mo's shoulders. "Think of the money! It's an easy gig."

That was another part of the problem. Contracts like this didn't come around very often, and the more Mo thought about it, the more it felt too good to be true.

"You're too much of an optimist," Mo said.

"No, I'm a realist." Cass gave her another jostle, then dropped her arm and nodded in the direction they were going. "Looks like Kynn's here."

The Aurora was as unassuming as any other business in Kalyndra. Most of the buildings had the same simple exterior, whether white or tan brick or a blend of those and light metal. A glowing neon sign hung above The Aurora's entrance, and the thick doors muffled the loud bass thumping inside.

A small crowd milled around the entrance. Kynn was among them, dressed in black pants, boots, and his favorite dark green jacket. It didn't look like he had any weapons on him, but knowing Kynn, he had one stashed away somewhere. He'd had errands to run earlier in the day and agreed to show up first to try to get a read on their newest work partners.

"Took you two long enough," Kynn said, flashing that infectious grin of his as he met them in the middle of the road. His dark brown eyes crinkled at the corners.

"I don't work on the government's timetable," Mo said.

Cass fluffed up her hair. "Are they inside?"

"Saw five of 'em walk in about twenty minutes ago," Kynn said. "Not a hundred percent sure it's them but seems likely. They all had sticks up their asses, just like every other Vanguard I've ever met."

Cass gave an exaggerated groan, but Mo smiled as they headed inside The Aurora.

It was just as loud, dark, and horrible as it always was at night. She avoided places like this, hating the crowds and the noise in equal measure. But Ril Staga had told them they'd be meeting with a Vanguard Unit here, the group apparently in charge of security for this contract.

She wasn't sure meeting in a bar was the best place to discuss military business, but Mo always did what she had to do when it came to her jobs.

She tossed her long white hair over her shoulders and moved closer to Cass and Kynn. He was leading them toward the back of the building, past the other Syndicate members and wealthier merchants in this part of the city. There were plenty of off-duty soldiers, too, but none of them looked like Vanguards.

Vanguard Units were the best of the best in the Federation Space Command—supposedly. Mo, thankfully, had never had the displeasure of meeting any of them until now. Kynn had once been recruited for the Vanguard program but flunked out after only a few months, and so she'd been able to forgive him for ever siding with the FSC in the first place.

Perhaps that was hypocritical given she'd just accepted a contract from the military, but taking freelance work and actually *joining* their ranks was different. Mo didn't have the luxury of declining work except in very limited circumstances.

Slowing, Kynn tucked his hands in his front pockets and adopted the ridiculous swaggering steps he so often used in places like this. Mo rolled her eyes as Kynn stopped at a half-moon booth in the back corner of the club.

The low lights did little to illuminate the five sitting there. They were entirely out of place with their rigid posture, and the tallest of the group kept glancing around the room like someone was about to attack him. Mo rolled her eyes again. Even without their black fatigues marked with the FSC's insignia, it was painfully obvious who they were with.

"Commander Ezra Lyre?" Kynn asked.

"That's me," the tallest of the bunch said. His voice was rough and low, a bit rumbly but pleasant even with his posh Aerilian accent. He stood up from his seat at the edge of the booth and stuck his hand out for a shake. "You're Kynn Sathir?"

"That's me," Kynn said, all false pleasantness. "Pleased to meet you."

"Likewise." Ezra's attention shifted to where Cass and Mo stood just behind Kynn. "And you're the other two?"

"We have names," Mo snapped.

"I know. I read your files." Ezra folded his well-muscled arms across his chest. As he took half a step forward under one of the ceiling lights, Mo could make out his face better. His black hair was speckled with gray. It brushed his shoulders, and the top layers were pulled up into a bun. A neatly trimmed beard covered his jaw and cheeks. The bridge of his nose was slightly crooked, like it'd been broken but not set correctly. And his eyes were a beautiful forest green.

He was irritatingly handsome.

"The Demon and the Phantom," Ezra said, not taking his focus off them. "Mora Cevi and Cass Farr. What makes Miduna's best bounty hunters take a job like this?"

"It's easy and pays well," Mo said.

"So you like to take the easy way out?"

She pushed her shoulders back. "When it suits me, yeah."

Ezra rubbed at his jaw. "Huh."

"Only the galaxy's biggest fool wouldn't do so."

He smirked. "Sure."

Oh, Mo was going to find a very good reason to wipe that look off his face.

"It's nice to meet you, Commander Lyre," Cass said, nudging Mo with her shoulder as a silent reminder to make a good impression. "What do we need to know about this contract?"

Ezra relaxed at Cass's polite interjection. She always was better at that than Mo ever had been.

"Introductions first," he said, then gestured toward the table. Of the four still sitting, only one was Sorthian. The rest were Human.

"Sergeant Darius Kane, my second-in-command." Darius Kane looked like he had an even bigger stick up his ass than Ezra. He was the exact stereotype of a Vanguard: tall, buff, and clean shaven. His dark brown hair was cropped short and appeared almost black against his white skin.

"Specialist Talon Rive." Ezra motioned to the next man. Talon had black-brown skin, tightly coiled black hair, and a thinner build than Ezra and Darius.

"Specialist Jarek Voss," Ezra said, and Jarek—the Sorthian in the group—waved. He was shorter and leaner, with copper skin, white tattoos, and silky black hair tied back in a single braid.

"And finally, Private Kira Vael," Ezra said, gesturing to the one woman on the team. She'd buzzed her blonde hair, and her tan skin reminded Mo of the beaches on a small planet named Suna'tu out in the Kantar System.

"Nice to meet you all," Kynn said. "Shall we get a round of drinks? On me. You five could stand to loosen up."

"We're not here to fraternize," Darius said, his voice higher than Mo expected. "We're here to discuss the contract and establish the parameters of your involvement."

"A drink sounds great," Ezra said, giving Darius a pointed look. "Thanks, Mister Sathir."

"Call me Kynn, please," he said, flashing his best smile. "I'll order for us. Be back in a jiff."

As Kynn slinked off into the crowd, Mo tried to hold back a sigh. Really, she did. But as soon as Darius glanced in her direction, she couldn't help but let out a little huff. Something about his shadowed gaze made her skin crawl.

"You two don't seem very heavily armed for bounty hunters," Darius drawled as he leaned back in his seat. "I find it hard to believe you're the best Miduna can scrounge up."

Mo's hands balled into fists. Cass stiffened.

"Darius, come on," Ezra said, dropping into his seat. He pulled up the sleeves of his tight black shirt, revealing heavily tattooed forearms.

"What?" Darius waved a hand at the two of them. "They don't exactly look like they'll be able to handle anything."

"Dar—" Ezra started.

"Bold coming from a Federation snake like you, Kane," Mo said. "Want to go outside and see who has the bigger sword? I promise it's going to be me."

"Oh, sweetheart," Darius growled, "you don't want to go there."

Ezra may have been irritatingly handsome, but Darius Kane was just plain annoying.

As Mo leaned forward, Cass put a hand on her forearm. "Let's just play nice and get our money," she whispered.

Mo kept hold of her mask, the mean one she pulled out so often when she was doing her job. Cass was right; they needed the money. And Mo had meant what she said earlier, about this being an easy job for good pay. She wouldn't screw it up just because some asshole Vanguard decided to get mouthy and disrespectful.

And she *would* play nice.

Eventually.

The band's bass thrummed through every one of Mo's bones. She shoved her discomfort deep down and leaned across the table. Lowering her voice, Mo said, "Do you know why they call me The Demon?" Darius stared up at her with a blank face as she continued, "No? I could show you, but I don't think you'd like it. Let's just do our jobs, *Sergeant*, like the professionals we are. That's the only way this is going to work, and we both know the FSC wouldn't be calling in bounty hunters for security on a crapshoot job like this if your team wasn't woefully unprepared."

"Unprepared?" Darius snapped. "We're the highest-ranked Vanguard Unit in the entire FSC."

Mo straightened and raised her eyebrows. "That can't bode well for the rest of the military if they've got their best on a silly little side project like this, now can it?"

As soon as Darius shoved out of his seat, Ezra pushed him back down. "Don't let her get to you," he muttered before glancing up at Mo. "And you, take your own advice and be professional. We're all just here to do a job."

Mo gave him her fakest smile. "Aye aye, Commander."

Kynn's voice rang above the music and the crowd, and a moment later, he appeared behind Cass. An Ivari server with dark blue skin followed behind him, a drink-laden tray balanced on one palm.

"Good, no one's killed each other yet," Kynn said with a grin. "I got us all Midunian ale to start. Any complaints? No? Excellent."

The server set the drinks in the center of the table as Kynn pulled chairs up for himself, Mo, and Cass. Mo took both a seat and a drink grudgingly, only slightly amused as the two specialists and private on Ezra's team wrinkled their noses when they sniffed the green alcohol. Midunian ale was an acquired taste, one Mo didn't have either.

"Let's just get started," Ezra said, setting his drink to the side and sliding a small tablet to Mo. "Everything you'll need to know is on there. We're heading out to the dig site first thing in the morning, south of the Zinthian Pass. It's—"

"Very remote," Mo said as she turned the tablet on. The screen lit up, revealing a slew of files with maps, information about the archaeologists, and project schedule. She glanced up at Cass, who shrugged. They hadn't been given information this specific when they signed up for the job, but that wasn't unusual. "What in Voxarus's name is out there?"

"Ruins of an old temple built for Evlos." Ezra kept his voice low as he said, "The government believes it may be important to the Ascended, actually. That's why they're going to study it, and—"

"And why they're putting security on it," Mo finished for him. He pinned her with a look, but she ignored him.

As much as Mo liked to push buttons, the Federation Space Command wouldn't be sending any Vanguard Unit—let alone their best—on a silly errand like this if they didn't see a real threat—and real value—to it.

But what would be so important about some ancient place that the military would send precious Vanguards all the way out here or spend all this money on three bounty hunters?

The Ascended still worshipped the old gods, though the Federation didn't—mostly didn't. There were still sects all across the empire dedicated to their worship and study.

There was Voxarus, Eternal One of Mystery and Death. Krytix, the Eternal One of War and Destruction. And of course, Evlos, Eternal One of Creation and Knowledge.

Mo didn't believe in the Eternal Ones. She never had. People had once used them to explain the development of all the different species in the galaxy, to explain the existence of magic. But the Eternal Ones were clearly just old stories, made up long before people had a real understanding of the world around them.

Mo's particular magic—psionic magic—was supposedly connected to Evlos. She briefly wondered if the FSC somehow knew about her power but decided they likely didn't. It was something she rarely showed the world, and those who did see it usually ended up dead.

"Why would the Ascended care about some broken down temple?" Cass asked before taking a sip of her ale. "I mean, surely they have enough temples on their own planets. Would they really target this one?"

"I think Aerilia's just being cautious with so much going on at the front," Ezra said. "There've been some other sites that have been targeted. But I think we're too far into Federation territory for that to be an issue."

Mo wanted to ask why he would think that when his government was spending so much money on this contract, but the irritated look on Darius's face made her keep her mouth shut.

"The archaeologists are good people," Ezra continued, "and easy enough to work with if you don't get stuck in a conversation with one of them."

Conversation, great. Just what Mo wanted.

None of this was what Mo wanted, but she and Cass needed this money. She had to remember that. If they kept taking big jobs like this, they'd be that much closer to retirement. To the quiet life they both wanted. It might take another year or two, but it felt more within reach than it had in a long time.

"Sounds like an easy gig, as expected." Kynn finished the last of his beer, then slammed the glass down on the table. "So, who's getting the second round?"

Chapter 6

Mo stared up at the dark metal ceiling of her bedroom on *The Revenant*. She sucked in a deep belly breath, held it for eight seconds, then blew it out for another eight as she eased her leg out in a shallow stretch.

Her knees were hurting worse than usual, a deep, aching pain that had kept her up more than half the night. The other half, she'd been alternating between fits of sleep and ruminating over this assignment.

After Kynn had ordered the table another round of drinks, the Vanguards still hadn't loosened up. They'd all remained tight and irritating, just like Mo's joints. Darius Kane had been the worst of them, always shooting glares in Mo's direction whenever Ezra Lyre hadn't been paying attention. If anything, it seemed to Mo that Darius was in charge despite his lower rank, especially with the way the younger three all looked up at him—literally.

She shoved the thought away. Vanguard politics were *not* her problem. She needed to get her joints under control, not just for her own sanity but because they'd be landing near the dig site soon. Mo usually liked to pilot, but Cass had insisted on taking over. *Probably for the best*, Mo reminded herself.

Stretches wouldn't help her today. No, she was going to need a numbing salve and a shit load of patience to get through the day feeling like this.

With a heavy sigh, Mo forced her aching body off the ground and shook out her arms. She rolled her neck several times, then went to the drawer on her small bedside table. Everything about this room was small, from the bed that would barely fit two adults to the metal furniture to the narrow porthole at the top of one wall. But it was *her* room, and as long as she kept it organized, the size wasn't an issue.

After coating her major joints in salve, Mo grabbed a black leather chest piece from the wardrobe and slid it on. It was a familiar weight and far more comfortable than her full suit of armor on a day like today. She braided her hair, attached her sword's hilt to her belt, and headed out.

Everything about *The Revenant* was compact, from Mo's room to the common area and command room. Even the crew quarters downstairs—where Kynn was sleeping for the duration of the contract—and the two small bathrooms were tight. Mo circled the holo table in the middle of the command room, then pushed the button to open the cockpit's sliding double doors.

"Heya, Mo," Kynn said from the copilot seat. He grinned over his shoulder. "Good timing. We're just about there."

Outside, trees went on as far as the eye could see, even covering the beginnings of the Zinthian Mountains. Miduna's northern hemisphere was covered in evergreens like this, and the local population had set up laws generations earlier to protect the forests. Mo loved these forests; she and Cass left the capital often to get away from all the people and noise.

Cass began their descent and landing sequence, flipping switches and pushing buttons as she navigated them down to the surface. Several large military transport vessels were already in the clearing below. They were ugly, boxy ships with the FSC's insignia painted on the sides.

"With all the money the government has," Mo mumbled, "you think they'd design more attractive ships."

"As long as they fly well, who cares?" Kynn asked. He also flipped a few switches, then cut off the engines and engaged the thrusters.

"*You* care," Mo said. "Why else would you get that ridiculous paint job on your ship?"

"Jealous much?"

"Absolutely not."

Cass gave them a wide berth and landed *The Revenant* a fair distance away from the FSC ships. Just seeing the soldiers milling around outside was giving Mo a headache. She left her friends to finish powering down the ship, instead going to prep her suit for later. She'd give herself the reprieve from it now, but she couldn't do her job without the security that armor provided.

As she headed back down to the lower deck and opened a wall panel, someone else clanged down the ramp. She ignored them, focusing instead on the black, gray, and blue armor nestled inside the compartment. Everything was where it needed to be.

"So." Kynn drew out the word and stopped next to her.

Mo kept her attention trained on her armor, counting the scuffs on the chest plate and legguards. She'd need to buff those out eventually, once her joints stopped hurting. Maybe she could bribe Kynn to do it for her.

She'd never actually have to bribe him. He'd do it just because she asked. He'd always been generous with his time and energy, even when they were kids. He'd always watched out for her and Cass when they were too small and weak to look out for themselves.

"So," she said, finally daring to look up. "What do you want?"

"Ouch." He rubbed the spot over his heart. "You wound me with your impatience."

"Sorry." Mo forced a smile.

"Listen, I know you don't like me telling you what to do, but—"

"Oh, good, here we go." Mo started to heft up the panel to set it back in the wall, but Kynn took it from her. "I could've done that."

Kynn pinned her with a look that was somehow both unrelentingly stern and terribly understanding. "We both know you could have, but you're not moving well. Save your energy for the job."

And there it was. Mo huffed.

It wasn't that she was ungrateful. No, she loved and appreciated Kynn and Cass both, for their understanding, their patience, their empathy. They'd never judged her the way others in the guild had, the ways others had when they'd first arrived on Miduna twenty years earlier, all of them just kids suffering after the Fall of Veronis I. None of them were blood related, but they were her family and had been for most of her life. They only had each other. It was why they were here now, working together.

But Mo hated that she needed help sometimes. Life was so much easier when she could just go about her business without a second thought. Lately, those independent days were harder to come by. She'd been pushing her body too hard, and she knew it. But out here, in the far reaches of the Federation? Sitting around wasn't a luxury she could afford.

She didn't know how to get over feeling like she burdened her friends. She didn't know how to tell them she felt that way. So, she didn't.

"Right," she finally said. "The job. Still can't believe we agreed to this."

"Eh, the commander's not that bad," Kynn said as he moved around her to go to the thick, black metal weapons locker on the far wall. He punched a code into the keypad, then opened its doors. "The rest of them are about as fun as a pile of wet rags."

Cass's loud snort came from the ramp leading up to the higher deck, then her boots appeared as she descended. "As long as they can work together and leave us to do *our* jobs, I don't really care if they're fun."

Kynn waved a hand as he began pulling out a series of small blasters. Despite them not being her weapon of choice, Mo took one when he offered it to her and hooked it onto her belt. Both Kynn and Cass forwent their armor, though Kynn grabbed two more guns for himself *and* his sword hilt, and Cass strapped her favorite rifle to her back.

"Let's head out," Kynn said, tilting his head toward the ship's exit. He pushed several buttons, and the familiar hiss of the external ramp's descent filled the space.

"Why are we letting him think he's in charge?" Cass whispered as Kynn strutted out the open door into the fresh air beyond.

"It's good for him every now and then," Mo said, and Cass snorted again.

"I heard that!" Kynn called over his shoulder.

As they followed him down the ramp, the chatter of the archaeologists and soldiers alike drowned out the sounds of the forest. Thick evergreens towered above all the ships, dwarfing them completely. Up ahead, the five Vanguards stuck out in their heavy black armor. A few other soldiers were intermixed, clearly hanging on Commander Lyre's every word.

Of course they were.

"... and that'll be the best way to split up the schedule," Ezra continued as Mo and the others walked up to the back of the group. He didn't even bother welcoming them. "You can take that back to the rest of your squads and let them know. Find one of us if you have any questions. Dismissed."

The soldiers saluted Ezra and, as they turned, eyed Mo, Cass, and Kynn warily. But then they were off.

People were always being so dramatic about bounty hunters. It wasn't like they were there to kill anyone. Mo had a very strict policy about not taking kill contracts. Deadly force was only to be used in dire circumstances, not because someone had a vendetta but didn't want to get their own hands dirty.

"I see you three finally showed up." Darius dragged his gaze up and down Mo's form. Whether he was just sizing her up in the daylight or had other ideas, Mo wasn't entirely sure.

"Try me," she mouthed at him.

Darius's eyes narrowed, but he glanced back at Specialist Jarek Voss. The younger man pushed his silky hair behind his ears, one corner of his mouth twitching. Ezra seemed oblivious to all of it.

"We aren't even a minute late," Kynn said. "How's everyone getting settled in?"

"We'll be heading east to the ruins in the next half hour," Ezra said. "We'll hike back here to the ships every night before dark."

"What, afraid of the monsters in these woods?" Mo asked.

"You never know what's lurking in the shadows," Ezra said. "Suit up, then I'll give you your assignments."

Kynn might have thought Ezra Lyre wasn't that bad, but something about him set Mo on edge. His whole team set her on edge, the way they looked like predators on the hunt. As soon as this job was done, she was collecting her pay and washing her hands of the FSC.

The only thing worse than keeping her guard up around the Vanguard team was the way the archaeologists wouldn't stop *talking*.

Mo held back a groan as one of them began asking Kynn about his "adventures," as the woman put it. And Kynn, of course, was happy to regale her with an overexaggerated tale about hunting down a criminal across some of the most dangerous parts of the Federation. He leaned against a dilapidated stone column, hands waving wildly in the air as his story reached its crescendo. Several of the nearby scholars stopped whatever scans they were completing with their tablets to listen in. Darius Kane was nearby, his expression tight. Private Vael loitered half a step behind him, one hand on the gun at her hip.

"Is any of this true?"

The deep voice and smooth Aerilian accent behind her belonged to Ezra Lyre. Mo peeked over her shoulder. In the late afternoon sun, his green eyes seemed almost brighter. And this close, she could make out several small, pale scars along his cheeks and near his forehead.

"He did catch the man," Mo said.

"That doesn't answer my question."

Mo shrugged one shoulder. "Kynn partakes in the time-honored tradition of exaggerating your successful contracts."

"Do you do that as well?" Ezra asked.

"Nope."

"Why not?"

"Seems unnecessary."

The truth of the matter was that Mo didn't *need* to exaggerate anything. She got her work done efficiently and with brutal precision. If a mark needed to be brought in the hard way, she did it, and she did it well. If they were an easy catch, that just made her life easier.

"I'll admit I've never been particularly fond of bounty hunters—" Ezra started.

"Feeling's mutual." Mo folded her arms over her chest. "The FSC is nothing but a bunch of elitists who put themselves above the rest of us."

Ezra arched one thick eyebrow. "Wow, and here I was thinking you wouldn't be honest."

"What do you want, Lyre?" Mo asked. "Can you even tell the truth with a surname like that?"

"I've heard that shit my entire life." He rolled his eyes. "I came over because I need you and Cass to come with me."

"Why?"

"You'd be a terrible soldier," Ezra said. "We don't ask why; we do as we're told."

"Good thing I never wanted to be a soulless automaton like you."

He scowled at her. "Will you please come with me? Cass is waiting."

Cass's voice echoed in her head, a needed reminder. *Be nice.* Mo wouldn't be nice because this military man wanted her to do something; she'd be professional because they had a job to do.

Mo kept pace with Ezra despite his much longer legs. He was easily eight inches taller than her, if not more. He was even taller than Kynn, almost unnaturally large.

They picked their way around the professors, the ruins, and the endless ferns covering the ground. Mo and Cass escaped the capital often to spend time in nature, and although they'd traveled near this area on foot before, the ruins were easy to miss. Mo had to look incredibly carefully among the underbrush to find bits of stone and brick. Whatever had once been here had been absolutely obliterated.

Just a few hundred feet ahead, Cass leaned against the thick trunk of a tree, arms folded loosely over her abdomen. She was the perfect picture of boredom, especially as she brushed a few strands of purple hair out of her face.

"What did you want to speak to us about?" Mo asked once Ezra stopped in front of Cass. The area was suspiciously quiet. Mo's hand drifted to her belt, just inches from her hilt.

"I wanted to ask if you meant what you said earlier about monsters in this forest," Ezra said, voice low.

Mo stared at him for one heartbeat, then another. Then, she laughed. It was a loud, obnoxious sound, the only appropriate response to his ridiculous question. Even Cass snorted.

"You actually thought I was being serious?" Mo asked. "Lyre, there are no monsters here, unless you count your people."

Ezra's jaw tightened. "No reports of Ascended?"

"Wouldn't your military be the one to know if the Ascended were skulking around Miduna?" Cass asked.

"Oh, that might be giving them too much credit," Mo quipped, making Cass laugh again.

Ezra huffed. "There's always a risk of an attack, anywhere in the Federation. I wanted to know if you two had heard anything, any whispers in the Syndicate's network."

Cass glanced at Mo, some silent question hanging between them. They hadn't heard anything about the Ascended, nothing beyond whatever the media outlets reported about the war.

"No," Mo finally said as she looked up at the Vanguard. His face was hard, intent. "Nothing like that."

"Really?" he asked.

"Why would we lie about that?" Cass asked.

"You clearly don't like the military."

"No, but we're not fools," Mo said. "If we knew something, we'd tell you."

"I certainly don't have a death wish," Cass said. "The fact that you think it's even a possibility we'd hide it from you is insulting."

Ezra watched her for a moment. "And the Separatists?" he asked. "The government says there's been a lot of talk among them out here."

"Yeah, *talk*," Cass said. "Not that I can blame them."

The ferns under Ezra's boots crunched as he shifted uneasily. "Are *you* Separatists?"

"The way I see it, it doesn't matter who's in charge," Mo said. "System's broken. Federation, Separatists trying to create their own version of the same shit—doesn't matter. I don't blame them for being fed up with Aerilia, though. Life's hard out this way. Wouldn't expect you to understand that, Lyre."

The intensity in Ezra's expression softened slightly, but he schooled his features before Mo had a chance to really study him. "So they're all talk?"

"As is their right, or at least it's supposed to be," Cass said.

"I'm not here to make anyone give up their ideals," he said, and Mo found herself grudgingly respecting the man for it. "I'm just trying to do my job and keep these civilians safe. Thank you for the information."

Shouldn't the FSC have given Ezra and his team all the information they needed to get this work done? Shouldn't he have been briefed about Miduna's political leanings and position in the war before arriving?

The FSC's shortcomings on that front weren't her concern. She doubted Ezra would tell her the truth either. He'd probably say it was classified or some other nonsense.

"We're here to do *our* jobs," Mo said. "If you have other questions, ask. I don't want to endanger anyone just because you didn't want to admit you didn't know something."

Ezra's jaw muscle ticked again. "I'd like you two to take over patrolling the northern edge of the area. Take over for Specialists Voss and Rive. I'll find you when it's time to relieve you from your shift."

Ezra stalked off through the forest and ruins. As Mo tracked him, she found Sergeant Kane standing a few dozen feet away near a clearing full of professors. He was watching Mo like a hungry animal, his posture tight and stare intense.

Cass leaned toward Mo and whispered, "What's that all about?"

Ezra met up with his second-in-command. Kane clapped him on the shoulder, sparing Mo one more disdainful glare before walking off with Ezra. Something unpleasant tingled in Mo's belly.

"I don't know," she said. "Do you think there's something off with Kane?"

"He's an asshole."

"No—well, yeah, but I meant something ... else. I can't put my finger on it."

Cass shrugged. "They all seem off. Ezra's not so bad, I guess."

Mo pressed her lips together. She didn't know what it was. Some men—some *people*—just rubbed her the wrong way. But Cass was right. Ezra Lyre was the only soldier there who didn't entirely give Mo the creeps. He seemed uptight but not *off.* Maybe it was her general distrust of the military that was clouding her judgment.

She'd have to keep an extra close eye on the Vanguards just to be sure.

CHAPTER 7

Kynn Sathir made the best coffee on this side of the planet, and Mo had never been more grateful to have him on her ship.

Sure, there had been a few times where the circumstances were far more dire and Kynn's presence had been a blessing, but after the day she'd had? Coffee was the only thing that would help. Mo accepted a thermos from him as she met him in the kitchen. Cass was seated at the table in the corner, yawning.

"How was your shift?" Mo asked.

"Uneventful," Cass said with another yawn. She rubbed at her eyes. "Voss wasn't all that talkative. Kept giving me dirty looks."

"They all do," Mo said. For the last couple of days, the Vanguards had been standoffish. Ezra hadn't been too unfriendly, but even he was on edge. "What's bothering them, the war?"

"It's simple," Kynn said, pouring coffee into a second thermos. "They don't like us. When I was at the academy, everyone who found out I'd been raised in the Syndicate immediately started to distance themselves from me."

"Seems unfair," Mo said.

Kynn shrugged. "It's not like we treat them any differently."

"Told you we should play nice and try to make a good impression," Cass said.

"Nah." Kynn waved his hand. "I don't think that'd help us here. Maybe it'd help with Ezra, but the other four are exactly what I expect of Vanguards."

"Stuck-up, self-important assholes?" Cass drawled.

"Exactly." Kynn screwed the lid onto his thermos and nodded. "At least we know one thing about the rest of this job will be consistent."

Cass yawned again, her eyelids drooping. After their first day out here, Ezra had been assigning her late shifts. Now they were about to switch off.

"You should get some sleep, Cass," Mo said. "There's Epzilian tea in the cabinet if you want some. Made sure to get you extra."

Cass often had a hard time sleeping when they were away on missions, and Epzilian tea was supposed to help. Cass said it only worked half the time but that it was better than nothing.

"I don't think I need it today," Cass said as she stood. "Good night. And good fucking luck out there."

She trudged through the kitchen and down the short hallway to where her and Mo's bedrooms were, the officer's and captain's quarters, respectively, based on the ship's blueprints. There wasn't any substantial difference between them, though.

Mo frowned but followed Kynn downstairs. The sun was out, and the air was unseasonably cool. Mo wasn't going to complain; she much preferred mild weather over the heat that sometimes clouded Miduna.

They headed over to the meeting point. The Vanguards weren't there yet, but a handful of the professors were already milling about and talking excitedly with a few of the soldiers. Everything seemed to be in order.

"Where's the commander?" she asked.

"Saw him and the others run up into one of their ships about twenty minutes ago, but they haven't been out since," Kynn said. "What do you think they could possibly be doing in there, just the five of them? I've sensed some tension between them."

The self-satisfied smirk on his face made Mo groan. She shoved him in the shoulder. "Oh, grow up."

He chuckled. "Don't tell me you didn't pick up on it too."

Mo opened her thermos and took a sip of coffee, watching as the Vanguards began filing out of their ship one by one. The only one missing was Jarek Voss, who had been on the overnight shift with Cass. Ezra was at the front, wearing just his black fatigues and a short-sleeved white shirt that showed off his ink and muscles.

"Not that kind of tension," Mo murmured.

No, she didn't think there was anything romantic going on between the Vanguards. But *something* was off, especially the way Darius Kane brought up the rear and barely looked Ezra in the eye.

Maybe there had been romantic entanglements that had gone all wrong? Or maybe Darius Kane wanted to be in charge. Ezra's more easygoing nature seemed to irritate him.

Ezra's pleasantly deep voice echoed through the encampment as he called out, "Circle up!"

Mo and Kynn made their way over, planting themselves at the back edge of the group that had gathered around the commander. He began their briefing by going over the night watch's notes, then assigning shifts to some of the low-ranked soldiers. As he talked, Darius shifted uncomfortably. Kira, the blonde on the team, pressed her lips together.

Interesting. Mo took another sip of her coffee.

"And I need someone to go out to the far northern edge of the ruins with Professors Oron and Akidi and their teams this morning," Ezra said.

Darius perked up. "I'll go."

"I'll go too," Mo said.

Ezra finally looked her way, the first time he had all morning. His eyebrows furrowed, but he nodded. "Kane and Cevi it is, then. Rive, you're going with the group heading south. Vael, Sathir, you'll go east. I'll stay in the middle with some of the platoon. Meet back here in six hours to change things up."

Good. Mo had six hours to figure out why the fuck Sergeant Darius Kane set her on edge.

As the others scattered, Mo pulled Kynn back toward their ship. Lowering her voice, she said, "Keep an eye on Vael today?"

"You really think something's up with them?" he asked.

"I told you, there's some kind of tension. I'd like to at least try to figure out what's going on with them and if it's going to hamper them if things go south." The last thing Mo wanted was to get ambushed by the Ascended and have a bunch of useless Vanguards.

Kynn glanced over at the Vanguards' ship. "I'll try," he said. "She hasn't been very receptive to chatting so far."

"You've always been the most charming out of the three of us," Mo said. "Do your best."

With a lazy mock salute, Kynn said, "Yes, ma'am."

Mo hurried up into the ship to grab her gear. She didn't want to be late.

Dappled sunlight filtered through the treetops, and a cool breeze kissed Mo's skin. Far in the distance, the sky shifted from blue to dark gray.

"Hopefully we can wrap up our work today before the rain sets in," said a rough, feminine voice. Professor Akidi, a Sorthian woman and one of the leads on this dig. She had light brown skin and hair as white as

Mo's, and based on the wrinkles around her eyes and mouth, had to be the better part of seventy years old. Circular white tattoos spread from her forehead down around both sides of her face.

Mo had been following her around for the last hour, watching as the professor oversaw her students' work. They'd found what they thought was a buried statue—or part of a statue—and they were carefully attempting to dig it out.

Darius Kane was on the other side of the clearing, shadowing Professor Oron, a Luxinae man with blue-white skin, a goatee, and geometric midnight blue markings. He was the more talkative of the two professors, and Kane's discomfort was obvious even from a few hundred feet away. *Good.* Mo wanted him to get uncomfortable. People were more likely to show their true selves under pressure.

"Hopefully," Mo said when she realized Professor Akidi was watching her.

"How's the weather been around these parts recently?" the professor asked as she went back to typing something into her tablet.

"Fine enough, I guess."

"That's good." Professor Akidi wandered away, yelling instructions at some of her students to be careful.

Mo surveyed the area again, then headed for where Kane was following Professor Oron. They'd stopped near one semi-intact pillar, which Oron was scanning with some strange device.

Sidling up to Kane, Mo dropped her voice and said, "All's good on my side. How are things over here?"

He didn't deign to look at her. "Fine."

"Nothing I should be aware of?"

"No."

"Huh." Mo hadn't thought this would be *easy*, necessarily, but Kane really did not want to look at her. She shifted her weight to one leg. "Akidi's worried about rain."

"Reasonable, considering"—Kane gestured vaguely toward the sky—"the look of things."

"Think we should lead them back early?" Mo asked.

"No."

"You have a problem with me or something?"

Kane's gaze snapped down to hers, his jaw tight. "Excuse me?"

"You've barely looked at me or spoken to me since we met," Mo said. "I'm not saying we need to be best friends, and I know we didn't get off on the right foot, but damn. Lighten up."

"You called me a Federation snake," Kane said.

"And you insulted my ability to do my job," she retorted. "I don't like that. So really, what's the issue?"

"You are a bounty hunter."

"So?"

Kane pivoted to fully face her. He towered over her, obviously trying to intimidate her. "I am a Vanguard."

"*So?*" Mo asked again as she held his stare.

"You are a bounty hunter. You sell your loyalty to the highest bidder. You"—his thin upper lip curled—"and this mission are beneath me."

Kane knew nothing of her loyalties. He knew nothing of *her*.

"That's the second time you've told me you're too good for this, and yet here you are." Mo stretched her arms out wide. "Your superiors must *hate* you if they sent you all the way out here. Something happen to get Lyre knocked down the list?" When he didn't budge, she asked, "Or something to get *you* in trouble, and you're just dragging the rest of your team down with you?"

Kane's body trembled. She had him. Once you knew someone's buttons, it was easy to rile them up or get them to spill the truth. Kane sucked in a sharp breath as if to speak, but the professor cut them off.

"You, Vanguard," he said, not looking over his shoulder.

Dammit.

Kane closed his eyes and sucked in a deep breath. "Yes, Professor Oron?"

"I need your help," the professor said.

After checking that his weapons were secure, Kane closed the distance between himself and the professor. "What can I do?" His tone was far lighter than it had been a moment ago.

"I need you to hold this scanner while I circle around with my other one," the professor said, already passing the strange device to Kane.

If Mo wasn't going to get answers out of the Vanguard, she could at least try to get some out of the professor. She hadn't really spoken to the civilians much yet.

"So, Professor," Mo said, trying to keep her voice casual, "what exactly are you looking for out here?"

"This is an old religious site," Professor Oron said as he circled around the pillar. He took several steps back, then pulled another scanner from his belt and began tapping its small screen.

"Right," Mo said, "but why's it so interesting? I mean, we're a long way from Aerilia."

"A long way indeed," Kane muttered so low that Mo almost didn't hear him.

"It's important to study ancient sites," the professor said, almost bored. "It's important to understand the past so that we can understand the future. It's especially vital when that past is connected to your enemy."

"You think this'll reveal something about the war effort?" Mo asked. All around them was just forest and a whole bunch of rocks and debris. Nature had reclaimed much of the site.

"The Ascended still value the Eternal Ones and old beliefs. If we continue to better our understanding of all three, it may give us deeper insight into the Ascended's ethos, what drives them."

"We don't know that already?" Mo's schooling back on her home world, Veronis I, hadn't covered more than the basics about the Eternal Ones. That education had been disrupted when she'd been evacuated to Miduna, where the Syndicate took over every aspect of her life. They certainly hadn't discussed the Eternal Ones in depth. And besides, this war was being driven by greed, not ancient history.

"There are always gaps in our knowledge that can be filled," the professor said.

"This temple was dedicated to Evlos, right?" Mo asked.

"Indeed," said Oron. "Eternal One of Creation and Knowledge."

"What kind of knowledge?" Mo asked, and Darius shot her a glare over his shoulder. She just smiled.

"All knowledge," said Oron. "Everything, since the beginning of time. She was responsible for shaping our Universe, or so say the old stories." His scanner beeped several times, and he slapped its side with his hand. "Damn tech."

"What's wrong with it?" Kane asked.

"They've been on the fritz on and off since we got here." Professor Oron shook his head. "Of course they'd break now."

Kane shifted uneasily. Mo frowned. What about that would make him uneasy?

"Could be the weather," Kane said slowly. "Or if there's any radiation out here."

"My suit would be going off if there was radiation," Mo said.

His jaw muscle ticked. "There are a thousand reasons tech could be going bad."

With a scoff, the professor lowered his tablet and pinched the bridge of his nose. "That doesn't help me do my job."

"This one's still working," Kane said, shifting again. "My team could look at your equipment later, see if they can find the problem."

"Much appreciated," the professor said as he circled the pillar. "Thank you, Sergeant."

Mo slipped away and headed back toward her half of the survey site. One thing was clear: Darius Kane knew something. Now Mo just had to figure out what that was.

Chapter 8

Three days in the forest with a bunch of overexcited professors and sarcastic—if not indifferent—bounty hunters was three days too many for Ezra.

So when he finally had a chance for a twenty-minute break at the end of the third day, he took it. He settled down on a nearby pillar, a canteen of coffee in hand. Shit, he missed good coffee. *Real* coffee, like the stuff served on the southwestern side of Aerilia. It was strong and smooth, perfect. This? It was watery and weak, as it always was when they were out in the field. How the FSC had managed to perfect energy weapons but not a decent form of portable coffee was beyond him.

"Commander!" Kynn Sathir stopped a few feet away, one hand resting loosely on the blaster hanging from his hip. "What're you doing over here all by yourself?"

Ezra gestured vaguely to the forest surrounding them. "Sitting, watching."

They were a few hundred yards away from the rest of the group, which was gathering up for some kind of meeting between the dig teams. One had found a large statue of Evlos, which they were thrilled about, and the other had apparently found some destroyed pieces of a wall that were marked with strange carvings none of them could decipher. He assumed more had been found, especially if they were stopping their work to discuss like this again.

Darius, Talon, and Mora—Mo, as Kynn and Cass called her—were loitering at the edges of the group, as were several of the enlisted soldiers still on duty. Others were spread out, patrolling the borders of the site.

Kynn pursed his lips as he turned and watched everyone. "Your team's seemed a bit restless."

"What makes you say that?"

"Don't tell me you can't see it," Kynn said. "Sergeant Kane is rigid—"

"He's always been like that, ever since we were in Vanguard training," Ezra said. There were so many instances of Darius being uptight or moody that Ezra could no longer count them on two hands. "He likes doing things a certain way."

Even as Ezra watched him now, Darius's posture was too stiff, as it had been since they'd left Aerilia. This was unusual, even for him. He'd only gotten more tense since they'd found out they were working with the three Starlight Syndicate members.

On principle, Ezra didn't like bounty hunters, but Mora Cevi, Cass Farr, and Kynn Sathir weren't *terrible*. Kynn was the friendliest—this was not their first conversation of the mission—and the two women were tolerable and seemed competent. And besides, everything had been going smoothly.

Ezra took another sip of his pitiful coffee and tried not to cough. He often abstained from it altogether when they were on assignment for this very reason, but he hadn't been sleeping well these last couple of nights in the woods. He'd been in far worse places—in far worse situations—and slept better. What was wrong with him? It was like there was something in the air.

Maybe that was why Darius was so on edge. The anxiety about the war, partnering up with bounty hunters, and lack of sleep. Even seasoned Vanguards couldn't keep it together all the time.

"Aren't you their leader?" Kynn asked.

"Yeah, but Darius has it covered right now," Ezra said. When Kynn still didn't look convinced, Ezra added, "Look, I don't know how bounty hunters do things, but this is why there's a hierarchy on our teams. When I need a break, he can take over. Leaders need to breathe too."

"I'm not saying they don't, but—"

One of the professors shouted incoherently and gestured at the data pad they were holding. Darius loomed over the other man as he shouted back.

"That doesn't look much like him 'taking over,'" Kynn said wryly.

Swearing, Ezra set his canteen on the ground, then jogged over to where the rest of the group was squaring up. Kynn followed him. The archaeologists began organizing themselves on one side, Ezra's team on the other. And the civilians continued shouting, pointing at their tech and then at the Vanguards.

"Hey!" Ezra yelled as he closed the distance. "Hey!"

Darius and the others ignored him, zeroing in on Professor Oron instead. He was at the head of the civilian group and, from the looks of it, ranting at Darius.

I take a break for five minutes and it all goes to shit. Ezra skidded to a stop near the outskirts of the group.

"You told me this tech would be fixed!" Professor Oron bellowed, his blue skin turning periwinkle with rage. "We were told the FSC was sending you to guard us, but you've done nothing to help!"

"We are—" Darius started.

"Isn't tech important for our safety?" Oron shouted. "You just said your own systems were on the fritz!"

"Our comms systems going in and out for a few seconds hardly counts as on the fritz," Darius snapped.

There'd been some issues with tech across the board out here in the woods, especially away from the ships, but nothing that concerned Ezra too much. Anything could affect signals and battery life, something he'd learned long ago.

"Aren't you supposed to be protecting us from the Ascended?" Oron's chest heaved. "How are you going to do that, *Sergeant*, if our sensors aren't even reading consistently?"

"*Your* sensors are not my problem," Darius said.

"You said you'd fix our scanners, but nothing seems to be fixed!"

"I said we'd take a look. I didn't make any promises," Darius said. "I'm a soldier, not a fucking engineer."

"And it's a good thing too. None of you would even pass basic classes, I'm sure."

Darius's hand tightened into a fist, poised to strike.

"Hey!" Ezra shoved his way through the crowd and blocked Oron from Darius's sight. "Hey, what the fuck is going on over here?"

Darius lowered his arm slightly. "He—"

"Your team isn't doing their job, Commander," Oron said.

Ezra turned. The professor was an older man, unarmed and much smaller than Darius, hardly a threat. For Darius to be escalating this to physical blows ...

"I thought everything was going alright until now," Ezra said, voice steady. Behind the civilians, he spotted both Mo and Kynn, watching intently. Ezra looked back at Oron. "How are we failing, Professor?"

"You know the tech's been spotty," Oron said.

Ezra nodded. "Yes."

"Your sergeant there said your team would fix our scanners and data pads, but the problem's persisted, and I just heard them talking about how their suits were acting up!"

"How are we supposed to feel safe when even Vanguard suits aren't performing as intended?" Professor Akidi asked as she stepped up on

Oron's left. "How are you going to protect us from any Ascended threats?"

"The ships' sensors have been reading just fine," Ezra said. "We have teams back there at camp. If anything was going wrong, the ships would tell us."

"And what about comms?" asked Akidi.

"If there was a threat and we weren't answering, those at the camp would know how to respond," Ezra said. "They wouldn't just leave us out here in the dark."

She pressed her lips together and gave Ezra a disbelieving look, but she didn't argue the point.

"Listen," Ezra said, turning to fully face the archaeological team, "I know how frustrating it is when tech breaks down, and I know how terrifying it is to even think the Ascended might have their sights on this location, but I promise, we're not going to let anything happen to you."

"You can hardly promise us that," Oron said.

"All due respect, Professor," Ezra said, "but I've gotten more civilians out of far more dangerous situations unscathed. We all have." He gestured back at his team. "And this job isn't going to get done if any of us are busy pointing fingers and yelling at each other."

Oron and Darius both huffed.

"All of us need to stay focused on our jobs," Ezra said. "You all on your dig, and us in the FSC on security. Alright? That's the only way this is going to work." When nobody answered, Ezra said, with more force, "Alright?"

"Alright," Professor Oron said. "Alright."

"Everyone back to work," Ezra ordered.

As the professors scattered and Darius went to leave, Ezra grabbed the sergeant by his arm. Darius glared at him, and the others stopped mid-stride.

"We need to talk," he growled at his team. "All of us. After dinner."

Darius wrenched his arm away. "Yes, Commander."

Ezra's jaw clenched, but he let Darius and the others walk away. He just needed them to get through the next couple of hours without making things into a shit show. Maybe a walk would clear their heads.

He was supposed to have another ten minutes on his break, but Ezra wasn't going to take it. Not now, when tensions were still so high he could practically see the change in the air. He headed back to where he'd been sitting earlier, took one more drink of coffee, and then put his helmet on. He had work to do.

By the time dinner was over and the professors were safely tucked away in their shuttles for the night, Ezra had a blinding headache. It was only made worse by the fact that Darius and the others were a dozen feet away, talking quietly among themselves.

Ezra hated pulling rank. Really, he did. But he would.

"Hey."

Ezra's voice made the entire team go rigid. Their faces were hard to see in the low light. The sun had long since set, and neither of Miduna's two moons were visible thanks to the dark clouds that had rolled in around dinner time. The only lights were one on the outside of the bounty hunters' ship and a low-burning campfire.

"Yes, Commander?" Darius drawled.

Ezra rolled his eyes. "Don't get smart, Darius. What the fuck was that earlier? I thought you were seriously going to hit the professor."

"He insulted us."

"So?" Ezra asked. "That doesn't give you a right to fight a civilian."

Darius shrugged.

"This isn't like you." Ezra glanced at the rest of the team, but they all shifted uneasily in their spots behind Darius. "What's going on?"

"Nothing," said Jarek.

Kira just shrugged one shoulder, and Talon pressed his lips together. Ezra scowled at them. "Well?"

"Just itching to get back to our real work," Darius said.

"That doesn't give you an excuse to talk to the professors like that," Ezra said. "You know better. That's not who we are, who the FSC is."

Darius stared at Ezra for so long, he wasn't sure the sergeant would answer. But finally, Darius sucked in a deep breath and crossed his arms over his chest. "Sorry."

"Don't apologize to me," Ezra said. "Just get your shit together."

"Are we still on watch tonight?" Talon asked.

Ezra nodded. "I still need you to do your jobs. No more arguing with civilians."

"Should be easy with them asleep," Jarek said, and Talon elbowed him in the ribs.

Ezra fought the urge to roll his eyes again. "Like I said, get your shit together. Go take a walk or something if you need to. Dismissed."

Darius gave Ezra one last unreadable look, then stalked off. Jarek, Talon, and Kira all followed him like ducklings running after their mother. Ezra pinched the bridge of his nose.

He needed some sleep, but he was restless, ready to run or fight or something. Anything. But running off into the woods hardly seemed like the brightest idea, especially since Darius and the others left the camp. He couldn't just leave the enlisted here alone.

Ezra circled around the clearing, weaving in among the shuttles and soldiers. He checked in with the squad leaders who were still awake. Nothing else had gone amiss that day, at least. They'd even successfully brought some large artifacts back from the ruins, things the professors thought were important to study on Aerilia instead.

And that was where he found Mora Cevi, studying a stone slab. It was nearly as tall as her and filled with strange carvings, everything from letters to loops and swirls. Ezra guessed they were decorative, but what did he know about ancient sites? Not a damn thing.

"Shouldn't you be asleep?" he asked.

She didn't flinch or even look at him. "Shouldn't you?" she asked. "I figured putting your team in their place would've really taken it out of you."

"What's that supposed to mean?"

"You're trying to wrestle control back from them." Mora finally turned toward him. "Right?"

"No," Ezra said. "The situation is very much under control."

"Then why were they getting into fistfights with civilians today?"

"Look," he said, keeping his voice low, "just do your job, alright? Let me do mine."

"I always do my job," she said. "And I do it well. You don't have to worry about me."

Despite her poor attitude, Ezra knew Mora was telling the truth. She'd been completing her assignments and checking in as required. She asked questions and pushed back sometimes, but the bounty hunters were the least of Ezra's worries. He just needed to figure out how to keep both the archaeologists and his team in check.

CHAPTER 9

An obnoxious beep pierced the night, filling the small cabin of the FSC shuttle and startling Ezra out of a pleasant dream about his favorite tea shop on Aerilia.

Groaning, Ezra rolled over on his cot. A blinking red light illuminated the darkness, and the beeping made Ezra's ears ring. Why'd this shit have to go off now?

On the opposite side of the cabin, Kira sat up in her bunk and rubbed at her face. "Ezra?" she asked.

"Some kind of alarm," he muttered, forcing himself out of bed. As soon as he reached the dashboard in the cockpit, he pushed a few buttons. Something blinked on the radar, unmoving. A ship? A weapon? It was some kind of energy signature.

Outside, several shadowy forms moved around, then a white light flickered on and off. It was Darius, saying they needed the rest of the team outside.

"Something's up," Ezra croaked, then rubbed at his face. "Suit up. Darius says he needs us."

"Ascended?" Kira asked.

"Don't know."

The radar couldn't tell Ezra exactly what it was they were dealing with, but if it *was* Ascended, they'd be moving, not stationary, right?

Shaking himself awake, Ezra snatched his gear from where he'd discarded it just a few hours before. He'd been hoping for a break from wearing it, but duty called. He grabbed his weapons, then followed Kira out the door into the cool night. Darius, Jarek, and Talon were all in a loose semicircle at the bottom of the ship's ramp. All of them wore their helmets, obscuring their faces.

"What's going on, Darius?" Ezra asked.

"Some kind of energy reading," Darius said.

"Yeah, I got that already. Do we have eyes on the source?"

"No."

"Do we know where it's coming from? Ground or air?"

Jarek pushed a few buttons on a panel on his gauntlet, no doubt moving through information inside his visor. "Looks like it's coming from underground, about two klicks northwest of here."

"There's a series of caves that way." Mora Cevi's soft voice made Ezra jump. "Scare you, Lyre?"

"What do you know about this?" he asked as he faced her.

Her long white hair fell around her shoulders in loose waves, and she wasn't in her armor. Like that night at The Aurora, Mora was dressed in fitted pants, a loose tunic, and tall boots. A silver hilt was strapped to her belt.

She frowned at him. "*I* don't know a gods damn thing about this."

"Then what're you doing out here?"

Mora lifted her round chin. "I was waking up for my shift, *as assigned*, and saw your buddy signaling with his flashlight. Is it a crime for me to check in when there's an issue at my job?"

It *was* just about time for them to rotate watch. Ezra studied Mora's rosy cheeks, her hard periwinkle eyes, and her rigid posture. She looked annoyed, as she often had the last couple days. She certainly didn't look guilty of anything. And besides, the bounty hunters had actually been a helpful addition to the mission. He didn't see a motive for them to set up some kind of rogue attack.

"Have you seen these caves?" Ezra asked his team.

They all shook their heads.

He glanced at Mora again. "I assume *you* know how to get there?"

"As a matter of fact, I do."

"Then you're with us."

"What about Cass and Kynn?" she asked.

"I need them to stay here," Ezra said. "You too, Kira, Jarek. Keep this place locked down until you get the all clear from us. Be ready to leave in five, and keep an eye on those readings."

Ezra strode away from his team, leaving them to get sorted. He needed to go speak with the dig team and—

"Cass and I work better as a pair," Mora said from behind him.

Ezra stopped short and turned on the bounty hunter. "I need her and Kynn here."

"But—"

"What, are you scared or something, Cevi?" he asked, only getting a hint of satisfaction from throwing her earlier taunt back in her face. Now wasn't the time to be petty.

She squared her shoulders. "Of course not. I'm just trying to tell you how we work best. Aren't leaders supposed to think about that shit?"

He *was* supposed to think about it, but Ezra's understanding was that Cass Farr was one of the best sharpshooters in the entire Federation. The file he'd been given said she'd even been approached by FSC recruiters, but they hadn't been able to convince her to join. With a shot like that, Ezra wanted her out in the open where she'd be useful, not stuck in a cave.

"She stays here," Ezra said. When Mora started to argue again, he said, "That's my final decision. Are we clear?"

Mora gave him a withering stare. "Crystal, *Commander*." She spun on her heel and headed back to her ship without another word.

Good. Ezra just needed her guidance to these caves, and then he could figure out what they were dealing with.

— ·····⟩ ·····✳·✦· ☀ ·✦·✳· ⟨····· —

Wind gusted through the forest, a sign of the storm front rolling in from the west. At least, that was according to the readings popping up on Ezra's visor. They needed to get this done and get it done fast.

"Jarek?" Ezra said over comms.

The speakers in his helmet buzzed lightly, then Jarek's smooth voice came over. "Yeah, boss?"

"Sending you our coordinates." Ezra punched a few buttons on his armor gauntlet. "We're less than half a klick from the caves. Follow us out this way if you don't hear from us within the hour."

"You got it, boss."

Ezra continued following Mora into the shadowy forest, Darius and Talon not far behind him. Mora took slow, steady steps, like she was expecting something to jump out at her.

"Keep going, bounty hunter," Darius said.

Ezra frowned, sure that Mora would turn around to give Darius a piece of her mind. But she just kept walking. Ezra edged closer to her, both hands on his blaster as he scanned the area. His suit wasn't picking up any life signs other than the four of them. The only disturbance other than the weather was that damn signal. His suit let out a quiet beep every few seconds, warning him.

"You really don't think it's some covert Ascended group, Lyre?" Mora asked.

"No, I don't," Ezra said, though he couldn't actually be sure.

This wasn't like any Ascended attack he'd ever seen. They had a vicious military—not that the same couldn't be said about the Cosmic Federation. Ezra wasn't naive enough to think the FSC wasn't brutal when needed. But they weren't actively trying to encroach on Ascended territory. They were only vicious in self-defense.

The beeping grew louder.

"We're almost there," Mora said.

"Fall back, Cevi," Ezra said, and to his great surprise, she did.

Ezra took the lead, Darius on his right and everyone falling in line behind them. It'd been a long time since Ezra had been out in the wilderness like this, not just because of his recent station on Aerilia but because of *all* his missions in recent years. He was always being sent to other planets and cities under attack, mining colonies being raided by the Ascended or cruisers and shipping vessels under siege. Never the forest of an outer systems planet to investigate a fucking energy signature.

A small blue light flashed in the upper right corner of Ezra's visor. He punched another button on his gauntlet.

"You're quiet," Darius said. He'd switched comms channels, away from the one everyone else was using.

"Just trying to focus," Ezra said.

"You think this ain't right?"

Ezra grunted. "I just assume there's more going on than we know."

Command had their secrets. So did the Triumvirate, the executive branch of the Cosmic Federation's government. Ezra wasn't foolish enough to think they didn't. Command had said the archaeologists wanted to study the ruins to better understand the Ascended attacks on similar sites, but what if they knew there was something here, whatever this signal was? If they did, why not brief Ezra on their theories or at least warn him?

"Guess we'll find out soon enough," Darius said.

Their boots thunked against the hard ground, scratching against brush and debris. In the faint glow of their suits' lights, Ezra could make out the trunks of trees and silhouettes of rocky outcroppings. The blue dot in the corner of his visor was joined by an indigo one.

As soon as he switched over to the team channel, Mora said, "Cave's entrance should be just a few hundred yards up to your right."

Ezra ran. Despite not knowing what they were headed into, stretching his legs like this felt good after days spent patrolling.

"Up ahead." Mora's breath came in short gasps. "Those rocks."

The rocky hills were littered with moss and other flora. A few scraggly pines grew near the hilltops, and beyond that were the beginnings of the mountains at the northern edge of the forest. Lightning flashed in the distance, and thunder followed a moment later.

Ezra slowed as he neared the cave's entrance. "Sensors aren't showing shit." His visor screen showed no heat signatures, no signs of life, and no damn energy readings.

"I got nothing either," said Darius. "It's like it just disappeared."

"How the fuck is that possible?" Mora asked.

"Could it be some random local experimenting with tech?" Talon asked. "Someone with a workshop out here?"

"Nobody's building fucking workshops out here," Mora said. "Believe me."

"Don't know that I'll take the word of a bounty hunter." Darius pushed farther into the cave as a flash of lightning lit up the space. "You do work for the highest bidder."

"And that's your government, asshat," she muttered.

"Enough," Ezra said. "We need to—"

"There it is!" Talon cried just as Ezra's visor lit up with a blue signal that pulsed like an erratic heartbeat.

Ezra didn't like this, not one bit.

Darius disappeared past a shadowy boulder, and Talon bolted after him, both moving in the direction of the energy spike. *Shit.* Whatever this was, they needed to take care of it fast.

Drawing his saber hilt, Ezra crept into the darkness. He pushed the power button with his thumb, and his blade flared to life, casting golden hues through the cave. The whole team barely fit inside.

"Doesn't look like much," said Talon.

"There's a tunnel," Darius said from the front of the line.

"Guess we have to—" Talon started.

Ezra's visor beeped slowly once, twice, a third time before spiking and screaming again. Ezra braced himself, boots sliding across stone. The sound was familiar, a warning from over a decade of battles against the Ascended. But the attack he expected never came. The beeping stopped as quickly as it had come on.

"Looks like it came from underneath us," Talon said, punching buttons on his gauntlet.

"Can we trust you to keep this strictly confidential, Cevi?" Darius asked, unmoving. "The FSC will need to debrief you, depending on what it is we find, and—"

"Fuck the FSC," Mora snapped. "If something's wrong on Miduna, our people have a right to know."

"Then you're not coming in with us," Darius said.

"Like the Void I'm not," Mora hissed. "I was hired for a security job. Whatever *that* is"—their suits began beeping again—"might be a threat. I'm only taking orders from whoever issued this contract, and I know that wasn't you, *Sergeant.*"

Darius stiffened. Dammit, that was only going to piss him off. Darius hated when people threw his rank in his face.

"I'll see to it that she's properly debriefed as needed, Darius," Ezra said. "Let's just go before we lose the signal. Now."

With a grunt, Darius continued forward. They had to move through the tunnel in a single file line. Ezra's breathing was steady. His hands didn't shake like they used to when he was new to the job. That probably should have concerned him, but he *needed* to be steady in his line of work.

The lights on top of their helmets helped illuminate the thick shadows, as did Ezra's saber. Mo drew hers, too, sending a cascade of white light across the rocky walls. The ground continued sloping downward, and the tunnel began to twist around itself.

As the ground evened out, the tunnel straightened again, ending at a carved archway several hundred yards ahead. Columns decorated the sides, damaged by time and the elements and probably people too. No way Midunians—or Ascended—hadn't been down here at some point.

"You know this place, Cevi?" Darius asked as the group approached the arch.

"Why would *I* know this place?" she asked.

"You said you knew these caves."

"Sure, but I've never actually explored them."

Darius clicked his tongue.

"What?" Mora asked.

"Nothing."

She huffed. "What's he on about, Lyre?"

"Fuck if I know." Ezra didn't have time for either of them to fall into petty arguments. "Signal came from in there. Let's move."

Up ahead, in the room beyond the arch, was a soft glow. There were still no life signs, but a faint energy reading blinked on Ezra's visor.

"You see that?" he asked.

"I'll check on it," Darius said.

"Easy," Ezra warned.

Darius signaled that he'd heard. He crept into the darkness beyond the arch, his boots barely making a sound. He inched closer and closer to the glow, until finally, he stooped and picked something up off the ground. Darius lifted it up, illuminating his form in shades of gold and indigo.

"It's a crystal," he called.

A crystal?

Ezra stalked forward, Talon and Mora shuffling in behind him. The crystal pinched in Darius's fingers couldn't have been more than six inches long and wide. Its iridescent surface shimmered with a mix of golds, purples, and blues.

"This is what's sending off the energy readings?" Ezra asked.

"Looks like it," Talon said as he tapped a button on his suit. "The energy it's putting off now matches pieces of the signature we saw before."

"Is it dangerous?" Mora asked. Her voice strained in a way Ezra hadn't heard before. "Like radiation or something?"

"Doesn't seem to be," Talon replied.

Crystals had their uses in all manner of tech, though they were most common in energy weapons, serving both as conduits that helped the weapons work *and* aesthetic choices. It was why Ezra had paid a hefty price for the rare golden crystal that gave his blade the same color. He imagined that, if he took this crystal in Darius's hand and put it into his sword's hilt, the output would be amazing.

But he wouldn't risk that.

Although Ezra wasn't necessarily the smartest man in any given room, he didn't know of any crystals that put off energy like *that*. That glowed so brightly and emitted energy surges that would make military sensors go off. Their sensors were carefully calibrated, especially for Vanguards.

Whatever this was, it wasn't normal.

"Could it be Ascended tech of some kind?" Mora asked.

"Don't know." Ezra stretched his open hand out to Darius. "Let me see it."

Darius's visor blocked his expression completely, but it was as if Ezra could sense him looking between the crystal and his hand.

"No," Darius said.

"No? What do you mean no? We need to take this back to Command and—"

"*We* aren't taking this anywhere," Darius said. "At least, you aren't."

"Lyre," Mo said, a warning in her voice.

Ezra whirled, raising his sword. Talon had two blasters out, one pointed at Ezra and the other at Mora. She angled her blade at Talon but didn't move a muscle.

"What the fuck is going on?" Ezra hissed.

"Nothing you need to worry about," Darius said.

Ezra pivoted back toward him. "You're betraying the FSC?"

Darius tucked the crystal into a pouch on his belt. "As I said, nothing you need to worry about." He nodded, then aimed his gun at Ezra. "Let us go the easy way."

Ezra's chest heaved as his mind scrambled to make sense of this ... whatever this was. "Is someone paying you?" he asked. "Did the Ascended get to you?"

It couldn't be, could it? Ezra had heard the stories, but his team ... they were not deserters. They were *not* traitors.

"Fuck no, not the Ascended," Darius said with a derisive snort. "I would never."

"Yet you're turning on me?" Ezra challenged, adjusting his grip on his sword. His magic buzzed under his skin, ready to be set free, but he wouldn't do that. Not yet.

"I didn't want it to come to this, but we've got to go." Darius looked over Ezra's shoulder. "Take care of this."

As Darius stormed past him, Ezra lunged, jamming his glowing blade forward. A heavy body tackled him, and Talon's voice rang in his ears. "Don't, Commander."

Ezra threw Talon off, jumped to his feet, and raised his sword. "You don't want to fight me."

"No, I fucking don't." Talon rolled forward and up, pointing his guns at Mora and Ezra again. "So I'm not going to."

Talon pulled the trigger. Ezra blocked with his blade, but the force made him skid back a few steps. Mora advanced on Talon, a blur of shadows and white light as she pushed him back toward the tunnels.

Ezra ran after them, shouting for Mora to move. She pivoted out of the way as Ezra charged Talon. He swiped at Talon's legs, but the man jumped back, raised his blaster, and fired. Ezra ducked. Mora swore.

The tunnel was too tight for them to fight in, especially with sabers. Ezra reached for the gun on his belt, but Talon was faster, his shot hitting Ezra square in the chest. Pain flared in his sternum, not because he'd been hit by the energy discharge but from the force of the blow. He tumbled back into Mora. She shoved his back and righted him.

Talon bolted up the tunnel. Ezra took off after him, heart racing. His comms became little more than garbled, static-filled speech. Was Darius somehow scrambling the signal? *Fuck me.* Whatever it was that Darius just stole, Ezra needed to stop him *now*.

"Talon!" Ezra roared as he reached the cave at the top of the tunnel. "Darius!"

Talon slammed into him from the side. Ezra hit the ground hard, and his view through his visor blinked in and out several times. He kicked up, forcing Talon off him. Rolling back to his feet, Ezra pulled on that familiar heat beneath his skin. A fiery shield burst to life in front of him, bright and hot like a star. With his free hand, he pulled his blade back out.

Talon hesitated before pushing a button on his arm. A dozen clicks echoed through the cavern. Talon bolted outside.

Even through the static clouding his visor, Ezra didn't miss the red flashes blinking around the perimeter of the room. Charges.

Oh, fuck.

Shit, they were going to blow this place up.

With Ezra and Mora in it.

"We gotta go, Lyre!" Mora barreled around the corner and grabbed Ezra's hand. She yanked so hard he nearly fell again.

"Yeah, I know!" he yelled, pulling his arm away.

"I'm not coming to save you if you get yourself blown up," she said, making a mad dash for the exit—and the pouring rain beyond.

Ezra's visor went dark. He groaned, punching blindly at his gauntlet until finally, his visor whirred and vibrated. It wasn't supposed to do that. It lifted, replacing the darkness of his tech with the darkness of the storm just outside.

Those small red lights blinked faster and faster.

Ezra sprinted forward, ignoring the pain burning hot and bright in his entire torso. He had to get out of there, and he had to stop Darius and the others from taking that crystal, even if it killed him.

If they were willing to betray him for it—betray the FSC for it—then it had to be important.

Ezra crossed the cave's threshold. Every breath was agony. He could no longer hear the faint beeps of the charges. All he could hear were his ragged breaths and the next crash of thunder.

Mora was already down the hill, yelling for him to hurry. Ezra pushed his legs faster. His boots hit wet ground. Rain soaked his exposed face.

Everything exploded.

Some invisible force threw Ezra forward, and it seemed like another pulled him from the opposite direction. He slammed against the ground amid a storm of rock and debris. Smoke filled his lungs. He choked and coughed as he stared up at the lightning-filled sky. His vision swam, but he swore he could see his team's transport ship flying away and leaving him to burn.

Chapter 10

Ezra groaned. His eyelids were heavy, and his body hurt. Badly.

A dark ceiling danced above him. Rain pounded on something metallic. He hefted himself up, hissing as his entire body protested. He was on a ship, but this was not an FSC ship. It was cramped and dark and old.

Shit.

Shit, his team really had left him.

If Kira and Jarek were still around, he would've been on one of the other FSC ships that had brought the whole archaeological squad here. He wouldn't have been on some random piece of junk.

This kind of betrayal …

It hurt in a way he hadn't felt before.

It was almost worse than all the ways his parents ignored him when he was young, all the teams he'd lost to the war or retirements or transfers. He'd only ever tried to get along with and support his team, and they go and stab him in the fucking back? They'd betrayed not just the Federation but everything the FSC stood for.

Ezra wheezed.

"In duty, we rise. With honor, we fight." There wasn't anything dutiful or honorable about what Darius and the others had just done.

He would find them. And he would make them pay. But first, he needed to get himself out of here and back to civilization. He had to warn Command about whatever it was Darius and the others were up to.

Unless Command knew? Would General San'ri have set Ezra up like that? Told Darius what to expect but not Ezra? Darius *had* gotten to that meeting first.

No ... that didn't seem right. San'ri had seemed genuine enough and always had in all the years Ezra had been working with her.

Did that mean Darius was siding with the Separatists? But why? And what would Separatists do with some glowing crystal? Or was it really the Ascended?

None of it made sense.

"Look who's finally awake," Mora drawled from a few feet away. She leaned against the doorframe, no longer in her armor but dark clothes similar to the ones he'd seen her in at that bar. "Want to tell me what the fuck all that was about?"

"Isn't it obvious?" Ezra grunted as he pushed to his feet. He was, unfortunately, still in his armor. He had no idea how the bounty hunters had gotten him back on their ship like this. "We got betrayed."

"You almost got me fucking *killed*," Mora hissed as she stalked forward, fists balled at her sides. She was a good deal shorter than him, but she closed the distance between them and pushed up on her toes so she was right in his face. "You almost got my friends fucking killed. Kynn and Cass almost died because of *your* team, Lyre."

"That's not my fault. I didn't know they'd pull some shit like this."

"Oh, no, of course you didn't," Mora said, voice laced with faux apologies. "Of course not. Unless you set us up to be betrayed somehow. Unless you wanted us dead."

"Why the fuck would I want the three of you dead?" Ezra shot back. His temper rose in his chest, but he tried to force it down. Mora obviously wasn't mad at him. Not really. She was worried about her people, and he could hardly fault her for that. "Think about it, Cevi."

"You don't like bounty hunters."

"Doesn't mean I want you dead."

She fell flat on her feet and took a step back. "No, of course it doesn't make sense for you to be involved," she muttered, rubbing at the knuckles on one hand.

"Did you get hurt?" he asked.

She ignored the question. "The rest of that platoon you all brought with you secured the professors and just took off for Kalyndra," Mora said.

"Any casualties among them?"

"Nothing serious."

Relief settled in Ezra's chest. Darius's actions weren't just about Ezra; a civilian could've gotten seriously hurt. "Good."

"We'll be headed back in a moment. Kynn's just finishing up repairs," Mora said as she headed for the door.

"Repairs?" Ezra asked, following her. The small bedroom he'd been in led out to a slightly bigger room, some kind of junction with five doors.

"Yeah, your asshole team damaged *my* ship."

"This is your ship?" he asked as they trudged out of the junction and into a rear cargo hold. It was fairly empty aside from a few boxes, drop benches bolted to one wall, and a ramp that led to the upper deck.

"Damn right it's my ship," Mora said.

"Seems like a piece of junk for a bounty hunter with your reputation."

Mora whirled on him. "She's been mine since I was twenty-one. I'm not going to let seven years of hard work and care go to waste because your traitorous friends wanted to sabotage her. Is that clear?"

Ezra raised his hands up in surrender. Mora Cevi was not one to be tested, that much was becoming clearer to him by the day. Her fuse was short ... although he probably also shouldn't have insulted her ship.

"Crystal," he said.

"Good. Now stay down here. We'll be back at your base by daybreak." Mora tossed her long hair over her shoulder and started up the ramp to the next deck.

Ezra ran a gloved hand over his face. He had an hour, maybe two, to figure out what the fuck he was going to tell leadership. Whatever that mission had been, he'd failed miserably, and Ezra Lyre didn't fail.

By the time Ezra reached the base on the far side of the capital, the sun had risen. The bounty hunters had dropped him off right outside the gates, and when the soldiers out front had saluted Ezra instead of hauling him inside in handcuffs, he assumed Command had nothing to do with the night's events. A brief chat with one of Command's staffers had confirmed that the base knew the team was on the run.

The medical staff had gotten his burns and blaster wounds healed quickly. He'd thought about doing it himself, but he didn't feel much like using his magic after the kind of night he'd had, and healing wasn't his forte anyway. After a few scans and tests, they'd also given him a prescription to rest, but Ezra didn't feel much like resting. He needed information.

While his suit was with one of the tech teams for repairs, Ezra was going to get his answers. Stepping out of the elevator, he pushed up the sleeves of his shirt and stalked down the hallway toward the base commander's office. None of the soldiers loitering around tried to stop him. Good. No low-level staffer was going to get in his way.

Colonel Thalora's metal door was closed. Ezra knocked once, then yanked it open and strode inside. She sat behind her desk, scrolling through a data pad.

"Where are Kane and the others?" Ezra snapped.

The colonel's gaze flicked up to meet his. "You're early."

"We didn't have an appointment," Ezra said, balling his hands into fists at his side.

"Commander, I'm in the middle of—"

"My team damn near killed me last night!" he shouted. "You wanna tell me what that's about?"

"Keep your voice down, Commander."

"I will when you give me some damn answers!"

The colonel pursed her lips. "I'd like to know what happened out there."

Ezra took a steadying breath. Getting agitated would get him nowhere. So, Ezra explained what had happened, from the team's stand-offish behavior to finding the crystal to the way they'd left him to die. His heart pounded in his ears the entire time, but he managed to keep his voice calm and even, as he'd been trained to do.

"I see." Thalora steepled her short fingers in front of her mouth.

"That's it?" he asked. "You *see*? You don't even have questions for me?"

"No," Thalora said. "You're a good soldier, Commander. Your account matches up with what the professors told us and the data we pulled from your suit." She sighed, then added, "We suspect they've defected."

"To the Ascended's side?" Ezra asked.

"What? No." Thalora shook her head. "Probably to the Separatists. They've been growing in number all across the Federation. It's certainly not the first time this has happened."

"I've never heard of an entire Vanguard Unit defecting," Ezra said.

Thalora shrugged. "No, but plenty of others have abandoned their posts."

Ezra ground his teeth together. "And what would they want that crystal for? Do you know what it is?"

"There are lots of buyers in underground markets," said Thalora. "I debriefed some of the professors while you were with the med team. They said such artifacts are fetching exorbitant prices these days."

"Who would want to buy that?" Ezra asked.

"Maybe something the Separatists wanted, or some private collector. Maybe it was just a payday for Kane and the others. I don't know, Commander."

That didn't sound like Darius and the crew. No, Darius had wanted to climb the ranks, join FSC leadership, and even run his own base. And the rest of the team? Jarek, Talon, and Kira? They all had hopes of becoming trainers for the next generation of Vanguards, helping guide young soldiers through all that would be required of them to keep up the fight.

This didn't make any sense.

"Did anyone follow them?" he asked. "Where'd the transport go?"

"We scrambled a squad, but they just ... disappeared once they got past the second moon."

"And you didn't track them?"

"Couldn't," the general said.

"Or wouldn't."

She frowned. "Commander, do you understand what we're up against here?" she asked. "We're trying to monitor for Ascended attacks, coordinate with bases across the Federation, protect civilians, and deal with the Separatist threats so that our entire government doesn't fall apart. Your team running away is a blow, yes, but not one we have the resources to fight."

A blow? That was all the colonel could call it?

"If we manage to track them down, great. And if not, let's hope their ship gets blown to bits by someone else."

"That's it?" Ezra asked. "We're not going after traitors?"

"No." Thalora's eyes narrowed. "I was just reviewing your medical records. I suggest you follow orders and take a break."

He huffed. *No.* Of course the FSC wasn't going to go after the traitors. Why would they? Why waste that kind of manpower on four Vanguards? Yes, his team had been some of the best, but Ezra could see the writing on the wall. The FSC didn't deem them worth the trouble.

"In duty, we rise. With honor, we fight." Ezra couldn't help but stare at those words painted above Thalora's desk. Where was the fucking honor in letting traitors go? Didn't they have a duty to find some answers?

"Will I be assigned to a new unit?" Ezra asked. It was a question that still hurt no matter how used to asking it he was.

"We need to look into a few things, but yes," she said. "We'll get you transferred as soon as possible. Dismissed."

Ezra mumbled a "yes, ma'am" before turning and heading out the door. It was clear enough to him that Thalora—and the rest of Command—wasn't going to do anything, but maybe he could. He couldn't just let Darius and the others get away with whatever they were up to. Something in Ezra's gut told him this wasn't just about the Separatists. He had to figure out what.

First? He needed a fucking drink, and he needed help.

CHAPTER 11

The dark, quiet space of The Aurora had Mo relaxing into her seat. So did the alcohol she was nursing and the herbal lotion she'd put on that always made her tense muscles loosen. Some might say it was early for a drink, but after the night she'd had? Mo figured it was fine this once.

"Never imagined this shit would go sideways so fast," Kynn said before tipping back his ale. He flagged down a waiter for another one. "Never seen a contract go bad so soon."

"At least we're still getting paid." Cass cupped both hands around the metallic mug in front of her. "A few days of easy work and we made out like bandits."

"There's just the small bit where I was almost blown up by four traitorous soldiers," Mo said.

Kynn nudged her in the shoulder. "Ah, but you weren't!"

"Yeah," Mo muttered, glancing between the two of them. Neither one bore any scratches or bruises. They didn't even look all that tired. "You two are actually good?"

"Yes," Kynn said.

"How many times do we have to tell you that?" Cass asked.

"Until I believe you," Mo said.

It was hard to believe that in the chaos, neither Kynn nor Cass had been injured. According to them, the two Vanguards who had stayed behind at the camp had started firing just after the explosion, and things had only gotten worse when Darius and Talon returned. Kynn and Cass had worked with the enlisted soldiers to try to fight the rebellious Vanguards, but they'd still escaped.

And Mo had managed to get Ezra back to the camp with a little help from her magic. Telekinesis made for a decent makeshift stretcher, although the effort still had her head pounding.

At least it was quiet. This was the only time of day Mo actually liked The Aurora. Its usual patrons were gone, and only a few other Syndicate members filled the space. Nobody had approached to ask them about the failed FSC contract. Nobody needed to. Word spread like wildfire in Kalyndra, and everyone already knew Vanguards had defected.

It wouldn't be good for morale. Vanguards were the most honorable and capable among the entire military—or so all the government and media stations said. Mo supposed there had to be some truth to those claims, but unlike many, she didn't put stock in the government keeping any of them safe. The only two people Mo could rely on in the world were at that table with her.

"Room for one more?"

Commander Ezra Lyre stood a couple feet away from their booth. He looked like shit, from the bags under his eyes to the way he favored one leg slightly.

"Didn't someone bother to heal you?" Mo asked.

The corner of Ezra's mouth quirked up. "Hello to you too."

"Why aren't you on base?" Kynn asked. "Didn't they need to debrief you or something? That was some shit your team pulled."

"Can I sit?" Ezra asked.

Mo almost thought better of it, but the commander looked ... pitiful. She scooted over to give him just enough room to sit on the end seat. He lowered himself with a groan.

"Oi!" Kynn called, snapping his fingers at a passing waiter. The man stopped, glaring at Kynn. "Can we get a pot of coffee for the table?"

"I could use something a little stronger than that," Ezra said.

"And a round of shots," Kynn added. The waiter waved Kynn off, but he'd be back. With that settled, Kynn smiled at Ezra. "What can we do you for, Commander?"

Ezra leaned forward, elbows on the table. "I need your help."

Cass caught Mo's eye, and they both laughed.

"You need *our* help?" Cass asked. "Because that went so well for us last time."

"I need your help," Ezra said again, voice low and almost desperate. "The FSC isn't tracking where my team went. Said they couldn't get a signal, but I don't believe it. I don't believe they'd just run off like that."

"Good riddance," Mo said, tipping back the rest of her drink. The alcohol was smooth and almost unnoticeable. She rubbed at the bandages coiled tightly around her hands, compressing her joints. "Why the fuck do you care? They tried to kill you. And me."

Ezra glanced at her hands, then back up at her face. "What they did was wrong. We weren't best friends, but we worked together for years. This isn't like them."

"Lots of people are deserting with the war," Kynn said slowly.

"And more are looking for a payday," Mo said. "What was that crystal they took? Was it worth anything?"

With a small shake of his head, Ezra said, "Command isn't saying what it was."

"Because they don't know, or because they won't say?" Cass asked.

Ezra shrugged. "Both?" he offered just as the waiter returned with a silver coffee pot, all the fixings, and four shots of amber liquor. Ezra grabbed his shot and tipped it back. "My team doesn't look for paydays,

Cevi. They had career goals, things they were working toward. That doesn't just change because someone offers you money."

"Depends on how much money," Mo muttered. When Ezra glared at her, she said, "*I* wouldn't sell out my team just for a payday, but I know plenty of people who would." She knew people like that all too well. "Maybe you didn't know these soldiers as well as you thought."

"I knew them," Ezra said with such unwavering determination that Mo almost believed him.

"You said you wanted our help," Cass said. "With what, exactly? Tracking them or something?"

"If the FSC isn't going to use any resources to locate them, I will," he said. "I want to know why they did what they did. I want to find my team, and I want to find that crystal, and I want to get answers. I need to know why they tried to kill me."

Mo folded her arms across her chest. "Not interested."

"I can pay you," Ezra said.

"Nope."

"Why not?"

"They almost fucking killed me last time," Mo said. "I'm not exactly keen on tracking them down. It's not worth it."

He held her gaze. "Name your price."

"I hardly think you can afford me."

"Try me."

Mo willed her expression to remain neutral. "Twenty thousand credits." Cass kicked her under the table, so Mo said, "Each. Twenty thousand credits each."

No soldier would be able to afford that, not even a Vanguard. It was a ridiculous amount of money for—

"Done," Ezra said. "I can make it thirty each."

Mo's mouth dropped open. How could this man shell out almost a hundred thousand credits for this? And why did he care *that* much? Cass and Kynn were her family, but if they ever tried to murder her, she wouldn't drain so much of her life savings to hunt them down. She'd hope the Void would take them in due time and try to move on.

Ezra looked around the table at each one of them. "Thirty thousand each," he said. "We'd need to take one of your ships. I have enough leave time saved up; I'd just need to put in the request."

When Mo started to speak, he held up a hand. "Before you reject me again, will you just think about it?" he asked. "Please? Sleep on it. I have a few things I need to sort out. I'll meet you back here tomorrow, same time, for your answer."

Before Mo—before any of them—could object, Ezra stood, dropped fifty credits on the table, and strode out the door.

"Did he just pay for our drinks?" Kynn asked.

"I guess so," Cass said, finally taking her shot.

Thirty thousand credits each.

Mo grabbed her shot and downed it, cursing Commander Ezra Lyre for making her life that much harder.

When they were in Kalyndra, Mo sometimes liked to spend time around the Starlight Syndicate headquarters or exploring the markets, especially the night markets. They had the best food in the entire city, always made right in front of you and served fresh to go.

She and Cass had gotten dinner from their favorite stall in the southern market, one that had the best grilled meat and flatbread in the entire city. The edges of both were always perfectly crispy. But they'd brought it back to *The Revenant* early, and Mo had been in bed ever since.

Although Ezra had taken the brunt of the explosion out in the woods, Mo's body hurt even more than normal. She had her knees and hands wrapped in off-white bandages, trying to give them the compression and support they needed. She'd even tucked pillows under her knees, but that wasn't helping either.

She was just lying in bed like a starfish, begging her body to either pull itself together or let her sleep. But even if she hadn't been in pain, she wouldn't be able to sleep.

Thirty thousand each.

How the fuck did a Vanguard have nearly a hundred thousand credits to pay bounty hunters? And again, why was this *so* important to him?

With a groan, Mo pushed herself out of bed and tugged on her softest, loosest pants, then grabbed a sweater and pulled that on too. She wobbled out of her quarters and down the corridor to the common room that held their small kitchen and living space. Kynn and Cass were hunched over the table in the corner, talking in hushed voices. A teapot sat between them, and they both had mugs with steam curling from the tops.

"What are you two whispering about?" Mo asked as she made it to the small cabinet that held more mugs. She pulled one down, then joined them at the table and poured herself a cup. She wrinkled her nose; it was green tea, her least favorite.

"Oh, just that interesting offer we got today," Kynn said. "How're you feeling?"

"Fine," Mo said, and he immediately gave her a look that said he knew she was lying. "What about the commander's offer? We can't take it."

"Why not?" Cass asked. "It's thirty thousand credits *each*, Mo."

"I know." Oh, Mo knew. She hadn't been able to stop thinking about it all day. The repairs she'd made to her suit, the maintenance on the ship, dinner—none of it had distracted her from the siren song of that money.

"We could be up fifty thousand credits each for what, a few days of work?" Cass smiled a little. "That's huge. Puts us that much closer to retirement."

It was huge, yes, but the thought of taking *another* contract for someone tied up in the government made Mo's skin crawl. It was one thing to do it when it was the military issuing the contract, a security job that required very little until Darius Kane and those other assholes had fucked it all up. But taking a job from someone like Ezra?

For the last twenty years, Mora Cevi hadn't trusted the Cosmic Federation one bit. The government and the military were a huge part of why their home world, Veronis I, was gone. Why her family—Cass's and Kynn's families, and countless others—was gone. Veronis had fallen to the Ascended because of the Federation's shitty response at every stage.

They'd failed to anticipate the Ascended attack, and then they hadn't sent any fleets out in time to help during the first phase of the siege. They'd barely gotten any civilians evacuated before the fighting had quite literally destroyed Veronis. It was no longer a planet, just a massive debris field.

Mo, Cass, and Kynn had been lucky enough to get on one of those civilian vessels that day. They'd been evacuated and relocated to Miduna, one of the few planets willing to take survivors. That was how they'd fallen in with the Syndicate, who had helped provide resources for refugees. They'd provided food, shelter, education. They'd offered training to those kids they thought suited the work—which maybe wasn't all that ethical, but it had saved them. Mo didn't know where she'd be without the help she'd had in those early years. The Starlight Syndicate had taught her how to fend for herself, to fight for herself, because nobody else was ever going to fight for her.

The FSC and the Aerilian government hadn't done any of that. They'd failed not just Mo, Cass, and Kynn, but literally millions of people. Tens of millions.

They were managing to keep the Ascended at bay now, but when would they fail again? They already deemed a bunch of traitorous Vanguards not worth the resources. When would they deem a colony or planet under siege to be not worth it?

"Where'd your head go, Mo?" Kynn asked, tapping the top of Mo's hand.

The world snapped back into place around Mo, her friends' concerned faces the first things she saw. "I don't trust the FSC."

"It sounds like Ezra doesn't much either right now," Cass said. "Not going after *Vanguards*? It's weird."

"We'll probably find the traitors in just a few days," Kynn said. "There's only so many places runaway Vanguards can hide. You said that crystal was putting off a strange signal, right?"

"Yeah," Mo said.

"Then we take the contract, and we start with that," he said. "By this time next week, the commander will have his answers and we'll have his money. It's a win-win."

Thirty thousand credits each. It was more money than Mo had ever seen for one job. It was more money than she'd make in the next six months even with other decent contracts—plus no Syndicate fees to worry about. As Cass had said, they'd be that much closer to retirement. They might even justify a vacation with that kind of pay.

"C'mon, Mo," Cass said. "We can't do it without you. Please?"

Mo tapped her fingers on the cool, smooth tabletop.

A few weeks off did sound nice.

"Fine," Mo said. "But you two better not make me regret this."

Chapter 12

Ezra desperately needed some sleep. It had eluded him all night. Every tiny sound in the base had kept him up. There was no distant whir of machines and ships like at the Aerilian headquarters, and there were no sounds of the city to help him relax. It wasn't even like on an FSC ship, which were equipped with sound machines and whatever else soldiers might need to get some rest.

No, the Kalyndran base wasn't equipped with any of that, and the capital itself was eerily quiet in the late hours of the night.

Who was he kidding, though? All night, Ezra's mind had turned over the issue of his team again and again. He'd tried desperately to find some clue he'd missed in the team's behavior to indicate they were going to pull some shit like this.

Darius had always been moody. In all the years they'd known each other, Ezra had come to expect him to sometimes be off. That was just how he was. As for the others, although they hadn't been the best of friends, Ezra had thought he'd known their true colors. He'd believed what they'd said about career goals, ambitions, and values. Either they'd been lying the whole time or just recently changed their positions. He couldn't even pinpoint when their behavior had started to change. None of that helped him now.

Ezra stepped to one side, narrowly avoiding the speeder bike someone was driving recklessly through Kalyndra's crowded streets. At least The

Aurora was just a few blocks away. Hopefully all his prep work wouldn't have been for nothing, and he and these bounty hunters could get moving.

Everything was ready to go, except for the small problem of needing *someone's* help. Ezra supposed he could go to the Syndicate if these three refused and see who else might be willing to take on the job, but he already knew Mo, Cass, and Kynn. Or, he knew them as much as he could having only spent a few days working security together.

As he turned the corner, Ezra tried to force himself to relax. There was no way these three wouldn't jump at the chance for that much money, right? He'd happily part with it if it meant finding answers. Besides, he had plenty more where that came from.

A large hand clapped Ezra on the shoulder. "My favorite Vanguard!" Kynn exclaimed, steering him toward a clean alley to their right. "Come on, then."

"Where the fuck did you come from?" Ezra asked, trying to pull away.

But Kynn held him tight and gave his shoulders a shake. "Relax, Commander. We just want to talk to you."

"Relax?" Ezra muttered. Kynn Sathir wasn't the one with a traitorous team on the run, and he wasn't the one on a foreign planet, alone, being guided into an alley by a bounty hunter. "Where are we going?"

"If you want to work with me, you're going to have to trust me," Kynn said.

Work with me? Ezra thought. "Does that mean—"

"Shh!" Kynn put his finger to his lips. "Questions later."

Ezra huffed. They moved down the alley, and instead of going into one of the doors on either side of them, continued straight. Kynn dropped his arm from around Ezra's shoulders as they neared the street on the other side.

"Do me a favor and stay five paces behind," Kynn said. "Act natural. Don't get lost."

And with that, Kynn darted out into the crowded market beyond. It was full of colorful stalls, a mass of people, and smells of food. Ezra's stomach growled; he hadn't eaten at the base that morning. He'd been too worked up.

Once Kynn was a few feet in front of him, Ezra followed. Even though he was used to tracking targets, Kynn Sathir blended into the Kalyndran crowd very well. Too well, almost. But the occasional flash of dark hair above most other heads or Kynn's forest green jacket gave Ezra a trail to follow.

Twenty minutes passed that way, with Ezra following and Kynn leading him damn near through the entire southern quarter. Ezra was just beginning to think the bounty hunter was fucking with him when Kynn slowed down at the entrance to a shipyard.

"Passed your first test," he said, turning and grinning at Ezra.

"You think tracking you in a crowd is a test?" Ezra asked.

Kynn shrugged, a nonanswer. "Come along."

Ezra sighed and followed him through the tall gates. It wasn't the best shipyard; in fact, it looked more like a junkyard. Spare parts and half-assembled ships littered the bays on Ezra's left, and up ahead, only a few ships were actually waiting despite there being room for more. And one of them ...

It was the same silver ship the bounty hunters had brought out to the forest.

Kynn led the way inside, then up the ramp on the left side of the rear hold. It deposited them in a common area with a small kitchen, table that could seat four, and the beginning of a dark hallway. Kynn passed through a doorway and headed into a command room outfitted with a holo table, workbench, a brig, and a terminal of some kind. The more

Ezra saw of the ship, the clearer it became to him that this was an old FSC freighter, obviously converted for their needs.

"Found him," Kynn announced.

Mo and Cass waited on the far side of the holo table, a set of double doors at their back. That had to be the cockpit. Mo crossed her arms over her chest as she sized Ezra up.

He gave her a bored look. "Trying to intimidate me or something? I thought we agreed to meet at The Aurora."

"We did," she said, "but I figured you'd be eager to get out of here. Doesn't the FSC like to keep a tight schedule?"

"I—" Ezra started.

"Did you get everything organized on your end?" she asked.

"You're taking the job?" He didn't know why it surprised him, but Mora Cevi obviously didn't like the Federation Space Command, and she didn't seem to particularly like him.

"We'd be the biggest fools in the Federation not to take this job if you're desperate enough to offer us so much money," she said. "So, are you ready to go or what?"

"I just need to get my gear from the base." Ezra cursed himself for not already having it. But he hadn't thought he'd need it *now*. "And I'll transfer the first half of the payment to all three of you." They hadn't talked terms of the agreement, but Ezra wasn't about to let this opportunity pass him by.

"Fine," she said. "You have two hours to do what you need to do."

Mo stuck her hand out to him for a shake. Cream bandages obscured her knuckles and the back of her hand, winding all the way up under the dark sleeves of her shirt. When Ezra took her hand, he couldn't help but notice how his engulfed hers. Damn, did she have a firm grip. A little too firm.

"Deal," he said. "I look forward to working with you."

"Let's get going," Mo said, pushing past him. "Don't be late, Lyre!"

The longer Ezra was on Mo's ship—*The Revenant*, apparently—the more he was wondering if this contract had actually been a good idea.

He'd only been back for a half hour, and she hadn't stopped going through a list of rules.

"No eating in your quarters," she said. "I don't want a mess in there."

"I'm not a messy eater," Ezra said.

She glared at him. "No eating in your quarters. No piloting the ship without authorization from me and me alone."

"Why not Cass and Kynn?"

The other two bounty hunters had made themself scarce as Mo gave Ezra a "tour," if it could even be called that. Ezra had seen most of the ship already, but she'd laid everything out for him anyway. *The Revenant* had two decks. The lower deck contained the rear hold, two small crew quarters—where he and Kynn would sleep—an engine room, and a front cargo hold, used more for exercise than storage. The upper deck had the living area, command room, cockpit, and both Mo's and Cass's quarters, plus the brig. It was even outfitted with two small laser cannons and deflector shields.

"Because this is *my* ship," Mo said. "I'm the captain here."

The Revenant certainly wasn't much to look at compared to the new FSC fleets, but Ezra supposed it would do. It seemed solid enough, and it had a Class 12 hyperdrive, the fastest available. It'd beat most large FSC vessels to their destination in just half the time or less.

"Of course," he said. "Didn't mean to question your authority, Captain."

Mo sighed loudly. "Don't be a smart-ass."

Ezra tried not to smirk as he said, "I'm not."

Contrary to whatever Mora Cevi thought, she was not in charge here. He was the one who had issued the contract. But if she needed to think she had the power, he'd let her. He did need her help, after all.

"What else do I need to know?" Ezra asked as they stopped on the lower deck again.

"You're in that room," she said, pointing to the one on her right. "Bathroom's there." She pointed to a door next to it. "There's another bathroom upstairs. Weapons locker is there." She pointed again, behind her to the rear hold. "But I assume you have your own."

"I do." He tapped the hilt on his belt. "Would appreciate you loaning me a gun, though."

"Talk to Cass about it. You can charge your power packs for your saber in the locker." Mo flipped her braid over her shoulder. "Follow me."

She started up to the higher deck again, and he followed, trying not to sigh. It wasn't a very efficient tour. But at least Cass and Kynn were now in the cockpit, preparing them for takeoff. Cass was in the captain's chair, Kynn to her right in the copilot's seat. Mo dropped into the free spot behind Cass, so Ezra took the seat behind Kynn. It had obviously seen better days; the fabric was clean, but the padding was thin.

"Where we going?" Cass asked over her shoulder. "I need coordinates."

"Aerilia," Ezra said.

"Aerilia?" Mo asked. "Why the fuck are we going to Aerilia? I thought we needed to figure out how to track that crystal's signature."

"We do," Ezra said, "but I think we need to start in the capital. They all have apartments there. If we can get into them, we might be able to figure out who they were working for or where they'd head to next."

"You don't know where they'd go?" Mo asked.

"No, but I—"

"Fuck me," she muttered.

"I was going to say the only places I know of that they frequented were on Aerilia," Ezra continued. "If we weren't out on assignment or for military exercises, we were in the capital. That's where they all lived and played. I'd rather try to narrow down where they were going instead of scouring the whole fucking Federation for that crystal's energy signature."

Mo pursed her lips. "Where on Aerilia?"

"Northeastern quadrant," Ezra said, mostly to Cass, who was still watching him with narrow hazel eyes. "There's a public shipyard there not far from where we all lived."

Kynn punched a few buttons next to a screen to his right. "Does the FSC know you're doing this?"

"They'll know if and when they need to know," Ezra said, an uneasy feeling settling in his gut.

He didn't like doing this off the books. His whole life for the past seventeen years had been laid out by the FSC. His standard of dress, his assignments, training, actions. Sure, he'd deviated from some regulations, like not always hiding his tattoos in certain settings, but he generally followed orders.

But Command hadn't given him any choice. He'd needed them, and they hadn't come through other than patching him up, fixing his suit, and telling him to wait for his next assignment. It wasn't honorable or right. He had to make this right.

"They approved my request for leave time," Ezra added, "so whatever I do now is up to me."

Some unreadable look passed between the three bounty hunters before Mo said, "Settle in. We'll be there soon enough."

Chapter 13

Even traveling faster than the speed of light, it'd be a while yet before they made it to Aerilia. The Federation was far reaching, and while Miduna wasn't exactly on the Federation's border, Aerilia was at its heart.

Mo, Cass, and Kynn had taken turns piloting the ship—not that it needed much attention when it was programmed to fly to certain coordinates. But they all liked to keep an eye on things and make sure nobody was following them.

Mo's eyes fluttered open as she stretched out her sore limbs. They were feeling a little better after a full day of rest, but she didn't have the luxury of sitting around much longer.

She flopped into her bed and scrubbed her face. It had been a long fucking week. Longer than she cared to admit. But here she was, on a contract that was off the Syndicate's books. That wasn't technically a problem; bounty hunters could be hired privately. But it wasn't exactly smiled upon by Syndicate leadership. Ril Staga was going to have a fit when he realized what they'd done. It meant the Syndicate wouldn't get their cut of the contract fee.

Mo smiled at the thought.

Now all they had to do was find four Vanguards on the run with a strange crystal.

With a sigh, Mo heaved herself out of bed. The metal floor was cold under her bare feet. Outside the porthole near the ceiling, hyperspace streaked by in blurs of blue, white, and black. She went over to the dark screen near her bedroom door and tapped the surface. It glowed with no new updates; all systems were running smoothly.

She tried to relax. Really, she did. But Cass and Kynn needed a chance to relax, too, so Mo grabbed a pair of leggings and a loose black tunic out of a drawer built into the wall. She pulled her silky pajama top over her head and tossed it on the bed, and the matching shorts followed. It was probably silly, someone like her having soft and delicate pajamas, but it was a comfort to change into them after a long day. Kynn would never let her live it down if he saw her like this. It was Mo's secret—one she intended to keep.

After changing and sliding on her boots, Mo made her bed and headed out into the corridor. A warm, loud laugh echoed through the narrow space. Frowning, she headed into the common room only to find Kynn and Ezra there, a pot of coffee sitting between them.

"No shit?" Kynn asked. "You passed the advanced tactical operations class that soon? I failed during my first and only attempt."

"It's a tough course," Ezra said. His back was to the hall. "But beating the teacher usually means you get to move on pretty quickly."

Kynn shook his head and brought his mug to his lips. Mo crossed her arms over her chest, and the movement must have drawn his attention, because he looked up and nearly choked.

"Oh, hey, Mo," he said. "Ezra and I were just having a nice chat."

"I can see that," she said. "Where's Cass?"

"Flying. She just tapped in. I was going to go to bed soon, actually."

"I can keep an eye on things if you need me to," Ezra said, turning around in his seat to look at Mo. "I'm a good pi—"

"No," she said, ignoring Kynn's exasperated expression. "We've got it covered, thanks."

Ezra tilted his head slightly and raised one eyebrow. "Suit yourself." He pushed to his feet, grabbed his mug, and headed for the command room. "If you'll excuse me."

Once the doors closed behind him, Mo dropped into the chair he'd been occupying. "What?" she asked when Kynn cleared his throat.

"You could let him fly the ship for a few hours."

"Why? I don't trust him."

"It's not like he's going to kill us or something after he just paid us all that money up front."

"I didn't say I thought he'd kill us." Mo grabbed the coffee pot and one of the spare mugs from the middle of the table and poured herself a cup. "I just don't trust many people with my ship."

"Right." Kynn pursed his lips.

"Drop it, Kynn. If you wanted to let him fly, we could've taken your ship."

"You know it's too small for the four of us."

"Exactly." She smiled. "My ship, my rules."

Rolling his eyes, Kynn said, "No bandages today?"

Mo glanced down at her hands, at the smooth pinkish white skin and several small scars. She could actually make out the individual ridges of her knuckles, and her fingers weren't swollen either. "First day in a while they haven't been giving me trouble."

"That's good," he said.

"Yeah."

Really, it was because Mo had managed to secure a dose of soltherin before they'd left Kalyndra. She'd bought it the morning after the ambush, actually, but had only taken it shortly after they entered hyperspace. It had left her feeling sleepy, but that should wear off by the time they got to Aerilia. She needed to be at her best for this contract.

When Kynn yawned, Mo said, "Go get some sleep. I'll take over for Cass soon."

"You sure?"

"I'm sure. I can fly this thing even if my hands *do* hurt."

"Right, well." Kynn tapped the table with his palm. "See you in a few hours, then."

It wasn't until Mo heard Kynn's bedroom door close downstairs that she finally pushed out of her seat. She downed the last of her coffee, then headed toward the cockpit. If she relieved Cass of her duties now, Mo would at least have some quiet time to herself and something to keep her busy.

But as she entered the command room, that same warm laugh from earlier bounced around the space. Ezra Lyre's laugh was pleasant, yes, but he didn't need to be distracting any of them.

"I thought I asked you not to eat or drink in the cockpit," Mo said, crossing her arms as she stopped behind them. Cass was in the captain's chair, and Ezra had dropped into the copilot's seat. His coffee mug was still in his hands.

"You asked me not to fly your ship," Ezra said, "and eat in my room." His eyes flashed with something—mischief, victory, pride? "You said nothing about coffee."

Mo ground her teeth together. "If you spill that—"

"Relax, Cevi," he said, already standing up and moving out of the way. "I'm not going to spill my coffee on your precious ship. This mission's too important. I'm not going to fuck it up."

Cass shifted in her chair, enough to look over her shoulder at where Mo and Ezra stood just a couple feet apart. "I sure hope not," Cass said. "You're paying us a lot of money to see it through."

"I'm careful," Ezra said, moving around Mo to take his coffee far away from the cockpit. "See? Or do you want to lock me in your brig so I really can't cause any trouble?"

"As tempting as that may be," Mo said, taking note of how he so casually leaned against the brig's door, "what's the plan when we get to Aerilia?"

"I already told you," he said, "searching their—"

"Besides searching their apartments," Mo said. "What if we don't find anything there? Surely they weren't careless enough to leave something out in the open about this level of betrayal."

"Deserting *is* a big deal," Cass said.

Ezra's crooked smile faded. "I know it is," he said, voice hard. "Believe me, I fucking know." He ran a hand through his hair, making the sleeve of his shirt tug up slightly to reveal more of the colorful ink he was hiding.

"Were you close?" Cass asked.

He shrugged. "Darius and I did our training together but went through many different and separate teams before that one. I thought we'd all been friends, or at least friendly colleagues, but apparently they had other ideas."

"That's got to be hard," Cass said. "I'd kill Mo if she ever did something like that."

"Thanks a lot," Mo said.

Cass grinned. "Luckily I don't have to worry about that."

Ezra studied the two of them so intently that Mo had to stop herself from squirming. He sighed. "Yeah, well, I thought I didn't have to worry about that either." He lifted his mug to them. "How long have you two—or three, I guess—been working together?"

"Why?" Mo asked.

"I'm curious about the people I've hired," he said. "Is that a crime?"

"It's not a crime, but it's not necessary. We're professionals. We can get the job done."

"I don't doubt your abilities, Cevi," Ezra said. "I just want to know a little more about you."

"I thought you read our files or whatever."

Ezra scratched at his beard with his free hand. "They were rather sparse."

Good. The FSC didn't have that much on them, then.

"The three of us have been together since we were kids," Cass said. "The better part of twenty years."

Ezra studied them again, like they were a puzzle he was trying to assemble. "And you've been working for the Syndicate for … ?"

"For more than a decade," Mo said.

"You've been at this for a long time given how young you are."

Mo wasn't old by any stretch of the imagination—she was twenty-eight—but *young*? "The Syndicate knows talent when it sees it, however young," she said. "You're awfully old to still be a Vanguard, aren't you, Lyre?"

"They don't retire us until we're forty-five," he said. "Sometimes fifty."

"So you've got, what, five years left?"

The corner of his mouth lifted in a smile. "I'm only thirty-five. I've got another fifteen left in me."

That explained the bits of silver coming into Ezra's hair and beard. It didn't look bad. It suited him, actually.

Ezra pushed off the brig door. "I'm going to sleep; wake me if anything happens. And I promise I'll keep all food and drinks confined to the previously defined areas, *Captain*."

And with that, Ezra was gone again.

Shaking her head, Mo dropped into the copilot seat and began checking a few of the screens and panels. All the systems were operating at full efficiency. If nothing knocked them out of hyperspace, they'd be to Aerilia in just another twelve hours.

"I feel bad for him," Cass said, voice so low Mo almost didn't hear her.

"Who, Lyre?"

"Who else?"

"Kynn maybe."

Cass shook her head. "No, I just mean it's got to be hard, losing your team like that. Even if they weren't that close."

As much as Mo liked to think she wouldn't bother hunting Kynn and Cass across the Federation for that kind of betrayal, she understood Ezra's desire to find answers. She understood betrayal a little too well, had experienced it firsthand many years earlier. But she'd never gotten justice for it.

"Yeah," Mo murmured. "I'm still not letting him drink coffee in here, though. Or letting him fly the damn ship."

Cass let out a light, airy laugh. "I told him not to let you see that mug."

"I can take over here if you want to get some sleep," Mo said.

"Nah, I've been feeling restless." With a sigh, Cass settled back into her chair. "I don't like the thought of going to Aerilia."

"Neither do I."

Their last few trips to the capital hadn't exactly been fun or fruitful. Aerilia was both the capital planet and city, a city that spanned the entire planet. Many people liked it for its cosmopolitan and vibrant areas, but Mo knew a different side of that city. Different people. People who hunted bounty for money, and people who were being hunted by all manner of criminals and government agencies alike.

Mo had been hurt on Aerilia before, and she'd done some hurting there too. She wasn't keen on going back, but she couldn't avoid it forever. She'd always known work would bring her back someday. This was just a lot sooner than she'd expected.

Maybe she wouldn't have to confront the past this time. Maybe she could just focus on doing her job.

"You going to be good?" Mo asked.

"Yeah," Cass said. "You?"

"Always," Mo murmured.

After all, what choice did she have? This was her job, and she was damn good at it.

Chapter 14

As Aerilia came into view, with its glowing surface and numerous ships in orbit, Ezra wished he wasn't back.

Not on this foreign ship. Not with three bounty hunters.

Not like this.

That sight was usually such a relief, especially after hard-fought battles and months away on missions against the Ascended. Now, all it did was make Ezra's stomach churn with anger.

As Mo navigated them closer to the planet, Ezra asked, "You got my coordinates earlier, right?"

"For the last time, Lyre, I got your coordinates," she said as they passed a large FSC transport vessel, one that was easily fifty times bigger than their ship. "Relax."

Cass, who was in the copilot's chair, smirked. Ezra bit the inside of his cheek.

"Let Cass and I handle it," Mo said. "And strap in."

Ezra glanced at Kynn, who was sitting behind Cass. He just gave Ezra an easy smile, an expression he'd worn often since leaving Miduna. They both buckled their seat belt harnesses, though Ezra found it completely unnecessary. He'd jumped out of the backs of ships going faster than this and landed just fine. He'd gone through plenty of landings standing up or asleep in his bunk. But he didn't think testing Mo on the seriousness of her safety protocols was a particularly wise choice.

The next few minutes passed in awkward silence as Mo and Cass navigated through the atmosphere and then the crowded skies of Aerilia. Ezra, still restrained by his seat belt, leaned forward as much as he could to look out the view screen. It was nighttime on this part of the capital, and the city glowed blue and red, both a welcome and strained sight. Ezra's chest tightened uncomfortably.

After another half hour, they touched down in the shipyard Ezra had recommended, and Kynn unhelpfully told him that he could unbuckle his restraints.

Standing, Ezra rolled his shoulders and neck. If they were lucky, there'd still be some smaller transports they could rent, then head to his apartment and start—

"Lyre?" Mo asked. It sounded like it wasn't the first time she'd tried to get his attention.

Ezra shook his head and blinked a few times. Mo stood just a few feet away in the command room, arms crossed tightly over her chest. Cass and Kynn were already downstairs by the sound of it.

"Yeah?" Ezra asked.

"Now what? Where do you want us to go?"

"We'll go to my apartment first," he said. "I have keys for all their places. I just need to get them."

Mo arched an eyebrow. "You think they wouldn't have changed the locks?"

"I can't think of when they would've had time. And regardless, I know how to get in if the keys don't work."

"Then why waste time going to your apartment?"

"Because I don't want to just bust the door down," Ezra said. "Sometimes a little stealth can go a long way. Shouldn't you know that in your line of work?"

Mo shrugged noncommittally. "This seems time sensitive, that's all."

"Let's just get going." Ezra stalked into the common room and toward the ramp. When she made no move to follow, he called over his shoulder, "You coming or not, Cevi?"

Mo shook her head as if frustrated and started forward. "Lead the way."

Ezra worked quickly to gather the few things he thought he'd need in Aerilia, mostly just his sword and a gun borrowed from the bounty hunters. His suit would stay locked away on the ship, and he had plenty of changes of clothes in his apartment. In fact, he'd need to grab some before they left the planet again—if they left the planet again. Maybe they'd get lucky and Darius's buyer would be somewhere on Aerilia.

As he left his pitiful quarters and moved into the rear hold, Ezra paused. Mo, Cass, and Kynn were all heavily armed, Mo with two guns and the hilt of her energy sword, Cass with a rifle and two blasters, and Kynn with a sword and three guns.

"What are you doing?" Ezra asked.

"We're hunting," Mo said. "Your team already tried to kill us once."

"We're *searching*," Ezra corrected, "and you cannot go into this part of Aerilia looking like that. It's going to draw suspicion."

"What's wrong with how we look?" Cass asked, a clear taunt.

Ezra huffed. "Besides the weapons? You don't look Aerilian. At least not the type of Aerilian that'd be in this part of town."

"Oh, I get it," Kynn said with a sage nod and devilish smile. "We look like simple country ne'er-do-wells traipsing through the civilized and upstanding capital."

Frustrated as he was, lashing out would do no good. So, Ezra settled for a watered-down version of the truth instead. "You *look* like bounty hunters. Leave most of your weapons behind and you *might* pass as off-duty FSC members."

"I think I'd rather get all the dirty looks for being a bounty hunter than being mistaken for a soldier," Mo said, and Cass laughed.

Ezra tipped his head back. "Fuck me."

"We'll do it your way," Mo said, already taking one of the guns off her belt as she headed for the weapons locker. "Minimal weapons. Visible weapons, anyway."

Wincing, Cass unhooked her rifle from its strap. "I feel naked."

"I have everything we need at my apartment if something goes sideways," Ezra said.

"And if we aren't at your apartment when it goes sideways?" asked Kynn.

"Then we deal with it," Ezra said. "We won't be going far, anyway. We all live in the same neighborhood."

The three of them exchanged a look Ezra didn't even bother trying to decipher. He just waited for them to disarm to an acceptable level and resecure the weapons locker.

"Better?" Mo asked, hands perched on her wide hips.

"Great," Ezra said. "Now let's get going."

Despite easily getting a rental ship from the yard and there being little air traffic at this time of night, Ezra couldn't help but be on edge as he flew them toward his apartment.

This place was his sanctuary, far away from the FSC and the war and whatever other bullshit he had going on. He rarely let anyone inside, let alone bounty hunters he'd met only a week earlier.

"Intense views," Kynn said as he stared out the window.

All around them, Aerilia rose up against the dark night sky. Tall residential buildings, taller government ones, a myriad of sizes and shapes and colorful lights. Below, more buildings, ships, and even the small, vague outlines of people.

"We're landing in a moment," Ezra said. "Hang on."

He angled the ship right, then down, as they approached one impossibly tall building. Several shorter skyscrapers surrounded it, most of the windows dark. He circled around to the opposite side of the building, where a small launch bay's forcefield glowed blue. Ezra flew the ship inside and set it down in one of the empty spots.

"I didn't realize you could do that," Kynn murmured as he turned in his seat to look at the window behind him.

Ezra flipped a few switches as he began powering down the ship. "All our keys are coded to let us enter."

"We don't have anything like that on Miduna," Kynn said. "I've only seen that on—"

"As fascinating as the intricacies of Aerilian residential technology are," Mo drawled, "can we get going?" She rubbed one of her knees, which she'd been doing on and off since they got in the rented cruiser.

"My apartment's just a couple floors up," Ezra said, pushing a button and opening the door for everyone to climb out.

Mo stretched as they walked through the bay, and Cass whispered something to her, far too quiet for Ezra to hear. Mo shook her head.

Frowning, Ezra led them through the double doors at the far end of the bay and into the building. The interior was silent, not another soul in sight. Warm lights were spaced evenly along the ceilings, and the dark carpets and walls made everything both sleek and cozy. Ezra always appreciated returning here after missions away or long days at headquarters. Now it just made his muscles tense.

After a short elevator ride to the top floor, the trio followed Ezra down several more long, silent hallways before he finally stopped outside a door. It was the last one in that section of the building.

Ezra blocked the door with his body, then tapped in his code to unlock it. He reached for the handle.

"If there are codes to get in, why do we need keys for your team's apartments?" Mo asked.

"Because you have to have the code and the programmed key on your person to get in," Ezra said. On the one hand, it was a bit primitive—few things still required any kind of physical key—but Ezra also appreciated that a simple code wasn't the only method of security for his apartment.

"And does your team happen to have a key for *your* place?" Mo asked as Ezra pushed the door open.

"Yes," Ezra said, the word clipped.

"You think they wouldn't have come in here?"

He'd thought about it, but he wouldn't get an answer until they checked. "I'll have everything changed tonight."

That must have satisfied Mo because she kept her mouth shut as they walked into Ezra's dark apartment. As they rounded the corner of the entry hall and entered the main living space, Kynn and Cass both swore.

Wide windows lined the far wall, giving an expansive view of Aerilia with how high up they were. The city's warm lights cast a glow through the living room and kitchen, which were spotless thanks to Ezra's weekly cleaning crew. The last thing he needed was to come home from the front to a dirty house.

"Shit, Lyre," Mo said as she watched her friends move toward the windows. "How much money are they paying you at the FSC to afford a place like this?"

Ezra shrugged. His military salary was good, but that wasn't what allowed him to afford this place. That was family money, but he didn't like to talk about it. It was ... complicated.

Though Ezra came from a well-connected Aerilian family—very well-connected, both in government and business—he was the odd one out. Both sides of his family looked down on his decision to join the military. His parents were professors at the top of their fields, and most of his extended family were academics, politicians, or businesspeople who had no interest in *fighting* the war that kept them all safe. Only his paternal grandmother had ever supported his desire to move away from a more aristocratic lifestyle, and she had long since passed.

The money for this apartment had been a gift from his parents when he'd turned eighteen, one Ezra had grudgingly accepted. All kids in their family received a portion of their future inheritance when they turned eighteen. He hadn't known what to do with it, but buying the place had seemed like the right move. He'd put the rest into investment and savings accounts. He didn't regret taking their money, even if it had made him feel obligated to his parents for a few years. But when they still hadn't tried to understand his life choices or career, he'd cut them off for good.

"Let me just grab the keys," Ezra said over his shoulder as he headed for the study. "There should be food in the fridge. Help yourselves."

Bottles clinked in the kitchen. Good. He needed to keep them occupied while he got the keys from the safe and—

"You didn't use your military money to pay for this place, did you?"

Ezra jumped and found Mo leaning against the doorframe.

"You scared the shit out of me," he muttered.

She pushed off the wall and strolled inside his office, examining the books and awards carefully placed inside the wood shelves. "There's not even a speck of dust in this place."

"I like it to be clean," he said.

Mo paused in front of an antique copper teapot his grandmother had gifted him from her home planet of Cyranel. "It's like a fucking museum in here."

"That was a gift," he said, and she raised an eyebrow at him. "Can you please turn around? I need to get into my safe."

Mo actually laughed. She had a light, airy, beautiful laugh, a total contrast to her rough-and-tumble personality. "Since you asked nicely." She turned her back to him and focused on the shelves again.

When Ezra was certain she wasn't looking, he knelt and opened one of the built-in cabinets on the far side of the room. Inside was a safe. Its screen lit up. With one final peek at Mo, Ezra punched in the ten digit code, then opened the heavy door.

His safe held only a handful of things: his team's apartment keys, the spare one of his, an old blaster, and a few pictures from his childhood. He ignored everything but the keys and tucked them into his pocket, then shut the safe and the cabinet doors.

"Got what I need," Ezra said.

Mo was still marveling at the shelves on the far side of the room. "You have *real* books."

"Yeah."

"I haven't seen these in a long time."

"My mother collects them," Ezra said. "It rubbed off on me."

And that was the simple truth of it. His mother had always collected antiquities and rarities, including physical books. Basically everything was digital now, but Ezra liked the permanence of a real book. There was something comforting about them.

Mo sighed almost wistfully as her fingers ran along one of the spines. "So did mine."

Any other day, Ezra would be happy to let her look around at his collection, but they had things to do.

"Can we get going?" he asked.

Mo snapped to attention and, sending what could almost be called a glare his way, headed back toward the kitchen. Shaking his head, Ezra closed his office door and followed her.

Cass and Kynn were loitering near the kitchen island, a few glass bottles of lemonade and water sitting between them. Only the one closest to Kynn was open.

"Got what you need?" Kynn asked.

Ezra nodded.

Kynn gestured toward the front door. "Lead the way, Commander."

Chapter 15

Ezra's first order of business was getting his keys and passcode changed, which had only taken a quarter of an hour thanks to his building's efficient management crew. He didn't trust that his team wouldn't come back to finish the job after they'd failed to kill him—once they figured it out, anyway.

With that done, he escorted the bounty hunters through a tenth-floor walkway that connected his building to Darius's. He figured that was the best place to start. After all, Darius was the one who would have set this whole thing in motion.

He still didn't understand why, but hopefully the team's apartments would shed some light on the situation.

Darius's building—and the rest of them in the complex—didn't have the same dark luxury Ezra's did. They were still nice, more welcoming and open thanks to their lighter interiors. The hallways here were quiet, and a few paintings of Aerilia hung on the walls.

"Where's Kane's apartment?" Kynn asked as they stepped into the lift.

Ezra tapped Darius's key card to the touch pad, then punched in his access code. "Twentieth floor," he said as the elevator started ascending.

"That's barely halfway up," Kynn said.

Ezra shrugged.

"And yet you live on the top floor of your building," Cass said.

Ezra shrugged again. They could think whatever they wanted. He knew how lucky he was to have gotten any family money at all—not just because of his familial conflicts but because others in the Federation weren't so privileged.

As soon as they got off the elevator, Ezra strode toward Darius's apartment. When they reached the junction that would take them the last of the way, Ezra stopped and raised his fist.

"You see something?" Mo asked from right behind him.

Ezra peered around the corner and found an empty corridor. "Let me go first."

"You have to go first," Mo said. "You have the key."

Ezra huffed. That wasn't how he'd meant it. He wanted to check for any signs of tampering. Ignoring Mo's comment, he headed down the hall. The others were so quiet he had to check to make sure they'd followed him.

The door to Darius's apartment looked like it always had: light gray metal, touch pad on the right-hand side, and nothing more. There were no scuffs, burns, scratches, or indents that would suggest something had been done to the door.

Ezra didn't think Darius would do anything reckless like wire the door with explosives. Whatever he was after, it wouldn't be hurting civilians or possibly taking down an entire skyscraper. Darius may have betrayed the FSC—and Ezra—but Ezra didn't think he'd do something *that* drastic.

What choice did he have? Ezra just needed to go inside.

When he touched the key card to the pad, the screen lit up, prompting him to enter Darius's code. Ezra did and held his breath. The screen lit up green, then the door unlocked.

He pushed down on the handle. No clicks or other sounds to suggest anything had become armed. Ezra eased the door open and flipped on the light switch right inside. If anyone was watching for signs of life in

Darius's apartment, Ezra had probably just fucked this up, but he didn't want to risk missing anything dangerous.

There was nothing.

It was the same apartment, filled with Darius's things. Pictures on the walls of his family at his graduation and promotion ceremonies, of the team on missions and assignments all over the Federation. Ezra's heart squeezed, but he forced his gaze away. He wasn't here to feel sorry for himself. He was here to find answers.

"Place looks clear." Ezra entered the small kitchen and living area. He pointed with each assignment as he said, "Sathir, check the kitchen. Farr, living room. Cevi, office."

He ignored their questioning looks and headed down the short, dark hallway that led to Darius's bedroom. Ezra flipped one switch as he went, lighting the whole place up.

The white walls of Darius's bedroom seemed to mock Ezra, as did the plain bedsheets and empty drawers and closet. There wasn't a damn thing in this place to suggest where Darius may have gone or who he was working for. The few clothes he'd left behind didn't have any strange insignia, tracking devices, comms units, or anything.

Shit.

Abandoning the bedroom, Ezra went to the office, where Mo was still rooting through drawers in the sleek desk on the far side of the room. Her eyebrows pinched together.

"Find something?" Ezra asked.

"No," she said. "I was just marveling at how much shit he's put in here. Guess that's why the place looks so clean."

Ezra joined her and began sifting through what she'd already examined. Not because he didn't trust her to be good at her job but because he just needed to reassure himself there was *nothing*. And there wasn't.

There were more old photos, random tools, even notepads. There was a tablet too.

"I was going to bring that to you," Mo said, almost defensively, as Ezra picked it up. "I didn't know the code to get in."

"Wouldn't expect you to," he murmured as he powered it on.

The screen lit up. He entered the same code Darius used for everything, and the device unlocked. Ezra steadied his breathing as he began tapping through the most recently used programs and documents.

None of Darius's messages seemed out of place, encrypted, or otherwise coded. They were either to the team chat—which Ezra had been part of—or headquarters. There were no deleted or hidden messages either. The entertainment programs were just attuned to popular shows and a self-help book titled *The Path to Unstoppable Leadership*. Ezra scoffed and kept looking.

A recent bank statement saved to the device detailed Darius's savings, which were neither exceedingly high nor low, and recent spending. There were payments for taxi shuttles, food, and clothes. And then there were the repeating payments to—

"What's Vertex?" Mo asked.

Ezra jumped. "Fuck," he muttered, finding her peering over his arm to look at the tablet. "Do you always have to do that?"

"Shouldn't you be paying attention, Lyre?" she asked. "Pretty sure that's part of Vanguard training, being aware of your surroundings."

Ezra ignored her, instead saying, "Vertex is a bar north of here."

"So he likes to drink," she said.

"No, Darius doesn't drink that much, and besides, Vertex is *not* the kind of place he'd go."

"Why not?"

"It's …" How did Ezra put this? "It's just not the kind of place any of us go. It's where a lot of the politicians and high rollers spend their time and take meetings off the books."

"You're saying he's too poor to go there?"

"No. It's just not the kind of place the FSC goes."

In fact, it was the type of place Ezra preferred to avoid. It was the kind of place his parents and extended family might go on a night out.

"So he likes fancy bars," Mo said. "You don't know that about him?"

"He hasn't in all the years I've known him."

"Sounds almost like you don't know your team that well at all."

Ezra sighed and pocketed the tablet. "Put everything back in the drawers," he said, stalking toward the door. "We need to go."

"That's it?" Mo called after him.

"We're not done. We just need to keep moving."

Checking the other three apartments belonging to Jarek, Kira, and Talon revealed exactly what Ezra had both hoped and feared: they had various receipts for Vertex as well.

"There's no way that's a coincidence," Kynn said as he stared down at the four tablets on Ezra's kitchen counter. "Unless they really just needed a break from you after work, Lyre."

"Aren't they supposed to be professionals?" Mo asked. "What're they doing leaving all their shit around for people like us to find?"

Ezra couldn't even fake a laugh. "That's our next move. Vertex, I mean."

"Then let's go," Cass said.

"Can't." Ezra frowned. "It's closed."

"I thought nothing closed on Aerilia," Kynn said.

With it being nearly three in the morning, very few things would still be open, at least in this part of the city-planet. "Trust me, it'll be closed," he said, "and I really don't feel like breaking in."

"I'm surprised," Mo mused as she lifted herself to sit on the counter. "First your team's apartments, now this club? Doesn't seem like something a proper and respectable military man would do."

"Good thing I'm neither proper nor respectable, Cevi." Ezra swore one corner of her mouth curved up slightly, and he couldn't help but be satisfied with himself. "We'll go tomorrow, early afternoon, and see what we can find."

"Until then?" Cass asked.

Ezra shrugged. "Get some sleep?"

"We should go back to *The Revenant*," Mo said. "I know you cleared the place, but I wouldn't put it past those fuckers to come around and try to murder us in our sleep."

Ezra nodded. "I agree."

"Wow." The corners of Mo's mouth pulled up again. "The great Commander Lyre agrees with me."

Mora Cevi had been less than friendly to him in the last week, but even this hint of playfulness helped him relax just a bit. His chest warmed, and he couldn't help but wonder what it might take to get her to smile more often. She had a nice smile. He wouldn't tell her that, though.

"Enough out of you two," Kynn said. "Grab your shit, and let's get out of here. I'm beat."

Ezra grabbed the last of what he needed—a duffel bag full of clothes, extra toiletries, and his personal tablet—then the evidence they'd found, and followed the bounty hunters to the door. Before he flipped the lights off, Ezra took one last look at his apartment and sighed. He was usually glad to get to stay here, to be away from the front for a little while, but he couldn't wait to get back to *The Revenant* and get to work.

Chapter 16

Getting just a few hours of sleep had Mo's head pounding and body aching.

Not only had their search lasted long into the night, but just being on Aerilia had Mo on edge. What little sleep she did get had been plagued by blood, incomprehensible screams, melting steel, and a desperate panic she hadn't felt in a very long time.

Mo popped a few pain relievers she kept in a small bottle next to her bed, then grabbed the thick wraps she used to support her joints. Her left knee, right shoulder, and right hand were particularly painful, so she wrapped them all carefully. It helped a little, but she'd be feeling it all day.

With a groan, she pushed off her bed and got dressed, opting for a black tunic that stopped mid-thigh, dark gray leggings, and her tall boots. After attaching her hilt to her belt, Mo left her room.

Where she'd expected an empty hall, she instead found a muscled chest and strong hands grabbing hold of her.

"Shit, sorry," Ezra said, dropping her.

Mo blinked. Ezra was practically in her doorway, his tattoos on full display thanks to his short-sleeved white shirt. The black and white marks were actually making up star systems, Mo realized, connected by thin red paths that reminded her of fire. But she didn't dare study him too closely.

"What the fuck, Lyre?" she bit out. "Haven't you heard of knocking? Or using the comms system?"

"I *was* going to knock, but—" he started.

"Good morning!" Kynn said from just behind Ezra, right near the entrance to the common room. His voice was light, almost too friendly. "We ready to hit up the club?"

"It's a bar," Ezra said as he turned to face Kynn. "Not a club."

"My sincerest apologies, Commander."

"*Anyway*," Ezra said. "Yes, we need to go."

What was Ezra like when he wasn't fixated on a mission or having his buttons pushed? Mo didn't know why she was curious, but she was. His expensive, high-rise apartment and that collection of real books had her more confused about him than ever.

She shook it off. She didn't need to know Ezra Lyre to get this job done. She just needed to know enough about his team to figure out what they were up to.

"Can we take *The Revenant*?" Mo asked.

"I wouldn't," Ezra said. "Too big."

"My ship is hardly too big." She didn't even know why the insinuation offended her; there was nothing wrong with a large ship. Part of her just couldn't help but respond to Ezra; it certainly wasn't the most professional or mature option.

"Small as it may be," Ezra said, placing his hand on the ceiling as if to demonstrate, "it's too big for Vertex. We'll rent another shuttle."

"Fine." Mo sauntered past him. "It's your money. Waste it however you want."

Once Cass joined them, they headed out into the midmorning sun. Ezra led the way back to the shuttle rental booth at the shipyard and secured the same one they'd used the night before. Its seats were barely padded and only made Mo's body ache that much more. She tried to ignore it.

"What's your backup plan if we don't find anything at Vertex, Lyre?" Mo asked. "We won't be able to look for the crystal's signature if we don't know where to find your team."

"We'll go to the university," he said. "We'll ask around about the crystal. Maybe we can learn enough to figure out where to search."

"Right, because a glowing purple crystal found in caves on Miduna is *so* specific," Kynn said. "We know nothing else about it?"

"Nope," Ezra said, his voice strained.

Mo settled back into her seat and watched the city pass by. Air traffic wasn't terrible and kept flowing at a steady pace. Kynn and Cass chatted about lunch options—apparently Ezra had the perfect spot for sunburst wraps, one of Kynn's favorites—quizzed Ezra on Aerilian governmental affairs—which he seemed to know little about—and even shared with him some of the more innocent stories of their past visits to the capital planet. Mo kept her mouth shut.

After another half hour, Ezra navigated them toward a towering red spire that looked like it was made out of a giant crystal. Its edges were jagged and rough, and it was the tallest building for at least a couple of miles. In her past visits to Aerilia, Mo hadn't ventured anywhere near this part of the city-planet. That thought made her relax a bit.

"This place looks intense," Kynn said as Ezra pulled the ship into a bay much like the one back at his apartment. This one was nearly empty. "Is the whole place Vertex?"

Ezra began powering down the shuttle. "No, just the top few floors. Come on, let's try to catch them before they open for lunch."

Mo let both men exit first, trying to hide a wince as she stretched out her bad knee. She'd need to find another dose of soltherin soon. She couldn't work if her joints kept this up.

"Mo," Cass whispered from behind her. "You good?"

"No," Mo said.

But when she realized Ezra was watching her impatiently, she forced herself to walk as normally as possible. He couldn't know about her issues. He might fire her if he thought she wasn't fit for duty. She *was* fit to work, as long as she was able to take care of herself.

Even worse was the idea that he might pity her or judge her. It wasn't until after the Fall of Veronis I that Mo's joints had started acting up. The Syndicate had brought in specialists to take a look at her, but the only thing that could be done was take soltherin. One doctor had suggested she go see a healer—those sunshapers whose magic allowed them to heal people—but the Syndicate hadn't wanted to pay for it. Mo couldn't even blame them; she didn't want to pay for it now that she was on her own. Magical healing could last longer than drugs but was prohibitively expensive. Soltherin wasn't cheap, but it was slightly more accessible.

Some doctors had said Mo's joint problems were due to the stress of losing her home and family. Some said it was genetic. Others had no idea. Mo was pretty sure it was some combination of all of those things that plagued her. Bodies were complicated, but they were also resilient.

She just couldn't let Ezra—or any other clients—find out about it. Ril Staga knowing the truth was bad enough.

"You think *The Revenant* is small?" Mo snapped at Ezra as she walked by him. She made a show of stretching her whole body out. "That piece of shit you rented is a thousand times worse."

"That piece of shit got us here, didn't it?" Ezra asked.

Mo ignored him, and she ignored the admonishing look Kynn threw her way. Cass set one hand between Mo's shoulder blades, a reassuring feeling. Cass had always known about Mo's body and always supported her. She didn't act like Mo was too weak to handle the physicality their job demanded, though she did gently prod Mo to slow down as needed.

Mo would always appreciate Cass's steady hand. She just hoped she would always be able to support Cass the same way.

Ezra led them out of the bay and straight into a lobby. The ceiling extended up two stories, and the windows lining the far wall provided a view of Aerilia. The small lights embedded into the walls gave the appearance of stars among the swirls of black and red paint. Everything else was expensive, either leather, wood, or crystal and gold, all of it equally obnoxious.

"Could they have chosen a gaudier aesthetic?" Mo whispered to Cass.

She grinned. "Ril would like it."

"Maybe we can ship him off here next time he pisses us off."

"The only way you're getting him to leave office is the day he dies," Cass said.

Morbid as it was, it was the truth. Ril Staga would never voluntarily leave his position at the Syndicate.

Ezra strode up to the half-moon counter flanked by doorways on the back wall. He pushed a small buzzer with a label that read "ring for assistance."

The air stilled. Ezra didn't move a muscle.

What was he waiting for?

A short Human woman swept out from the left door. Her box braids were dyed rose pink, a beautiful contrast to her umber skin. The black and red dress she wore had to be some kind of uniform.

She raised one perfectly shaped eyebrow at Ezra. "We're closed."

Ezra pulled something off his belt—a badge? "You're open."

The woman pressed her full lips together as she glanced from Ezra to the badge and back again. "What do you want, Vanguard?"

"To ask your staff some questions."

"Fine, but you have to be quick," she said. "Don't want clients showing up and thinking we're in the FSC's pocket or something."

The woman turned on her heel and hurried back through the left door. Ezra followed her. Kynn shrugged at Cass and Mo, and they all stalked after the commander.

This place had to be the *real* Vertex. It was decorated much the same as the lobby, with lots of booths in shadowy corners. The stage where a band would normally play was empty and dark. A few staff in red and black uniforms were cleaning tables around the wide space, while others were stocking glassware behind the bar. A spiral staircase in the middle of the room led to a mezzanine on the second floor with more tables.

"Ausha!" the pink-haired woman called. "Ausha, this guy needs to talk to you."

One of the employees behind the bar lifted her head. Her white Sorthian tattoos nearly blended into her pale skin, and her hair was as white as Mo's.

"That's our manager," the pink-haired woman said. "You have fifteen minutes."

"I'm gonna need longer than that," Ezra said.

"Fifteen," the woman repeated, then walked off.

Ezra scratched at his beard. His jaw tightened. But he shook his head and headed over to where Ausha was waiting for them at the bar.

"What can I do for you?" Ausha asked. "We aren't breaking any laws, I promise."

"I'm not with law enforcement," Ezra said blandly.

"You sure don't look like a civilian." Ausha's narrow lips pulled into a smile. "None of you do. We don't get your type in here often."

"Really?" Ezra reached into his pocket and pulled out a small tablet, then turned it on to reveal photos of his team. "Because these four were in here a lot in recent weeks according to their bank statements."

Ausha pushed back from the counter slightly. "So?"

"They're Vanguards." Ezra set his badge on the bar top, its purple and silver crest shining in the bar's low lights. "You spotted us immediately, so how'd you never clock them?"

"You're all Vanguards?" Ausha asked.

"Fuck no," Mo said. When the woman raised her thin eyebrows, Mo didn't elaborate.

"Yeah, I've seen them a few times," Ausha said, glancing from Ezra to the photos again. "Especially this one, the tall one." She pointed at Darius's picture. "I definitely saw him. He wouldn't stop hitting on me."

Mo's upper lip curled.

"What else did they do while they were here?" Ezra asked. "I've heard Vertex hosts people looking for ... work."

Like bounties? Mo wondered. This place definitely wasn't associated with the Syndicate. One of the smaller guilds, then? She didn't think so. None of them had money for a place like this. It seemed more like a place where politicians and corporate leaders would gather and make backroom deals. The thought was enough to piss her off.

Ausha twisted a black towel between her hands. "Sometimes, yeah. Our clients are varied. We don't ask questions."

"Maybe you should start," Cass said, gesturing to the photos. "Those are some dangerous people."

Lowering her voice, Ausha leaned across the bar. "We get a lot of dangerous people in here. Dangerous people tend to have the money to spend."

Mo really did *not* like the sound of this.

"Any idea who this man was talking to?" Ezra asked, pointing at Darius. "Did he get work from someone?"

Ausha's lips pinched together. "There's been talk recently," she said. "Ask any of the servers in here. Several parties have been in here looking for hired muscle. I don't know what for; it's best that I don't ask questions."

The people Mo usually hunted down weren't prone to telling the truth. This Ausha, though? Mo believed her. She was just a bar manager who probably didn't get paid enough to deal with shitty customers all night. Mo had seen it often enough back at The Aurora in Kalyndra.

"Do you have any security footage?" Ezra asked.

"Yes," Ausha said. "But it gets deleted every morning."

"Doesn't seem very smart," Kynn said.

Mo had to agree. It was awfully convenient, too, that there'd be no trace of Darius or the others except for those receipts.

"Again, we get dangerous people in here who have money to spend," Ausha replied quietly. "It's not my job to question how things work around here."

And while Mo agreed with Kynn, she also understood why Vertex's owner would set the system up that way. If well-connected people were coming here to make deals, they'd expect a level of discretion and anonymity. Receipts for their drinks was one thing; video footage of them speaking with one another was different.

"Thank you for your time," Ezra said. "Can we speak to some of your staff?"

"Make it quick," Ausha said. "Some of our clients come in early. Don't need them seeing you here, Vanguard."

Considering there were clients looking to hire muscle, and someone had hired four Vanguards already, Mo found that comment strange. Maybe those clients hadn't realized Darius and the others were with the FSC? But Mo didn't push; it would just be a waste of time. Instead, she dutifully followed Ezra around the bar as they interviewed a few different staff. All of them said the same—or less—than Ausha.

"So," Cass said once they were safely back in their shuttle, "why would Darius and the others be looking to pick up work? I could maybe understand them taking a security job or something, but why betray their stations?"

Ezra eased the shuttle back out into the skies. He was tense, tight, perhaps more rigid than Mo's joints felt. He sucked in a deep breath as they merged into traffic and said, "That's what we're going to find out."

CHAPTER 17

Ezra tried to keep his cool as he piloted their shuttle toward Aerilia's foremost university, but he still found his hands tightening around the controls.

Darius fucking Kane.

Had whatever contract he'd taken stipulated that he had to kill Ezra? Or was he just unfortunate collateral damage?

Ezra wanted to pretend it didn't matter, but it did. If he was just collateral damage, that was unfortunate. But if Darius had been hired to steal that crystal *and* kill Ezra, that changed everything. And he would make Darius pay—especially if the FSC wouldn't.

Don't fixate, Ezra warned himself as he flew down to the university's sky gardens. He couldn't fixate on this. Not now. Not when there was work to do and when he needed to be in control. He couldn't have these bounty hunters thinking he'd completely lost his mind.

"Wow," Cass breathed as they climbed out of the shuttle.

Ezra had parked it with a few others on the perimeter of the gardens, which, as odd as it looked, was entirely acceptable. He knew because this was where his parents both worked.

His father, Kaden Lyre, was a famous architect who had designed countless iconic buildings across the Federation and won more awards than they ever had room for in their house when Ezra was growing up. He also taught a few classes every semester and had helped design these sky gardens decades ago. And Ezra's mother, Doctor Adira Valtor, was a mathematics professor. Last Ezra had heard, she'd finally had some new breakthroughs in her field of abstract algebra.

Ezra never had cared much for math or architecture. Hopefully he wouldn't run into either of them.

"This place is beautiful," Kynn said, turning in a circle as Ezra led them through the pristine paths cutting through the gardens.

They were filled with flora and fauna from all over the Federation, from glowing night flowers and moss to red-leafed trees and bushes with purple spots on them. The gardens started ten stories above the planet's surface and continued up for another five stories, each level home to some of the university's departments. The other parts of the campus weren't quite as beautiful, and that was where Ezra's parents *should* be.

"Yup," Ezra said.

"You don't think so?" Cass asked. "Or are you just spoiled because you see things like this all the time?"

"Nope," Ezra said. "Just don't care much for flowers and all that."

In truth, all Ezra wanted to do was get out of the open and find some of these professors who had been at the dig site. They'd left Miduna before Ezra and the bounty hunters, so they would surely be in their offices or lecture halls by now.

"It wouldn't kill you to stop and admire things, y'know," Kynn said, clapping his hand on Ezra's shoulder. "Might help you smile."

"I'm perfectly fine not smiling," Ezra said. "Let's go."

But Cass had stopped to read a placard, and Mo was just a few steps behind her. She'd been moving slower all morning than Ezra had seen before. He didn't think she'd been hurt in the ambush, but had he missed that just like he'd missed signs of his team's impending betrayal? He doubted it; he probably wouldn't hear the end of it from her if she had been injured.

Slowly, Cass turned to face Ezra, a sly grin pulling at her mouth. "Who's Kaden Lyre?"

Fuck me, Ezra thought.

"My father." He didn't see much of a point in lying.

"Your father designed this place?" Cass asked, drawing a surprised yelp out of Kynn and a confused look from Mo.

"He's designed a lot of places," Ezra said. "It's not important. Can we go, please? You three should know better than to be outside when Darius and the others might be tracking us or something."

"Let's get going," Mo said. She was clearly trying to walk without a limp, but she seemed to be protecting her left side.

"Let's," Ezra said, walking just half a step behind her.

He directed Mo to the archaeology building, a shining golden structure with a glass roof designed to look like a crystal. Cass and Kynn marveled at that, too, and any other day, Ezra would admit it was both beautiful and impressive. Today? Not so much.

"Professor Oron might be the one to talk to," Mo said, voice low as they entered the empty lobby.

Everything from the floors to walls was made of white tiles. The glass roof high above cast rainbows across all surfaces; it was almost like being in a prism.

"Is he the one who almost got in a fight with Kane?" Cass asked.

Ezra nodded.

"Before all that went down, some of his tablets and scanners weren't working, and he'd mentioned radiation as a possibility," Mo said. "Kane denied it but was uneasy about the whole conversation."

"You think Kane realized the crystal was disrupting some of the tech?" Cass asked.

"But why only some?" Kynn asked.

Mo shrugged.

After asking a few students, they found Professor Oron's office. It was on the building's fourth floor, set far away from that ornate lobby in a more practical part of the building with beige carpet and white walls. Announcement boards, display cases, and more peppered the halls, and more than one lecture let out as they were trying to make their way to the professor's office. But they made it, and to Ezra's great surprise, the man was actually in there, sitting behind his desk. His door was even open.

Ezra still knocked. "Excuse me, Professor Oron?" he called.

The professor startled and looked up from the tablet he was reading. "Can I help you?"

"I'm Commander Ezra Lyre—"

"Oh!" Professor Oron nearly jumped out of his seat, his cheeks flushing periwinkle. "Commander, I barely recognized you without your armor and weapons." It wasn't the first time Ezra had heard that. "Please, come in."

Ezra stepped aside so the three bounty hunters could enter, and once Ezra was inside, he closed the door behind them. The professor's office was large despite the furniture crowding the walls. Mo and Kynn dropped into the two armchairs in front of Oron's desk.

"Is this about the events on Miduna?" Professor Oron asked. "We were debriefed by military leaders both there and here on Aerilia when we returned—"

"Sort of," Ezra said. "I'm not here on behalf of the FSC. I'm looking for information."

"I see." The professor sat back in his chair and steepled his fingers in front of his mouth. "What kind of information?"

"Do you remember when Sergeant Kane and I were speaking with you, by that pillar?" Mo asked, and the professor nodded. "Did his team ever touch your equipment? The stuff that stopped working?"

"Indeed, they did."

"Could they have tampered with it?" Cass asked.

"I don't believe so," the professor said. "The FSC examined every-thing. I told them about that."

Damn. Ezra supposed that would've been too easy.

"Did the FSC tell you what Sergeant Kane and the rest of my crew found in that cave?" Ezra asked.

Oron's thick eyebrows furrowed. "No, they did not."

Shit. Now what was Ezra supposed to do? He doubted the FSC want-ed this information to get out. But if they weren't going to find Kane and the others, what was he supposed to do? Let them run off?

"Were you looking for something in particular at this site?" Ezra asked. "Any artifacts, statues ... crystals?"

"Crystals?" The professor chuckled. "Why would we be looking for crystals? We've got no use for them."

Fuck it.

"My team ambushed me after finding a small glowing crystal in caves north of the dig site," Ezra said. "It seemed to be putting off the strange energy spikes we thought might've been Ascended or Separatists."

"Energy spikes from a crystal?" Oron frowned. "Can they do that?"

"It might be why your tech was acting up," Mo said.

The professor sucked in a breath as if to say something, then shook his head and grabbed his tablet. He began tapping its surface furiously, almost like he was trying to find something. Kynn glanced back at Ezra, who shrugged.

"Professor?" Mo asked.

"Apologies." Oron still didn't look up. "Apologies. I had a thought ..."

"Would you like to share with the class?" Mo asked, earning her an exasperated look from the professor. Ezra suppressed a smile.

"My colleague, Professor Bas're. She's been conducting this research …" He tapped a few more buttons. "She'll be here in a moment. I've asked her to join us."

"What kind of research?" Cass asked.

"She's part of the archaeology department and focuses on religious studies."

"Why wasn't she at the dig?" Kynn asked.

"Her wife is sick," Oron replied. "She didn't want to leave her."

"Understandable," Ezra said.

Someone knocked on the door, then it slid open. A plump Ivari woman with light blue skin stood just outside, her icy eyes bright.

"Ah, Bas're!" Oron called. "Please, come in, come in. I'd like you to meet some folks." He tried to introduce the lot of them but didn't remember Mo, Cass, or Kynn's names. "They have a question about a crystal that was found on Miduna."

Bas're perked up. "Do you have it with you?"

"No, unfortunately," Ezra said. "It was stolen, found about one klick north of one of the main parts of the dig Professor Oron was on."

"Describe it for me," Bas're said.

"Six inches long, glowing, a mix of purple, blue, and gold," Ezra said. "It put off strange energy readings that triggered Vanguard suits. We thought it might've been an Ascended ship until we went to investigate."

Bas're pressed her thin lips together and toyed with the silver wedding band on her ring finger. "I see."

"What is it, Professor?" Cass asked.

"You know of the Eternal Ones?" Bas're asked.

Mo nodded. "What about them?"

"We continue to study them, though most believe they are nothing but fables," Bas're said. "My assistant and I have recently stumbled upon texts that suggest there were … artifacts … associated with the Eternal Ones."

"What kind of artifacts?" Ezra asked slowly.

"A sword and a key," Bas're said. "A crystal as well."

Nobody moved.

But then Mo snorted. "I'm sorry," she said. "You mean to tell me that whatever those fuckers stole was an artifact from the Eternal Ones? What, did Kane get himself involved with some religious zealots or something?"

"Cevi—" Ezra started, but she waved her hand at him.

"The Eternal Ones are *just* stories," Mo said.

"That's what people think," Bas're replied. "They think the Eternal Ones and their artifacts are just myths, meant to serve as moral lessons and cultural symbols, most now lost to time. But there are texts that speak of them."

Kynn leaned back in his chair and folded his arms across his chest. "There are texts that speak of many things. Why is this any different?"

Ezra tried not to sigh. Really, he did. But ancient artifacts? The Eternal Ones?

"More people are beginning to learn about them," Bas're said. "To return to our old beliefs. As life gets harder daily all across the Federation, people are looking back in time for answers."

"Shouldn't we be looking *forward* for solutions?" Cass asked, earning her a glare from both professors.

"Of course we should, but there's a comfort people find in an idealized version of the past," Oron said. "And of course, there are things to be learned too. It's why I have a job!"

"Philosophical questions aside, there have been rumors of people looking for these artifacts," Bas're said. "People who believe in them, as well as people who see an opportunity to make a fortune from them, as is often the case."

Was it as the staff at Vertex had suggested, that Darius and the crew had been hired by someone there to locate and steal one of these artifacts? Ezra had heard of far more outlandish things in his long career. This wasn't that implausible at all, even if he didn't believe in the Eternal Ones. Someone might pay a lot of money for something they *thought* was one of these artifacts, like the religious zealots Mo had suggested.

Or maybe the Ascended were looking to start more covert operations throughout the Federation?

Part of him still couldn't believe his team had gone through with any of this, nor could he fathom them betraying everything they fought for just for a big payday.

Ezra had no idea what to think anymore.

"Of course, I could be wrong," Bas're said with a smile. "Perhaps these thieves were mistaken."

"Maybe they were," Ezra said. "We appreciate your time, Professor. Both of you." He nodded to Bas're and Oron. "Can we stop by again if we have any other questions?"

"By all means," Oron said. "My door is always open."

"Enjoy the rest of your day," Ezra said over his shoulder, pleased to find the bounty hunters were following him. It was a good lead, even if he didn't know exactly what they'd just stumbled into.

Now they just needed to find *where* Darius and the others would be meeting their potential buyer.

Chapter 18

With a huff, Mo settled into her seat at the back of the shuttle. Her knee was bothering her more than she wanted to let on, but now, she had no choice but to stretch it out as much as she could. She rubbed it with one hand, and she didn't know if that made it feel better or worse.

As soon as Ezra closed the shuttle doors and dropped into the pilot's seat, he said, "We need to speak to the Triumvirate."

Mo actually laughed. She couldn't help it.

"Excuse me?" she asked just as Cass said, "Why?"

Ezra tilted his head back and sucked in a deep breath, then said, "My third cousin is one of the members."

The Triumvirate were at the top of the executive branch of the Federation. Each of the three members were elected for four-year terms. But with elections staggered every two years and a three-term limit, there was a fairly consistent change in leadership. They worked with the two legislative bodies—the Commons and the Senate—as well as the court systems, planetary leaders, and the military to keep the Federation running.

"No shit?" Kynn asked, the perfect picture of a casual listener as he slung one arm over the back of his and Cass's seats. But with his head tilted slightly to one side, Mo had a perfect view of the way his jaw muscle ticked. Kynn was angry. "Which one?"

Ezra finally looked at them again. "Chancellor Livia Valtor. I barely speak with her. I barely speak with any of my family."

"So your father's a famous architect and your third cousin's one of the most powerful people in the Federation." Cass pursed her lips and nodded. "That's just great."

"Anything else we need to know, Lyre?" Mo asked, trying and failing to keep the venom from her voice.

This was why she hadn't wanted to take this contract. The deep ties to the military first—and now the deeper ties to the government.

No wonder Ezra seemed to have endless money. He probably had all the fucking resources in the world with a family like that.

"Look, I know you three aren't fond of the government—"

"For damn good reason!" Mo cried. "They make most people's lives harder."

Ezra leaned forward on his knees. "I know that, Cevi. I *know*. I grew up around it. My parents are revered in their fields, and the rest of my extended family is either involved in the government, academia, or are executives at top conglomerates. I grew up around *all* the bullshit, all kinds of it." As he pinned Mo with those deep forest green eyes, she tried not to squirm. "That's why I left."

"You'd give up those kinds of connections?" Cass asked. "I can't decide if that's honorable or stupid."

"I like to think it was honorable," Ezra said.

"Because the FSC is *so* honorable," Mo muttered. "Not just another tool of the Federation."

Ezra sighed. "I was the odd one out in my family. I saw the bullshit and couldn't stand it. I think the others saw it but simply didn't care. When I told my parents I'd enlisted with the FSC, they nearly lost it. It was right after they'd gifted me part of the family estate. You wondered why I had that apartment? That's why."

"Are you still in contact with them?" Mo didn't know why it mattered; maybe it didn't at all.

"No." The word was clipped. "No, I'm not, other than occasionally letting them know I'm alive after some of the worst battles on the front. I haven't spoken to them directly in almost fifteen years."

"Wouldn't a family like yours tout your service?" Kynn asked. "Wouldn't they use it for some weird political gain?"

"They might, without my knowledge," Ezra said. "I wanted to join the FSC because I thought that was how I could make a real difference. I could actually be on the ground, connecting with people who needed help, who needed protection. 'In duty, we rise. With honor, we fight,' and all that."

Mo didn't hear the FSC's motto very often, and she preferred it that way.

Ezra's voice wavered and strained a little as he said, "And I've done that. Regardless of what you three think of the FSC, we've done some real good. I've helped with civilian evacuations, relief efforts, and saved entire towns from being overrun by Ascended attacks. But I lost my first family to do so, and now I've lost my team because they decided to betray what we stand for. They betrayed *me*. And if I need to suck it up and go back to my family to try to get some help and some answers, I will."

Mo kept her face a calm, neutral mask.

Maybe Ezra was right, that he had helped people. He probably was. Every single FSC soldier couldn't be bad. Not everyone who served in the government was bad, even if many were. And she had to admire him for turning his back on his family to stand up for something he believed in, even if she didn't agree with the organization he belonged to. Mo didn't even agree with the Syndicate half the time. Few things were so black and white as good and evil, right and wrong. Not when it came to something like this, anyway.

"I'm sorry they did that to you," Mo said.

Ezra's gaze snapped to hers. His eyebrows furrowed. "What?"

"It's a terrible thing, having people turn their backs on us like that," Mo said. "I know what that's like."

His expression softened. "Thank you."

She sucked in a deep breath. "Why do you think we need to go speak to your cousin?"

"Her civilian title is Doctor Livia Valtor," Ezra said. "She was elected two years ago. Her father, Doctor Marcus Valtor, is an archaeologist. I thought between her knowledge about the Federation and war and his knowledge about ancient history, we might be able to narrow down who we're looking for. Maybe she even knows if someone's targeting our family and that's why my team tried to kill me."

Mo hadn't thought that it could've been some kind of strange political hit put out on Ezra. It didn't seem to make much sense given his detachment from his family—assuming he was being honest. He seemed to be. But why would someone want to kill a third cousin of a chancellor?

"You haven't done anything that would warrant someone putting a hit out on you?" Kynn asked.

Ezra glared at him. "Seriously?"

With a laugh, Kynn held his hands up in surrender. "We need any and all information, man. You never know. People make enemies. Just ask Mo."

"I do not have *enemies*," Mo said. "I just have people I hate, and the feeling happens to be mutual."

Ezra laughed. It was a warm, beautiful sound. In the objectively short time she'd known him, she hadn't heard him laugh, not like that.

But he sobered quickly. "No one I can think of," Ezra said. "No one who'd be able to convince my team to desert and murder me, anyway. Nothing that serious."

"If you do think of anyone," Cass said, "let us know."

"I don't need you to be my security team," he said dryly.

"No, but I'd rather not be fucking killed because you forgot someone," Mo said. "So let us know."

Ezra gave her a small smile. "Fair enough."

"Will your cousin be available if we go see her now?" Kynn asked.

"Won't know until we find out." Ezra swiveled his chair around to face forward and began powering up the ship. "We should be there in an hour."

As the shuttle lifted off the ground and Ezra began piloting them to their next destination, Mo settled back in her seat and rubbed at her knee again. She'd never imagined herself going to speak with anyone from the Triumvirate, let alone to do so in search of information rather than giving them a piece of her mind. There was a lot she'd love to say to any government official who would listen, about Veronis, about the war, about every way the Federation failed its people.

But it wasn't like they'd listen to her anyway. So she'd keep her mouth shut and play along for the sake of the contract. The sooner they got this done and the sooner she got to go back to her life on Miduna, the better.

Chapter 19

Going to his family for help felt like defeat.

With the way they hadn't supported him or even tried to check up on him, Ezra had promised he wouldn't go back to them. Not his parents, not any of the extended family.

And now here he was, ready to ask the Triumvirate—well, his cousin—for help.

Ezra rolled one shoulder as he walked with Mo, Cass, and Kynn toward the ornate complex of buildings that made up The Sovereign Nexus, the public-facing portion of the Federation's executive branch. The off-white marble and glass domes of the three buildings gleamed in Aerilia's setting sun.

As they went up a ridiculously long set of stairs, Ezra glanced to his right, where Mo walked next to Cass. Mo seemed to be having trouble, but with the way her jaw was set, he wasn't going to ask. He didn't need to get his head bitten off by her before he walked into the lion's den.

Finally, they reached the top of the stairs. Ezra kept moving forward, past the colonnades on either side and heading straight for the massive double doors. Right inside was a security team, blocking most of the lobby from view.

"Names?" asked one Human man with pale skin and equally pale hair. He matched Ezra's height and was even broader and more muscular.

"I'm Commander Sergeant Ezra Lyre." He reached for the badge on his belt and offered it to the man. "These are my associates."

"Cass Farr," the sharpshooter said.

"Kynn Sathir."

Mo hesitated, but when Cass nudged her, she said, "Mora Cevi."

The security guard raised one eyebrow and handed Ezra's badge back to him. Usually his Vanguard status got him a little kinder treatment, especially around Aerilia.

"And your business here, Commander?" the man asked.

"I'm here to speak to Chancellor Valtor."

The man let out a low, deep laugh. "Not a chance."

"Why not?" Ezra asked. "She's my elected representative."

"The chancellor isn't taking any meetings."

"Perhaps you should let her know I'm here," Ezra said. "Ask her if my name means something."

One of the other security guards tapped the pale one on the shoulder. He leaned down so the shorter woman could speak into his ear. His attention turned back to Ezra.

"Apologies, Commander," he said. "Let me phone the chancellor's chief of staff and see if she's in."

"We don't mind waiting," Ezra said.

As the security guard returned to his desk, Mo stalked over to one of the stone benches against the wall and dropped down onto it. Cass and Kynn joined her.

"You good, Cevi?" Ezra asked as he followed them.

"Fine," she snapped. "I don't see the point in standing around for an hour while they try to chase your cousin down."

When she said *cousin*, Ezra checked over his shoulder. Sure, he'd thrown his weight around a little with the implication of some connection to Livia, but he didn't want to shout out to the whole world that he was related to one of the Federation's leaders. The security guards didn't seem to be paying attention.

When he focused on Mo again, he found her absently rubbing her knee. He was just about to ask her if she'd injured herself when the security guard called Ezra over to his desk. With a small huff, Ezra strode back over.

"Chancellor Valtor will see you and your team," the man said. "Do you know the way?"

"No, I don't." Ezra hadn't spoken to Livia in close to fifteen years other than exchanging a few digital messages, and he'd certainly never been to her office. "Can someone escort us?"

"Of course, Commander. I'll take you there myself."

Ezra motioned for the bounty hunters to join him, and only after a security sweep were they allowed to enter the building. The lobby was far grander than anything Ezra had ever seen, with looming pillars and a vaulted ceiling so high he almost couldn't see the top. The glass had to be coated on the inside, because even though Ezra could make out the faint reds and oranges of the sunset, there was no glare like he'd expected.

They followed the man deep into the building, going past corridors, closed doors, staircases, and lifts. They passed politicians, military personnel, and who Ezra assumed were lobbyists. He worked hard to memorize every step they took so that he could get them back out of the building.

As they came to the end of a hallway, it opened into a formal foyer. A thick, muted blue Sorthian carpet was rolled out over the stone floor, and overstuffed armchairs were in all four corners. It was almost old fashioned, ancient.

"Just let them know you're here," the security guard said, gesturing to the closed double doors before leaving.

Ezra didn't like this one bit. He didn't like the security cameras near the ceiling, the quiet stillness of the hallway and foyer, or the fact that his very powerful cousin was on the other side of that door. He and Livia had never had a bad relationship, unlike some of his other extended family, but they'd never been particularly close, either.

Word would surely get back to his parents soon, though. His parents and all the rest of them.

"Lyre?" Mo asked.

Pushing his shoulders back, Ezra knocked on the door. There were no obvious comms buttons, and they were clearly expecting them after security had called up.

They waited.

And waited.

And waited.

Cass huffed, and Kynn shifted uneasily. Mo muttered something disrespectful about the government.

Ezra held his breath.

The muffled clicking of heels came from the other side of the doors, then they opened. A Human woman dressed in an elaborate black gown smiled at Ezra.

"Commander Lyre," she said in the same posh, upper-rim Aerilian accent Ezra had. "Welcome. Chancellor Valtor is expecting you. Please, come with me."

As she walked deeper into the office, the long skirts of her dress skimming the ground behind her, Ezra took measured steps. The reception area was as strangely old fashioned as the foyer, with wooden tables, luxurious furniture, and ornate paintings of both Aerilia and past leaders of the Federation. The hair on the back of Ezra's neck prickled.

The woman—Livia's chief of staff, Ezra assumed—opened the door at the far end of the room and gestured for them to go inside. Ezra stepped into his cousin's office first, and only once the bounty hunters were inside with him did the woman close the door.

Livia Valtor stood up from her desk. Like many in the family, she was tall, though not nearly as tall as Ezra. She shared many features with Ezra's mother, actually, from her slim nose to her sandy complexion. It made sense, given she was his maternal cousin. The only difference was that Livia was a blonde while Ezra's mother had the same black hair he did. Livia's dark blue suit jacket was perfectly tailored to her slim frame, and the matching trousers were so wide at the bottom they almost looked like a skirt.

"Hello, Ezra." Livia smiled at him as she circled to the front of her desk, a data pad still clutched between her hands. "Welcome home."

"Thanks," Ezra said. "Nice office."

"The job has its perks."

"I hope we weren't interrupting anything."

Livia gestured down at her data pad. "Just going over notes for a speech I have in a few days," she said. "It's no interruption."

Kynn cleared his throat, and Ezra shook his head. "Sorry. These are some friends of mine, Kynn, Mora, and Cass," he said, pointing at each of them. Livia gave them all the same polite, well-practiced smile.

"What brings you all the way to Aerilia, and to my office specifically?" Livia asked. "Weren't you recently deployed?"

"Long story," Ezra said.

Livia gestured to the round meeting table in one corner of the lavish room. "Let's talk."

Ezra really didn't want to get caught up in the details of this mess again, but Livia always wanted things done a certain way. She was only seven years older than Ezra, but when they were kids, she'd always held that over him, saying she knew better than him about all things.

The group settled into the antique chairs circling the table. Mo and Cass both stayed rigid, but Kynn relaxed into his seat with a sigh. And when Livia offered them drinks, they all declined.

"I really don't want to take up too much of your time," Ezra said. "I'm sure you're a busy woman."

"I can make time for family," she replied, gaze darting to the windows to her right. They overlooked the gardens outside, where security guards patrolled. "Tell me why you're here, Ezra." She turned back at him, her green eyes bright. "Are you in trouble? Something with the FSC?"

He gritted his teeth. He'd never been in trouble with the FSC. "Not exactly," he said, then briefly explained the situation on Miduna. "After my team tried to kill me and absconded, I couldn't help but wonder if there have been any threats against the family. You know, considering ..."

"Considering I'm now Chancellor and everyone else has made names for themselves?" Livia sucked in a heavy breath and shook her head once, as if considering. "Indeed, there have been threats against *me* ever since I announced my candidacy, so it's not a stretch to assume some of my political enemies might start trying to go after the family."

"But me?" Ezra asked. "We're third cousins."

She shrugged. "Family is family."

"Any particular group issuing these threats?" Mo asked, the first words she'd spoken since they'd entered the room. Ezra was just grateful she hadn't taken the opportunity to go on some rant about the Federation. That none of the bounty hunters had, actually.

Livia pinned her with a look. "Mora, was it?" Then she smiled that practiced smile again. "The threats are everywhere, in every corner of the Federation. If it's not the Ascended, it's dissidents within our own borders, Separatists and other political groups who dislike my policies and the work the government does to keep everyone safe."

"And they'd target your third cousin to get to you?" Mo asked. "My understanding is that you're not very close."

Livia clicked her tongue. "Not close?" she asked Ezra.

"It's not like we're pen pals, Liv," he said. "Our work keeps us busy. Nothing personal from either side, I know."

She nodded. "No, I suppose it's not. Maybe we should get back into the old Valtor family habit of sending out holiday cards every summer."

Yeah, I'll get right on that, Ezra thought.

"Have you spoken with your parents recently?" she asked.

"Not in years."

"Still upset they don't support you?"

"I've moved on," he said. "How often do you speak with your father? You two still close?"

"At least once a week," Livia said. "It's a bit tough now, considering he's busy teaching again. Moved all the way out to Vonnoth about a year ago, to Atmos."

"Finally got tired of Aerilia?" Ezra asked.

"You might say that." Livia tucked a few strands of hair behind her ear. "Was there anything else you needed?"

"No, I guess that's it." Ezra didn't feel like he was any closer to an answer, but it helped to know the family was under threat. "Can you make sure my parents have security details?" He might not have gotten along with them, but he'd hate for them to get caught in the crossfire of Livia's political career.

"I'll see to it personally," she said.

"Thanks, Liv," he said as he stood.

"Anything I can do to help, just ask. But you'd better watch your back too, Ezra. Don't get yourself caught up in anything you shouldn't."

"That's the first thing they teach us at the academy. Been watching it for years." That was the sad truth to it, but Ezra had made peace with that fact long ago. Now he just had to figure out who had put the target there most recently.

Nobody said much as they flew back across Aerilia to return to the shipyard. Ezra preferred it that way. He was sure the three sitting behind him were only going to have questions, and he didn't have many answers.

In fact, none of them even spoke to him once they landed. They climbed out in silence and headed for *The Revenant*. Ezra tipped his head back toward the evening sky and sucked in a deep breath. He had a feeling he was not going to like whatever was about to come next.

He took his time walking to the ship and up the ramp into the top deck. Mo disappeared down the hallway to her bedroom; Ezra followed her. The door was wide open, and she was rummaging around inside an open wall panel.

"What are you doing?" Ezra asked as he poked his head into the room.

"You aren't allowed in my quarters," she said, not looking at him.

He rolled his eyes. "You saw *my* house."

Mo didn't respond. She tugged a jacket out of the wall—was she using it as some kind of closet? He didn't dare go in for a closer look—and tossed it on the wide bed behind her. Next was a roll of thick cream bandages.

"You feeling alright?" Ezra asked.

She slammed the panel back into place. "I'm good."

"I didn't mean to offend you—"

"Not offended," Mo said, grabbing both the jacket and the bandages. "Busy."

"Busy doing what?" Ezra asked. "We need to talk about what my cousin said."

Mo gestured vaguely toward him, almost as if she were exasperated. "So, talk."

"I thought we could, the four of us."

She muttered something under her breath. "I'll be out in ten minutes, okay? Get changed."

"What?" Ezra was wearing the black pants that made up his fatigues but had switched the usual shirt out for a short-sleeved white one. There were no stains or tears, not even scuffs on his boots. "Why?"

"Because you look like a fucking Vanguard."

"Is that a problem?"

"It's going to be tonight."

"What's going on, Cevi?"

"Go," she said, shooing him toward the door. "Ask Kynn for some clothes or something. I don't care. You just can't look like that."

Ezra really didn't like the sound of this. And despite telling himself he was in charge on this mission, it was like it was ingrained in him to follow orders, even from a bounty hunter.

Mo's bedroom door slid shut. Ezra imagined that if it wasn't a sliding door, she would've slammed it in his face.

Rubbing his forehead, Ezra returned to the "room" he'd been given. It was barely bigger than a storage closet, with a single bed better fit for a child than a man his size. He closed his door, then began disrobing. All the clothing he'd brought with him probably screamed Vanguard.

But that was his life. That was who he was. Why would he have clothing for anything else? The FSC *owned* you. They spoke of valor and strength, discipline and allegiance. Everyone who joined lived and breathed the military. *Almost everyone*, he thought ruefully.

Ultimately, he decided on a pair of dark green pants that still looked utilitarian, but in the way the bounty hunters did. He switched to a black short-sleeved shirt, then put his boots back on. And when he went into the hallway, he was immediately met with a sigh.

"All you did was change what colors you're wearing," Mo said.

Cass and Kynn stood near her, clearly *not* dressed to go out. They didn't even have weapons on them.

"This is as good as it's going to get," Ezra said. "No offense, but I don't think Kynn's clothes'll fit me."

"None taken," Kynn said with a grin. "Not all of us are monsters like you, Ezra."

It was meant in jest, Ezra knew, but that word—*monster*. It was just supposed to be a reference to Ezra's bulkier form compared to Kynn's leaner one. Nothing more. But coming from these three, it felt like an insult.

He shook it off. "Can we talk now?"

"I had an idea while we were flying back," Cass said, "and I hope you'll listen to us. We all agree it's a good plan."

"We need to see if anyone knows about these hit orders against your cousin and your family," Kynn said. "Who's going to know about contracts like that aside from bounty hunters?"

"It's time to do things our way," Mo said. "Between what your cousin shared and the information from Vertex, it looks like whoever paid off your team wanted to strike both at the Triumvirate and get into this archaeological underground market the professors mentioned. I don't really see the connection, but maybe they think all those old stories about those artifacts are true."

"Which means we should go to Vonnoth," Ezra said. "To Livia's father to see what he knows. He always had a fondness for the old beliefs."

"And we *can* go there," Kynn said.

Cass smiled. "But try it our way first."

Their way? How could their way possibly be any better than what they'd already been doing?

"I don't think that's—" he started.

"It's what you hired us to do," Mo said. "It's why you're paying us so much money. To find those bastards. We've done things your way. We've gone to the obvious sources. Let's stick to the shadows tonight and see what we find."

Oh, Ezra most definitely did not like this. But maybe she had a point. He *had* hired them for a reason.

"And what shadows are those?" he asked.

"The kind you typically avoid."

Chapter 20

Watching a Vanguard squirm—a Vanguard who was paying her a shipload of money—made Mo's night a little more tolerable.

So had the look on his face when she, Cass, and Kynn had sprung it on him that they were going to try things their way. Ezra had looked like a kid in trouble. And maybe he would be. She had no idea if he'd cleared any of this with his commanding officers. That wasn't her concern, though.

Her concern was the way he was so fucking awkward, walking through Aerilia's dark streets. Down here, everything was covered in shadows, whether from the towering buildings and layers of the city or the strange, harsh glows cast by neon signs lighting up the different bars and stores they walked past.

She hoped that Kynn and Cass were good. They'd offered to join Mo, but they really needed to resupply *The Revenant* if they were going to take off for Vonnoth soon. They needed fuel, a new injector, and food. And Kynn and Cass were far better with ship maintenance than Mo. Someone needed to take one for the team and work with the Vanguard one-on-one.

Besides, she was the one who'd been on *these* streets before. Those weren't good memories, but she could handle it. Nothing scared her. Not anymore.

As they passed one particularly rowdy bar and two patrons came flying out in a tangle of limbs and fists, Ezra flinched.

"Don't you like, stalk the Ascended or something, Lyre?" Mo asked, keeping her voice low. "Start acting like it. There's nothing to be afraid of."

"I'm not afraid," he retorted. "I'm *concerned* since you haven't told me where we're going."

"You'll find out when we get there."

"I need to know now."

Huffing, Mo stopped on the crowded street and whirled on him. "We're going to a Syndicate-run bar," she whispered, "and I'd really prefer you don't embarrass me while we're inside. Let me do the talking."

His forest green eyes darkened with the night. "Fine."

Mo continued on, leading him down side streets and alleys. They passed dumpsters and what were clearly illegal exchanges done in the darkness. Ezra almost stopped to intervene more than once, but Mo forced him to keep moving.

"How do you even know where we're going?" he asked once they hit an open street again.

This part of Aerilia was emptier, and they were only a block from their target now.

Mo shrugged. "I've been here before."

"When? Why? This doesn't seem like someplace you'd come willing-ly."

"These streets, or Aerilia?" she asked.

"Both."

"Yeah, well." She knew that didn't answer anything, but she couldn't bring herself to. "Here I am anyway. I told you, I know how to do my job."

The last time she'd been on Aerilia had been one of the worst days of her life, the day her partner of nearly two years had betrayed her in ways she hadn't realized he'd been capable of. She'd only been twenty, barely a woman. And he'd cut her deep.

They moved through one more alley, then turned right. And there, where it should be, was a white neon sign flashing the insignia of the Starlight Syndicate: a stylized star made to look like a dagger. Mo knocked on the door, and a slider opened to reveal a pair of all-white eyes.

"Name?" they asked.

Mo leaned closer. "Cevi, The Demon, from the Miduna chapter."

There was a pause, then a beep as a screen lit up. "Yes, come in," that voice said.

The door slid open, and a Luxinae enforcer stood just inside, almost as big and broad as Ezra. He motioned for them to go down the narrow hallway.

Mo led the way, but Ezra was right behind her. He put off a distinct heat and, no matter what clothes he put on, always smelled faintly of evergreens. It was irritating, if not pleasant, especially as the smell of smoke and bodies wafted down the corridor.

Fuck, it was going to be a long night.

The band's music thumped steadily in Mo's bones as she pushed into the wide-open bar. It was nearly black inside, with few sconces lighting up the walls. This was nothing like Vertex, with its shiny facade. No, this place was meant for deals made in the shadows. Backstabbings. All kinds of nonsense.

The bar was in the middle of the club, and several bartenders circled its perimeter, ready to take orders. A few spots were available on the far side, so Mo headed that way. A couple of booths along the wall were open, too, but they'd probably need to put themselves out there. Something Mo hated doing. But she was going to have to speak to people if she wanted to get information to get the job done.

Rolling her shoulders back, Mo took one of the open barstools near the end of the line. At least this way, her conversations could be a little more controlled. Ezra took the seat next to her, and no sooner had he sat down than a Human woman waltzed toward them and slapped two coasters down in front of them.

"What'll it be?" she asked in a thick accent Mo couldn't place. Her gold eyeshadow popped against her dark brown complexion, and the ends of her locs were tinged the same blue as the Syndicate insignia.

"Midunian ale," Mo said.

"Do you have any Ivari whiskey?" Ezra asked.

The bartender smirked and motioned to the wall of bottles behind her. "We've got whatever you want, sweetheart. On the rocks?"

"Sure."

When the bartender returned, she gave Mo a pointed look. "He new or something?"

"Something like that," Mo said.

They both looked at Ezra, who sipped his whiskey as if he wasn't under scrutiny.

"We're actually here with some information," Mo continued, keeping her voice low. "If you think anyone would be interested in swapping."

"Depends on what you've got," the bartender said, leaning her forearms on the bar. "Place is crowded tonight, only so much to go around."

"We heard there was some kind of scuffle near Kalyndra last week, something about the FSC and some of its members taking private bounty contracts. Know anything about that?"

"Heard whispers," the bartender replied, gaze sliding to Ezra. "He with them?"

"He's with *me*," Mo said, and she swore Ezra sat up a little straighter.

The bartender pursed her lips. "What are you looking for?"

"Information about any contracts taken out against the Triumvirate," Mo said. "Or treasure hunts."

The bartender's eyebrows furrowed. "Well that's a fucking combination."

"Don't I know it," Mo muttered.

"Enjoy your drinks," the bartender said, then walked away.

"So ..." Ezra's deep voice trailed off. "Now what?"

"Now we wait," Mo said. "She'll point the right people in our direction, or vice versa. If we haven't heard anything within an hour, we'll leave."

Hopefully the whisper network among Syndicate members would lead to something. Even if nobody in the Syndicate had taken on such jobs, surely *someone* would've heard about whatever it was that was going on. It was a small profession, all things considered. There weren't many secrets that could be kept, at least not when money was involved.

The loud patrons and thumping music made Mo's head spin almost as much as the worries poking at the back of her mind. Worries about this damn contract, about the past catching up to her. But on a city-planet of billions, with dozens and dozens of bars and hideaways for Syndicate members, Mo surely wouldn't have to worry too much.

She focused on the bottles of alcohol. All the vibrant colors glowed in the lights behind the bar, creating a rainbow of options. She'd never been very fond of alcohol, but she tended to get strange looks if she didn't order something. She wrapped one hand around her glass, her fresh bandages snug against her knuckles. Only her right hand was swollen, and not too badly at that. A small miracle, and one she needed.

As Mo flexed those fingers slightly, Ezra said, "So ..."

"Not this again."

"We're just going to sit here in silence all night?" he asked.

"I'd prefer it that way, yes."

"I wouldn't."

Of course she'd take a contract from a *talkative* Vanguard. "Then talk," she said. "I'll listen."

"It's more fun if both people are engaged in the conversation."

Mo finally peered up at him. He gave her a smug half smile, making the smallest dimple appear in his right cheek. It suited him somehow.

"Make it worth my while and I might," she said.

"Worth your while?" Ezra said the words as if they were some unsolvable puzzle to him. But after taking a sip of whiskey, he asked, "Have you always lived on Miduna?"

"Almost always."

"I was born on Aerilia," he said. "Born and raised."

"I can tell."

He didn't take the bait. "What about your family? Where are they?"

"Back on *The Revenant*."

"No siblings? Parents?" Ezra asked. "A partner?"

"Just me, Cass, and Kynn." That thought used to hurt, and maybe it always would in some way, but for the most part, Mo liked her life. *Their* lives. There was plenty she'd change about the past—and certain hopes she had for the future—but all things considered, life had turned out alright.

"Any schooling?"

"Just whatever the Syndicate wanted to teach me and whatever I've taught myself since." She took a drink of ale and scrunched her nose. "Really, Lyre, you've got to do better than that. This is boring."

With a sigh, he set his forearms on the bar. As he reached for his drink, the movement of his tattoos caught Mo's eye. They almost made up constellations, but none of them were ones Mo recognized. Or maybe it looked more like the swirls of a galaxy? She couldn't decide.

"You've got a lot of ink," she heard herself saying before she could think better of it.

That made his dimple appear again. "I do."

"What's the pattern supposed to be?"

Ezra's smirk faded, and a small crease formed between his brows. "Missions."

"Good ones?" Mo asked. "Bad?"

"All sorts." Ezra took another sip of his drink, then leaned toward Mo and whispered, almost conspiratorially, "Although most FSC bars I pass through give free drinks to people with enough tattoos, so it's more practical than sentimental."

Mo rolled her eyes.

"You do that a lot," he said, straightening again. "Rolling your eyes. Making faces when I speak."

"Say smarter things and maybe I'll stop."

That earned her a chuckle and another smile. What was with him?

"Maybe I'll get that tattooed next." He traced a long finger over his exposed forearm. "Right here."

"Why ruin the look?"

"Maybe I need the reminder."

"I won't let you forget," she said.

Ezra laughed again. "No, I'm sure you won't." He reached out to tap the top of her hand, but Mo pulled away quickly. "Don't mean any harm. I was just going to ask about why you keep bandaging your hands."

"What gives you the right to ask?" she snapped, her heart hammering in her chest. "And I don't like being touched."

"I thought it was fair after you asked about my tattoos. And noted. Sorry."

Mo forced herself to relax. "Old injury," she said. It was a partial truth and the best he'd get from her. "Bothers me sometimes."

"I can—" he started, but the bartender returned. Mo sent her a silent thanks.

"You've got incoming," the woman whispered as she set another ale in front of Mo. Her first one was barely half empty.

"Mora Cevi!"

That voice. Mo would know that voice anywhere.

She spun in her seat, finding a tall Human man with sand-hued skin approaching her. An Ivari woman with a snowy complexion and long, pierced ears followed.

"Bax," Mo said to the man. And to the woman, she said, "Amane. What are you two doing here?"

"The better question is what are *you* doing on fucking Aerilia?" Bax asked, wrapping an arm around her shoulders.

Mo tried not to flinch. Bax and Amane were two of her old teachers. Bax was only older than her by a decade, but Amane was two decades older. Ivari just aged differently, lived longer. Mo had never been the best of friends with them, but she'd liked them well enough. More than most of the people who'd tried to teach her anything back on Miduna.

"Long story," Mo said. "But I take it you might know some of it?"

"Some," said Amane, eyeing Ezra. Something about the way she sized him up didn't sit right with Mo.

"This is Ezra," Mo said. "We're looking for some information."

"Let's go have a drink," Bax said with a smile. "I've got a booth. Come, come."

Mo went to pick up both of her drinks, but Ezra took the new ale and his whiskey, leaving her with just one glass to carry. She shot him a glare before trudging through the crowd after Bax and Amane; she didn't need Ezra taking pity on her just because he thought she might be in a little pain.

"Here we are." Bax slid into one side of the crescent moon booth, and Amane joined him.

Ezra slid in on the other side, leaving the end for Mo. She settled in, wincing at the creak of the leather bench and taking note of the surrounding tables. The conversations kept rolling, but the way some of the other patrons shifted made the hairs on Mo's neck prickle. Any change in the room was bound to set the other bounty hunters on edge.

"Heard you might be looking for information about the Triumvirate," Bax said, his brown eyes settling on Mo and pinning her with a look she used to get from him all the time. "Heard talk of some bounty hunters going to meet with someone in the government this morning."

"Wouldn't know about that." Mo forced her posture to stay relaxed. "But I've heard rumors about people looking to hire for ... actions taken against any of the Triumvirate families."

"There've been whispers," Amane said. "None here, though. The Syndicate wouldn't tolerate it."

"You two here often, then?" Mo asked. "Never did hear where you went once you left Miduna."

"Not keeping tabs on me?" Bax asked with a grin.

"Fuck no! I was glad to be rid of you," Mo said. "Both of you."

Ezra cleared his throat, but Bax laughed and slapped him on the shoulder. "Easy, Ezra. Mora doesn't mean any harm. We go way back."

"How far back?" Ezra asked.

"We taught her and some of her friends while we were still on Miduna," said Amane. "Left about eight years ago to pursue other opportunities elsewhere in the Federation. We needed a more centralized base of operations."

"Hard chasing bounties from the opposite side of the Federation," Bax mused. "But I hear you're top of the class, Mora, as always."

"Something like that," Mo said. "You hear about any treasure hunters either?"

Amane's thin eyebrows rose. "As a matter of fact, yes. We thought it strange, but there was a group in here just last night, talking about a big bounty for anyone who can find Ascended treasure."

"What treasure?" Mo and Ezra asked at the same time.

"Didn't say." Bax grimaced. "Wish I'd stuck around to find out, but we had an"—he slid his arm around Amane's shoulders—"appointment."

"Disgusting," Mo whispered under her breath, but Bax just laughed again. She'd never been keen on hearing any details about Bax and Amane's marriage, and she still wasn't.

But at least they knew there were indeed those looking to harm not just Ezra's extended family but also those looking for Ascended treasure. That was close to the Eternal Ones.

"A bit odd, treasure hunters looking to hire help," Mo said. "I can't recall them ever looking for our help before. They never want to pay."

"Odd, indeed," Bax said. "But a ton of odd shit's been happening in the Federation lately, no? All the Ascended invasions, the Separatists, these strange contracts ... makes you wonder."

Ezra reached for his whiskey. "Wonder what?"

Someone at the table behind Amane shifted so they were partially facing Mo. The back of the booth was too high for her to make out a face, but they'd gotten someone's attention.

"What's getting into people," Bax said. "So much unrest, and for what? We need peace for once in our fucking lives."

Mo didn't disagree, but until the war ended and the government stopped screwing its people over, there would be no peace.

"A little advice, Mora," Amane said, leaning away from her husband and across the table. Her ears pinned back. "Don't get too involved in whatever drama Aerilia's creating. Do not fall into its trap."

"Like you did?" Mo asked.

"We stay far away from the drama of government and high society," Bax said, giving Ezra a pointed look. "Whatever it is you've gotten mixed up in, think about taking a step back. Nothing good is coming to this planet or this Federation, mark my words. Shit's been boiling up for years."

Tension had been simmering for far too long in the Federation. Something was going to give, sooner or later. Maybe Darius Kane and those other assholes had something to do with all that, or maybe not. Maybe they were just a bunch of jackasses who stole a crystal and tried to commit murder. It wouldn't be the first time people with delusions of grandeur and daydreams of power committed a few crimes. It also wouldn't be the first time Mo had been hired to find them and bring them in.

"Thanks," Mo said. "I'll keep it in mind. But we need to get going."

She stood and left her drink on the table. Ezra joined her, that faint scent of evergreen following her as she started back toward the bar—and the exit. She'd had enough of this scene and these people for one night. There was too much noise, too much smoke, too many drunkards.

And whoever had been at that table behind Amane had gotten too interested in their conversation. She didn't know if it was someone connected to these strange contracts or not, but Mo didn't like it, nor did she like that the very same person was now following them.

"Come on," Mo said to Ezra. "We're leaving."

"You see the guy from—"

"Yup," Mo said. At least she wasn't alone in this. "We can lose them outside."

"You sure that's a good idea?"

"Better than getting into a fucking bar fight," she said. "Now come on."

CHAPTER 21

Inches. They were literally *inches* from the door when the voice Mo had never, ever wanted to hear again slithered up her spine.

"Mora Cevi."

Tallas.

Tallas fucking Bara.

She wouldn't give him the time of day if he asked for it. She might just punch him in the face given the chance.

Mo kept walking. Ezra followed. They went out onto the darkened street, still crowded as Aerilia's nightlife began picking up. Good. Maybe she could avoid a fight tonight. Tallas didn't try shit when there were witnesses around.

"Mora!" he called again.

"Who's that?" Ezra asked as Mo stopped partway down the sidewalk and turned.

"Nobody," Mo muttered.

But there he was. The one man she'd ever been afraid of. Every part of her screamed for her to run, an instinct from long ago. Mo refused to be afraid of him now. He had no power over her. Not anymore.

"There's a face I haven't seen in a while," Tallas said, smiling as he approached. Even in the neon lights of Aerilia's underbelly, his white skin and short blond hair had a healthy glow. His blue eyes were clear, focused. He wasn't nearly as tall as Ezra, but he was still a good bit taller than Mo. Time had been too kind to him.

Mo crossed her arms over her chest. "I thought I told you I'd kill you the next time I saw you."

Tallas flashed one of his fakest, smoothest smiles, the kind that had won over all the other mentors at the Syndicate, the kind that had won Mo over when she'd been young and naive. When she'd still believed many people were good at heart. She knew better now.

"Oh, Mora," he said with a practiced laugh. "I never quite understood your sense of humor." Tallas tilted his head at Ezra. "Who's this?"

"Ezra Lyre," he said. "Who are you?"

"Mora hasn't told you about me? Momo, I'm hurt."

That nickname.

Despite her racing heart, Mo forced herself to remain calm, steady. She had to be steady. Tallas always wanted her to react.

"I'm Tallas Bara." He rolled one shoulder, the long pole of the glaive on his back glinting in the lights. "Mora and I were romantically involved. Hunting partners too."

"I thought the Void would've taken a miserable bastard like yourself by now," Mo said.

"There you go again," he said, laughing. "What's this I hear about you looking for treasure hunting contracts?"

"I'm not looking for shit," Mo said.

Ezra nodded. "Just went in for a drink."

At least Ezra knew how to play along.

Mo's fingers twitched, eager to reach for her blade or gun. Anything to distract her from how the signs were too bright, how Tallas was too close, how her chest was too tight. She hated him. Hated seeing him. Hated knowing he'd been watching her. It was just like how she used to feel around him, like she was never safe from prying eyes.

"A drink," Tallas mused. "I heard you talking to Bax and Amane, Momo."

"Can't talk to my old mentors?"

"If you were doing the rounds, why didn't you talk to me?" Tallas asked. "I was your mentor once too."

Mo hated him, but she might've hated herself more for ever falling for a man like Tallas Bara.

Although Bax and Amane had been mentoring Syndicate members for years by the time Mo, Cass, and Kynn arrived in Kalyndra, Tallas was different. He was Veronian, too, and had been evacuated from the planet along with them. Mo hadn't even known him then, as he was a few years older than her and from a different part of Veronis. But when he'd started teaching some of her classes when she was eighteen, he'd abused their shared connection. He'd used it and twisted it—twisted her—until she hardly knew up from down anymore. Until she hardly knew herself anymore.

Ezra didn't move a muscle.

Good. Mo would handle this.

"What do you want?" she asked. "We need to go."

"I want to hear about your new job. He's clearly someone you're working for," Tallas said, eyeing Ezra again. "No offense, Ezra, but you don't exactly look like one of us."

She didn't see the point in trying to lie to Tallas, not with the way he'd clearly been watching her. And besides, Ezra was easy to clock in a bar full of bounty hunters and their clients. He just wasn't the kind of person usually seen there.

"There's nothing to tell," Mo said. "You know that. I don't discuss work unless it's with my client or my team."

"Ah, your *team*." Tallas chuckled. "Where are Cass and Kynn? I haven't seen them in years."

"Count yourself lucky." Mo looked up at Ezra and tried to ignore the small furrow between his eyebrows. "Come on."

Mo started down the street, eager to put distance between her and Tallas. Ezra kept pace with her. As she was about to turn a corner, Tallas slid in front of her, blocking her path.

He grabbed her forearm. "What if I told you I had information?"

He was fucking with her, just like he always had. Trying to claw his way back into her life.

Mo rammed her knee into his crotch. He dropped her. With one hand, she grabbed the hilt of her sword, and with the other, she shoved Tallas back against the nearby alley wall so hard she thought she heard his skull crack.

It wasn't her body that kept him there but her magic, the mindbender magic she so rarely wielded. It was like a forcefield, preventing him from moving.

She ignited her blade, then brought it just inches from Tallas's throat. Its white glow lit up his face, making him look like a ghost. His thin lips pulled up, revealing sharp canines.

"You think this is funny?" Mo hissed. "I told you last time I saw you that if you *ever* touched me again, I'd fucking kill you. And here we are."

"You won't," Tallas taunted. "I know you, Momo. Your bark is bigger than your bite."

She pressed harder against his throat. "Try me."

"You won't," he whispered. "Not with Ezra right there. Not when you just showed him the thing you never show anyone."

Fuck.

Fuck, Tallas was right.

Mo never used her magic in front of people. Didn't want people to know about it. They were quick to judge mindbenders.

And he was right that she was no killer. Not unless she absolutely had to be. Tallas was a hateful, abusive man, but did that mean he had to die by her hand tonight?

Her magic wrapped aubergine tendrils around his body. "Leave me the fuck alone, Tallas," she said. "Crawl back into whatever pit of hell you came out of."

"So *sensitive*, Momo," he cooed. "As always."

Shit, Mo really wished she was a cold-blooded killer. That she could truly be that brutal, ruthless person she showed the scum of the Federation on a daily basis. Then she could be done with him for good.

She squeezed her magic tighter around Tallas's body. "Get the fuck out of my sight, jackass, and don't come near me again," she said, then flicked her fingers. Mo and her magic tossed him down the alley like the trash he was.

The purple swirling around him died as soon as he slammed into the ground. Tallas sputtered and cursed as he staggered to his feet and shouted, "You'll regret that, Mora Cevi!"

The only thing she regretted was not throwing him farther and harder.

"Come on," she said to Ezra as she headed back into the street. She hurried along, desperate to put space between herself and that alley. She didn't even care if he followed her.

But he did. As soon as they made it several roads over, Ezra asked, "What the fuck was that? You're a mindbender?"

"I don't want to talk about this, Lyre," Mo muttered. She was too hot. She was on fire, and her heart was beating too quickly.

Tallas fucking Bara. She'd thought that on a city-planet of billions, she wouldn't run into him. Not even at that bar. Bounty hunters were always coming and going, away more than they were home. The chances of running into him had been so small. And there he'd been anyway.

In some far-off corner of her mind, Mo heard Ezra call out to her again. She forced herself to stop walking; she didn't even know where she was going. She was just going away from wherever Tallas was.

"Hey, Cevi," Ezra said as he caught up to her. "Come on."

"What?" she asked, glaring up at him.

He held his palms up in surrender. "I'm not mad or anything. I was just going to get us a cab back to the shipyard."

The streets were emptier than before. Dark skyscrapers rose up around them, the sounds of Aerilia's nightlife nothing but distant rumbles. Whatever shops and offices were around here were closed for the night. High above them, air traffic was light and moving at a steady pace. A few cabs were hovering on the nearby corner, green lights indicating they were available for hire.

"Oh," she said.

To her great relief, Tallas hadn't chased them down, and Ezra didn't prod her for any more information. As he went over to speak with one of the cab pilots, Mo sucked in a deep breath, held it for eight seconds, then blew it out for just as long. Ezra waved her over, then climbed inside the small shuttle.

Mo gave herself a mental shake and joined him. She needed to focus on her job, not the past. She needed to focus on exactly what was in front of her: hunting down the people who had betrayed Ezra, much the way Tallas had betrayed her. Maybe she wouldn't ever get closure, but she could help Ezra get his.

By the time they made it back to the shipyard, it was nearing midnight. All Mo wanted to do was collapse into bed and put the day behind her, but she'd been serious about getting back to work. About focusing on her job.

"Cass? Kynn?" she called as she stormed into *The Revenant*. All the lights were on, and upstairs, she heard their faint chatter. "Cass?"

The chatter stopped.

"Mo?" Cass's voice was tinged with worry.

"Tallas is back!" Mo yelled as she stalked into the common room. She bypassed where Cass and Kynn were sitting, instead heading for her bedroom. She ripped her jacket off and dug her fingers into her hair.

Tallas was back, and she'd just exposed her magic to a fucking Vanguard.

Mindbenders weren't illegal or anything of the sort. No. They were just part of nature, like all other magic users. Some had telekinesis, like Mo. Other mindbenders were tactile telepaths or even empaths. Despite trying to learn those other skills, Mo had only ever been able to tap into that telekinesis. People often didn't trust that she was honest about her abilities, and who would? If she were a telepath, she'd probably lie and say she wasn't.

She'd shown Tallas her magic a few times when she was young and stupid, cocky in her ignorance. He'd wanted to use her magic for his own gain, to put it to the test on contracts.

Shit, Mo felt like she was going to be sick.

Someone knocked on her doorframe, then came a deep, unwanted voice. "Cevi?"

Mo couldn't let Ezra see her like this. Not when he'd already seen her crack.

Fluffing out her hair, Mo pulled on her neutral mask and turned around. "We need to talk," she said as she passed him, barely avoiding shoulder-checking him in his chest. "All of us."

Behind her, Ezra sighed. Mo ignored him and hurried back into the common room, where Cass and Kynn were both standing worriedly. Of course they were worried. They knew Mo's history.

"You ran into Tallas?" Cass asked.

"Did you get what we need?" Mo asked in response as she headed for the cockpit.

"Yeah, everything's good. Supplies, systems, everything. Why?"

"We need to leave," Mo said.

She couldn't stand the thought of being on this planet a moment longer, and besides, they needed to leave to continue working the contract. Several sets of footsteps followed Mo into the command room.

As Mo opened the cockpit doors, she glanced over her shoulder at the commander standing silently behind Cass. "Still want to go to Vonnoth?"

To his credit, he didn't miss a beat. "Yes. Maybe Liv's father knows about the crystal or can tell us if he received any threats."

That was good enough for Mo. It was the only logical next step anyway. The trail had gone cold. Maybe it had never really been warm in the first place. Maybe Doctor Valtor could help them change that.

And at least Ezra didn't seem disturbed by the revelation about her magic.

Mo dropped into the captain's chair and started powering up *The Revenant*, running through as many system checks as quickly as she could. Her hands trembled as they moved over the controls.

"Mo, what happened?" Kynn asked as he settled into the copilot seat.

"Tallas happened," she muttered. "Let's jump, then we can talk."

Cass and Ezra strapped into the back row while Kynn helped Mo get everything flight ready. Soon, they were off. As the ship flew high into the atmosphere, she and Kynn plotted a course to Vonnoth. Even traveling in hyperspace, it would take over half a day to reach the planet. It wasn't in the Federation Core—the innermost collection of planets, and some of the wealthiest—like Aerilia was, but rather within the boundary of the Inner Systems, well-off and well-protected worlds surrounding the Core.

As the ship's hyperdrive kicked on and the computer took over navigational controls, Mo finally relaxed into her seat. Tallas was already far, far away. Soon, there would be light-years between them.

She didn't know why he still held so much power over her. Why he still irked her so much after all these years, or why her body held so much fear. After all, Mo could squash that pathetic excuse of a man in seconds.

"Mo." Cass's voice was as soft as the hand she set on Mo's shoulder. "What happened?"

"Sorry," Mo said. "Sorry. One second."

As Kynn left his seat and moved away with Cass, Mo sucked in another deep breath and let it out slowly. They'd only left the planet a half hour earlier, but Mo couldn't believe she'd just ignored everything else to escape.

It was as she said earlier, she *really* needed to focus on doing her job. Not on the past.

Mo didn't like leaving the helm unattended, but the autopilot feature would be fine for a few minutes. As she stood, Mo squared her shoulders and followed the other three back into the common room. Kynn dropped into one of the seats by the kitchen table and groaned.

"I found Bax and Amane," Mo said.

Cass's eyebrows raised as she lowered herself into the seat next to Kynn. "Are they still married?"

Ezra busied himself with getting a glass of water.

"Yes, disgustingly so," Mo said, to which Kynn laughed. "They've heard some rumors of treasure hunters looking to hire Syndicate folks—and others—as well as rumors of the threats made against Chancellor Valtor and Lyre's family. They couldn't give specifics."

"Of course they couldn't," Kynn said.

"At least we know we're not the only ones looking for this shit," Cass said. "There's got to be a way to figure out who bought off Ezra's team. You really don't know anyone who would do this?"

"Not a damn clue," Ezra said as he joined them. The glass in his hand was only half full.

"Let's hope Doctor Valtor knows something, then," Kynn said.

"What about Tallas?" Cass asked. "Was he at the bar?"

"He was, and he was listening in on the conversation we had," Mo said. "He said he had information, but I think he was just trying to get to me. You know how he is."

"I hate to sound uninformed," Ezra said slowly, "but who is Tallas Bara? Besides obviously being some sort of bounty hunter."

"He's a member of the Syndicate," Kynn said.

Cass nudged him in the ribs. "He's a real fucking piece of work is what he is."

"*Obviously,*" Kynn drawled. "I thought a little professional context might be important."

"What's so bad about him?" Ezra asked.

"He's a liar, a cheat, and a thief ... generally known for being a piece of garbage." Mo didn't want to get into the details. "All the traits you'd assign to a bounty hunter, probably."

Ezra's eyebrows furrowed. "I don't think all bounty hunters are garbage. I'm insulted you'd even say that."

"Darius sure thought so."

"Yeah, well, Darius was a piece of work too, apparently. Whatever he said, he certainly doesn't speak for me. You're not bad people."

Mo wasn't sure she believed him, but she'd let it go for now. Maybe he was telling the truth. She should probably at least give him the benefit of the doubt.

"You're not freaked out that I'm a mindbender?" she asked Ezra, and Cass's eyes widened. "Yeah, as soon as Tallas laid a hand on me, it just came out," she said to her best friend. "Flexed a little too much, probably. He said I'd regret it."

"Tallas always talks shit," Kynn said. "He always did."

Mo knew that, but she didn't want to give Tallas any reason to come looking for her. She didn't need him interfering in her work or her life.

"I really do not care that you're a mindbender," Ezra said to her. Fire sparked to life over his palm. "I can do this, remember? Magic's just magic."

"And yet your kind aren't feared like mine are," Mo said, hating the bitterness coating her words.

"People fear what they don't understand," Ezra said. "Are you a telepath too?"

"No," she muttered. "Only telekinesis."

He dismissed his flame, then nodded at Cass and Kynn. "What about you two?"

"That's all you have to say?" Mo asked.

Ezra shrugged again. "Magic's just magic."

"Nothing from either of us," Cass said.

"And thank goodness for that, because I already have enough to manage without throwing that into the mix," Kynn said.

Many people were jealous of magic users, but Mo's ability had never caused any tension between her, Kynn, and Cass. It was just something she could do, something she used sparingly and only when necessary on contracts.

Ezra nodded. "We should get some rest, unless you want me to fly for a while?"

"No," Mo said. "You can go sleep. All of you. I'll wake you up in a few hours, Kynn."

Ezra pinned her with a look, but she wasn't going to budge on her rules. She needed one thing to be normal, and this ship was normal. Her rules were normal.

As Ezra and Kynn headed back downstairs, Mo started for the cockpit again. Cass followed, her footsteps barely audible on the metal floor.

"Mo," she said as she dropped into the second chair. "You don't have to put up a front when it's just me."

"I know."

"Do you?" Cass asked, her face and voice filled with concern.

"Of course I do. I just hate that he snuck up on me. That I didn't expect it, that I wasn't ready."

"We can't be ready for everything all the time."

"Sure wish we could," Mo mumbled.

"That'd be nice, but it's just not possible," Cass said. "It sounds like you put him in his place. That should keep him off your back. You're not some kid anymore."

"I appreciate you, Cass," she said, giving her a small smile. "Always have."

"I know." Cass smiled back. "We got some custard buns on top of all the other supplies. You want one? Did you eat?"

"Always trying to feed me," Mo said.

Cass poked her in her thigh. "You'd forget half the time if we didn't remind you."

Mo couldn't deny it. She often didn't realize she was hungry until she was starving, or she'd get so focused on doing something else—tracking targets, making investments in their futures, helping fix their weapons or figuring out ship maintenance—that it just slipped her mind. Sometimes she hated that she got like that and that she needed Cass and Kynn to step in, but she was also grateful they didn't judge her and didn't mind.

"Well, thanks. I'll get one in a bit," Mo said. "I think I'd rather be alone for a while, if that's alright."

Cass stood. "Of course. You know where to find me if you need me."

"Get some sleep!" Mo called over her shoulder.

Mo scrubbed at her face. Cass was right. Mo wasn't a kid anymore. She was a strong, powerful woman, one of the best bounty hunters in the Federation. She wasn't going to let Tallas Bara fuck with her, and she certainly wasn't going to let Darius Kane get away with attempted murder. Mo was sick and tired of shitty men getting away with terrible things, and she was finally going to make them pay.

Chapter 22

Ezra stared up at his bedroom ceiling, counting each panel over and over again. There were only eight of them, all large, plain rectangles. A pair of silver knitting needles and a skein of yarn sat untouched on the mattress beside him. He'd meant to start a new project to pass the time—it was something he used to do with his grandmother and a simple distraction on flights—but he just couldn't focus.

Mora Cevi was a mindbender. A fucking mindbender.

He'd meant what he'd said earlier. It didn't scare him. He'd known a few mindbenders in the FSC, but they'd never shown restraint like Mo did.

Honestly, he was just impressed that she'd managed to hide it so well.

But that begged the question of what else she might be hiding.

Not that he really had any business digging into whatever secrets she might want to keep, but the more time he spent around her, the more he wanted to know her. He was so damn curious about her. She was strong, but she showed restraint. She clearly liked things being done a certain way and being in charge. She had a seemingly quick temper, but that softer side she showed Cass and Kynn was ... different. It seemed like a great privilege to get even a glimpse of it. Ezra had the distinct feeling that Mora Cevi rarely showed anyone that part of herself.

Had she shown Tallas Bara those secret pieces of her heart? Had he used it against her? He'd obviously hurt her—maybe Cass and Kynn too.

And why did Ezra even care? It was probably ancient history between competitors and former lovers. He'd also meant what he'd said about thinking Cass, Kynn, and Mo were decent people, but bounty hunters weren't known for being friendly. By the nature of their work, they couldn't exactly create too many personal attachments.

Ezra sighed. He wasn't getting any sleep, not with such wandering thoughts and certainly not in this damn bed.

He stood and ran his fingers through his hair, then tied it back into a short braid. After getting dressed, he left his cabin.

Kynn's door was closed. Upstairs was quiet.

Ezra climbed the ramp as silently as he could. The ship rattled for a moment, no doubt some bump in space. It happened sometimes, more easily felt on older, smaller ships like this. He continued climbing up.

The doors between the common area and command room were closed, but through the windows, he could see the cockpit was open. Mo was stretched out in the pilot's chair, all lazy limbs and slouched posture. She twirled a piece of long white hair between her fingers. It looked more silver in the ship's lighting. He'd noticed that earlier on Aerilia, too, and back in the forests on Miduna before that. When the sun hit it just right, her hair almost sparkled.

She said something to herself, then sighed and shifted.

Well, shit. He'd better just go in there before she caught him and thought he was spying on her.

He opened the doors, then called, "Cevi?" as he strolled into the command room.

Mo whipped around, already watching, waiting. On alert.

"What's wrong?" she asked, eyebrows furrowing.

"Nothing's wrong," he said, stopping just a couple feet from her. "I can't sleep. Do you always give guests the smallest bed? And does this ship rattle this bad all the time?"

The wrinkle in her brow deepened. She frowned. "Don't insult my ship."

"It's an observation," he said, dropping into the seat next to her. "Why don't you get it fixed?"

She immediately busied herself with checking some of the screens lighting up the dashboard. The radar was empty—as expected when traveling at this speed and in this part of the Federation—and everything else seemed to be in order.

"Getting it 'fixed,' as you call it, is very expensive," Mo said. "Though I'm sure that's nothing you've ever had to worry about."

"I've certainly never owned my own ship. I can't imagine the cost."

"Take my word for it." She glanced sidelong at him. "If you trust me, anyway."

"You haven't given me a reason not to trust you."

"Not even the mindbender thing?"

"I swear," he said, "that really doesn't bother me. That's not something you have to disclose. Not unless you're FSC, of course."

"Like that'd ever happen." Her words were clipped, almost angry. "How long have you known about your magic?"

"Since I can remember," Ezra said. "I'm a healer too. In case you didn't know that."

"I didn't."

"Well, I am." Healing was the gentler side of Ezra's magic, life-sustaining rather than destructive and uncontrolled. He wasn't a miracle worker—wasn't as strong as some of the most talented healers in the Federation—but he could stabilize someone until the real doctors arrived. He'd used that gift many times over the years for his team. Maybe he shouldn't have.

She started to say something more, but heavy footsteps sounded behind them. Kynn ran a hand over his cropped coils, all smiles as he circled around the holo table.

"Go to bed, Mo," he said. "You look like shit. I'll take over."

"Fuck you," Mo said with a laugh as she pushed out of her seat.

She shoulder-checked him as she passed, and Kynn chuckled. Something tugged at Ezra's heart, but he didn't want to examine whatever that feeling was too closely. He'd always longed for that easy rapport, the heckles and jokes, that so many teams seemed to have. That he'd only experienced in fits and starts throughout the war.

"You good, Lyre?" Kynn asked as he dropped into the pilot's seat. "I'm surprised she even let you up here."

"Kinda snuck up on her," he admitted.

Kynn clicked his tongue as he checked a few of the screens. "Never sneak up on Mora Cevi."

"Why not?"

"She'll kick your ass, and I'm pretty sure I still have my bruises to prove it."

Ezra smiled a little. "Has she always been like that? She's got a pretty short fuse some days."

Shifting in his chair, Kynn studied Ezra's face. He tried not to squirm under the bounty hunter's scrutiny, but something about Kynn's gaze was unnerving.

"She's not the most patient person I've ever met," Kynn finally said, "but there's a lot more to Mo than her temper."

"I gathered. Most people are more complicated than that."

"She's not actually that complicated once you figure her out."

"And you won't tell me?" Ezra asked.

Kynn grinned. "Nope."

Dammit.

"Why do you care?" Kynn asked. "We'll be done with the job soon. Clients don't usually care to get to know us. Most of them just hire us and send us on our way, preferring to stay back."

"You're interesting," Ezra said, mostly the truth. "And I'd really like to know why she still seems to hate my guts when you and Cass don't. Did I do something to offend her?"

Again, Kynn laughed, a warm and pleasant sound. "You're a Vanguard. That's enough for Mo."

"Yet she accused me of having negative opinions of all bounty hunters earlier?"

Kynn shook his head once. "That's Mo."

"That doesn't explain anything!"

With a sigh, Kynn said, "We've all been let down by the FSC. Mo just holds a meaner grudge than Cass and I do. And I think deep down, Mo knows you're not personally at fault for the FSC's failings, but you're in front of her, in her house, giving her a paycheck. I was hoping it wouldn't make her that prickly, but ..." He shrugged.

"I know the FSC isn't perfect." Ezra had all the proof he needed just from the fact that Command wasn't willing to look for Darius and the others, not to mention all the times they'd failed in battle, failed to save civilians, or even silenced their own. "But we do good work. We really try to do good work."

"I'm not the one you need to convince," Kynn said.

Ezra didn't know why this was so important to him, proving to Mo that he wasn't someone she needed to hate. Maybe he couldn't change it. Maybe she was an orphan of some Ascended attack or had lost her parents to the military. There was no fixing that.

"What about that Tallas guy?" Ezra asked. "What's his deal?"

"Tallas ..." Kynn clicked his tongue. "That motherfucker."

"Why?" Ezra pressed. If Mo's ironclad control had snapped so easily, the man had to be bad news.

"That's not my story to tell."

"Come on, you won't tell me anything?"

"Let's just say Mo might be able to relate to you a bit," Kynn said. "The whole 'someone I care about tried to murder me' thing."

Ezra's eyes widened. "He tried to kill her?"

"Tried to kill all of us."

"Why?"

"Greed? Arrogance? Tallas Bara is many things, but his motives are simple enough."

Ezra stared out at the blue, white, and black streaks of hyperspace. "What else did he do?"

"You'll have to get that story from Mo," Kynn said, his voice going ice cold. "I'd kill Tallas if I saw him. He's lucky I wasn't there tonight or any other night he tried to hurt Mo. Very lucky."

Tallas must have done something awful—worse than just trying to kill them—because Ezra had a feeling Kynn wasn't exaggerating. He seemed like the most easygoing of the trio, but the tight set to his jaw and clenched fist said otherwise.

"Well, thanks for that much, I guess," Ezra muttered.

"Just be patient with Mo," Kynn said. "Keep proving you're a halfway decent guy. She'll come around."

"And if she doesn't?"

"Then you won't even have to worry about it, because soon, we're going to find those fuckers who tried to kill you, and we'll be done with this mission."

Ezra sure hoped Kynn was right. He needed to stay focused on this mission, not on winning over Mora Cevi. And he needed to get some sleep.

Pushing to his feet, Ezra clapped Kynn on the shoulder, bid him good night, and headed out. The hallway that led to Mo's quarters was dark, and her door was closed. Ezra shook his head. He really needed to focus.

Chapter 23

As they dropped out of hyperspace and into the far outer reaches of the Rueli System, Mo blew out a deep breath. That had felt like one of the longest flights of her life despite not even being a full day.

"Contacting Rueli's monitoring stations," Cass said from the copilot's seat.

She pushed several buttons, and as the high-pitched voice of some system worker echoed through the cockpit, Cass responded with their ship name and destination of Atmos, a midsize city in Vonnoth's northern hemisphere. When they received clearance to proceed, Mo slid the acceleration lever forward, and soon, they were back on track.

Mo watched on one of her screens as they passed through the outer edge of the Rueli System. Outside, through the cockpit's view screen, was mostly darkness, except for the smatterings of far-off stars and worlds. They were heading sunward, toward the inner rings of the solar system that actually had habitable planets instead of gas giants and space stations.

Cass pushed a button in the middle of their long, shared dashboard. "Kynn, Ezra, we're making our final approach."

Mo had been avoiding Ezra since the night before. She really didn't care for him to get more involved in her life than he already had, but Tallas's bullshit and her own secrets were making that very difficult.

As much as she hadn't liked him initially—for no real good reason, she'd admit to herself—Ezra wasn't terrible. They were working well together. Maybe he wouldn't be an asshole about her past—all of their pasts—if she told him. But did he need to know? He was a client. Clients didn't need to know shit.

Kynn's loud laugh pierced the upper deck as he strode into the command room. Ezra followed, grinning like a man who'd just heard a joke for the first time in his life.

"What's so funny?" Mo asked.

"Nothing," they said in unison, but the glint in Kynn's eye suggested there was something more to it.

"Just realizing we have a lot in common," Kynn said, and Ezra laughed again.

That was a ridiculously vague answer. If they didn't want to tell, she wouldn't prod.

"We're approaching Vonnoth," Mo said. "Should break the atmosphere by the top of the hour. These still the right coordinates, Lyre?"

Ezra leaned between Mo and Cass's seats, his hand resting on the back of Mo's chair. He was so close that Mo could smell the evergreen radiating off him. It was stronger than during their misadventure on Aerilia, or maybe he was just closer. She tried not to breathe him in as he examined the screen.

"Yeah, that's right," he said. "That'll bring us to a shipyard right outside of Atmos. The university is in that quarter of the city, so we should be able to make this a quick trip."

"You make it sound like you've been before," Cass said as Ezra straightened and took half a step back. He didn't move his hand.

"I have," Ezra said. "Mission here a few years back. A group of radicals had captured one of Vonnoth's senators, so we were sent in to extract her."

"Was that with Darius and the others?" Kynn asked.

Ezra nodded.

"Do they know Doctor Valtor lives here?"

"He wasn't here at the time."

"I still don't like that they know this place," Mo muttered.

"We've been all over the Federation," Ezra said. "To hundreds of cities, outposts, and worlds."

While that was surely true, and while the Federation was enormous—with over a thousand inhabited worlds, plus more outposts and newly colonized planets and moons—alarm bells went off in Mo's head.

"If they were hired to take out your family, he might be high on their list of targets," Kynn said.

"We should still be careful," Mo said. "Never know who or what is lurking around. I think last night proved that." She would not be caught off guard again.

Ezra's grip on the back of her chair tightened. "Fair enough."

As much as Mo enjoyed bringing criminals into custody, she couldn't stop thinking about going home. Back to the status quo, to Miduna, where things were relatively calm and normal, where she knew who was coming and going from the Syndicate and Kalyndra. She'd never been to Atmos.

Soon, the blue-green mass that was Vonnoth came into view, along with all the small satellites and space stations in orbit. With approval from landing crews on the ground, they began their descent. High-traffic planets like Vonnoth always had some kind of protocol for takeoffs and landings.

The ship rumbled as they cut through the atmosphere, and Ezra muttered a curse as he and Kynn both strapped into the two rear seats. The vibrations didn't bother Mo. They were familiar, and both she and Cass always said that feeling such movement helped them pilot better.

Unfortunately, the shipyard Ezra had suggested they use was full, as were the other two on the outskirts of the city. They ended up landing in a clearing not terribly far outside of town, which was fine with Mo. At least it didn't cost anything. They grabbed their weapons and headed out.

Atmos was a bit larger than Kalyndra, both in terms of square mileage and population. Several million people lived within its immediate borders, and more had built sprawling estates in the hills above the city proper. The blue and white buildings amid the sea of green trees were almost happy.

"Did you manage to free that senator who'd been taken captive?" Kynn asked Ezra as he led them through the foreign city. "You never finished the story."

"Of course we did," Ezra said. "We didn't fail. We never failed."

"Which certainly bodes well for us considering your team's new direction in life," Kynn quipped.

"The good news, Kynn," Ezra said, "is that I don't fail either."

Mo raised an eyebrow. She didn't know the Vanguard well enough to judge that for herself, but he clearly had a strong track record. Besides, even if *he* failed, Mo didn't. Cass didn't. And Kynn—all jokes aside—really was the best bounty hunter on Miduna behind Mo and Cass.

After walking for more than half an hour—most of it in silence—the roads and tall buildings gave way to a fenced-in courtyard, along with a sign advertising Atmos's university. At least that had been easy enough.

Given it was only midday on the planet, students and faculty alike milled around the tree-laden campus, whether lounging in the grassy central courtyard or on the stairs leading into the buildings surrounding it. Some small part of Mo's mind wondered what it was like for all these young people to be off on their own, enjoying school and not worrying too much about the ways of the world. Had any of them learned to survive the hard way like she had? Like Cass and Kynn?

Ezra led them into a building marked as anthropology and history. It wasn't all that dissimilar to the one on Aerilia, though it lacked the same distinct crystalline roof and bright floors and walls. Instead, warm wood and metal accents filled these halls, a mix of old and new.

Students they passed by gave them confused or dirty looks, which Mo was happy to give back to them. They had more important things to do than worry about making a few young adults uncomfortable. People walked around armed all the time.

After asking several students and professors, they were able to find Professor Marcus Valtor's office deep within the building's third floor. The door was closed and locked.

"Damn," Ezra muttered, pushing the button on the frame again and again. It *should've* worked, but obviously the professor wasn't in. "Could he be teaching right now?"

"We should've just gone to admissions," Kynn said. "Saved ourselves the trouble. We can't feasibly check every classroom."

"We could wait," Cass said.

"Oh, great." Kynn rolled his eyes. "Just a bunch of bounty hunters and a—"

"Excuse me?" A high-pitched voice with a thick Aerilian accent echoed down the now-empty hall. A few dozen feet down, a young Luxinae woman with snow white skin and curly white hair frowned. Luxinae all had distinct patterns on their skin, almost like a fingerprint. This stranger had dark blue markings that reminded Mo of a circuit board. "Can I help you?"

"We're looking for Professor Valtor," Ezra said. "Do you know if he's teaching right now?"

"Professor Valtor?" The young woman moved closer and pushed a few stray curls away from her forehead. "Why?"

"We wanted to ask him about—"

"Not this," the Luxinae replied with a groan.

Ezra raised an eyebrow. "What?"

"People are *always* wanting to talk to him about his ... unique interests." She extended a hand to Ezra for a shake, then the others. Mo declined. "I'm Professor Taera Rionis," she said.

Kynn leaned against the wall next to Valtor's door. "Awfully young to be a professor, aren't you?" he asked.

She straightened and adjusted the collar of her maroon shirt. "Youngest ever to graduate with my doctorate as a xeno-archaehistorian."

"Do you know Professor Valtor well?" Ezra asked.

"No, nor do I care to," she said. "He's one of the more ... fringe elements here on campus. Why?"

"As we said, we need to speak with him," Mo said, deciding it was best not to offer specifics if this woman didn't think very highly of Professor Valtor. "Do you know where we can find him?"

"He hasn't been by all week," Taera said.

"Do you know where he lives?"

"Why?"

"We're actually here on behalf of his family," Ezra said. "They asked us to check in with him." When Taera's eyebrows furrowed, he pulled out his Vanguard badge. "All above board, I promise."

Taera pressed her thin lips together, then nodded. "He lives in one of the estates in the hills outside the city. Do you have a tablet?"

Kynn passed her a small tablet he must've taken off the ship. Taera tapped its screen a few times, then handed it back to him.

"The coordinates," she said. "Good luck. And if you find him, let him know nobody in the department is willing to cover his classes this week. Admin's pissed. He needs to get his ass to school."

As Taera stalked off, Kynn passed the tablet to Ezra and said, "Well?"

"Guess we've got our next destination," Ezra muttered. "Let's get going."

Mo was getting tired of traipsing around the Federation looking for whatever meager information they could find about Ezra's team. The more time passed, the longer they had to find a good hiding spot, which was just going to make Mo's job that much harder.

Thick ferns and underbrush slapped her shins and crunched under her boots. The coordinates Professor Rionis had given them weren't all that far outside the city, so they'd decided to walk. When spending so much time in space, it was good to be planetside for a little while—even when Mo was exhausted. They'd passed half a dozen other small estates on the walk out here, all of them beautiful and made of stone and glass.

What was this professor up to? It seemed unusual that someone of his tenure would be skipping out on work. Based on what Ezra had explained, Professor Valtor was a veteran of academia. Maybe he'd gone on a bender of some kind and didn't even know what day it was. Maybe he'd gotten lost in his studies, or maybe he'd just gotten sick of teaching.

Or maybe someone had already gotten to him. Mo tried not to think too hard about that one; even if that was true, they needed to locate him.

"How much farther?" Cass asked from the back of the group.

"Not even a full klick," Ezra said. "Just over that ridge, and we'll almost be there."

They started up the well-worn path that led over the next ridge, right into a clearing with a three-story mansion made of a mix of wood and metal. A place like that on Miduna would've cost at least a million credits—far more than *The Revenant*. It probably cost even more here.

Mo shook her head as she trailed after Kynn and Ezra, but as they entered the slightly overgrown courtyard, she paused. Something wasn't right.

A few of the pavers on the ground were damaged. Up ahead, the front door was ajar. Cass nudged her shoulder and began reaching for her weapon. Mo did the same, her finger hovering just over the trigger that would engage her sword.

"Lyre," she said. "Kynn—"

Ezra slowed and reached for his saber. "I see it."

The high-pitched whine of blaster fire rang in Mo's ears. As she ignited her blade, she cursed herself for not stopping back at the ship for her armor. She knew better when on a hunt. Her blade blocked the first shot, and Kynn blocked the second.

Ezra planted himself at the front of their group, a large, fiery shield bursting to life in front of him. Its flames made his saber look more red than gold.

"It's them," he said over his shoulder. "It's my team."

"You're sure?" Cass asked from the back, guns drawn.

"Positive."

Mo understood. She'd know Cass's shots anywhere after so many years together.

"Get the fuck out of here, Lyre!" came a voice Mo hadn't heard in a while. Darius Kane.

That motherfucker.

This was no fucking coincidence.

"Not a chance, Darius!" Ezra shouted back.

"You were supposed to be dead."

"And yet here I am."

Mo scanned the building in front of her. They were at a disadvantage. Ezra's team had the high ground, the cover, everything.

It was a good thing Mo worked at a disadvantage half the time.

"Lyre, you and I are going in," Mo said. "Kynn, Cass, go around back."

To her great surprise, Ezra didn't disagree.

"On my mark," he said instead. "One."

Mo braced herself.

"Two."

She tightened her grip on her weapon.

"Three."

Mo darted forward, following half a step behind Ezra as he charged the front door. They drew heavy fire from his team through the upper windows, but they zigged and zagged out of the way. Mo barely caught sight of Cass and Kynn as they sprinted around the corner of the house, a blur of blue and purple.

The outside stone gave way to smooth wood floors and one of the worst messes Mo had ever seen. Furniture toppled over, books and papers thrown around, pottery and art destroyed. Ezra pushed through the foyer and an archway leading into the next large room. A staircase was at the far end, and above, soft footsteps.

Ezra tilted his head toward the stairs. Mo nodded.

Another door squeaked open, and the blue glow of Kynn's saber lit the hallway to Mo's left. When his face appeared amid the shadows, Mo mouthed, "Upstairs." He nodded and ushered Cass away to try to find another way up.

Mo and Ezra cleared the lower level before beginning to climb the stairs. The floors squeaked again.

"Darius!" Ezra called. "Let's talk this out. It's just me."

"And some fucking bounty hunters!" Darius called back, his voice coming from somewhere above them. It was partially muffled, almost like he was behind several walls or doors.

Behind Mo, Cass and Kynn started their way upstairs. Obviously they hadn't found an alternate staircase or anything of the sort, but maybe it was best they stuck together.

"What'd you expect?" Ezra shouted. "You tried to fucking kill me!"

"Really didn't want to, Ez."

They reached the top of the stairs, and Ezra motioned for Mo to follow him to the left. Cass and Kynn went to the right.

Blaster fire erupted from both ends of the hall. Mo spun around Ezra, blocking each round with her saber. The weapons' energy ricocheted off her blade, creating an eerie mix of blue and white.

A door slammed open. One former Vanguard charged Mo, sword drawn. She parried and stepped back toward Ezra. He moved to her right, blocking their attacker with his golden sword. Mo couldn't tell who it was with their helmet on. Not Darius; they were too short to be Darius.

They reached for their gun. Ezra tackled them. Their sword clattered to the ground, the blade disengaging on impact. Mo reached her hand out, tendrils of her magic snaking around the weapon and pulling it to her. Ezra had already seen her magic; she might as well put it to good use. She stormed down the hall, one hilt in each hand, toward where more blaster fire came from.

She dodged and deflected each shot of energy with little effort, as if fighting against a child or new recruit back at the Syndicate. Mo kicked the door in as soon as she reached it, lifting one weapon in front of her face. Its white glow lit up the room, revealing a Vanguard in dark armor to her left.

Mo sidestepped and spun around to face her attacker. They aimed their blaster at her face. As they pulled the trigger, she deflected, batting the energy away like it was little more than a game. They fired again and again, but they weren't even close to hitting Mo, especially not when she had two swords.

It had to be Darius, as he was nearly the size of Ezra.

She thought only for a second to redirect one of those shots at the Vanguard, but no. She was not here to kill. She was here to subdue, just like on any other mission. Darius Kane was not hers to kill.

"Sergeant," she said through clenched teeth. "Stand down."

Darius started forward, but Ezra crashed into him from behind, tackling him to the floor. Darius's gun fell, and Mo kicked it away. She pointed both blades at the Vanguard as he tried to wiggle free from Ezra. He had Darius pinned to the ground.

"Don't make me hurt you, Darius," Ezra said.

"Fuck you."

Ezra forced Darius up, then wrenched both hands behind his back. Then he pulled something out of his back pocket, just a long line of flexible steel. Ezra bound Darius's wrists, but Mo wasn't sure that was going to hold up. Not against a Vanguard in their gear. Energy cuffs would've been better. Too bad she hadn't brought any.

In the hallway beyond, Cass and Kynn were already standing guard over the other three of Ezra's team members, all of them bound and looking particularly pissed now that their helmets were off. Mo disengaged her blades, then grabbed Darius's discarded blaster and attached it to her belt. No use leaving it around in case the fucker got loose.

"Downstairs," Ezra barked at the rest of his team. "Now."

As they marched their captives downstairs, Mo looked over Cass and Kynn. They were both walking fine, no limps or awkward gaits. No marks on their clothes or other signs of injury. Ezra didn't seem to be hurt either. Good.

Ezra ushered his team into the kitchen. It was a large, beautiful space with a view of the forest outside. The cabinets were dark wood, the counters white stone, and the floors were a mess of broken items and flowers knocked from vases. Ezra forced the traitors to sit in a row on the floor against the kitchen island. Cass and Kynn spread out, weapons drawn. Mo circled around and planted herself between Cass and Ezra.

Ezra crossed his arms tightly over his chest. "Explain," he barked.

"Ez—" the woman, Kira, started.

"It's Commander Lyre."

"But—"

"You lost the right to think of me as anything other than a very angry superior officer when you all tried to murder me and ran off with that crystal," Ezra said. "Where is it?"

"What crystal?" Darius asked.

"You know the one," Ezra said. "The one from the cave. Purple, blue, and gold."

Darius pursed his lips, then shook his head. "Sorry, Ez. No clue what you're talking about."

"You stupid motherfucker." Ezra's hands tightened into fists at his side. "All of you. What the fuck is wrong with you? Why would you betray the FSC?"

Ezra may not have said it out loud, but Mo didn't miss the question he wanted to ask: *"Why would you betray me?"* It was a question she was all too familiar with, one she couldn't examine too closely right now lest her mind stray back to Tallas.

The four disgraced Vanguards stared up at Ezra, defiant sets in their jaws and glints in their eyes. Mo may not have loved the Federation or its military, but this was cold. Cruel, even. Ezra wasn't a terrible man. He didn't deserve to be betrayed like this, not by the people who were supposed to have his back.

"What is all this about the Eternal Ones artifacts on an underground market?" Ezra asked. "What does that have to do with killing members of my family?"

Though they remained silent, Talon and Kira had the good sense to look away from their former commander. What was making them so resigned to their fate as captives? Mo wanted to knock them around a bit to try to get them to talk, but she didn't think Ezra would want to resort to such tactics. And this was his contract, so she'd follow his lead for now.

"Where's Doctor Valtor?" he asked.

Still, silence.

"Will one of you answer me?" Ezra shouted.

Darius glared up at him. "You're unprepared for what's coming," he said, voice low.

"What the fuck does that mean? Unprepared for what?"

Darius just spat on the ground at Ezra's feet.

Mo's jaw tightened. These pricks.

At least these four would be in FSC custody soon. Even if Ezra wasn't going to interrogate them further, there was no way the military would stand by and let these four keep quiet. They'd have telepaths of their own, plus more direct ways to put pressure on the traitors to talk.

Ezra's voice turned cold and lethal as he crouched in front of his former team. "Here's what's going to happen," he said. "We're going to take you back to town, pass you off to the base, and wash our hands of you. Maybe I'll see you when you get court-martialed, but you four can rot in prison for all I care." He pushed to his feet and didn't even spare Mo, Cass, or Kynn a second glance. "Twenty minutes for me to search this place," he muttered. "Then we're leaving. I can't look at them a second longer."

Pressing her lips together, Mo watched him stalk off. This was how contracts always ended. Irritatingly quiet marks—most of the time—who were angry you'd managed to catch them. This was nothing new to Mo, Cass, or Kynn. It was the way their world worked.

But she also understood why Ezra was so bothered by it. She actually felt bad for him.

Darius and the others shifted on the floor, their bodies tensing as they watched Ezra leave.

Mo reached for the finely carved silver hilt hanging from her belt. She unhooked it and pointed it at Ezra's traitorous team, then put on her meanest smile.

Darius scowled at her. "Fuck you."

"Don't tempt me, Kane," she said. "Unless you want to finally find out why they call me The Demon."

"I'd like to see you try," he snapped.

Cass raised her gun, pointed it at his head, and fired. The shot slammed into the cabinet behind him, leaving a smoking hole no more than a half an inch from his ear. "Want to see what happens when I don't miss on purpose?"

Darius held their stares for only a moment longer before he finally looked away and his posture relaxed. *Coward,* Mo thought.

Ezra might've left to go continue his search, and he might've thought the steel cuffs would hold these four, but Mo wouldn't let her guard down. She had to stay vigilant until these four were out of her hair.

Chapter 24

Ezra picked his way through the mess of furniture, glass, and other debris in his cousin's house. What could someone have been looking for in here? He knew his team wouldn't confirm *they* were the ones who had made the mess, nor would they deny it even if it were true. They just weren't going to talk to him. He had to assume it was them.

Ezra made his way to the office on the far side of the house and began sifting through the tablets and notebooks strewn around the room. Glass crunched behind him.

"Thought you could use some help," Kynn said.

"Yeah," Ezra muttered. "What about the team?"

"Cass and Mo are scarier than me," Kynn said with a wink. "I think they've got it under control."

Right. Cass and Mo were clearly more than capable of handling themselves. He'd seen Mo that night in that alley, how quickly she'd reacted to that prick, Tallas. And he'd seen her just minutes earlier, the way she'd held off Darius like it was little more than a training exercise. Her skills were wasted as a bounty hunter. She would've made an excellent Vanguard with reaction times like that.

Ezra gave himself a mental shake. "I'm looking for anything about the doctor," he said. "About this crystal, or where he might be if he's not here."

"Could he have been their buyer?" Kynn asked as he picked up a notebook and began leafing through its pages. "I mean, he has an interest in all this ancient shit, right? And your family obviously has money. He could buy it."

"But why try to kill me?" Ezra stooped and picked up a tablet, cursing when the damn thing wouldn't turn on. He tossed it aside. "That's what doesn't make sense."

Doctor Marcus Valtor had always been a bit of an aloof uncle to Ezra, never quite as wrapped up in strange family politics as most everyone else was. They'd never been close, but he'd never seemed to hold anything against Ezra. He didn't think Marcus would've taken a hit out on him ...

"Maybe he knew something about the crystal, then," Kynn said. "You know, if it's true, all the stuff about the Eternal Ones."

Ezra was certain none of it was *true*, but maybe Kynn was right. Maybe the doctor had been looking into something. That other professor did say he was on the "fringe" side of the department on campus. If he knew something, that could've been enough to get him targeted by the real buyer.

Could it have been the Ascended? Darius had said Ezra was "unprepared for what was coming," whatever that meant. The only thing he could fathom was the Ascended preparing some kind of massive assault on the Federation.

Twenty minutes wasn't nearly enough time to search, but Ezra did find a framed photo of the professor at a cabin in the woods, and Kynn found several more tablets that all needed a charge. Maybe there'd be something in those. If not, they could go back to the university and ask for more information. Right now, they really needed to get Darius and the others into FSC custody.

When they returned to the kitchen, everything was as Ezra expected to find it: his former team looking enraged, and Cass and Mo with their weapons drawn, smirking as if this were some kind of game. At least he could count on one thing.

"Find what you wanted, Ez?" Darius asked.

Ezra ignored him. "Let's get out of here."

He did a brief sweep of the property inside and out as his bounty hunters searched and secured the traitors. No sign of the crystal—not that he'd actually expected it to be here. There *was* a small shuttle hidden in a clearing in the far back of the property. It wasn't the military one his team had absconded in, but of course they wouldn't keep it. It would've been too easy to track. And this new ship, of course, had no obvious ties to whoever had hired them. It was some rental shuttle, a basic model you could find in any city across the Federation. They'd left it unlocked, and Ezra had searched it, too, but found nothing.

Ezra hurried back to the house, where Mo, Cass, and Kynn were bringing the traitors outside.

"We good to go?" Cass asked.

"Found their ship," Ezra said. "This way."

After a quick walk through the woods, they forced the traitors inside their own shuttle. Mo and Cass secured them while Ezra and Kynn got the ship powered up and airborne. Ezra found the nearest FSC base just outside of Atmos on the navigation screen, then set a course.

Ezra had half expected his team to start up with their nonsense, but they were resigned, like they'd accepted whatever fate awaited them. He was surprised they weren't trying to fight back more, but maybe they knew what was best for them. At least he could wash his hands of them soon.

The flight was short and easy, not even taking a half hour. Bold of his team to risk coming so close to the base, but obviously they'd wanted or needed something in that house. Ezra just hoped he was able to figure out what, or that maybe the FSC would finally take him seriously.

There was no door to seal off the cockpit, so as they made their final approach and received a comms request from the base, Ezra had no choice but to let the unfamiliar voice ring out through the small ship.

"VRS-9271, this is Federation Space Command Base Serenity."

Behind Ezra, Mo snorted. He suppressed his sigh.

"Please identify your purpose and confirm your trajectory toward Base Serenity," the unfamiliar voice continued.

"FSC Base Serenity, this is Vanguard Commander Sergeant Ezra Lyre piloting VRS-9271. I've apprehended four criminals on charges of desertion and attempted murder." Ezra's throat tightened around those last few words. "Requesting permission to land and bring them into Serenity's custody, for immediate transfer to Aerilia."

A long pause. Ezra held his breath.

"Commander Sergeant Lyre, this is Base Serenity. Permission granted."

Ezra kept their course steady as they crossed the last of the distance to the base, and he managed a smooth landing despite the way his heart hammered in his chest. He was never this nervous on missions. His body was used to the danger, the fight. He supposed he couldn't expect himself to just get over his team's actions, though.

"Really, Ez?" Darius drawled as Ezra and Kynn finished powering down the ship. "*Criminals?*"

"Plain and simple," Ezra said as he got out of his seat.

"Yet you'll work with these three?" Darius's nose wrinkled as he nodded toward Cass and Mo on the opposite side of the cabin, then Kynn, who was just behind Ezra. "Typical."

"Bounty hunting isn't a crime, unlike murder," Ezra said. "And these three have been nothing but helpful."

Cass passed him a blaster. Darius's, actually. He'd recognize the thing anywhere. Darius had once had the barrel inlaid with three thin stripes of indigo nepaxite. It had always seemed silly to Ezra; a weapon was just a weapon. But Darius had loved this gun and its reflection of the FSC's colors.

"Because you bought their loyalty."

"Looks like someone bought yours too," Mo said, flashing a mean smile as Darius's jaw tightened. "We're not so different after all, *Sergeant*."

Ezra waved the gun at his team. "Get your asses up. We're ready to go."

One by one, they stood and shuffled toward the door. Cass opened it, and they started outside without a fight. Ezra let out a slow breath as he watched them go. Kynn followed them out into the open courtyard.

"He's an asshole," Mo said, voice low.

"That he is," Ezra muttered, then stalked off.

Outside, a tall Sorthian woman waited, her crisp black uniform and dozens of tiny badges above her heart denoting her rank. Her black hair was pulled into a tight bun, and swirls of white were tattooed all over her brown skin. Her lip curled as she surveyed Darius and the others.

"Commander Lyre," she said once Ezra left the ship. "I'm Colonel Leski."

"Colonel." Ezra nodded at her. "These are Vanguard Sergeant Darius Kane, Specialists Talon Rive and Jarek Voss, and Private Kira Vael. They deserted on a mission on Miduna over a week ago and attempted to kill me and this woman, Mora Cevi."

Mo's spine straightened.

"I've read the reports," Colonel Leski said. "My people will handle their transfer to Aerilia. In the meantime, may I speak with you in my office? Just you."

As a group of soldiers began cuffing Ezra's former team and leading them off, Ezra shot one look at the bounty hunters. Kynn gave him a nod, as if to say, "We'll be right here." Ezra needed to talk to them. Technically, their contract was fulfilled—they'd only agreed to find Darius and the others—but he needed to convince them to stay on, at least until he knew more about the crystal and where Professor Valtor was.

"Sure thing, Colonel," Ezra said as he followed her.

Base Serenity was like most FSC bases, with an array of buildings, bunkers, and hangars circling a central courtyard. Soldiers practiced drills in the distance. They walked on in silence. Leski led Ezra into the tall building in the middle of the base. They turned down crowded hallways and empty ones, took several sets of stairs, and finally stopped in front of a simple black door.

After punching a code into the pad embedded in the wall, Leski went inside. Ezra followed. It was a large, tidy office. Windows lined the back wall, providing a view of where they'd just landed the ship. Ezra could still make it out, but he didn't see the bounty hunters. They'd probably gone inside.

Leski cleared her throat as she sat down behind her glass-top desk. Ezra shook himself mentally and positioned himself in front of it, arms crossed behind his back like the good soldier he was. It was how he was supposed to stand in front of a superior officer.

"So, Commander," Leski said, tapping a few buttons on the tablet she picked up. "As soon as my flight coordinators relayed your name to me, I did a little digging. It seems your mission was unauthorized."

Shit.

"Yes, ma'am, you might say that."

"Might?" She arched an eyebrow.

"Permission to speak freely?" Ezra asked. He really did not want to deal with any hierarchical bullshit today.

"Granted."

He let himself relax. "After my team tried to kill me on Miduna, I approached the base commander there about finding them. She told me that Aerilia had already decided not to pursue the matter due to lack of resources and the difficulties in tracking them down."

"But you didn't like that answer?" Leski half stated, half asked.

"Nobody gets to betray the FSC like that and get away with it," Ezra said. "I decided to use my leave time and personal resources to pursue them. And I found them."

Leski pursed her lips. "Did you find the crystal? Aerilia wants to know."

"I didn't. My former team wouldn't engage when I tried to question them, but they did warn me I'm not ready for what's coming."

"What does that mean?" she asked.

Ezra shrugged. "Maybe something with the Ascended? Separatists? The crystal may be tied to an underground market for old religious artifacts. It seems someone hired them to retrieve it and take me out at the same time."

Leski's eyebrows furrowed.

"I don't see the full picture either," Ezra said. "I was hoping the FSC might be able to get more information out of them."

Leski nodded. "Indeed. Aerilia's interested in doing so as well. They have, however, requested that you cease all investigations."

"What?" Ezra tried hard to swallow but barely could. "Why?"

"They will take over," Leski said. "You are to return to Aerilia."

Shit. Now what the fuck was he supposed to do? He was so close to finding Professor Valtor, to figuring out what all of this had been for. He couldn't just give up, especially not when he was right on the trail of ... something. If he had to go back to Aerilia and Command and explain all of this, then bring a team of investigators up to speed, it was going to take forever. The trail would go ice cold.

"Listen, Colonel, I'll be honest, the last couple of weeks have been hard on me mentally and physically," Ezra said. "I'll forward all the information I have to Command, but I'd like to use another week of my leave time to pull myself together."

It was a weak attempt at best, but it was all Ezra could think of on the spot. He even let his shoulders roll forward, and he forced out a short sigh.

"Vanguards are trained to keep going," Leski said.

"Nothing can prepare you for your own team betraying you. I was so focused on finding them that I didn't process it."

She scanned his body, her expression skeptical. "I can't make that decision, but I'll connect you with Command."

Leski tapped a few more buttons on her tablet, then a few on the surface of her desk. She stood, then motioned for Ezra to take her seat. "I'll be right outside," she said to him. "Good luck, Commander."

Ezra settled into Leski's stiff chair and waited for the familiar crackle of a long-distance transmission to come in. He needed to be convincing and make this quick. He needed to meet up with the others and get them to work with him for just a little longer.

Chapter 25

It took nearly an hour, but Ezra laid out everything he'd discovered in the investigation and convinced the leaders back on Aerilia to let him take another week off duty. He'd really had to lean into the story about his team's betrayal and even had to agree to schedule a psych eval when he returned to the capital. He didn't think he needed one, but he was willing to do whatever it took to see this through.

As he exited Base Serenity's central building and stepped into the sunshine, Ezra breathed in deep. There was no sign of his team—his former team—anywhere. Good. He could let the FSC do their job now, and he would continue on his own mission.

He approached the borrowed ship and, thankfully, found Kynn, Cass, and Mo all lounging around inside. They each had a tablet in hand, and another was charging in the cockpit. That had to be a good sign, right? That they were going through the professor's files?

"I explained everything to the higher-ups at the FSC," he said. "They're going to extradite Darius and the others to Aerilia. They should be able to get information out of them."

"Was telling them wise?" Mo asked.

"Why wouldn't it be? They already knew the Ascended were targeting sites like that."

Mo pressed her lips together.

"Find anything?" Ezra asked. "FSC's not going to look for Valtor unless there's a clear tie between him and Darius."

"Yeah, I found out something alright," Cass muttered. "This man does *not* have a clear organizational system. He doesn't even have a standard way he names his files. I mean, how does he find shit?"

"Not all of us are masters of organization like you, Cass," Kynn said without looking up from his tablet. "Did you know that once, when we were just kids—"

Cass groaned. "Don't start."

"—Cass took it upon herself to entirely reorganize not just my quarters but Mo's? This was on Miduna. Terribly small living accommodations we received, but Cass knew exactly how to get it to work. She also reorganized the training rooms without any authorization."

Ezra arched an eyebrow.

"Nobody ever put the weapons racks in a way that made sense," Cass said. "So I like things to be tidy. Sue me."

"Maybe I will." Kynn gave her a cheeky grin but sobered up as he turned back to his tablet. "Looks like Valtor has another house higher up in the mountains. Found some bank notes about it, along with the coordinates."

"Seems like someplace he'd go if the university hasn't heard from him in a while. We should check it out." Ezra dropped into the pilot's seat and found all three bounty hunters watching him expectantly. "Assuming you're all agreeing to extend your contract, at least until we find Professor Valtor. Another five thousand credits each, and we'll renegotiate if this drags on after the end of the week."

Cass and Kynn agreed. Mo's eyebrows drew together.

"Cevi?" Ezra asked.

"Fine," she said. "But once we find him, I'm done."

"Alright." He nodded and spun his chair around to face the control panel in front of him. "Shall we take this, or do you want to go back for *The Revenant*?"

"Back to the ship," Mo said. "I'm not going in there without my armor. That's the second time someone's tried to kill me in a very short period of time."

"Keep looking for anything useful in his files," Ezra said as he powered up the engines. "We'll get back to your ship soon."

He needed to make the most of their help while he had it, and he had a feeling that was going to be longer than they were willing to stay on.

Soon, they were all fitted out in their gear and back in their newly acquired shuttle. It was so small it didn't even have a name, just the signature VRS-9271. They'd all agreed to leave *The Revenant* where she was, as they weren't clear on how much space Professor Valtor's cabin would have for a larger vessel.

"This place is in the middle of nowhere," Cass murmured as she peered out one of the windows. Far below was nothing but evergreens and trees with blood red leaves.

"My last visit here for that civilian extraction was a few hundred klicks west of here," Ezra said. "The mountains run that far west, as does this forest. Creepy place; not many people live that way and for good reason. All kinds of monsters live in those woods."

"Including whoever it was that kidnapped a senator," said Kynn.

"They wanted attention, not to hurt the woman," Ezra said. "We defused the situation, and everyone walked away with their lives."

"Like you defused it earlier?" Mo asked.

He glanced over his shoulder. "You know I didn't defuse a damn thing," he said, and he swore the corner of her mouth quirked up for a second. Ezra turned back around. "We were just better than them."

"Of course we were," Kynn said. "You didn't hire amateurs."

Ezra couldn't help but laugh a little. No, he most certainly had not. Even if sheer luck had been on their side for half of this search, Ezra knew, without a doubt, that the three bounty hunters would've found his team. He was confident they would help him wrap this all up, too, to hand to the FSC in a neat package.

After a few more minutes of flying above the red trees, Ezra guided the small ship down and around the side of the nearest mountain. They landed in a clearing that was only a quarter klick away from the house's coordinates, then headed out.

The mountain air was cool and crisp, and a rough wind whipped its way through the trees. The skies were overcast, but it didn't look like rain or storms were on their way. The last time Ezra had been in this mountain range, the weather had been decidedly colder to the point that it had snowed.

The trees thinned out again, giving way to a rustic cabin—one that was designed to look rustic, anyway. It was made of expertly carved logs mixed with metal and glass, and its location and second story made of all windows surely provided a panoramic view of the forest. Ezra shook his head. His family—and others in the upper echelons of Federation society—liked to pretend they were roughing it, when really they were in comfortable second, third, or even fourth homes with all the tech and equipment they could need.

"Looks empty," Kynn said from the front of the group.

Indeed, it did. There was no sign of a ship or other vehicle. In fact, there wasn't a hangar or garage of any kind. No lights were on despite the growing darkness.

"If we came all the way out here for nothing ..." Mo muttered.

"Let's just take a look around," Cass said. "Might as well make the trip worth it. Maybe he's just asleep."

Ezra doubted it.

He led the way to the front door and drew his sword, but he didn't engage the blade. When he knocked, there was no answer. He tried the handle, and it opened with ease.

"Don't like that," Mo whispered.

"Doctor Valtor?" Ezra called as he stepped inside. "Marcus?"

No response.

There was only silence and another mess. Ezra flipped several light switches, and a warm glow illuminated the house. Just like back at the estate near Atmos, this cabin had been ransacked. Furniture was tipped over, decor smashed, pictures knocked off the walls. Ezra bit back a string of curses.

"Spread out," Ezra said. "Find him."

"You think he's here?" Kynn asked, voice low.

"Unless he managed to get off planet, yes." The knot building in Ezra's gut was rarely wrong about these things.

Mo and Cass split off to search the second floor while Kynn stayed downstairs with Ezra. They cleared it room by room, from bedrooms to the living area and kitchen. In the final hallway, they found a half-closed door. Ezra pushed it open.

If he'd been anyone else, had any different training or life experience, he would've gagged or turned away. But this was just disappointing. Not even shocking. Just disappointing.

Doctor Marcus Valtor, with his graying hair and familiar dark spectacles, was slumped over his desk. A blaster wound bloodied his temple. Ezra didn't need to go over to check if he was dead.

"Fuck," Kynn muttered. "Guess you were right."

"I'd guess my *team* was here," Ezra said as he stalked into the room. "I don't think he was the buyer."

"Guess not," Kynn said. "So they were here for what, exactly? Information?"

"If he's got fringe theories about the Eternal Ones, then probably," Ezra said. "But was he killed for knowing too much or refusing to give up information my team needed?" That was what he intended to find out, but it wasn't like there was anyone he could ask. Maybe military interrogators could get the answer now that Darius and the others were on their way to Aerilia.

Ezra and Kynn began combing through the professor's wrecked office, from papers to books to crushed-up artifacts he must've had on display. There wasn't much of anything useful—until Ezra moved closer to the body. A tablet was under the professor's cheek. Ezra grabbed it, and to his great surprise, the thing still had charge.

"What's it say?" Kynn asked as he peered over Ezra's shoulder.

"He was writing a letter," Ezra said. "To Livia. It says he's sorry, but that's it."

That was *it*. A simple start to the correspondence: *I'm sorry, Livvi.*

What was Ezra supposed to do with that? Sorry for what? Would Livia know? Had there been some ongoing conflict between them? Ezra certainly had no idea what was going on with most of his family nowadays. For all he knew, there'd been all kinds of drama and issues between them. Between any of them.

Ezra tucked the small tablet into a pouch on his belt. "I don't think we're going to find much else here," he said. "I'll report it to the FSC when we get back to the ship. Livia's got to know what happened to him."

Fuck. Not only had his lead gone cold, but now he was going to have to tell the family what happened. Maybe he could just have someone from Command inform Livia. She was, after all, part of the Triumvirate. Someone higher up the chain of command probably *had* to be the one to tell her. There was probably some strange political bend to all of this that he just wasn't seeing.

"Lyre?" Mo called. "Kynn?"

"In here!" Kynn yelled, and both women appeared in the door.

Cass grimaced as her gaze landed on the body. "That's terrible news."

Ezra shrugged. It *was* bad, but he was just going to have to figure something out. "We need to get back to Atmos," he said. "Or at least to the ship so I can contact Base Serenity. Someone needs to come take care of this."

"And what will we be doing?" Mo asked.

"Sticking around to see if we can find anything else useful. He was killed for a reason."

Mo huffed, but Ezra stormed past her and headed for the shuttle. The FSC needed to get out there immediately, and then he needed to make sure his bounty hunters didn't run off on him. He still needed their help.

CHAPTER 26

Mo couldn't take any more bad news.

"What do you mean Darius Kane and the entire team are dead?" Ezra stared at FSC Colonel Leski.

She'd met them at Base Serenity as soon as their small shuttle had touched down. Ezra had wanted to return to ensure the proper authorities went to retrieve Doctor Valtor's body, only for them to be met with this news.

Nothing was going right on this fucking contract. Well, some of it had, but *dead*? Darius Kane and all those other Vanguards were *dead*?

"We only turned them in six hours ago," Mo said. "How are they already dead?"

"It's best we go into my office," the commander said.

Leski's stern brow and even sterner tone suggested she didn't tolerate any nonsense, nor would she welcome any protest on Mo's part. She also walked too quickly for Mo's needs, but she forced herself to keep up despite the ache building in her bones. They'd been going nonstop for hours, and her body was not happy with her.

Rest later, Mo told herself. This was almost done. She'd find out what happened to Darius and the others, then leave Ezra to figure out the rest. They'd more than fulfilled their contract. Maybe he wouldn't be satisfied with the turn of events and not having more concrete answers, but there was no way they were going to find that crystal unless they knew who had killed Darius, and besides, it wasn't like Ezra had hired them to find the crystal specifically.

All Mo wanted to do was get back to her routine and take a break.

Colonel Leski led them through the labyrinth of a headquarters, then into what had to be her private office. She ordered Ezra to close the door behind him.

Mo's skin crawled as she took in the cold office, no sign of personality or emotion. There were no rich goblets or expensive wine or tapestries and rugs with colorful stories behind them like Ril had back in his office on Miduna. There wasn't even so much as a picture. This was impersonal, purely functional. And Mo wasn't one for design—she appreciated function—but it just reinforced what she hated about the FSC.

This was not where she belonged. She needed to get out.

"Darius is really dead?" Ezra asked as Colonel Leski circled her desk.

"Sergeant Kane and the other three are all dead," she said with a grave nod. "Happened about two hours ago. Nobody knows how, but it looks like their ship was attacked. The whole prison transport crew is dead."

"Do we have any ship signatures?" Ezra asked. "Anything we can use to track them?"

"Everything was scrambled," Leski said. "The transport was completely obliterated. Forced out of hyperspace, then attacked. There aren't even logs to pull from. We believe it was the Ascended."

"We'd know if the Ascended had gotten this far inside our borders, Colonel." Ezra folded his arms across his chest. "I mean, we're within the Inner Systems. There's no way we wouldn't have detected an Ascended ship."

Leski shook her head once.

Ezra sighed. "What's Command saying?"

"They're still investigating, but they agree that it was the Ascended. It's the only logical explanation."

Ezra scoffed.

"Believe what you want, Commander," Leski said, "but you have been ordered to step back from this. You already went against your promise to take leave time to recuperate."

Another thing Mo didn't appreciate about the FSC: they even dictated how you got to take a vacation. Maybe Ezra *wanted* to investigate. Maybe he found it relaxing. And it wasn't like the military was doing anything to help. They should be grateful he'd found those traitors in the first place. That *they'd* found them.

"Fine," Ezra said. "Fine, Colonel. I appreciate the information about my team. I'll do as I promised. I'll leave Vonnoth soon."

"Stay on planet if you want. I don't care, Commander," she said. "Just stay out of our way, and go back to Aerilia when your time is up. That's an order."

Ezra agreed, and then they were all dismissed. That was another thing Mo didn't like, that these commanders thought they could boss Mo and her team around. They didn't answer to anyone, not even the Syndicate.

At least we're out of there. She would finally get to go back to *The Revenant* and Miduna. No more working with Vanguards or the government, just her and her two best friends going where they wanted, when they wanted.

They all climbed back into the small ship, and Mo tried to relax into her seat. Really, she did. The skies were nearly dark, and the day had been too long, filled with too much death.

"I don't think this was the Ascended," Ezra said as soon as he had the ship off the ground and heading back to where *The Revenant* awaited.

Mo groaned. "Drop it, Lyre."

"What?" he asked. "It wasn't them. It doesn't make sense for it to be them."

"Why? If they were hired by the Ascended to steal that crystal and try to destabilize the Triumvirate somehow, they were just cleaning up loose ends."

"It wasn't them," Ezra said. "No way could an Ascended ship have made it through FSC security measures at the borders."

"The Federation is a very big place," said Kynn. "Surely there are weak spots in our defenses somewhere. It's hubris to think there are none."

"Fine," Ezra conceded. "Maybe so. But this isn't what the Ascended do. They attack planets. They go after resources."

"Wasn't your team just another resource?" Cass asked.

"That's not what I mean," Ezra said. "Every time the Ascended has launched an attack on the Federation, it's been about expansion and resources. They need more of both for their population size, and taking our worlds is easier than terraforming new ones."

"But haven't they been attacking planets with sites connected to the Eternal Ones?" Cass asked. "I thought there was supposed to be some kind of pattern there."

"Those planets have plenty of resources too," Ezra said. "Maybe that's how they choose their targets. I don't know."

"But why would the FSC insist this was the Ascended if it doesn't actually seem possible?" Mo asked.

Ezra didn't reply, and Mo really didn't like that.

"Here's what we know," Ezra said. "Threats are being made against my extended family due to Livia's position in the government. Someone did try to kill me. Those same people wanted to find this so-called ancient Eternal Ones crystal, and one of the people who most likely knows about those crystals is also dead. The crystal is gone. There's an underground market of buyers who are also looking for this treasure, and it's *possible* the Ascended also want it."

"That sounds like a fucking mess to me," Mo said. "Could the Federation be involved somehow?"

"Why would they try to kill me if that was the case?" Ezra asked. "Why not just recruit me to the cause? And what would the government even need these artifacts for? It's not like they need the money."

Mo pursed her lips. Maybe he had a point.

"Even if it was just to keep them away from the Ascended," Kynn said slowly, "it still boils down to why try to kill you?"

"Right," Ezra said.

"Whatever kind of conspiracy this is, it's a poor one," Mo said. "There's no clear-cut reason for any of this."

"Right," Ezra said again, as if that was precisely why it all made so much sense.

"Explain," said Cass.

"Obviously we're missing part of the picture," Ezra said. "What is that crystal? What's so important about it that people are seemingly getting killed over it?"

Maybe Ezra had a point, but it wasn't Mo's job to worry about this. The FSC could solve this—if they weren't entirely useless, anyway. Or involved.

"We need to figure this out," Ezra said. In the forest below, *The Revenant* came into view, and the edge of Atmos was visible in the distance. Ezra piloted them down to the ship.

"No, *you* need to figure it out," Mo said. "We've fulfilled the contract. It's time for your government to take over and do their jobs."

"My government? This is *our* government." Ezra powered down the ship and spun around in his chair. "Do you two agree with her?" he asked, gesturing to Cass and Kynn.

Cass shrugged. "It's not like there's much left for us to do. The trail's gone cold. We don't have the ability to track an unknown ship."

"Kynn?" Ezra asked.

"Look—"

"Fuck." Ezra fisted his hair, which he'd long since taken out of its short braid. "Fuck, why don't you three care? It could be the Ascended, sure. Maybe I'm wrong about that. But it could be the Separatists or someone else! This is bigger than we thought."

"So let someone bigger than us handle it," Mo said.

"Why don't you care?" Ezra asked, voice strained. "Why don't you care that someone could be trying to take down our government? That they're putting hits out on Vanguards and politicians?"

Mo had heard enough. Ezra may not have been the worst Vanguard in existence, but he didn't understand. He would never understand what it was like to be on the outside, to not have your government care about you. He would never understand what it was like to lose not just your family but your entire home.

She pushed out of her seat and opened the shuttle door. As she stormed outside, Ezra called after her, but she ignored him.

"Cass, Kynn," she said as they followed her, "can you please get the ship ready? I'll be inside in a moment."

"You sure?" Cass asked. "We can just leave him here."

"I won't leave him here unless he wants to stay," Mo said, unsure why she was even contemplating taking him back to Aerilia. He could find his own way. He just needed to pay them first. She passed her helmet to Cass. "But he needs to get some things straight if he's coming back with us. I'll take care of it."

Cass pressed her lips together, but Kynn ushered her away, muttering something about "Mo handling it."

Footsteps crunched in the grass behind Mo. She turned slowly, finding a fuming Ezra behind her. His green eyes were almost black in the growing darkness.

"You three really won't continue on?" Ezra asked. "The Federation has hurt you so much that you'd risk people's safety?"

Mo tried to take a deep, cleansing breath. Instead of bringing calm, all it did was ignite the fire in her veins.

"Your precious Federation has never cared about us," she hissed. "You asked about my family, if I had any besides Cass and Kynn. You want to know why I don't? Why *we* don't?"

Mo never told anyone this, but she'd already shown Ezra her magic. How much worse could it get?

Before he could reply, she snapped, "We're orphans of Veronis, Lyre. Your beloved government and military did nothing to help my people. Did nothing to help us. They didn't care when the Ascended came for us. They didn't even try. So excuse me for not exactly caring if the Ascended have come for them, or the Separatists, or whomever it is you want to blame for your shitty team's behavior. I need to watch out for myself and Cass and Kynn, and getting involved in some wild, aimless chase is *not* it."

Mo stalked off, fists clenched at her side. She needed to go help Cass and Kynn, but she also needed a moment to breathe. Being trapped in that ship was not going to be fun, even if they did leave Ezra here in these woods.

"That's terrible," Ezra said from behind her. Of course he wasn't going to drop this. "The Fall of Veronis I was a terrible tragedy, but can you really turn your back on civilians if it means preventing other planets from being destroyed the same?"

"Why do you think this is going to lead to planets being destroyed?" Mo asked. "That's a huge jump in logic."

"Because shit like this doesn't happen if it's not a weapon," Ezra said. "Or if people don't believe it's a weapon, anyway. They don't issue kill contracts just for a sparkly thing that'll get them paid."

"They do in my world," Mo said. "I see shit like that all the time. People get killed for far less in my line of work."

"Well, that's not how it works in *my* world."

"Just drop it," Mo muttered.

"I'm not willing to drop it," Ezra said. "Even if it's just some rock and not important at all, it's already gotten people killed. I'm not willing to take the chance that it's nothing. Are you?"

The thought that maybe, just maybe, this could get other civilians—other kids—in trouble made Mo pause. He had a fucking point, unfortunately. But there were plenty of capable people who could handle it. Plenty of people who would handle it soon. Aerilia had the resources.

A twig snapped behind Mo. The hair on the back of her neck prickled. She spun, one hand already unlatching the silver hilt at her side. The whine of a blaster exploded behind the tree line. Mo's blade ignited. The phaser hit her saber, bouncing back exactly where it had come from. Another shot came, and again she deflected it back to its source.

Mo's heart pounded in her chest. She bolted forward, and Ezra wasn't far behind. She skidded to a stop among the trees and found ...

A Vanguard?

A Vanguard lay at the edge of the woods, their black armor smoldering and broken where Mo had aimed their attack back at them.

"What the fuck?" Ezra whispered. He put his sword away and stooped, then pulled their helmet off.

Inside the suit was a Human woman with curly blonde hair and skin as pale as Mo's.

"Not Ascended," Mo muttered.

Maybe Ezra was right. There had to be some larger conspiracy going on. With another Vanguard attempting to kill—

Ezra whirled just as the whine of an energy rifle exploded behind them. A fiery shield burst to life in front of him, absorbing the shot that was ...

Aimed right for Mo.

The shot made contact with his shield right where Mo's forehead was.

A head shot meant for her.

With his free hand, Ezra grabbed his sword hilt and ignited his blade. "You see them?" he asked, voice low.

"Almost directly across from me," Mo said. There was the faint glow of a rifle. Mo had seen a similar blue glow a thousand times from Cass's favorite weapon.

But that wasn't Cass.

Cass and Kynn scrambled down *The Revenant*'s ramp, weapons in hand. Mo couldn't make out their faces; they were in their full armor, including helmets. Mo cursed herself for ever handing her helmet off to Cass in the first place. This would be a lot easier if she was in her full gear. Ezra didn't have his on either; he must've left it in the shuttle.

"Let me draw them out," he said.

"I can—"

"Cover me." He passed her the blaster previously attached to his hip. "Get back to the ship."

Mo ground her teeth together. She didn't need him giving out orders like she was some soldier to command. Still, if this was another Vanguard … She might as well shut up and listen to Ezra.

She took the gun. As his shield disappeared and he sprinted into the night, Mo took aim. There it was, that glow of blue again, as their attacker prepared to fire.

Mo pulled the trigger. A burst of white shot out from the gun, whizzing past Ezra's head and into the forest beyond. It didn't hit its target, but Mo drew their fire away from Ezra, and that was good enough.

She ran for *The Revenant*, shooting in their attacker's general direction as she went. One shot exploded at the ground near her feet, either a warning or bad aim.

"What's he doing?" Kynn asked as Mo skidded to a stop at the bottom of the ramp.

"You see him?" Mo asked Cass instead.

She already had her rifle aimed. "I see him."

Ezra's golden blade drew arcs in the air beyond the VSR-9721, clashing with a blue energy axe. Another shot came, this time hitting the side of *The Revenant*. Mo cursed. It was one thing to attack her, but her ship?

"Take that sniper out," Mo said. "Kynn, cover me."

Mo ignited her blade and sprinted toward where Ezra was locked in battle with another Vanguard who had not one but two energy axes. Ezra ducked, narrowly dodging the blow aimed for his throat. Mo jumped in, blocking one crackling axe as the attacker aimed for Ezra again. A sparkle of blue and white set the air alight as Mo came face to face with a black Vanguard mask.

Mo shoved hard against her attacker, forcing them both back a step. Mo's chest heaved as she circled the Vanguard. Ezra lunged from behind, but the Vanguard spun out and met his attack.

The three of them locked in a dance of complicated lunges, deflections, and dodges, weapons clashing but never landing a direct blow. Mo's arms shook with the ferocity of the Vanguard's attacks and her own. Whoever this was did not want to lose.

In the distance, the familiar echo of Cass's rifle went off, and all other fire ceased. She'd hit the sniper. Mo didn't need her helmet or comms to know that for a fact.

But this third attacker was not giving up. Mo drew them away, deeper into the dark forest. Ezra followed, his blade disappearing as he stalked from behind. Mo readied herself.

The Vanguard lunged. Mo deflected, her muscles trembling as the attacker pushed harder against her. They were taller and stronger, and her joints *hurt*. This was too much. Too much for one day, certainly.

But Mo would not be beaten. She forced their axe to the side and stepped back, putting little more than an arm's length between them. They brought both axes up, prepared to bring it down on her. Mo readied herself to parry again, but the orange-gold glow of Ezra's saber lit up the night as he put himself between Mo and the Vanguard.

He threw them off balance, pushing them farther and farther back. He swung again and again in violent arcs, finally overpowering the would-be assassin. And then he rammed his blade through their armor and chest. Their axes fell to the ground, the energy dissipating. Their knees hit the forest floor with a heavy thunk. Ezra withdrew his weapon, chest heaving.

"You didn't have to do that," Mo said. "I had it handled."

He actually smirked at her over his shoulder. "Figured it was only fair that I got this one considering you got the first."

"Are you serious?" She huffed, still trying to catch her breath.

Ezra ignored her and crouched near the fallen Vanguard. He pulled off their helmet, and sure enough, it was an Ivari man, this one with green hair and pale, freckled skin.

"Fuck," Ezra muttered, his head rolling back as he stared up at the canopy and dark sky above. "What the fuck."

"We need to go," Mo said. She was sweaty from the effort of the fight, and her whole body felt like it was one big bruise. She hadn't been hit directly, but it had been too much. And she needed to make sure Cass and Kynn were okay. "Back to the ship."

"We can't just leave them here."

"Sure we can," Mo said. "They tried to fucking kill us."

"They were Vanguards."

"And?" Mo asked.

Ezra pushed to his feet. "We at least need to search them."

"Then search them," Mo said. "I'm going back to the ship. Don't get yourself killed."

Ezra scoffed, but Mo continued on. Ezra could obviously take care of himself, and she would let him. She pushed her tired, aching body into a jog as she headed back toward *The Revenant*. Cass and Kynn met her halfway, their dark visors still obscuring their faces.

"Third one is down," Mo said. "Ezra's searching them. Any others?"

"Doesn't seem like it," came Kynn's slightly modulated voice. "You shouldn't have run off like that."

"We're fine," Mo said. "You?"

"No worse than that time on Kesatera's moon," Cass said.

"I told you to never bring that up again," Kynn replied, but his voice was light.

"So, a bruised ego at worst," Mo said. That contract had been one they'd taken a few years earlier, with Cass having to step in to save Kynn's ass when he found himself in hot water with a small band of pirates.

Footsteps crunched behind her. "Definitely Vanguards," Ezra muttered. "I found their badges. Synced up with my suit."

"Which means?" Kynn asked.

"Either the government is trying to kill us, or more Vanguards have been bought off," Ezra said.

Mo didn't know which one was more likely. It seemed the second, but she just didn't know anymore. And Mo didn't like being uncertain.

More than that, she really didn't appreciate being the target of an assassination attempt. What had happened on Miduna had been a coincidence. What had happened at the professor's estate, that shootout with Ezra's team, had been part of the job.

But this?

Mo turned to Ezra, to his pained expression and heaving chest. "I'm back in."

His brow furrowed. "What?"

"I'm back in," she said. "You wanted to extend the contract. I accept."

"Why?"

"They tried to blow my brains out, Lyre. I don't care who hired them or what we have to do. This is fucking personal."

Ezra's expression was too shadowed to decipher, but Mo could feel his eyes searching hers. She held his gaze until he finally glanced over her shoulder. "What about you two?"

"Clearly this isn't going to stop," Cass said. "Not when whoever sent them realizes they failed, just like your team did. I'm in."

"Can't let you three have all the fun," Kynn said, a smile in his voice.

Ezra held his hand out to Mo for a shake. She took it and said, "Now let's get the fuck out of here."

Chapter 27

The four of them agreed immediately on two things. The first was that they were going to leave the assassins where they were, out in the middle of the woods. The second was that they needed to go back into Atmos proper and visit the university again before leaving Vonnoth.

With that settled, they managed to find a shipyard with empty docking ports on the southern side of the city. It wasn't ideal, given how far it was from the university, but it would have to do. It was better than a night in the woods. They were far less likely to be targeted by more assassins if they were around city guards and watchful civilians alike.

Mo still thought perhaps the FSC was out to get Ezra, but it didn't make sense. As he'd said, why try to take him out? Even if he was a somewhat distant cousin of Chancellor Valtor, trying to kill him still didn't make much sense. She considered that it might be a military-led coup, but why not either try to recruit Ezra to the cause or take them all out the minute they were alone with Base Serenity's leader?

Something else poked at the back of Mo's mind. She wasn't sure what that intuition was about, but something told her it wasn't the FSC. That still begged the question of who was behind this, and unfortunately, it wasn't something she could figure out in one night.

Now that they were relatively safe within the Atmos city limits again, Mo took a few moments to herself. They had their plan, and they just had to wait until sunrise to get back to work.

Mo pulled out a fresh roll of bandages, stripped down to her under-wear, and sat down on the edge of her bed. With careful hands, she began wrapping her joints. For her knees, she wrapped partway down her shins and up her thighs too. For her hands, all the way up her forearms and down in between her fingers. She couldn't do much for her shoulders or hips; this would have to be enough for tonight.

Just the extra pressure and support of the thick cloth bandages made her joints hurt a little less. She let out a relieved sigh. She really needed to find more soltherin soon. Maybe she could go out in the morning—

A knock sounded on her door.

"Yeah?" she called.

"Cevi?"

Shit.

"One second!" Scrambling out of bed, she grabbed a fresh set of leggings and a new tunic, forgoing her boots as she tugged on her clothes and approached the door. She opened it, only to find Ezra standing there with wet hair and in a change of clothes himself. "What?" she asked.

"I don't know about you, but it's been a long fucking day," he said. "Want to get a drink? Cass and Kynn already turned me down."

Did she ... want to get a drink? With Ezra? With a *Vanguard*?

"Please?" he asked. "I could use one, and you don't have anything on the ship."

Any other day, Mo would decline. And maybe it *was* that it had been a frustratingly long day, or maybe it was the way he looked almost haunted, but Mo heard herself say, "Sure."

It wasn't late, at least not late enough that the bars and taverns around Atmos would be closed. Going out for one drink wouldn't hurt. Besides, it might help her get her mind off her joints. She certainly wasn't going to sleep anytime soon, and lying in bed feeling sorry for herself never helped.

Mo finished getting dressed, then grabbed both her saber hilt and two extra blasters from the weapons locker. Yes, she was confident nobody was going to try to kill them *now*, but she also wasn't taking any chances. Not tonight.

After checking in with both Cass and Kynn, who wanted to go to sleep, Mo followed Ezra out of the ship. They ambled through Atmos in silence. The city wasn't nearly as loud as Aerilia had been. It reminded Mo of Miduna quite a bit, actually, with its neatly organized streets and crowded bar scene. It didn't matter where you went in the Federation; people loved to eat and drink their troubles away.

Ezra led her to a bar several blocks away from the shipyard. A few of the tables on the sidewalk were occupied, and inside had a respectable crowd but wasn't overstuffed. He moved to the back of the bar, then got a curved booth in the corner of the building. The lights were dim, and the interior design was casual, relaxed. Rather than a live band, quiet music floated down from overhead speakers.

"And you didn't even take us to an FSC bar," Mo said as she slid into the booth next to him. She left a couple of feet in between them, getting close enough that he could still hear her if she spoke quietly.

"Of course not," Ezra said. "I don't know who to trust right now besides you three."

Ezra trusted them? She supposed he had to, given the situation. Something in her chest tightened, but she shoved the feeling away.

"Evening." A waitress stopped in front of their table and slapped a few napkins down. "What do you want?" She didn't smile, nor introduce herself, or anything for that matter. She just stared at them expectantly.

"Two Twilight Twists and whatever the kitchen's still serving," Ezra said. "Thanks."

"You ordered for me?" Mo asked, glaring at him.

"Just try it," he said. "Trust me."

Mo rolled her eyes harder than necessary. Ezra laughed good-natured-ly, but an awkward silence soon settled between them as they waited for the server to return. What had Mo been thinking, agreeing to this? It was too late to back out, though.

When the waitress returned a few minutes later, she set down two tall, skinny glasses filled with magenta and purple liquid. She left, then reappeared again with a long plate taken up almost entirely by a flatbread covered in cheese. Mo's stomach growled.

"Kitchen's closed now, but the bar's open," the waitress said.

Ezra tossed a handful of credits onto the table. "That'll be all for us, thanks."

"Presumptuous," Mo said, already reaching for a slice of flatbread. "Ordering for me and assuming I don't want another drink?"

"You seem easy enough to please."

Mo choked on her food. She coughed, then reached for her drink and took a sip. It was mild and fruity, with barely any alcohol in it. "I'm easy to please?" She scoffed. "You clearly don't know me, Lyre."

"No, I clearly don't. But I'd like to."

She scoffed again. Nobody wanted to *know* her. Not like Cass and Kynn did.

"Why do you think it's ridiculous?" Ezra asked, a real challenge in his voice. "Why do you think I'm ridiculous?"

"I don't think you're ridiculous," Mo said. "I think we're different people, from different worlds."

"Yes, you're Midunian and I'm Aerilian. I thought that was already well established."

"Smart-ass."

He smirked, and the dimple in his right cheek appeared. "Seriously, why don't you like me?"

Mo took another bite of food, barely tasting it as she tried to buy herself time. Shit, she *should've* backed out. She hadn't been ready for an interrogation.

"Why does it matter so much to you?" she asked.

"Because most people find me irresistible."

"Does that line work for you or something?"

He laughed again. "No, but I thought it was worth a try."

With a sigh, Mo leaned back in her seat. "I don't know how to make it any clearer to you. I don't dislike you, but we're just ... different."

"I don't think we are," he said. "We must have something in common besides our family's interest in literature. Name something. Anything."

Perhaps, since it seemed they'd be working together for a while longer, Mo needed to play nice with him.

So, she said, "I hate when people chew their food loudly."

"Me too!"

She pinned him with a look. "You just happen to agree with the first thing I say?"

"Seriously," Ezra said. "That asshole?" He pointed to a Human with auburn hair and a goatee. He was hunched over the bar, chewing with his mouth wide open, but he was too far away for Mo to hear. "Just watching him makes my skin crawl."

Mo grimaced and turned back toward Ezra. She had to agree; she couldn't watch that. "Fine, so we have one thing in common."

"I prefer nights to mornings," he said.

"I really don't care either way."

"I have trouble sleeping."

"Doesn't everyone?"

"No, not everyone. Dar—" Ezra's face fell, as if realizing exactly what he was about to say. He reached for his glass and took a long drink.

Mo pressed her lips together, desperate to get rid of the heaviness falling over their table. "It probably doesn't mean much, coming from me. But I know what it's like to get hurt by the people you're supposed to be able to trust," she said quietly. It felt like as close to the truth as she could tell him about Tallas. "I'm sorry your team betrayed you, and I'm sort of sorry they're dead. It must be hard."

Ezra heaved a sigh and shifted so he faced her fully—and so he was nearer to her. "It's funny," he murmured. "We have training as Vanguards to not let fallen brethren faze us, to keep pushing through. We have to, considering some of the things we see. I just can't ..." He shook his head. "I can't fathom any of it. Why they did it. Who they were working for. What Darius meant when he said I wasn't prepared for what was coming."

Unfortunately, Mo had none of those answers. "Whatever it is, it sounds like it's going to be a pain in my ass."

Ezra laughed. "Do you regret taking my contract?"

"Changes by the hour."

Another chuckle. "I appreciate you staying on," he said. "Even if it was only for personal reasons."

An unexpected stab of guilt lanced Mo's belly. It hurt more than her joints did. "I *am* a bounty hunter," she said. "It's not just for myself. It's my job."

"Right ..."

"You seem disappointed in that answer."

He smiled. "Thought you might've started to like me."

"It's as I said before, we're from different worlds. You're looking to buy someone's loyalty, and I'm willing to sell mine. It's a mutually beneficial relationship."

"So cold and calculating, Cevi."

She shrugged. "Don't we have to be? You and I both, in our respective worlds."

"I suppose you have a point. A bleak one."

She shrugged again. "Life's bleak."

"Damn. Maybe I should've gotten you another drink. Would that get you to lighten up?"

"We've almost been killed several times in a very short period and you want me to *lighten up*?"

He moved closer again. "Why not? We've got to find a little happiness, don't we?"

Mo had found her happiness, with Cass and Kynn, back on Miduna, whenever they went on hikes and escaped the city. When it was just the three of them, a family without ties to the Syndicate or any bullshit. But that happiness was fleeting in the Federation. There was always more work to be done, more criminals to hunt, and more money to be made.

"I don't think happiness is meant for someone like me," she said. "That's a luxury I can't afford. That most people in the Federation can't afford."

"I wish it wasn't like that."

She gave him a small smile. "Me too."

"See?" He nudged her shoulder playfully. "We do have things in common. You just have to let yourself see it."

Maybe she did. Maybe she needed to let herself see it, to trust Ezra Lyre.

He *had* saved her life that night. But was it because he was paying her? His duty as a Vanguard? Or was that just who he was? Mo didn't yet know, and trust was a fragile thing. She couldn't just place her life in anyone's hands. She couldn't just let anyone into her world. She'd made those mistakes before, had learned those lessons the hard way.

Enjoying Ezra's company would probably be easy if she let herself. She just didn't know if it was worth the risk.

By the time they'd finished their dinner and drinks, Mo was no clearer on where she stood with Ezra.

They'd steered the conversation away from darker topics and settled on mostly mundane things like Ezra's favorite bars on Aerilia and Mo's affinity for hiking, Kynn's enjoyment of reality shows, and Cass's love of food. It had seemed safer, not talking about the hard things like traitorous teammates and complicated backgrounds.

The bar was finally shutting down, and they were two of the last people inside. Their waitress from earlier in the night had been shooting them dirty looks for the last fifteen minutes, and they'd decided it was time to go.

Mo started to scoot out of her side of the booth only for her body to scream in protest. *Fuck*. Had she been alone, Mo would've let herself cry it out before figuring out how to make herself more comfortable, but she absolutely could not let Ezra see her cry.

Sucking in a deep breath, Mo pushed through the pain and got to her feet. She adjusted her belt and weapons, and when Ezra gave her a confused look, she glared at him.

"What are you waiting for?" she asked. "Let's go."

"I'm going, I'm going."

He said it with a smile, yet Mo felt bad for snapping at him. She usually only ever felt bad for snapping at Cass and Kynn.

Outside, the streets were still flooded with light from other bars and streetlamps, as well as the twin moons passing through the sky. Mo tried to keep up with Ezra, but her body just hurt too much.

"Lyre!" she called.

He glanced over his shoulder, eyebrows furrowing as he obviously took in the distance between them. He turned fully and waited for her to catch up to him.

"Sorry," Mo said. "It's been a long day. I don't mean to offend your Vanguard sensibilities on fitness or speed."

"We're not on the battlefield," he said. "No need to rush around."

"It's starting to feel like we are," she said as they set out toward the shipyard again. Every step made Mo wince, and of course, Ezra noticed.

"You're hurt," he stated more than asked.

She waved him off. "Old injury, I told you."

"All over your body?" He gestured to her hands, then at how she was limping along. "Did someone break all your bones or something?"

"Something like that," Mo muttered. She had always been prone to inflammation and pain, but the day Tallas had left her for dead hadn't exactly been easy on her body either. "I just need to sleep it off."

Ezra grunted but otherwise walked on in silence. To his credit, he kept pace with her. Mo wanted to thank him, but that somehow felt like admitting defeat. Maybe it was a childish thing, to still be so stubborn about her body, but it was hard not to get frustrated by it sometimes.

"I'm sorry about before," Mo said. "When I snapped at you in the bar. I have a short temper when things hurt."

A warm, low chuckle burst free from Ezra's chest.

"What could possibly be funny?" she asked. "I'm trying to be nice."

"A temper when things hurt? Your temper's been short since the day we met."

She almost told him that things hurt all the time. She never stopped hurting, in one way or another. But that seemed dangerously close to telling him too many truths about herself.

"Sorry," she said again instead. "I'm working on it. With people who aren't assholes, anyway."

"So you think I'm not an asshole?"

"Not entirely."

For some reason, that seemed to satisfy him. Ezra smiled. Mo didn't understand him or what he wanted. Why get to know her? They'd part ways soon enough. Clients never wanted to know about her, and she never wanted to tell them.

As they turned down the street that would take them to the shipyard, Ezra said, "I could heal you, you know."

"I'm fine." Mo's response was immediate, instinctual. She always refused help. She didn't like owing anyone anything. It made for bad things down the road when people wanted to call in favors. "If I can find a few doses of soltherin before we leave Atmos, I'll be fine."

"Why won't you let me help you?"

"Don't waste your energy."

"It's hardly a waste if it means you'll get sleep and be at the top of your game."

Mo's chest heaved. That ... hurt more than she could ever have imagined it would. She hadn't even realized she was hoping he wouldn't say something like that.

So this *was* about her work. Of course. He needed to make sure his investment in their team wasn't wasted.

"I'll be fine," she said. "Just need to sleep it off for tonight."

"Then at least let me help you get to bed, Cevi. You can barely walk."

Ezra was, unfortunately, right about that. Even just a few blocks was proving to be too much. Mo really did want to cry now. She shouldn't have agreed to go out. She should've known this was coming.

But she pushed her shoulders back and blinked a few times, clearing any tears. "Fine." Her ego was bruised, but she didn't want to wake Cass or Kynn to get their help. If Ezra wanted to protect his investment, fine. She would let him protect it.

They made it back to *The Revenant* in silence. Nothing was amiss in the shipyard, nor was anything wrong in their ship. Everything was as it should be—except for the Vanguard waiting to help Mo crawl into bed.

Ignoring the weight of Ezra's stare, Mo punched in the code to lock the ship for the night. The ramp retracted, and the doors closed, keeping them safe from any potential assassins or other strangers. Then Mo hobbled upstairs to her bedroom and punched the button to open the door.

Her bed. What a glorious, beautiful sight. Never had she been so happy to see her bed.

"What's your routine?" Ezra asked. "Do you need anything?"

"Nothing you can help with," Mo mumbled. "I'll be right back."

She made her way to the lavatory next to her room, then washed up as quickly as she could. She would've braided her hair, too, but couldn't bear to make her aching fingers move. She'd just deal with it.

Mo limped back into her quarters, where Ezra was leaning against the wall near the door. She went straight past him and dropped onto the edge of the bed. Ezra started to ask her something, but Mo gestured to her boots. "Just untie them," she said, then added a quick, "please."

Ezra knelt before her on one knee, his long fingers making quick work of the laces on her black boots. Mo shooed him out of the way, then toed them off herself.

"You're sleeping in that?" Ezra asked, tilting his chin toward her tunic and leggings.

"You're not getting me naked, Lyre, as much as you might like that."

He didn't even bat an eye. "Don't be so shy. You should be comfortable."

"I'm fine, thanks."

"If you're sure."

"I've never been more confident in my life."

He smirked, as if he'd won somehow. It was most definitely not what Mo would choose to sleep in, but she would *not* be letting Ezra Lyre help her change into pajamas. No way. That was a line she couldn't cross.

"Ready?" Ezra asked as he stepped closer.

"What?"

"Are you ready?"

Mo started to answer, but Ezra had her in his arms, then settled comfortably on the bed before she could even think to protest. She sputtered an unintelligible string of sounds, which just earned her another smile as Ezra grabbed the light gray blanket from the end of the bed and draped it over her.

"You're sure you don't want me to heal you?" he asked.

"I'm fine."

He sighed. "Alright. Anything else?"

"No, thanks." Mo didn't even know what happened. Had Ezra Lyre really just tucked her into bed?

"Shout if you do," he said, already backing toward the door. "Good night, Cevi."

His fingers lingered by the light switch, then he flicked it off and went out into the hall. Mo's door slid shut.

She didn't even have it in herself to be mad or embarrassed or anything. She just didn't know what to think anymore. It had been a very long, mostly bad day, yet here she was, settled safely in bed thanks to a Vanguard.

Not just *a* Vanguard. Commander Ezra Lyre.

And it was as she contemplated that very idea that she finally fell asleep.

Chapter 28

Steel groaned. Fire raged on around her, singeing her skin and the ends of her hair. Smoke filled her lungs.

She was going to die here.

"This is what happens when you deny me."

Her eyes burned as she stared up at a familiar pale face obscured by the dark miasma.

"This is what happens when you don't listen to me."

She couldn't breathe.

"Good luck getting back to Miduna, Momo."

He raised his blaster and pulled the trigger. The shot pierced her armor and seared her skin. She screamed. He walked away, never looking back as she cried until her throat was raw. Metal crashed down around her. She had to find a way out, a way to survive—

Mo jolted awake with a gasp. Her brow was slick with sweat, and her chest rose and fell in quick, shallow bursts. *Fuck.* She hadn't dreamed about that night in so long. It hadn't happened like that, not exactly, but her dreams were never the same.

Fuck, she thought again.

Groaning, she rolled onto her side and focused on the gray metallic wall across from her. She needed to get up and do something. Her body still hurt, and Ezra would probably never let her live down the fact that he'd had to help her get into bed, but she didn't care. She couldn't just lie there while her mind taunted her with visions of the past.

Mo gathered all the energy she had, then sat up and swung her legs over the side of the bed. She wasn't as wobbly on her feet as she had been the night before. She could actually take a halfway decent step, and her fingers flexed more easily. She made quick work of tidying herself up, including changing into a fresh set of clothes, before she stormed out of her room and across the hall.

She knocked on Cass's door, and it slid open a second later. Cass ran a hand over her face and yawned.

"Mo?" she asked.

"Can we talk?"

"Sure?"

Cass was clearly still half asleep; Mo didn't even know what time it was. The rest of the ship was quiet, and in the narrow porthole above Cass's bed, a hint of orange was visible. It had to be early, maybe sunrise.

"Did I wake you?" Mo asked, already regretting her decision to run over here. She was usually good about regulating herself, not relying on others. She'd just been in such a panic—

"No," Cass said, pushing past her. "I was up, just need some coffee. Couldn't sleep much."

"Why?" Mo asked as she followed Cass toward their small kitchen.

"Been a shitty few days." Cass made her way toward the cabinet where they kept the supplies to make coffee and began prepping a pot that would easily serve six. "Don't think I'll sleep well until we're back on Miduna, honestly."

There really was no place like home. Out on contracts like this, *The Revenant* offered some semblance of safety, but so much could go wrong. Someone could attack them, even while they were onboard. Someone could follow them through space to their next destination or engage them in a battle among the stars. Home—Miduna—at least meant the relative protection of the Syndicate base and larger community. Fellow bounty hunters may have been their competition, but most Syndicate members wouldn't let harm befall their colleagues.

Unless they were someone like Tallas Bara.

Or unless there were exorbitant sums of money involved.

Mo dropped down onto one of the seats at the corner table. "We'll be home soon," she said, though she knew she couldn't promise it. She always hated when Cass couldn't sleep. Kynn, at least, seemed to be able to sleep wherever and whenever he wanted. They both envied the man. "We'll be done with this soon."

Cass peeked over her shoulder. "Do you actually believe that?"

"I want to believe that."

"Hm."

"What?" Mo asked.

Cass turned back to the coffee. "So you think this is going to be a long-haul contract."

Mo sighed. "Don't you want to figure out why someone tried to kill us?"

"Of course I do. I'm also trying not to get my hopes up about going home anytime soon."

This was why they needed this money. They'd be so much closer to leaving the Syndicate and bounty hunting for good, closer to the quiet life they wanted.

Maybe, if this really was some conspiracy to take down the government like Ezra thought, they'd even get rewarded for helping uncover all of it. Hopefully that hypothetical reward would come in the form of credits rather than some useless medal.

"I suppose that's smart," Mo said as Cass set a full coffee cup down on the table in front of her. Steam curled up, and the sweet, earthy scent helped Mo perk up a little. "Thanks."

"Distract me," Cass said. "Don't let me fall into homesickness. It's not good for me."

"I don't exactly have anything fun to talk about."

Cass brought her own mug to her lips, took a sip, and sighed contentedly. "Don't care."

Mo cared. She'd give anything for a positive distraction right about then.

"Mo?" Cass asked as she took a seat across from her.

"Do you ever think about that day?" Mo murmured.

"There've been a lot of *days*," Cass said. "You'll have to be more specific."

Mo's throat tightened. "That day on Aerilia. All that time ago."

Tallas Bara hadn't just betrayed Mo. He'd betrayed Cass and Kynn too.

They'd been inseparable once upon a time. With their mutual connection to Veronis and Tallas teaching some of their classes despite not being much older than them, they'd bonded quickly. Tallas had been—still was—an incredible fighter. And while he'd seen Cass's and Kynn's skills, he'd taken a special interest in Mo. He'd always told Mo that her magical gift and general talents made her unique. She'd felt wanted for the first time in a long time, by someone other than Cass and Kynn. He'd made her feel special. He'd gained all of their trust with promises of camaraderie, and they'd been so young they couldn't see that he just wanted to use them for his own gain.

"Of course I do," Cass said. "Not as often as I used to, but I don't think that's something I'll ever forget."

"Do you think ..." Mo swallowed hard. "Do you think it's ever going to get easier? It was so long ago."

Eight years. Mo had been just twenty when Tallas had betrayed them.

Their relationship had started off strong, at least in Mo's very inexperienced opinion. But as time wore on, Tallas became more volatile in private, criticizing her and putting her down, proving his seniority, demeaning her on days when her joints betrayed her. She hadn't known any better. He always claimed to do things out of love, that he only cut her down to make her stronger, that nobody else would care for her the way he did, that she *owed* him after all the affection and energy he'd given to her, all the help he'd provided.

She'd gotten so twisted up and turned around that she kept those comments to herself and tried to be better. Cass and Kynn had never known. She hadn't wanted them to know, because something in Mo's gut had told her none of it was right.

But by the time she listened to her intuition, it had been too late.

They'd been working a contract in some of the less than desirable sections of Aerilia, places where only arms dealers and other "suppliers" ventured. Things had taken one wrong turn after another. Mo had confronted Tallas about his behavior when they were alone, and that was when things exploded. They'd argued and shouted, and that had almost escalated to physical blows. She'd wanted to break up. Not just their romantic entanglement; she'd wanted to get Cass and Kynn away from him too.

During that argument—that distraction—they'd been attacked by the mark they'd been hunting. A whole gang, larger than they'd realized. In a bid to save himself, Tallas had abandoned all three of them. He shot Mo in the shoulder, told her she deserved whatever fate she met, and then he'd run like the coward he was.

She'd managed to kill nearly every member of the gang. It had been self-defense. They would have done far worse things than kill her if she hadn't protected herself. It was the only way she'd reunited with Cass and Kynn. And those she hadn't killed, Cass and Kynn had helped take down as they fought their way out of that terrible situation.

That day, Mo had promised herself that she wouldn't ever let another person into her world. She'd been foolish and softened by promises of love and appreciation. She'd almost paid with her life.

Bounty hunting didn't give her the luxury of trusting people and getting burned. She had to put herself—put Cass and Kynn—first. She had to protect herself and her family above all else.

Even people like Ril Staga tried to hurt them in small ways, like skimming off their payouts and stealing from them if they turned their backs. They always had to be on guard.

"There's no shortcut to healing," Cass said.

"You and Kynn seem to handle it better than I do."

"Yeah, well, he didn't treat us as badly as he treated you. I would've beat the shit out of Tallas if he'd crossed paths with me the other night," Cass said. "Kynn would've killed him. I hardly think we're handling it better than you."

Mo shrugged. "I just figured it wouldn't hurt so much after all this time. That it wouldn't be so hard some days. I hadn't thought about it in a long time, actually."

She may not have thought about it, but the scars of that betrayal were still branded into her skin and her soul. She knew that, and she still couldn't change it.

Was this how Ezra felt? Did it feel better knowing his team was dead? Tallas had never faced any real consequences. He'd lied to Syndicate leadership and said he thought the three younger members of his team had all been killed in the chaos. He'd acted so surprised and relieved when they'd shown back up at Midunian Syndicate Headquarters; it had almost made Mo throw up. Only Bax and Amane had believed her side of the story, but that didn't matter to Syndicate leadership. After all, she hadn't had any evidence to prove her accusations. The only good thing to come out of those hearings was that Tallas had decided to leave Miduna. She hadn't had to see him in years, until the other night on Aerilia.

"Maybe it'll always hurt," Cass said. "Maybe it'll just dull with time, like every other wound."

"Maybe," Mo whispered. Here she was, all turned around again. She needed to focus.

"Did you actually go out last night with Ezra?" Cass asked.

That made Mo's eyes snap up from her coffee. "What?"

"You went out with him last night, right?"

"Yeah. Everything was fine. Nobody seemed to be following us or watching the ship."

"That's not what I was asking."

Mo frowned. If not that, then what?

"How was it?" Cass asked as she leaned forward and lowered her voice. "Awkward? That was why I didn't want to go. I never thought you would."

Tapping her fingers on the table, Mo sighed. Of course it was *awkward*. How much did she tell Cass?

"It was fine, I guess. We ate, he paid. He wanted to try to get to know me on a personal level, said he thought it was important or whatever."

Cass snorted. "Mora Cevi, making small talk?"

"Barely." She scratched at the back of her neck and sighed again. "My joints took a beating after yesterday. He had to help me into bed, but only because I didn't want to wake you or Kynn."

Cass erupted in a full-on belly laugh. "Fuck, I'm surprised he's even alive this morning after all that."

Mo couldn't help but smile. Cass's laugh always soothed her aching heart. It was so full of joy, even after all the shit they'd seen and done.

"I tried to be nice," Mo said. "He saved my life yesterday."

"As he should."

Mo shook her head. "It's only because he hired us."

"He wouldn't help you into bed if it was just about hiring us for a job, Mo."

Mo wouldn't normally think so either—it felt too friendly, too personal—but that was what he'd said. He needed her "at the top of her game." He wanted her to be ready to work, not stable and comfortable as a person. That was the way it always went.

She was about to argue the point with Cass when footsteps sounded on the ramp. Ezra entered the common room, somehow managing to look refreshed and sprightly in the early hours of the day.

"Morning," he said a bit too cheerfully. He had a small black bag in one hand, which he placed on the table between Mo and Cass.

"Sleep well?" Cass asked, turning to watch him make himself a cup of coffee.

"Not really," he said. "You need a better guest room. I was telling Cevi that the other day."

Mo rolled her eyes. "I didn't design the damn ship."

"No, but maybe it's time to get yourself an upgrade." Ezra returned to the table and sat between them, then nudged the black bag toward Mo. "Here."

"What's this?" she asked warily.

"Just open it." As he waited for her, he lifted his mug to his lips and took a long sip.

Mo slid the bag toward herself. It was a smooth waterproof material and no bigger than a standard blaster either. What could Ezra possibly have to show her?

As she finally unzipped the bag, she stifled a gasp.

There, twinkling under the kitchen lights, were ten vials of soltherin.

"Lyre?" Mo asked.

"You said you needed some, so I went out this morning. Cleaned out three nearby suppliers."

Ezra said it so casually, so calmly, that it was almost like he thought this was normal. Like this was something reasonable, or perhaps even something expected.

This was ... This was something only Kynn or Cass would do for her, and even then, they wouldn't get her this much. Not because they didn't want to but the sheer cost. This was thousands of credits worth of medication.

Mo blinked, then slowly lifted her gaze. Ezra was the perfect picture of a relaxed, off-duty soldier as he sipped his coffee. There wasn't so much as a wrinkle in his tight white T-shirt, and he'd trimmed his beard and pulled his hair up in a messy bun.

"How much do I owe you?" Mo asked.

He frowned. "Nothing."

"I can't just accept this."

"Sure you can," he replied as he leaned forward conspiratorially. "You just say, 'Thanks, Ezra.' Really, it's not hard."

Was that some kind of taunt?

"Dock the cost from my share of the contract fee," Mo said.

"No."

Mo huffed and looked at Cass. She needed backup here. Mo did not like owing anyone anything, and in the last eighteen hours, she'd managed to build quite the list of things she owed Ezra Lyre.

But Cass just gave Mo an easy smile, as if to say, "Take it, dumbass."

Mo wanted to fight him on it, but she was too damn tired. She'd try again later.

"Thanks, Lyre," she finally said as she zipped the bag shut again. "When do you want to get started today?"

"Figured we'd wait a couple more hours until the campus opens, then go back to talk to that professor," Ezra said. "We've got a while yet. Where's Kynn?"

"Still sleeping," Cass said.

Ezra waved a hand. "Let him."

Mo did the only thing she could do. She settled back into her seat and picked up her coffee. She would find some way to pay Ezra back, even if she had to forcibly give him the credits. She wouldn't let her debts continue to grow, and she certainly wouldn't fail on this mission.

Chapter 29

Had Ezra gone too far?

Mo usually had a good poker face, but when she'd opened that bag of drugs at breakfast, he'd thought she might actually pass out or kill him.

He didn't see what the big deal was. She needed the medication, and he'd been able to locate some. He also happened to have a grotesquely large bank account, and buying that many doses hadn't made a dent. Money could make people cruel—he'd seen that with his family—but it also guaranteed access to much-needed things: food, medication, safety. He had more than he could ever want. Why not use it for something important?

Apparently Mo didn't see it that way. He certainly wouldn't be taking anything from her as payment. Maybe he could get her to renegotiate their contract to include him supplying *all* necessary items, from transport to weaponry to medical care. That would make her happy, right? Or at least it might help her relax.

He'd worry about it later.

As they walked toward the university gates again, Mo at least seemed to be moving better. She was even joking around with Kynn, another good sign—which also had the side effect of getting people to stop looking at them so suspiciously. Ezra supposed they stuck out like sore thumbs amid the professors and students milling around.

They headed straight for the archaeology building again, cutting through crowded atriums and narrow halls until they found themselves in front of Professor Taera Rioris's office. Her door was closed.

"Shall we see if anyone's home?" Kynn asked, already reaching for the comms button embedded in the doorframe. He pushed it, but nothing happened.

"Maybe she heard about the murder and decided to stay home," Cass said.

Ezra hadn't even thought that might be why the other professors and students had been looking at them strangely. Surely word had begun to spread about Professor Valtor by now. That couldn't be good.

Kynn pushed the button again and waited. With a huff, Mo leaned against the wall near the door and folded her arms over her chest. She wouldn't look Ezra in the eye or spare him any attention. Maybe he really had gone too far.

"Cevi," he said.

She glared at him, her expression warning him he had about five seconds to say whatever it was he wanted.

"I'm sorry if earlier made you uncomfortable, but—"

Professor Rioris's office door slid open with a quiet swish. Frowning, she poked her head out. "Come in, quickly."

It was a tiny room, and Ezra had to nearly fold in on himself to not squish Mo or Cass where they stood in the back.

"Professor Rioris," Kynn said with a smile. "I assume you've heard the bad news by now."

"You mean that Valtor is dead?" Taera asked as she circled her desk. "Of course I've heard. What do you want?"

"We wanted to know more about what he was studying that put him on the 'fringe,' as you called it," Kynn said.

"Is that what got him killed?" Taera asked.

"That's what we're trying to figure out," Mo said. "Can you help us?"

Taera's pale eyes searched the room. "You're serious?"

"Completely," Cass said.

"I thought he was a strange man," Taera said, "but it's a shame he was murdered. No one deserves that fate."

"Agreed," Kynn said lazily. "So, what was he studying?"

"He was looking into the Eternal Ones," Taera said. "Into their connections to magic and these old artifacts."

Ezra shifted his weight to his left leg, then back to his right. Valtor was looking into *that*? Maybe it really had gotten him killed.

"Like what?" he asked Taera.

"I don't know any specifics," she said. "You should speak to Professor Kirak. He's just down the hall. Knows all about whatever Valtor was working on."

Great. Another professor to track down. Ezra was getting tired of this dance.

"Is he in now?" Ezra asked. "We need to make this quick if we're going to find Valtor's killer." He was fairly certain he already knew who had killed Valtor, but this woman didn't need to know that.

"Let me call him." Taera sat down in her slim desk chair, then pressed a button on her desk. "Aelith? You there?"

A moment later, a deep voice replied, "Yes, Taera?"

"I'm sending some folks down to speak with you about Valtor's work."

"Fine."

Taera glanced back up at them. "Six doors down on the right, Professor Aelith Kirak. Not that friendly, and just to warn you, he thought Valtor had lost his mind too."

This was just getting better and better.

"Thanks," Ezra said, already turning to leave the room.

They shuffled down the narrow hallway and found who had to be the next professor—a large Sorthian man with amber skin, black-brown hair, and an aggressive frown—waiting just outside his office.

"Professor Kirak?" Ezra asked.

"That's me," the man replied.

"We need to speak with you about—"

Kirak spun on his heel and stomped into his room, his loose white robes flowing behind him. "Come inside before the students hear you," he called over his shoulder.

Thankfully, Kirak had a larger office than Taera. The four of them were able to spread out, and Ezra didn't miss the fact that Mo kept Cass solidly between them. Truly, how could providing her medicine make her so much more prickly? It was like every time he thought he took a step forward with Mo, he actually did something to set himself two steps back.

"What do you want to know about Valtor?" Kirak asked as he leaned against the front of his black desk.

"What was he working on recently?" Ezra asked. "Professor Rioris mentioned that he'd been working on something with the Eternal Ones and some ... artifacts?"

They'd learned a bit about this back on Aerilia, but Ezra thought it best to act clueless. If Kirak thought Valtor was "fringe" for studying this, already having some background on the subject might make them seem suspicious too. And they were probably already suspicious.

"He was," Kirak grunted. "We were just discussing it a couple of weeks ago. You see, long ago, people in this galaxy worshipped the Eternal Ones and believed they brought magic to inhabited worlds. Some believed this magic was tied to artifacts left by the Eternal Ones after they disappeared."

"Why'd they disappear?" Cass asked.

"No one knows," Kirak said.

"What do you believe?" Kynn asked.

"That they were never real, nor are these relics," the professor said. "A bunch of nonsense to get collectors to pay out for false rarities. You know how the market goes."

"Sure," Kynn said, all smiles.

"Valtor believed he'd found the location of a sword called the Star Eater," Kirak said. "And last I spoke with him, he also wouldn't shut up about the Genesis Crystal and how it had once been on Veronis."

Mo didn't even flinch. Ezra had thought for sure that would get some reaction from the bounty hunters, given it was their true home world, yet they didn't react at all. But if the Genesis Crystal had once been on Veronis, what was it Darius and the others had stolen on Miduna? Professor Bas're had said that there was a crystal, a sword, and a key. Ezra had just assumed they found that crystal, or at least something they thought was that same crystal.

"Why would he talk to you about it if you obviously believe it's all fake?" Mo asked.

"I study the Eternal Ones as well," Kirak said, "and despite him being on the fringe of our field, I once respected him greatly."

"This fixation on the artifacts was new?" Mo asked.

"Seemed that way to me, unless he harbored those ideas all along and only just got the courage to speak to them," Kirak said.

"Do you have any of his notes?" Cass asked. "Files? Whatever he was studying?"

"I believe some of it was at his home," Kirak said. "Some should still be in his office."

"Can we have access to it?" Ezra asked.

"Sure, what do I care?" Kirak muttered. "You with the police or something? Why are you investigating his death?"

"We've been asked by his family to look into it," Ezra said.

"Bounty hunters, then."

Ezra didn't correct the man.

"Fine," Kirak said. "Take whatever you want. I'll let you in."

At least they had a somewhat easy win. Ezra and the others followed Kirak down the hall to Valtor's office, where he punched a code into the pad by the door. It slid open. Inside was a bit of a mess but nothing that looked out of place for a normal private office.

Kirak oversaw their effort, which consisted of gathering any data pads and handwritten notes they could find. It took the better part of half an hour to ensure they'd found anything that might be stashed away, whether out of paranoia or privacy. Valtor's office didn't have many personal effects and really did focus on his work.

By the time they were done, Kirak seemed more annoyed than before, like this was a great imposition. They certainly didn't *need* him there to watch over them.

"Before you go," he said as Kynn started for the door, "just ... be careful, with whatever it is you're investigating."

"You don't need to worry about us, Professor," Kynn said.

"Perhaps not, but if this really did get Valtor killed, then we all need to be looking over our shoulders," Kirak said. "You know the way out?"

"We've got it, Professor. Thanks for your help," Ezra said, then nodded at Kynn to leave. They had a ton of information to get through and not much time if they wanted to get ahead of whatever it was they'd stumbled into.

After stopping on the way back to the shipyard to grab food, Ezra and the others settled in around the upper deck to plug in tablets and data pads to begin sifting through everything. Kynn took over the handwritten notes, as he was the only one able to decipher Professor Valtor's messy scrawl.

Much of it was stories Ezra knew of the Eternal Ones: their origins from the creation of the Universe, their connection to various planets across the galaxy, and their bestowing of magic onto mere mortals.

Widespread belief in the Eternal Ones waned over the last two millennia, starting before the Federation was founded. Pockets of believers still existed, of course, as was their right. Ezra wouldn't begrudge anyone their right to their own beliefs. The Ascended had retained more believers, and that was actually part of why the Ascended broke off from the early Federation to form their own empire.

During the Great Schism, ongoing issues around things like trade policies, genetic enhancements, resource management, and religion had played a role in the split. The Ryperion species had led the charge and established Sorvath Prime as the Ascended Empire's new capital planet, where they'd continued tending to beliefs in the Eternal Ones and pursuing other policies Federation leadership disagreed with.

The differences in philosophical beliefs wasn't the cause of their current conflict. Both the Federation and the Ascended wanted and needed more resources. The Ascended were just pushing into Federation territory to try to do so, while the Federation was exploring its own territories for untapped resources instead. It took a great deal of energy and space to sustain such massive populations.

For nearly two millennia, the Federation had been expanding and changing. It started out as just Aerilia and a handful of other systems and now encompassed thousands of light-years of space. The Eternal Ones just hadn't stuck around—or come back—as part of those changes. Ezra himself believed it was all myth. There were no gods out there.

"Listen to this," Mo said. She was lounging on the floor on the opposite side of the common area, almost lazy in her posture, like she didn't care. "'I located a monk on Thalindor who spoke of a different history of the Eternal Ones, one of war and death that spanned star systems. She said that after a narrow victory, the Eternal Ones left pieces of themselves scattered among the Federation and Ascended territories, waiting to be reclaimed when they could someday return.'"

"Victory against who?" Cass asked. She was sitting at the table, legs folded under her slim frame. She didn't take her eyes off her own tablet.

Mo tapped the screen of her pad. "Doesn't say."

"That's helpful," Ezra muttered.

"Sounds like the artifacts Professor Bas're mentioned," Kynn said, adjusting his position on the floor and rummaging through the mess of Valtor's handwritten notes.

"Didn't Kirak say Valtor had a map in here or something?" Ezra asked. "Bas're mentioned the underground antiquities market. We should figure out where more of these artifacts are. Maybe that'll lead us to whoever it is that's willing to kill to get them."

Ezra would've gone that route before, but it hadn't been readily available. Chasing his team down had been the top priority. Would they still be alive if he hadn't turned them over to the FSC? Probably not, or if they were, their days would've been numbered. He couldn't think about that right now.

"It's got to be in here somewhere," Kynn said, mostly to himself as he began sifting through more paperwork.

Ezra went back to his own tablet, tapping through files for Valtor's classes, messages from the department heads about his lack of attendance, and more. This was going to put Ezra to sleep.

"I think I got it." Cass's eyebrows furrowed, then she hopped out of her seat. "Holo table."

They all followed Cass into the command room. She pushed a few buttons, and a holographic map popped up in the middle of the table. It took them on a path from Vonnoth through the Federation and to a far-off planet called Mor'vex. Ezra hadn't ever heard of it; there were too many inhabited worlds in the Federation to name them all.

Cass zoomed in on Mor'vex, right to what appeared to be mountains. "His notes mentioned this particular volcanic region and wanting to 'study' here."

"Are any of you familiar with this planet?" Ezra asked.

Kynn shook his head. "Never heard of it."

"Let me check the Syndicate database," Mo said as she strode over to the comms terminal on the opposite wall and began furiously tapping buttons.

Ezra waited quietly as they worked. He hated feeling left out of the loop, but they clearly knew what they were doing, and wasn't this why he'd hired them? They had resources, especially now that he had none, other than the large bank account.

"Let's see ..." Mo nodded. "Mor'vex is the only habitable planet in the Bolmera System, but looks like it's largely abandoned at this point. Stripped of its resources. Most of the local population has fled in the last century ..."

"Oh, lovely," Kynn said. "Just where I've always wanted to go, an abandoned and desolate world."

"No place is ever *abandoned*," Mo said. "A few small settlements are listed in the database. They're probably filled with scavengers or even crime lords trying to hide their stock."

"An absolute hellhole," Kynn quipped. "Even better."

"And this is where Valtor thought one of the artifacts was?" Ezra asked.

"I assume so, since Professor Kirak said Valtor thought he'd identified the location of the Star Eater," Cass said. "Anyone find that in their notes?"

"No, but I'll keep looking," Ezra said. "Didn't he mention the Genesis Crystal too?" Again, he watched the bounty hunters carefully, but none of them flinched. "That Valtor thought it had been on Veronis?"

"That's what he said." Mo's answer was clipped.

There, he had her.

"You three ever heard anything about that?" he asked.

"Heard all kinds of things," Mo said, leaving the holo screen up and stomping back to her earlier seat far away from Ezra.

He didn't think it was egregious to ask them. Mo had told him about their real home world. Why was she acting so brusque about it?

"Mo," Cass said.

Mo looked at her, and though their expressions hardly changed, Ezra assumed they were having some kind of silent conversation. Finally, Mo rolled her eyes.

"Yes, we've heard some things about it," Mo said. "Every child on Veronis heard of such stories, about crystals that gave Veronians a higher chance of being born with magic. Crystals, plural. I *suppose* that could be some kind of remnant story about the Genesis Crystal, or whatever Kirak called it."

"Nobody ever connected it to the Eternal Ones," Cass said. "At least, not my family or teachers."

"They were just stories," Kynn said. "You know, like nursery rhymes and shit. We know magic is passed through family lines."

"Even if it was there, even if it was real," Mo said, "it's gone now. It's all gone. So I don't really see the point in debating this."

"I wasn't looking for a debate." Ezra sighed. Could he do nothing right when it came to Mora Cevi? "I just wanted to know what you might've heard as kids, if anything. I didn't mean to offend you."

Heavy silence fell between the four of them.

"Do you think that was the crystal they stole on Miduna?" Kynn asked.

"I'd been wondering that," Ezra said, "but wasn't sure how it would've gotten there if it had originally been on Veronis. I guess someone could have moved it, but why? When? And how'd it end up on the floor of a cave?"

More silence.

"Maybe this is about the Ascended," Mo said. "If they want these artifacts, too, and they thought the same about the Genesis Crystal, maybe that's why they went to Veronis. Maybe that's why it's gone."

Shit. Ezra really hadn't thought of *that*. It seemed he truly couldn't do anything right. He just wanted Mo to be comfortable around him, and here he was, fucking it all up.

"I didn't mean to bring up painful memories for you," Ezra said, then looked back at Kynn and Cass. "For any of you. I'm sorry."

"Not your fault," Kynn said. "What's done is done. We may never know if that's why they were going for Veronis. We don't even know if any of this is real, after all."

"Seems like our best bet is to assume it is," Cass said.

Mo nodded. "Then let's go to Mor'vex. We can try to find this sword, or hopefully whoever it is that's put a hit out on us."

Chapter 30

Getting to Mor'vex was going to require them to cross nearly half the expanse of the Federation. Even with *The Revenant*'s Class 12 hyperdrive, they were going to have to travel for almost a week to get there.

And a week cooped up in Mora Cevi's ship was hardly Ezra's idea of a good time.

He'd gotten used to the way the ship rattled after their first few jumps into hyperspace, but Ezra was having a hard time not running into Mo, and she didn't seem to want to be around him at all. Which was fair enough. He wouldn't make her do anything she was uncomfortable with. But he hated feeling like an intruder.

There also wasn't anything to do to pass the time. He caught up on some news from the capital—including a headline that Livia was set to make a speech about her father's death—and he found a few novels in the ship's databases that he'd never read before. But they were only on their second day of travel, and Ezra didn't know what else to do with himself. He didn't feel much like knitting. He needed to work out, but he didn't feel much like doing that either. His mind wouldn't stop running through recent events over and over again.

Fixating on it would do him no good.

Ezra abandoned his quarters and headed for the kitchen. He really would've liked a drink, but these bounty hunters didn't keep any alcohol on board. Figured.

As he reached the top deck, he found a blur of black and purple hair moving around on the kitchen side of the common room. Cass slammed a cabinet closed. "Hi, Ezra."

Whatever she was cooking smelled good. "Didn't mean to intrude," he said. "Just needed a change of scenery."

"Want something to eat?" Cass asked. "I'm making Kantarian noodles."

"Sure." He didn't want to piss off Cass if she was actually tolerating him being around. Besides, he hadn't gotten to spend much time with her alone, and he had questions, if she was willing to answer. He grabbed a few Korlan plums from the fridge in the meantime—dark purple fruit originally from the planet Korla but now grown across the Federation.

"Thank goodness someone does," she said. "Kynn says they're too spicy."

"No such thing," Ezra replied, and she actually shot him a smile over her shoulder.

"Is this usually how you spend long-haul flights?"

"Sometimes, but we usually know we're going and have time to prepare," Cass said. "We usually have updated entertainment files. And we sleep a lot. Or play cards."

"Any favorites?"

"I like Serpent's Bluff."

"Ah," he said. "Deception."

Serpent's Bluff was a strategic game of deception in which players had to bluff their way through bets and card exchanges. The player with the highest-value hand at the end of the round won. Serpent cards could be ascribed any value individual players wanted, but too many serpent cards in your hand at the end meant you'd be penalized. Ezra often watched the enlisted soldiers gamble away weeks' worth of pay on the game.

"It's fun," Cass said, stirring the noodles in her pan. "Mo hates it."

"Why?"

"She's not good at keeping a straight face."

Ezra thought Mo was pretty good at that, but instead he asked, "And you are?"

"You've got to be neutral as a bounty hunter," she said. "Mo's good at it on the job, but not so much when it's just us. Which isn't a bad thing. Unless we're playing cards."

"Does Kynn always come with you?" Ezra asked. "My understanding was that you don't always work as a trio?"

She pushed a few stray hairs out of her face and smiled. "Not always, no. Often enough, though. He just likes to be on his own sometimes."

"And you and Mo don't?"

Cass shrugged. "We trade off on sleep anyway when it's just the two of us, so we get our alone time."

"I can't remember the last time I was alone."

He hadn't meant to say it aloud, but there it was. Ezra was so used to always being around others, whether his former team, his commanding officers, younger soldiers ... someone. And despite that, Ezra often felt alone, surrounded by plenty of well-meaning people but nobody he ever truly clicked with.

Cass turned off the induction cooktop and grabbed two plates out of the cabinet above her. She served them both—a much bigger helping for himself, Ezra noticed—and brought it over before he could even offer to do anything. Steam curled up from the red noodles.

"Mo and I have had this thing since we were kids ..." Cass smiled a little as she sat across from him. "It sounds silly, but we called it 'being alone together.' We'd each do our own quiet activity in the same room, just for company."

"That's not silly," Ezra said. "It sounds nice, actually. And makes sense given your ..."

"Given that our home world was obliterated? Yeah." Cass nodded. "None of us liked being alone for the longest time."

"I can't imagine what that was like," Ezra said. "Not as an adult but certainly not as a child."

"Hard," Cass said. "Indescribably hard."

That didn't seem to even scratch the surface, but what other way could Cass even try to explain it? As much as he could empathize with them, Ezra wouldn't pretend to truly understand.

"I'm sorry," he said.

"Why?" Cass glanced at him through the steam wafting up from her noodles as she combed her fork through them. "It's not your fault."

"No, but ..." Ezra drummed his fingers on the table and sighed. "Before those Vanguard assassins came after us, Mo told me the military and government didn't come to Veronis's aid. That's not how it was taught to us, but given how they've responded to everything else going on, I guess I'm not surprised."

Ezra had expected far more from the FSC. He shouldn't have had to hire bounty hunters himself. He shouldn't have had to take this mission on his own. In fact, he shouldn't have been on it at all. The FSC should've headed the investigation, and he should've recused himself and only answered their questions to help them.

But that wasn't how any of this had actually played out, and he almost couldn't fathom it. There was no chance they would be happy to hear he was still investigating despite orders for him to stand down. Going against orders made him uneasy, but Ezra couldn't let this go. Not then and not now.

"It's hard to question your own organization." Cass twirled some noodles around her fork, took a bite, and groaned. "Shit, that's good." She took another bite and groaned again, then got up for a glass of water.

As she returned to the table, she said, "It's hard when you believe in the mission and they don't, or at least not as much as you do."

"You say that like you've experienced it," Ezra said.

Cass shrugged one slender shoulder. "The Syndicate isn't perfect either. They talk about serving the bounty hunters and creating a more fair and stable environment for us, but they skim off our profits when they think we aren't looking and try to take more than their fair share. I don't think any organization is perfect or ever can be. They're run by people, and people are flawed. We just have to decide how we react to those imperfections and what we want to do about them."

Ezra nodded. He'd known of military failings in other areas, and perhaps it made him a bad person, but it wasn't until they'd failed him so recently that he'd really, *truly* considered what those other failings might mean. How many other soldiers had they failed? How many powerful people had they let hurt the FSC and his fellow soldiers with no consequences?

"No wonder Mo can't stand me," he murmured. "If the FSC is as bad as they look to me right now ..." Mo had to see much worse when she looked at him.

Cass shrugged again. "Are they *that* bad? I don't know. They've failed us before, and they'll surely fail us again. But I won't hold that against you personally. You're not them."

Cass may not have seen Ezra as the FSC, but that was how he saw himself. For seventeen years, he'd been serving in their ranks. Believed in the mission, the honor of the fight and protecting the people of the Federation. He still did. He was part of a broken system, but weren't they all? Everything felt broken with the war raging on and nobody doing anything to stop it on either side.

He pinched the bridge of his nose. He was too tired to think about this. He still had a fucking mythical sword to find ... or find whoever it was that wanted to buy the damn thing, if it existed at all. Maybe once he figured out why someone wanted him dead, he could think about the bigger problems plaguing the FSC.

And to figure out why someone wanted him dead, he was going to need not just Cass and Kynn's help but Mo's too.

Ezra had spent much of his night the same, either chatting with Cass while she cooked or with Kynn while he monitored everything from the cockpit.

Then had come another sleepless night. He couldn't get Mo's anger out of his head, her frustration over the Fall of Veronis I and the pain in her eyes right before they'd been attacked. Yes, she'd said this mission had turned personal, but with the way she was avoiding him now, it was only going to make the next portion of their contract so much harder.

He sighed and set down his knitting needles. He'd started working on a blanket, a basic pattern he knew by heart, thanks to his grandmother starting him on the hobby when he was still in grade school. But it wasn't helping today. Not being able to pilot or anything just made him feel useless. He needed to clear his mind.

Ezra tugged on a short-sleeved white shirt, black training pants, and his boots. He'd go to the front cargo hold for a bit and try to quiet his mind with movement. There was room in there to do some basic bodyweight exercises—not what Ezra was used to with the FSC, but it'd do for now.

As his door slid open, Ezra barely avoided barreling into Kynn. "Shit, sorry," he said, stepping back. The "crew quarters," as Mo called them, were basically just two closets next to each other. It made for a very tight squeeze.

Kynn chuckled. "Going somewhere?"

"Exercise," Ezra said. "You done flying?"

"For now. Time for some shows."

"Didn't you finish them already?" Ezra asked. The night before, Kynn had confessed to already finishing up what little new entertainment he'd happened to have on hand, some reality survival show set on the moons of Trilia, a colony in the outer reaches of the Federation.

"Yeah, but what else am I gonna do?" Kynn asked. "Helps me fall asleep."

"Enjoy," Ezra said.

Kynn gave him a mock salute as he headed into his quarters. Ezra just shook his head and went on his way. He didn't see the appeal of such shows, but maybe he'd end up watching one with Kynn. They still had a few days before they'd reach Mor'vex.

As Ezra navigated the narrow corridors toward the front cargo hold, he ran through a few circuits in his head, trying to decide what would be the best use of his time. But as the door opened, he didn't move a muscle.

Mo was inside, her back to Ezra as she rolled her body forward into a stretch. She didn't get far, like her joints and muscles were stiff. She muttered a few choice curse words under her breath.

Ezra tried very hard to keep his eyes to himself. He generally considered himself a respectful person, but he found himself almost unable to rein in that desire to look at her. She was beautiful. He'd noticed before, of course, but it was harder to ignore when she wasn't in armor of some kind. Tight shorts hugged her wide hips and thick thighs, and her tank top was so oversized that it exposed more skin than it covered. Even her slightly mussed braid suited her perfectly somehow.

"Need some help?" he asked.

Mo snapped upright, turning to glare at him. Just behind the left-hand strap of her top was the unmistakable mark of a blaster wound. Long since healed, of course; it was little more than a thick, knotted scar that was slightly more pink than the rest of her pale skin.

"Oh, good," she said. "What do you want, Lyre?"

"To exercise." He couldn't help but notice that neither her knees nor hands were bandaged. There was a small bruise on her thigh, though. Had she taken some of the soltherin?

She waved a hand at him.

"So, can I come in?"

"Fine." She stalked across the room to where a water bottle and towel sat on top of a large crate. After taking a healthy swig, she said, "Talk, Lyre."

"How do you know I want to talk?" he asked.

"Because you're just standing there." She gestured toward where he was still near the door, then started undoing her braid. "And you seem to always have something to say."

Ezra rarely got nervous, but Mora Cevi staring him down certainly had him on edge.

"I genuinely came in to work out," he said. When she pinned him with a look, he decided to throw caution to the wind. "We never really got to talk about it since, you know, someone tried to kill us, but I'm sorry about Veronis. I understand why you wanted to stay out of this. I only know what I was taught about the loss of your home world, but recent events have shown me that maybe I don't know the FSC as well as I thought. I never would've thought they'd just blow off what happened on Miduna."

As she ran her fingers through her loose hair, Mo raised an eyebrow at him. "That's what you wanted to talk to me about?"

"And to thank you for extending the contract." Ezra moved in closer, leaving just a few feet between them. Sweat beaded on her forehead, her cheeks were splotchy and red, and her chest rose and fell in shallow bursts. "I know it's not easy considering what I must represent."

She continued watching him.

"Well?" he asked.

"I don't really know what to say. Thanks, I guess?"

"You guess?"

Mo stopped fiddling with her hair and leaned back against the crates. "I don't know what you want me to say. It's not *your* fault."

"No, but I make you uncomfortable."

"So? Lots of people make me uncomfortable."

"I don't want you to be."

She sighed.

"Just like I'm sorry if I overstepped by getting you so much soltherin," he added. "You needed it, so I did what I could, but like I said, I don't want to make you uncomfortable. We can just roll it into the contract and make all supplies, including medical, part of what I cover."

Mo sighed again and whispered something about "being too tired for this shit." Ezra didn't think that was entirely fair; she could've denied him the opportunity to talk. She could've even sent him away now, or she could've walked away herself. But she didn't.

Instead, Mo peered up at him. "Why do you care?"

His eyebrows furrowed. "What?"

"Why do you care?" she asked again. "Why do you care about making me comfortable?"

Was this some kind of trick question? Ezra didn't think there was a wrong answer, but knowing Mo's short temper, maybe there was.

"Because we're working together," he said. "A team needs to work well together, and everyone needs to be comfortable to do that."

She sighed a third time.

"What?" he asked. Apparently he *had* said the wrong thing.

"Thanks for the chat," she said. "Now leave."

"What's so wrong with my answer?"

"Nothing." She pointed to the door. "There's the exit."

"Why?"

"My ship, my rules. Or did you forget I'm the captain here?"

"I'm not leaving," Ezra said, making her face flush a deeper red. He folded his arms across his chest. "I'd like to know what's so wrong with what I said. You, Cass, and Kynn obviously care about each other's comfort and safety. You said that to me the other day, back on Vonnoth. You didn't want to drag Cass and Kynn into some mess. You want to take care of them. Why can't I help take care of all three of you? You're my responsibility."

Mo's eyes narrowed. "I am *not* your responsibility," she hissed. "None of us are. You're acting like this is the fucking FSC or something. It's not. We can take care of ourselves."

Ezra dropped his head back and stared at the pipes and tubes running across the exposed ceiling. This was not going well, not at all.

"Obviously you can," he said, meeting her cold gaze again. "I understand that. I've seen what you can do with your saber."

"So?" she asked. "What is it, then?"

"I'm not allowed to want to help people?"

"Nobody 'helps' without ulterior motives, Lyre."

"That's one of the bleakest things I've ever heard."

"It's true." She crossed her arms over her chest—a mirror to his stance. The movement pulled her tank top strap slightly to one side, revealing more of that scar. "In my world, it's true. And you know it's true for Aerilia, where politicians are only doing things to gain favor with each other or with business leadership."

"I hardly think trying to ensure you had medication or that you three don't die means I have ulterior motives," Ezra said.

Mo huffed, as if he was missing some glaringly obvious point.

"The only people who have ever cared about me and haven't hurt me are Kynn and Cass," she said. "Otherwise, people *always* want something. My time. My skills. To use me to grow their own bank accounts or otherwise."

"People like Tallas Bara?"

Ezra didn't know where the question came from, but there it was, floating heavy in the air between them.

Mo's jaw tightened. "Yes. People like him."

A thousand more questions burned in Ezra's mind, but her rigid posture said he was already on thin ice. His attention flicked to that scar again. Had that been the result of some brawl on a contract? Or had Tallas done it to her? Kynn *had* mentioned that Mo could relate to what Ezra was going through.

"Whatever he did to you, I'm sorry," Ezra said. "But I don't think you can judge me based on his actions, nor can you judge me for something the FSC did twenty years ago."

She searched his face for what felt like an eternity. Ezra's heart beat wildly in his chest.

"Maybe not," she conceded with a frown.

"I know what it's like," Ezra said, "to be seen only for what you can do and not for your humanity. It's how the FSC treats us. We're soldiers and numbers, not people. That separation helps us sometimes but hurts us many others. I thought my team saw that difference and cared, but apparently not."

"But you saw them as more than that."

He nodded. "I did. And for what it's worth, I see Cass, Kynn, and you as more than that too. You're not just your skills. You're people. And I care about people. That's why I joined the FSC. I just want to help, but if it makes you uncomfortable, I'll stop."

"How noble of you," she said, the words somehow sharp but soft. Her poor attempt at a joke, probably. She scrubbed at her face and groaned, as if whatever fight she'd had in her left. "Fine, we can make supplies part of the contract."

"Thank you."

"You're very strange." Mo grabbed her water bottle and towel off the crates behind her. "Most clients try to pay us as little as possible."

"I'm not most clients, Cevi."

"No," she said, pushing past him to leave. "You're not."

With a satisfied smile, Ezra turned and called, "Next place we get supplies, I'm buying alcohol. Is that okay, Captain?"

His smile grew as Mo's cheeks reddened. Maybe he was making some progress with her after all.

CHAPTER 31

Having visited far more planets in the Federation than most people could dream of, Mo didn't usually find herself reacting to views of new worlds as she flew toward them.

But something about the dark clouds swirling around Mor'vex was unsettling. The hairs on the back of Mo's neck prickled. Her fingers tightened around the steering yoke as she piloted the ship closer.

"Is it just me," Kynn said from the copilot seat, "or does this place feel wrong?"

"Not just you," Mo murmured, trying to pull her attention away from the planet and focus on the dashboard lighting up in front of her.

Something about this place didn't feel right at all. Mo's mind and gut screamed at her to turn the ship around and head straight back to Miduna. She *had* survived several recent assassination attempts, and more than that, she had Ezra's strange sincerity to deal with. Maybe she was just more rattled than she realized.

When Ezra had interrupted her a few days earlier in the gym, Mo hadn't wanted to hear a thing he had to say. But he'd made her listen—something only Cass or Kynn usually managed to do—and he had, unfortunately, made some good points. They still hadn't discussed that chat. She knew she should just take the win—if Ezra was any other client, she'd be grateful he wanted to pay for all supplies and costs—but it was hard. Something about Ezra made her ... nervous. She didn't like the way her chest got a little tighter or her face a little warmer whenever he was around. She didn't like that he was in control of this contract, and his seemingly sincere desire to help had her on edge.

Mo forced the thought away. She needed to focus. They had a warlord or some Ascended to find—or whoever else might be behind all this madness.

The Revenant bumped and rumbled as they began their descent to the surface. According to what they'd pieced together in Professor Valtor's notes, they would need to visit a volcanic chain near the planet's equator. Although he hadn't said it explicitly, it seemed he thought the Star Eater might be there. It was as good a clue as they had.

Besides, this was what Mo, Kynn, and Cass did regularly as bounty hunters. They took whatever data points they had and combined them with educated guesses and experience to find what they were looking for. And if they didn't find the sword, they could at least start visiting the settlements on the planet to look for information about whoever wanted Ezra—whoever wanted all of them—dead.

The closer they got to the surface, the thicker the cloud cover. The turbulence only grew, prompting both Ezra and Cass to hurry into the cockpit and strap into the empty second row.

"Fuck," Kynn said with a laugh, one hand on his controls and the other flipping a series of switches on the dash as they both tried to level out the ship. "This reminds me of that time on Belvars II."

It had been a tough contract, one they'd taken shortly after Tallas had betrayed them. They'd had to track and capture an entire clan of illegal arms dealers on a planet only recently colonized, which had very little Federation backup. She, Kynn, and Cass had worked that one with Bax and Amane. The criminals hadn't surrendered without a massive fight first, and a few had even died in the process.

"I think I'd prefer that," Mo muttered. At least on that contract, she'd known why she had a target on her back.

"Me too!" Cass called from behind her.

"You put in the coordinates?" Ezra asked.

Risking a peek over her shoulder, Mo found that he hadn't yet secured his harness. "No," she said, "I'm actually taking us to the other side of the planet just to spite you."

"You might," he replied with a smirk.

Mo huffed. "Strap in, Lyre."

"Yes, Captain."

She glared at him, and he just winked before buckling his harness. With a heavy sigh, Mo focused again, not just on the dashboard in front of her but the feeling of the controls under her fingers and the way the ship moved through the air.

Soon, the sky outside cleared from thick, dark clouds to a rust red haze. Jagged mountains stretched all around the basin below them, almost unnatural in their location and form. The navigational system had them descending into the basin and toward the far end of the mountains, where the ground was nearly black.

Mo's gut screamed at her again, but she ignored it. She ignored the way Kynn shifted uncomfortably in his seat too.

The closer they got to the earth, the clearer their target became. At the end of the basin, nestled right at the bottom of the tallest peak in the ring, were several enormous statues. That had to be where Valtor thought the sword was. No way that was a coincidence.

"We landing there?" Kynn asked as he stared outside.

"Yeah," Mo said. "As close to that thing as we can get."

They circled around, choosing a spot about half a klick from those statues. As they set the ship down, black dust and debris clouded up in front of the view screen.

"This is going to be fun," Cass said as she unlocked her seat belt and hopped to her feet. "Truly, can't wait."

"What do you think those statues are?" Mo asked, standing and heading for the command room.

"No idea, but it sure looked like someplace connected to some gods, at least from what I could see," Cass said, following right behind her.

The four of them made their way down to the lower level. Mo headed for the weapons locker near the cargo doors, then grabbed her silver hilt. She hooked it to her belt, then opted for a small black blaster and slid it in her holster on her thigh.

"We assuming our target's in there?" Cass asked.

"Let's not take any chances," Mo said, "unlike Kynn on that contract on Zolibos."

"Hey!" Kynn shouted as he grabbed his saber. "That's not fair."

"What's not fair?" Ezra asked.

"So I accidentally stumbled into our target's lair, unarmed, *one time*," Kynn said. "I wasn't feeling well that day. My head wasn't clear."

"Your head wasn't clear because you spent the entire night before drinking with that blonde," Cass said as she strapped her rifle to her back. "And stayed out with her and that Sorthian guy until dawn."

Kynn grinned. "Isn't getting to know new people half the fun of a contract?"

"No," Cass said.

He rolled his eyes. "And they were more than friends, just for the record."

"Oh?" Ezra asked, taking his saber and a single gun.

"The commander's looking for juicy details." Kynn slapped him on the shoulder. "They invited me to join them, but I declined. They were nice enough, but I need a more emotional connection, y'know?"

"I do, actually," Ezra said.

Mo cleared her throat. "If we're done talking about Kynn's not-dating history, can we get going?"

Cass grabbed two more small pistols, then slammed the weapons locker shut. As the others finished suiting up, Mo made sure her braid was tucked up into her helmet, then punched in the code to unlock the ship's rear doors and lower the ramp outside.

"Let's go see where your fringe cousin's ideas took us, Lyre," she said. "You all can gossip later."

"What does his being my cousin have to do with this?" Ezra asked through their comms channel. His voice was laced with a touch of static.

Probably just interference from something on the planet, Mo thought. After all, that crystal back on Miduna had seemed to do some odd things to tech. If Professor Valtor was right and this place really did hold some ancient artifact, who was to say it wouldn't deteriorate the quality of their tech?

"You hear that?" Mo asked.

"Could be those clouds," Cass said, "or something else around here."

"Don't get separated," Mo said as she headed for the ramp, Cass on her right.

When Mo punched a button on her gauntlet, an overlay lit up her visor. There were no signs of life other than the three people with her. Not even animals. The blackened ground looked like layers and layers of volcanic ash. Hopefully this chain was dormant, as the Syndicate database had claimed.

They continued on, trudging through the dark ash and windy basin. It was like whatever wind blew into the crater became trapped and swirled in on itself, creating a vortex. It was almost hard to walk. Mo gritted her teeth as they got closer to their target coordinates.

When they were just a quarter klick away from those enormous statues, the ground gave way, dropping off at sharp and awkward angles. The dark earth made it hard to see; it all blended together in a mix of stygian black and charcoal gray. But yes, there was a chasm separating them from the base of the mountains.

"That way," Ezra said, pointing to their right.

Amid the blackened landscape was an equally dark bridge, so flat and colorless that it was camouflaged by their surroundings. The garnet sky did little to offer light or contrast.

As they approached the bridge, Mo stuck an arm out, stopping Cass from going any farther. "Are we sure it's stable?" Mo asked. She doubted that, in a place as desolate as this, anyone had been by to check the structural integrity of the damn thing.

"Only one way to find out." Ezra started forward. He made it three steps across the bridge, then stopped and turned toward them. "See?" The metal groaned, then quieted again. "It's fine."

"Make it to the other side first," Mo said. "Then we'll see about crossing."

It was like she could see Ezra roll his eyes despite his opaque visor. He finished crossing, then put his hands out to either side and said, "See?"

If a man as large as Ezra could make it over, the bridge would surely hold, at least if they crossed one by one. Mo went next, then Cass and Kynn followed her over. The bridge continued to protest, but Mo paid it no mind.

The closer they got to the statues, Mo was able to make out some of the features—long spears held in each statue's hand, heads bent in reverence—though most of the minute details had been broken or worn away by time. In the stone behind them were more carvings, these ones of fire and stars.

And in between the two statues was a shadowy passageway covered by a rocky overhang. They seemed to be guarding it.

"What is this place?" Kynn asked.

"Definitely a temple or something," Cass said. "Maybe dedicated to Krytix. Look at the fire." She pointed at some of the carvings on a nearby wall.

"We should go inside," Ezra said, already starting up the wide path between the statues. They towered high above, easily two stories tall, and the passageway was taller still.

The hairs on the back of Mo's neck prickled again as the wind kicked up—not that she could really feel it with her armor on, but her visor told her the conditions were changing.

"Let's be quick," Mo said, hurrying after Ezra.

They passed the statues, stopping as they came face to face with enormous double doors. Mo could barely make them out in the darkness; it was like this place was void of light despite the open air behind them.

As Mo switched on her helmet's external light, Cass and Kynn did the same. Ezra, however, summoned fire over his palm. His sharp breath clouded the comms.

"Ezra?" Cass asked.

"It's like ..." Ezra audibly swallowed. "It's like my magic is drawn to this place. I'm having a hard time controlling it."

Mo did not like the sound of that at all. Cass had to be right that this place was connected to Krytix, who had supposedly given sunshapers their magic. But even if that was the case, why was it making Ezra react? And why hadn't her magic reacted in the ruins of Evlos's temple on Miduna?

"Look," Kynn said, swinging his light to the left. He pointed. "They're broken."

Sure enough, one of the doors was chipped and cracked at the bottom. The jagged opening was maybe four feet tall and a few feet wide, but they could fit through. Mo didn't see any other way; doors that big would be too heavy to open by hand or even with her magic, and there were no mechanisms or levers to help them.

Mo stalked forward and dropped to the ground, silently cursing the entire situation as her knees popped in protest. Yes, the medicine Ezra had provided helped, but that didn't mean she was entirely pain-free.

She crawled through the opening. Once she cleared it, she pushed up to her full height. As the others came in behind her, Mo took a few tentative steps forward. Her helmet's light did little to illuminate the cavernous space around her. Wherever she turned, shadows swallowed up the building. The place went up multiple stories; there were windows several floors up that she could barely make out, as well as doors, stairs, and more. The hallway continued on for an immeasurable length.

Kynn picked up a small rock and threw it hard. As it landed with a thunk, echoes reverberated around them. "Well," he said, "this is a fucking nightmare."

Cass snorted. "Afraid of the dark?"

"No, but shit, how are we going to find this sword?"

"We split up," Ezra said. He'd put out his fire and switched his helmet light on too. "Cevi and I will head down this passage. Cass, Kynn, up those stairs." He pointed to a set of dilapidated stone steps to their right. "We reconvene in an hour. Stay connected on comms."

Mo almost asked what gave him the authority to separate them, but they'd never cover this much space without splitting up. And as much as she would've preferred to work with Cass, Mo was the only other magic user here. If Ezra somehow lost control of his fire—if this place overwhelmed him for some reason—she had the best chance of subduing him.

"Fine," she said. "One hour. If we don't find the sword or any evidence, we leave."

"Agreed," Ezra said.

Cass tilted her head at Mo, the only sign of her question. Mo gave her a quick nod, which Cass returned, then followed Kynn over toward the stairs. They split up often on contracts, but only in the sense that Mo went into battle close-quarters while Cass stayed long-range. This was different, unusual for them. One of the last times they'd split up like this had been when they were on that gods forsaken contract with Tallas.

Mo wouldn't think about that now. Instead, she switched to another comms channel, then motioned for Ezra to go ahead. "Lead the way, Commander."

"Very funny," he said, but he started down into the dark anyway.

Their footsteps echoed around them as they went. Mo's visor lost track of Kynn and Cass's heat signatures, but that was no surprise given the stone architecture and that they were headed in opposite directions. It still made Mo uneasy.

"You ever seen something like this?" Ezra asked, voice low.

"When would I possibly have seen something like this?" she asked. "Have *you*? You're the one with rich parents. Surely you traveled a lot."

"They never took me someplace like this," Ezra said. "Just resorts and cosmopolitan cultural centers."

"Sounds boring," Mo quipped.

She had the suspicion he was telling the truth as he said, "It really was."

"Miduna has nothing like it," she said. "We went all over for Syndicate training, but we never saw anything other than ruins or other settlements."

Mo wished she'd seen something like this before. She wished she had some training around it, something to make her feel more prepared.

The farther into the darkness they went, the more the place began to feel the same. More statues popped up at even intervals, cloaked figures holding weapons or carved flames above their hands. Mo still didn't understand why this place would affect Ezra's magic, but it seemed like it had been built either for or by sunshapers.

Just as the timer in the top right corner of Mo's visor ticked to the fifteen-minute mark, Ezra stuck his arm out to stop her from going any farther. She was about to ask him what his problem was, but he tilted his head toward the floor.

Stairs dropped off just inches from the edges of Mo's boots, winding down into the dark. It looked an awful lot like that chasm outside, only this wasn't something meant to be crossed. A wall extended up beyond the stairs, blocking their path forward.

"Guess we're going down," Mo said, nudging Ezra out of the way to keep going.

The walls along the circular stairs were carved with more images—of the stars and moon, the sun, eclipses, warriors armed with all kinds of weapons—and strange letters Mo couldn't read. Ezra ran his gloved fingers over them as they walked.

"What is it?" she asked.

"I've been forced to study a lot of languages, but this doesn't look anything like the common alphabets."

"It's probably some ancient, dead language." Wasn't that obvious to him? It was to her. "Let's go, Lyre."

"Just wait." He took a step back from the wall, then pointed his light at those peculiar letters. He pushed a few buttons on his gauntlet, then nodded at her. "Pictures," he said. "In case we need to take them to someone."

"Oh." Now Mo felt a little silly. "Good idea."

He chuckled, a smooth, low sound, as he skirted past her. "Never thought you'd give me a compliment."

"I can admit when someone has a good idea," Mo protested as she stomped after him. "Sometimes."

He laughed again, and Mo's chest warmed. She actually laughed a little too.

"And you think I'm funny?" he asked. "Where are Cass and Kynn to witness this when I need them?"

"Be quiet," she said, but the words held no bite. "Focus up. Let's get this done."

"Right," he said, amusement thick in his voice. "I think we're almost at the bottom."

The timer on Mo's visor said it was already twenty-two minutes into their hour. This place was even bigger than she'd thought. Whoever built it must have carved out an impossible amount of space under the mountains to achieve this.

Ezra reached the bottom of the stairs first, his helmet lighting up the next passageway spreading out before them. It was narrower than the one upstairs, and the ceiling was shorter too. No statues sat along the walls, nor were there inscriptions or carvings here. Just smooth stone and a door at the far end.

"There's more around this way," Ezra said as he moved toward the narrow space behind the stairs. "But most of it is blocked off. It looks like part of the tunnel collapsed."

"Because that makes me feel so much safer down here," Mo muttered, and Ezra laughed again. "Let's check out whatever's this way, then head back. It's taken us long enough to get here."

In fact, it had been too long since she'd heard from Kynn or Cass. If they'd tried to reach out, Mo's visor would have gone off. She tapped a button on her gauntlet and switched back to the team comms channel.

"Cass? Kynn?" She waited. No response. "Cass?"

Just as Mo's heart began to beat faster, a garbled, static-filled reply came in. "We're here," Cass said. More static, then, "Bad connection."

"Yeah," Mo said. "You good?"

"Good, but nothing yet," Cass said. "See you soon."

That was good enough for Mo. She moved back to her channel with Ezra. "They haven't found anything yet."

"So I heard," he replied. "I'm beginning to think this was a waste of time."

"At least we ruled it out," Mo said, following him as he strode toward the closed door on the far side of the corridor. "Maybe we can even take those pictures to Bas're and see what she can tell us."

"Maybe." As he neared the door, Ezra slowed. He pushed on it, but it didn't budge. "Do you see a way to open it?"

Mo searched the wall closest to her, but there were no buttons, levers, or switches. She felt along the stone for any imperfections but found none. Ezra did the same on his side and grumbled a curse as he came up empty-handed.

As much as it might have been a long shot, Mo decided her next idea was worth a try. "Stand back," she said.

"What?"

"Stand back, Lyre."

Ezra hesitated, then circled behind her. Mo focused on the well of power deep in her core, the way it swirled and pulsed if she really listened to it. She pulled on that energy, concentrating it in her hands before letting it out with an explosive, silent command. Purple tendrils slammed into the metal door. It didn't fly off the hinges, but its front was dented, and there was a clear gap between it and the wall.

"Shit," Ezra said. She glanced back to find his head tilted slightly to one side. "That's one way to get in."

"Any other obvious things you want to point out?" she asked. "Or will you just try to open it so I don't waste all my energy?"

"Damn," he said with a laugh. "Fine. Here." Ezra moved to the door again, leaving just enough space that he could kick it. After a few attempts, it swung open. He turned to Mo and motioned for her to enter. "Ladies first."

As she shoved past him, she muttered, "Shut up."

The door opened into a relatively small alcove that held only an unlit brazier and another door. Mo groaned as she looked at the timer on her visor again. Thirty-three minutes had gone by already.

"Fuck me," Ezra said from behind her.

He sounded almost out of breath. From kicking one door in? Mo expected more stamina from a Vanguard.

"We trying that again?" she asked.

"No."

"Tired already?"

"No," he said again. "My magic—"

Mo reached for her hilt. "Lyre—"

"No." He shook his head. "No, I have it controlled. But it's even worse down here, *in* here. I think ..."

"The pictures," Mo said. "The statues. The ones wielding fire. I get it. Something's up."

Ezra moved toward the unlit brazier near the door. Flames roared to life over his palm, and he guided them in place. As soon as the brazier lit, he snuffed out his magic and shuddered.

The ground rumbled, and the door began sliding open.

"Good work," Mo said.

"Two compliments? I'll remember this day forever, Cevi."

"Your ego's already inflated enough. That's the last one you'll get for a while." She nodded toward the fully open door. Darkness waited beyond. "Come on."

She stepped in first. The chamber was small, maybe large enough to fit six men Ezra's size. In the center was a stone pedestal, untouched by time. And in the middle of that pedestal?

A gold and black hilt, not unlike one Mo might find at a high-end weapons dealer's shop on a planet like Aerilia. Onyx stone was inlaid into the gold, swirling around the entire hilt like smoke curling up from a fire.

"Shit," Ezra whispered as he stopped beside her. "Is that it?"

"How should I know?" Mo asked. The professor's notes hadn't said *what* this supposed gods-given sword looked like. "I assume so. Or something people think is the sword. We should grab it and leave."

Ezra reached for the hilt. As soon as his fingers curled around it and he lifted it from the pedestal, the ground shook.

Mo whirled. The door slammed shut with a thud. The ground rumbled again. She tapped on her gauntlet to contact Cass and Kynn, but all she got was static before everything went black.

Chapter 32

"Fuck." Ezra slammed the hilt back down onto the pedestal, but the door remained shut. He hadn't been able to see a brazier before their suits cut out. He yanked his helmet off. "Cevi?"

"I couldn't get in touch with Cass or Kynn," she said. Her voice wasn't muffled, so she must have taken her helmet off too.

It was the first time he'd ever heard panic in Mo's voice.

Ezra let go of the tight control on his magic, welcoming his fire as it flooded his veins. It was a relief, like releasing a pressure valve. A spark danced above his right palm, illuminating just enough of the small space to see there was no brazier or torch or anything on this side of the door to unlock it.

Mo's eyebrows knitted together. "I'll try using my—"

A sharp crack echoed through the room as the ground shook again. Were they under attack?

"No, Human, you are not under attack," said a deep, resonant voice. It was all-encompassing, like thunder during a bad storm, making the inside of Ezra's head rattle around.

"What the fuck was that?" Mo asked, whipping around in a circle. Nobody else was in the room with them.

"I have had many names," that voice said, *"but you know me as Krytix, Eternal One of War and Destruction."*

Mo laughed. It was a low, full-body laugh that made her whole frame shake. "Alright, so I've lost it," she said. "Is there a speaker in here somewhere? Someone's fucking with us. Probably whoever wants to kill you, Lyre."

But Ezra's body tingled with awareness, with *magic*. He breathed in slowly, and that power burning under his skin grew. It wanted to expand, take hold. If he let it, the small flame above his palm would turn into a raging inferno. It was only with great control and effort that Ezra managed to keep it from exploding.

"This is not a joke, Silver-Haired Human," that voice—Krytix?—said. *"I am real."*

"Then show yourself!" Mo called, reaching for her hilt.

"I cannot, nor can you attack me."

"Of course I can."

"I do not exist in your plane," Krytix said.

"Prove it!" Mo shouted toward the ceiling.

Ezra didn't believe in the Eternal Ones. He didn't believe in any of it. But the way his entire being hummed with unfamiliar energy, the way he felt so intrinsically connected to this temple, had to mean something. It seemed impossible. Unfathomable. And yet ...

"I think it's him," Ezra said.

"Bullshit," Mo snapped.

"He is right," said Krytix. *"I will show you."*

An invisible force snuffed Ezra's fire out. Darkness swirled around him and Mo. The ground fell out beneath them, and Mo actually stumbled and grabbed Ezra's arm. He tugged her to his chest and wrapped an arm around her, trying to hold her in place as the world spun around them both, tossing them around like they were just leaves in the wind.

And as suddenly as it started, it stopped, replaced by a sky-high view of the very temple they were in. It was as if they were on a ship, looking down on the planet's surface. It was like they were floating, yet they were standing still.

Impossible. Completely impossible, but Ezra couldn't deny it was happening.

"What's going on?" Mo asked. "What is this?"

"*I told you, I am Krytix,*" the god said again. "*Eternal One of War and Destruction. You have entered my sacred temple, and you have taken the Star Eater. Who are you?*"

"Commander Sergeant Ezra Lyre, Vanguard in the Federation Space Command," Ezra said. "And Mora Cevi, bounty hunter."

Mo shoved him, but Ezra held on tight. He didn't think they'd fall—didn't know how they would if a god was doing this—but he wouldn't take that risk.

"*Ezra Lyre and Mora Cevi,*" Krytix said. "*Why are you here?*"

"We came looking for answers," Ezra said, "about why someone is trying to kill us, and why they want your sword."

Krytix hummed, but it sounded more like powerful ship engines firing up. It surrounded them, swallowed them whole.

"*Who seeks to kill you, Ezra Lyre and Mora Cevi?*"

"We don't know," Ezra said. "But they want that sword. They want all the artifacts, it seems."

Ezra certainly hadn't been sold on the idea that these things existed, let alone that the gods were real. If Mo hadn't been there next to him, he probably wouldn't have believed any of this was happening. He'd call it a hoax. But it was as real as anything he'd ever felt.

"It might be the Ascended," Ezra said. "Do you know about them? And the Federation?"

"*Mortal wars do not concern me,*" Krytix said.

"Is that a yes?" Mo asked.

"*Yes, Mora Cevi. I know of your squabbles.*"

"If these artifacts are real, we're fucked," Mo said. "It's going to turn into something far worse than a squabble. People are already killing to get them."

Darius had said Ezra wasn't prepared for what was coming. Was this it? An escalation in violence thanks to these god-touched relics? He didn't know what they were capable of, but if anyone controlled them, disaster surely waited on the horizon.

"I agree, Ezra Lyre," said Krytix.

"You can read my mind?" he asked.

"We know and see most things."

"Most, but not all?" Mo asked.

"As I said, I am not on your plane, Human."

"Why not?" Mo asked. "If you're real, what happened to you? Where'd you all go?"

The image of the temple began spinning again. It was like a transmission being rewound and replayed, the image shifting from that barren, desolate landscape to one filled with lush vegetation and humanoids dressed in dark robes.

"My siblings and I once walked among you," Krytix said. *"We aided mortal beings, gifting them with magic, and in return, they served us. But all was not well among our kind."*

The image turned again, from the peaceful forest to violent volcanic eruptions, the vegetation being replaced by fires and lava and ash. Again the vision shifted, from those volcanoes to violence across planets, thousands of them, as if Ezra could see and know all that had ever happened. His head pounded in time with his heart.

"Chaos spread throughout your galaxy, thanks to my sister, Ikna."

Ikna? Ezra had never heard of Ikna. There was Krytix, and then there were Evlos, Eternal One of Creation and Knowledge, and Voxarus, Eternal One of Mystery and Death.

"Ikna is the one of Change and Chaos," Krytix said. *"She holds sway over the most unpredictable forces in the Universe, across all planes. She seeks to disrupt the natural order."*

"Why don't we know about her?" Mo asked.

"Because she is responsible for what you see now," Krytix said. *"Many of our siblings died in our fight against her. Evlos, Voxarus, and I worked hard to defeat her, locking her away in a prison among the stars before she could give her magic—chaos magic—to any mortals. But this weakened us greatly, and she managed one last feat."*

The wars playing out before them disappeared in a blink, replaced by shadows and smoke. A slew of magical pulses tingled against Ezra's skin, and then four items appeared. A much larger version of the purple crystal they'd seen on Miduna. *"The Genesis Crystal,"* Krytix said. The gold and black hilt Ezra had just touched. *"The Star Eater."* A disc glowing with green energy. *"The Void Key."* And finally, a crystal bleeding red. *"The Chaos Shard."*

The items disappeared, and Ezra's mind stretched with the vision, as if watching the objects being flung across the galaxy. Mo tensed in his arms.

"All are dangerous," said Krytix. *"Ikna managed to send our artifacts away from us, the very things that helped us imprison her. We were too weak to get them, so we tasked trusted mortal champions with finding and protecting these items for us as we went into our slumber again."*

That explained the sword being hidden in the bowels of an abandoned temple, but why was no one guarding it now?

"I do not know why my order has abandoned this place," said Krytix. *"But now that I have awoken, I felt the pull of my sword again."*

The world shifted around them, and solid ground formed under their feet. They were back in that chamber, and Ezra was able to summon his flames again. As he did, he took in Mo's wide, concerned eyes.

"So why don't you come get it?" Mo asked.

"I cannot," Krytix said. *"Not yet."*

"Then we should destroy it," she said. "If it's really powerful enough to cage a god. We can't let the Ascended—or anyone—get it."

"It's neither yours to destroy, small Human, nor possible," Krytix said. *"Just as it is not yours to use."*

"How do we know any of this is real?" Mo asked. "How do I know this isn't just some elaborate projection?"

"Some things require faith," Krytix said.

"Yeah, well, I like a little evidence before I start trusting disembodied voices."

"Belief without evidence is foolish, and I can tell you are no fool, Mora Cevi. If what I have shown you did not convince you—"

The ground rumbled beneath their feet, but the image didn't change this time. The ceiling shook, too, and small pieces of debris and dust fell around them.

"It is too late," Krytix said. *"This once sacred place has been discovered."*

"We're under attack, you mean," Mo said.

"Yes. The temple is under attack."

Fuck. "The Ascended?" Ezra asked, his pulse roaring in his ears.

"All I know is this," Krytix said. *"The stars are sundering. Ikna is awake, and she* will *return. She will seek vengeance. You must protect the Star Eater, and you must find my siblings' artifacts. Not everyone will be your ally in this fight."*

And just as quickly as Krytix had appeared, the pressure in Ezra's body released.

"Krytix?" Mo shouted. "Hello?"

"I think he's gone," Ezra said. The chamber door rolled open. "Or, I guess he's gone now."

"What the fuck was that?" Mo cried, spinning around to look at the open door. Only darkness awaited outside. Even the flame Ezra had put in the brazier earlier had been snuffed out. "Was that really a god?"

"I don't know for sure, but I think so."

She huffed. "Now what?"

"It sounds like Ikna wants to finish whatever it was she started back then," Ezra said.

He wished Krytix had revealed more. Actually, he wished the god had never spoken to them at all. Ezra was *not* interested in whatever he'd stumbled into. Whatever his team had stumbled into. But as the temple shuddered again, and as something exploded in the distance, Ezra knew he had no choice. He was in the thick of it, and if he had to find these artifacts to prevent whatever it was Ikna wanted, then he would.

"Get your helmet," Ezra said.

Mo shoved her helmet back on. Ezra did the same.

He snatched the Star Eater off the pedestal again, then grabbed Mo's hand and ran for the exit. She swore, then swore again as the door slammed shut right behind them. They'd barely made it out in time.

Mo tore her hand away from his, furiously pushing buttons on her gauntlet. "Cass? Kynn?"

No response came through Ezra's comms other than a mess of static.

Shit. He had no doubt Cass and Kynn could take care of themselves, but still. They needed to reconvene, and they needed to get the fuck out of there.

Another muffled explosion sounded in the distance. More debris fell from the ceiling. Ezra double-checked that he had the Star Eater safely attached to his belt, then bolted for the stairs. Mo followed him. Their comms weren't working at all, between them or with the others.

Ezra had been in worse situations. They could get out of here. They had to.

His heart pounded in his ears with the effort of the run up the winding stairs. He forced himself to take in even breaths, just as he'd been taught. He was a Vanguard. He did not forget his training.

As he cleared the top of the stairs, Ezra skidded to a stop. Up ahead, far down the corridor, the colorful glow of energy weapons lit up the darkness. One of the doors had been blown open, but the other was still standing. *Fuck.*

Mo nearly slammed into him, grabbing his arm as she steadied herself. "Oh, fuck," she said. Ezra could barely hear her through the chaos of the fighting ahead or her helmet.

Mo frantically pushed several buttons on her gauntlet, and static filled Ezra's ears for a moment before Cass shouted, "Mo!"

"What's going on?" Mo asked, her breathing labored.

"Looks like the Federation and the Ascended," Cass said. "We've got eyes on them."

"How close are you to the ship?" Ezra asked.

"Close," she said. "We can get there."

"Go," Mo said. "Start her up. We're on our way." Then, to Ezra, she said, "We fighting our way out or what, Lyre?"

"Seeing as we have no fucking choice," he said, "yes."

The Ascended were bad enough, but the Federation? That did not bode well. Either they knew he'd disobeyed orders to stop his investigation and were looking for him, or they were hunting down these artifacts now too.

Maybe they always had been.

Ezra couldn't focus on that right now.

"Stay on me, Cevi," Ezra said. "Don't get separated."

It sounded like she scoffed, but another explosion rocked the temple. They just had to get out of there. They just had to make it a half klick back to *The Revenant*, and then they could figure out what was going on.

Ezra charged forward. He unhooked his hilt but didn't ignite his blade. Not yet. He only would if he had to. He didn't check to see if Mo was behind him; he had to trust she would follow orders, especially now.

As he ran, Ezra tried to count how many soldiers were fighting in the grand hallway. There were at least a dozen, but in the darkness and the chaos of energy blades and blaster fire, he couldn't get a good read. Maybe it didn't matter. He would only retaliate if attacked first.

An Ascended soldier jumped out from behind one of the statues they passed, his purple spear casting an eerie glow over his white armor and illuminating the Ascended's sigil, a stylized star rising above a curved horizon. The soldier was massive, far bigger than any of the Federation species, as many Ascended were thanks to their frequent use of genetic engineering in the military.

The Ascended attacked. Ezra ignited his blade, parrying quickly. Their weapons clashed in sparks of gold and purple, Ezra attacking with such force that the Ascended stumbled back. He dodged Ezra's next assault, just in time to parry Mo as she barreled into the fight. Mo twirled out of the Ascended's way, leaving an opening for Ezra. He advanced. The Ascended parried again, a growl erupting from behind his mask.

Ezra moved in again, alternating parries and attacks, dodges and swings, as he still tried to keep track of Mo's white blade amid it all. She danced in whenever she had a shot, but the Ascended blocked everything. Ezra roared, frustrated, as their weapons clashed again.

They did not have time for this.

"His left side—" he started.

"I know."

White flashed through the air as Mo circled to the Ascended's left. Her blade glowed brighter, then sliced through the man's armor and the middle of his torso, stopping halfway across. He didn't even scream as he dropped to his knees, then toppled over, unmoving.

Mo sprinted for the fighting near the doors, and Ezra followed hot on her heels. Maybe, with his armor, it would at least prevent the Federation from attacking them.

She skidded to a stop as another huge Ascended soldier jumped in her path. Ezra spun around her, blocking the strike with his fiery shield. Mo circled in front of it, slicing their open side again.

On and on they continued, dodging where they could and attacking where they had to as they moved for those doors. Ezra's mind zoned in on the fight, as it always did, tunnel vision as he waded through the violence and bloodshed. It was the only way to the other side.

A path nearly straight through the two sides opened up. Mo ran. Ezra followed. Someone shouted at Ezra—someone from the FSC—to ask where he thought he was going. Well, shit. So they thought he was running from the fight. Vanguards didn't do that.

He'd worry about it later.

Outside was a mess of black soot and red blood, bodies of the fallen and reinforcements trying to pile in through the half-open doors. Mo slashed and dodged, taking the brunt. Ezra tried to get to her, but she was swarmed as she got closer to the bridge.

"Behind me, Cevi!" Ezra yelled.

She fell back, her hand pressing the armor between his shoulders. Ezra unleashed the magic burning in his veins, still humming with the intensity of Krytix's temple. A swirl of fire erupted around them, like they were the sun emitting impossibly hot flames. Ascended and FSC alike put space between themselves and Ezra's fire. He continued on, picking up the pace once he was sure Mo was moving with him. They blazed their way past the reinforcements on the bridge in a blur of flames and heat.

Rows and rows of Ascended and FSC shuttles had landed in the clearing beyond the bridge, though *The Revenant* remained largely alone on its own side of things. More shuttles dashed through the red sky, as did small attack ships from both sides.

The Revenant's cargo doors were still open, the ramp still down, but the engines were kicking up black dust and sending out waves of heat that called to Ezra's magic. He made a beeline for it but stopped as Mo cried out and swore.

He skidded to a stop, kicking up more soot. Mo was sideways on the ground, her thigh smoldering. She'd been shot.

Fuck.

"Cass, Kynn, we need cover!" Ezra yelled through comms. "Now!"

He put his blade away, grabbed Mo's, and scooped her up. She protested weakly, something about "killing him" if he didn't put her down. Ezra barely heard it as his blood pounded in his ears and he watched *The Revenant*.

Cass came down its ramp, her opalescent armor gleaming in the red sunlight. She lowered her rifle, took aim, and fired at something behind Ezra. She fired again and again, presumably hitting her targets given Ezra was able to make it to the ship without being attacked.

He hustled up the ramp, still holding Mo close to his chest as he and Cass burst into the ship's lower deck. Cass began the lockup sequence, and Kynn lifted the ship off the ground before the doors even finished closing.

"Go, Kynn!" Cass yelled into her mic. "They're onboard."

The doors locked as Kynn punched it. Ezra managed to keep his footing despite the change in speed and headed for crew quarters. Cass followed, slamming her fist on the button that opened Ezra's door.

"I need to go help Kynn," she said. "Take care of her."

"I will," Ezra said.

Mo began to protest again.

"Shut up, Mo," Cass snapped. "I gotta go." And then she was gone.

Ezra set Mo down on his bed, then ripped his helmet off. Mo yanked hers off too. Her usually pale skin was flushed red, whether from anger, exertion, or embarrassment, Ezra had no idea. Maybe all three. She wheezed and dropped her head back against Ezra's pillows.

As he tore his gloves off, Ezra knelt next to the bed. "Let me look."

"Leave me alone," Mo hissed.

"You'd rather have a fucking hole in your leg than let me look at it?" Ezra asked. "Fuck, I knew you were stubborn, but this takes it to another level."

"I don't like to be touched," she said, a weak excuse if Ezra had ever heard one. Her breathing turned ragged and labored. "Shit. Fuck me."

Whatever—or whoever, and Ezra had a very good guess as to who—had made Mo so resistant to help was truly a pain in Ezra's ass. All he wanted to do was help her, save her. She was beginning to sweat, and her skin had lost all its color. He'd seen this before, the shock of taking a laser straight through the body.

"Cevi," Ezra said, lowering his voice. "Mo, look at me."

Her chest shuddered as she met his gaze. Her eyes were half closed, cloudy.

"I need to heal you."

"But—"

"You heard Cass. You want me to make her come down here?" As if on cue, the ship rumbled, like they'd just been hit. "She's probably manning the guns right now," Ezra said. "You really want to take her away from that? Risk the ship?"

Mo deflated more, as if that were possible. "No."

Ezra reached up, hesitating before he brushed some loose hairs away from Mo's eyes. "Relax," he whispered. "I've got you, alright? I've got you."

Mo sagged into his bed. Ezra ripped off her legguards and the leggings underneath. She didn't even protest. Her skin was bleeding and raw, torn open by the blaster hit. He couldn't tell for certain, but it looked like it had come awfully close to a major vein, if not hit it and cauterized it again.

Ezra slid both hands onto her exposed skin, pulling on that ever-present warmth that lived near his heart and in his belly. Fire ignited in his veins, like that of a hearth on a cold winter night. It was gentle but true, and his hands began to glow with that same heat. The same intent, healing and comfort rather than the destruction so easily wrought by fire.

Her skin began patching itself together, scarring over pink and a little jagged. Healers with more training could usually prevent such things, but Mo was stuck with him. He had the raw power but not the finesse. A scar was better than her dying.

Ezra pulled his hands away, now sticky with her blood. He glanced up at her, but instead of finding an irritated expression, he found her unconscious. He checked her pulse; she was still breathing. She'd need to sleep it off.

Ezra pressed his forehead to the mattress and squeezed his eyes shut. "Fuck."

The knot in his chest loosened. They were all safe. Him, Cass, Kynn. Mo was safe. Not without a few scratches, but alive, tucked away in his bed, on her ship. He reached up, brushing stray hairs from her face again. And even when his fingers lingered on her cheek, she didn't stir.

Ezra sighed. He didn't know what to think of the last few hours.

Maybe he didn't need to figure it out in that moment. They still had to get away from this system and away from both the Ascended and

Federation. They had to buy themselves time while they figured out what was going on with the Eternal Ones.

But first, Ezra really needed to wash his hands of Mo's blood, and he really needed to talk to Cass and Kynn. They had so much to figure out.

Together, they'd make a plan.

Chapter 33

Ezra wasted no time. He hustled to the lavatory, washed his hands, and scrambled to the top deck, all three sword hilts jostling against his hip as he went.

Kynn and Cass were both in the cockpit. Outside, where there would usually be the vast blackness of space, were ships. Dozens of ships, some as small as *The Revenant* and others so large they could house thousands of soldiers. They were Federation and Ascended alike, an amalgamation of classes and colors, all taking aim and firing at each other.

"Can we use this as cover to get out?" Ezra asked. Somehow, nobody seemed to be targeting them specifically.

"Trying," Kynn said from the captain's chair.

Not seeing Mo there was strange. Ezra really hoped she'd sleep the injury off and leave the rest of them to sort this out. The last thing they needed was an angry and injured Mo trying to climb up to this deck.

The ship banked right, then left again, not so extreme that Ezra lost his footing but enough that his stomach dropped. He gripped the backs of both seats, his knuckles turning white.

Cass fired at an oncoming vessel, a starfighter built for speed and attack power. Ezra had seen ships like that hundreds of times fighting the Ascended. Her shot landed, and the ship exploded, creating an opening for them to fly through.

Again and again, Kynn pivoted the ship and Cass took aim. She was an incredible shot, both on the ground and in space. Ezra hated not being able to help, but she had it covered.

They broke through the last lines of Ascended starfighters, some kind of half-assed blockade to get in or out of the system. As soon as they cleared them, Kynn said, "Firing up the hyperdrive."

"Better be quick," Ezra said. "They'll recover fast. Ascended always do."

"Heard." Kynn's fingers flew across the dashboard, tapping colored buttons and flipping switches. "Ready?" he asked Cass.

She punched a few things into a screen on her right, then said, "Yup."

"Where are we going?" Ezra asked just as the ship jumped into hyperspace. There was always a strange lag, an unsettling feeling in Ezra's body as the speed kicked in. But it was gone almost as quickly as it came on, and he relaxed.

"The Eibos System," Cass said.

"Isn't that far from here?" Ezra asked, racking his brain.

"Sure, but we don't want to stay close," Kynn said. "And there's a planet there, Zerathia, where we can get repairs done."

"We need repairs?" Ezra asked.

"Ship took a few blows; they disabled one of our shield generators while still on the ground," Kynn said. As Ezra's eyebrows furrowed, Kynn added, "Relax. I rerouted everything. We'll be fine until we make it to Zerathia."

"Relax?" Ezra cried. "We need full shielding!"

"So it's not ideal," Kynn said, "but it's just a blown regulator within the power relay. If we stay vigilant, we can make it to Zerathia in one piece."

Ezra did not like the sound of this, not one bit. But what was there to do? They had to get away from all that fighting on Mor'vex. He had to trust Kynn to get them to their destination in one piece.

Cass slumped back in her seat and huffed. "How's Mo?"

"Sleeping," Ezra said. "Bad shot to the leg. I healed it. Doesn't look pretty, but she shouldn't have any lasting damage."

Cass nodded once. "Alright, good."

"What the fuck happened in that temple, Ezra?" Kynn asked.

"I was going to ask you what the fuck happened outside," Ezra retorted. "Maybe Mo should be here for this."

"Why?" Cass asked.

"So I don't sound like I'm completely out of my mind," he said. "Let's just say everything I thought I knew about the Universe may not be true. We spoke to Krytix."

"What?" Kynn and Cass yelled at the same time.

"See? It's better if she's here to corroborate. I hardly believe it myself."

Kynn pinched the bridge of his wide nose. "Fuck me."

"We need to consider that we're being followed," Ezra said. "Someone on the ground may have been tracking our ship. They'll realize soon enough that what they want isn't in that temple, and they might realize we have it."

"You found it?" Cass asked. "The sword?"

Ezra unclipped the hilt from his belt and held it out for the other two to see. "Apparently it's exceedingly dangerous, especially in the wrong hands. Krytix warned us not to use it at all."

"Better our hands than their hands," Cass murmured.

Although he didn't like the thought of having such a weapon, Ezra was inclined to agree. The Ascended certainly couldn't have it, and at this point, he didn't know what to think about the Federation.

"You should go get some sleep," Cass said, startling Ezra. "And take a shower."

Ezra examined himself. His armor was covered in black dust, and he was a sweaty mess otherwise. Besides, his body was ready to give out. The exhaustion came out of nowhere and nearly knocked him over.

"You two good up here?" he asked.

"Yeah," Kynn said. "We'll wake you when we need you. Should be about a day before we get to Zerathia if I can keep pushing the hyperdrive, maybe a little longer."

Ezra reattached the Star Eater to his belt. "Wake me as soon as you need me. Don't hesitate."

They waved him off, and Ezra forced his tired body down to the lower level. He never got exhausted like this, not even after a fight. Maybe it was just everything finally catching up to him.

Ezra returned all three swords—his, Mo's, and the Star Eater—to the weapons locker. Then he took extra care removing and cleaning his armor before setting it inside his room. Mo hadn't moved at all; she lay in the same position on his bed. He checked her pulse again. It was steady and strong.

Satisfied, Ezra grabbed a change of clothes and headed into the bathroom. It was claustrophobic, the shower barely big enough for him. He made quick work of the task, then changed and started back for his room.

Shit. Mo was in there. And he didn't dare move her, not now.

But her room was empty, and he'd wake up before she did. Surely she'd understand, right? A clean bed was a clean bed, and he needed to sleep as much as she did.

Ezra shoved down his reservations and went upstairs into her empty room. Everything was tidy. There were very few personal effects, other than a few pictures of Mo, Cass, and Kynn in frames studded to the wall.

A data pad sat in a charging station on her bedside table too. Otherwise? Nothing of note.

Though he'd just gotten dressed, Ezra stripped off everything but his black boxer briefs before collapsing into Mo's bed. The gray sheets smelled like her, just a faint hint of vanilla and cinnamon. He hadn't even realized that's what she smelled like, but it was. He hardly got close enough to her to be able to tell. She never let him get close enough.

He hadn't thought that bothered him, either, but after today? Working with her, making her laugh like he had? Yes, they traded jabs often—her more than him—but something about today had made him ...

He wanted more of that. He wanted to get closer to her, not just to figure her out but because he liked her laugh. He liked *her*, prickliness and all. They made a good team. She'd probably try to kill him if he ever told her that.

Besides, there was so much they still needed to untangle. But nothing could be done right now. Even if he'd gone over their encounter with Krytix in detail with Cass and Kynn, there was nothing to do until they fixed the ship and determined their next destination.

So, Ezra listened to the hum and familiar bumps of the ship as he settled the blankets over himself, and soon, blissful, peaceful sleep pulled him under.

CHAPTER 34

Mo woke with a gasp, visions of fiery worlds, endless battlefields, and elusive gods still dancing in the dark recesses of her mind.

Her fingers curled around unfamiliar blankets. Her eyes took in an unfamiliar room.

No, not entirely unfamiliar. The spare quarters on *The Revenant*. She was on the ship. And with the way it bumped and hummed, she guessed they'd jumped into hyperspace.

Fuck. Her leg hurt. Not in the way it usually did. Mo brushed the spot with her fingers, finding a raised, slightly uneven scar and dry blood.

Right. Ezra had healed her.

Fuck me. She didn't even know where that shot had come from. Maybe a sniper? Maybe just someone getting off a lucky blaster shot. She hadn't exactly been covering her back, other than Ezra's flames, which weren't a perfect shield. They couldn't be in a situation like that. Magic never was.

She blinked against the fog in her mind. Ezra's armor was on the floor just a few feet away, and it was then that Mo realized a piece of one of her legguards was missing. *When he healed you,* she reminded herself. Of course he'd had to take it off.

Mo pushed to her elbows, then swung her legs over the side of the bed. With painfully slow precision, Mo unhooked the rest of her armor, then set it on the floor next to Ezra's. His was clean while hers was covered in soot and blood. She'd need to fix that later.

But now, she needed a shower and a gods damn coffee to wake up. Then she would check in and see where they were going and what had happened in the time she'd been asleep.

Mo trudged upstairs and went straight for the bathroom. She tried to keep the shower as quick as possible, not only because the water was freezing but because she'd been unconscious for far too long. How long, exactly, she wasn't sure, but any length of time was too much given what had just happened on Mor'vex.

Krytix. The Ascended. The fucking Federation.

There was a lot they needed to figure out.

She skipped washing her hair. All that mattered was that all the blood and sweat was gone. Mo turned the water off, grabbed a towel, and cursed herself. She hadn't grabbed clean clothes, and there was no way she was putting her old ones on before they were washed at least twice.

Grumbling, she dried off, then wrapped a fresh towel tighter around herself. She hurried the short distance to her room and pushed the button to open it. She fumbled around for the light switch. As soon as she flicked the lights on, Mo stifled a curse.

Ezra was in her bed.

He was in her bed, lying on his side, hugging *her* pillow to his chest, and wearing nothing but his underwear. His torso and back were on display to her, a patchwork of colorful tattoos and faded scars.

When was the last time a man was mostly naked in her bed? Almost a decade, but that wasn't important.

"Just going to stand there, Cevi?" came Ezra's voice, raspy with sleep. He peeked at her over his shoulder, his black hair unkempt and almost wild now that it wasn't swept up in its usual braid or bun.

"I—"

He rolled over with a chuckle. "What a way to wake up." His gaze barely flicked to where she clutched her towel just beneath her collarbone. He focused on her face again.

Her cheeks burned, and something in her belly flipped uncomfortably fast. She was completely covered thanks to the nearly blanket-sized towels Kynn had insisted on buying for whenever he stayed on *The Revenant*, but Mo couldn't wrap her head around this.

Ezra, almost fully undressed, in her bed.

Herself, wrapped just in a white towel.

"If you wanted to say thank you for the healing," Ezra said, a smirk pulling at the corner of his lips, "there were a dozen other ways you could've done so that involved more clothing. Not that I'm complaining."

"What the fuck are you doing in here?" Mo snapped.

Ezra held his hands up, palms out, as he swung his legs over the side of the bed. "Before you throw me into the wall with your magic, I didn't want to disturb you while you were recovering. I needed some sleep." Mo's face burned even hotter when he didn't bother trying to cover himself up at all; his chest was full of tattoos too. "Didn't mean to scare you," he said, all traces of teasing gone. It was like he knew she would bolt. "I'll get out of your way. I'll wash your sheets if you want me to."

Her chest heaved as she watched him pull his clothes back on, those scars and tattoos disappearing in the blink of an eye. He gave her a tight smile as he slipped past her and headed for the door.

Mo turned on her heel. "No."

He paused at the threshold, thick eyebrows furrowed. "No?"

"Don't wash them. You ... you have to buy me new ones."

It was decidedly not her best comeback. It hardly qualified as one at all. She didn't know why she was so slow or so flustered. Maybe she hadn't slept long enough.

His lips twitched. "Oh?"

"Gods forbid I touch them again," she said, trying to infuse some hardness into her voice. But it came out all choked and wrong.

"Right, what a travesty *that* would be."

Ezra turned to leave again. Despite the words building in Mo's chest, she couldn't get them out. She owed him even more now; he'd saved her life twice. And while he didn't seem to think much of it … she did.

She let him go. When her door slid closed, Mo's head rolled forward until her chin touched her chest.

"Pull yourself together, Cevi," she whispered. There was so much they had to untangle, and so much she needed to catch Cass and Kynn up on—if Ezra hadn't already.

She'd let herself have a few minutes, but then, she'd go back out there, Ezra be damned. She wouldn't be embarrassed just because they practically saw each other naked. It was bound to happen on a ship this small. She'd accidentally seen Kynn naked more than once, and they could laugh about it. Why wouldn't she be able to laugh about it with Ezra too?

Mo took her time getting changed into a loose tunic and leggings, then her tall leather boots. She even made time to brush out her hair and braid it in one long plait. She hardly felt any more prepared to go out there, but Cass and Kynn would need her, and she refused to be shy around Ezra.

With one last deep, cleansing breath, Mo headed out into the hall. It was quiet. Ezra was nowhere in sight. She moved through the ship toward the cockpit, grateful to find that her thigh only twinged a little. She'd received sunshaper healing a couple of times before, and that pang always seemed to work itself out eventually.

Up ahead, Cass and Kynn were both at the helm.

"Hey," Mo said as soon as she approached the open doors.

Cass jumped out of the copilot's chair and pulled Mo into a tight embrace. She hugged her back. Neither were prone to hugging, but after all that? Mo could use one, and she guessed Cass could too based on the haunted look on her face as she pulled away.

"How long was I out?" Mo asked as Kynn and Cass traded places. While Cass and Mo weren't prone to long embraces, Kynn loved them. She leaned into him now.

"Only a few hours." Kynn ran one large hand down the back of Mo's head and tugged lightly on her braid, something he used to do all the time when they were kids. "Before you freak out—"

"What happened to my ship?" Mo asked. Nothing too terrible could've happened if they were indeed traveling with the hyper-drive—which they were, based on the rumbles and the blue-silver glow filling up the view screen.

Kynn laughed, a low, warm sound. "Damn, that obvious?"

"Why else would I freak out?" Mo asked.

"Fair enough, I suppose." With a sigh, he squeezed her shoulder, then returned to the helm. "One of our shield generators was disrupted before you and Ezra even got to the ship, but I've got a workaround until we get to Zerathia."

"That's where we're going?" Mo asked.

"Figured we needed repairs and some distance between us and … whatever that was," Cass said.

Mo nodded. It was as good an option as any other. "Were either of you hurt?"

"No." Cass shook her head and crossed her arms over her chest. "No, we weren't."

Mo pressed her lips together. "And Ezra?"

Not only had she not thanked him for saving and healing her, but she hadn't even bothered to ask how he was feeling or if he'd been injured.

Mo knew she was standoffish with everyone except Cass and Kynn, but Ezra deserved better than that. He'd proven time and again that he was on Mo's side, even if only for the contract. Even that much was rare in her line of work. People wanted the job done, not to be a team.

"I'm fine, thanks," he called from behind her. "Figured we need to talk about what happened back there."

"That was a complete cluster," Mo said, ignoring the way her face warmed as Ezra's arm brushed hers. He put a little distance between them and dropped into the seat behind Cass's. Mo took the one behind Kynn.

"Ezra said something about Krytix?" Cass asked, pointedly ignoring Ezra and looking at Mo.

She nodded. "I haven't really had time to consider it but ... but we definitely were speaking with someone who wasn't on site. He claimed to be Krytix."

"More than claimed," Ezra said. "Showed us impossible things, things only an Eternal One could show us." When Mo began to protest, he added, "Nobody has holograph technology that advanced. Not in the way we were taken to ... well, I can't even describe it."

Mo couldn't describe it either. It had been a completely out-of-body experience, and yet she'd been able to feel Ezra as he held her tight during whatever it was Krytix had done in that room. If it really was a god, could it have been some kind of astral projection?

"I suppose that's true." She fidgeted with the hem of her tunic before meeting Cass's questioning gaze. Kynn was still focused on the navigational systems. "Krytix showed us the past, as if we could see everything all at once. He told us ..."

So much. Krytix had told them so much and yet so little. Mo didn't even know where to begin. Couldn't fathom any of this being true, although the more she sat with it, the less she could deny that it had all happened. Krytix had told her there was no belief without evidence, and he'd certainly given her *some* evidence to work with.

As much as she wanted to deny it and call all this a hoax, Mo couldn't. Not with what she'd seen and experienced firsthand. As Ezra said, nobody had tech that could create the same results. And even if they did, something in her gut told her that really was Krytix they'd spoken to. There was something ... *different* about what she'd felt in that temple.

"Basically, it looks like the Eternal Ones are real," Ezra said. "Krytix, Evlos, and Voxarus fought a battle long ago to lock their sister, Ikna, away in a prison."

"Ikna?" Kynn asked.

"Eternal One of Chaos and Change," Ezra drawled. "Apparently she scattered these relics—there are four, and it seems like hers is linked to chaos magic. Krytix said they did not allow her influence among mortals for a reason. She's trying to come back and start something, but the other Eternal Ones are still trying to gather their strength again."

"Huh," Kynn said.

"What?" Cass asked.

"Krytix suddenly appears and paints himself as the good guy in all this?"

"Chaos magic doesn't exactly sound like something that should be unleashed among the populace, Kynn," Cass retorted.

He shrugged one shoulder. "Fair. This is just a little hard to believe."

Mo understood. A lifetime of nonbelief didn't just disappear thanks to one experience, one Kynn hadn't witnessed directly. They'd all need some time to wrap their minds around this.

"Did he give you anything else?" Cass asked.

"He said we need to find the artifacts," Mo said, "and keep the Star Eater safe. It's too powerful and destructive to fall into the wrong hands." She glanced sidelong at Ezra. "We should destroy it."

Ezra huffed. "Krytix said it's impossible."

"Nothing's impossible."

"He said it wasn't yours to destroy."

"It sure is if it's on this ship," she said. "I won't have some godsforsaken artifact blowing us out of hyperspace and into the Void."

"I'm with Mo," Kynn said. "Destroy the damn thing. Attach some explosives to it, then send it out the airlock."

"I thought you didn't believe any of this?" Cass asked.

"If there's a chance this is all real and that sword is that dangerous, I don't want it near us."

She scoffed. "Fine, but I'm with Ezra. If Krytix is real, and this Ikna is trying to break free from her prison, couldn't the sword be important? I doubt mortal weapons are going to take her down."

"Fuck me," Mo muttered. That was a very good point. "I don't want it falling into the hands of the empires, though. Who knows what they want to do with it."

"I know what the Ascended will do with it," Ezra said. "They'll use it to wreak havoc on the Federation."

"And the Federation?" Kynn asked, turning in his seat to look at Ezra. "What the fuck were they doing there at the temple?"

Ezra shifted uneasily. "I don't know. Maybe looking for me and got swept up in things? I did disobey orders."

"Disobeying orders shouldn't result in them sending a fleet of ships after you," Cass said. "One or two? Sure. Not that many."

"You may have a point." Ezra ran a hand through his tousled hair. "Maybe they started looking into everything we told them when we turned over my former team. Maybe they were able to figure out what we did and went looking too."

"Which means they want the artifacts," Mo said.

"Or to stop the Ascended from getting them," Ezra said. "Maybe *that's* why they were there. Fleets will be deployed the second they detect Ascended ships in our borders."

"You still believe the government isn't connected to this?" she asked, frustration building in her chest and throat.

"I'm just saying I don't know what to believe," Ezra said. "My entire worldview has collapsed in the last few weeks. I'm a little turned around. I mean, the fucking Eternal Ones are real."

Mo scrubbed at her face and groaned. "Don't remind me."

How had she taken a simple contract to hunt down some traitors and it turned into ... Mo didn't even know what it had turned into. Something far bigger than herself. Something cosmic.

Exactly what she didn't want or need.

At least Ezra was being normal about the towel thing. Her one saving grace in this conversation.

"What about the Genesis Crystal?" Mo asked, forcing herself to look Ezra in the eye. "The one Krytix showed us was a lot bigger than what Darius stole."

"How much bigger?" Cass asked.

"Several times its size."

"One of the professors said the crystal was thought to have been on Veronis originally, right?" Kynn asked. "Maybe someone stole a fragment of it. Maybe that's all that's left."

It *was* possible someone had gotten just a piece of it off planet before the Ascended attack. "But why leave it there, in a cave near a ruined temple to Evlos?" Mo asked.

"I don't know," Ezra said, though with the way he stared ahead, he seemed half lost in thought.

Maybe it wouldn't be a bad thing that only part of the Genesis Crystal still existed. Mo would rather that whoever had stolen it only had *part* of a powerful, divinely infused artifact rather than the whole thing. They would need to keep digging through Valtor's notes to see if he had any other theories.

"So ..." Kynn let the silent question hang in the air.

"We go to Zerathia and we regroup," Cass said. "Repair the ship, then figure out where the next artifact might be."

"And get my armor patched up," Mo said. "Back on Aerilia, Bax and Amane said there were more calls for treasure hunters. Obviously the Ascended and Federation know about all this. Maybe it's not just warlords out to get it. We should stop in with the Syndicate base when we land and see if they have any contracts out for something like this."

"None of this answers why I was a target to be killed," Ezra said.

Mo shrugged. "We can still assume familial connection, right? Valtor found the Star Eater, so maybe someone was trying to eliminate anyone even moderately close to him."

It didn't entirely make up the full picture to Mo, but unless there was some enormous piece of information Ezra was withholding—and she didn't think there was—it was the only thing that currently made sense.

Ezra scratched at his beard, then said, "Fine. Sounds like the best plan we have."

"It's really our only option," Kynn said. "No way are we making it back to Miduna with some of our shields down. I'm not risking it. Especially not if we're possibly being tracked."

Mo's heart jumped to her throat. Right. Of course. There'd been so many witnesses to their escape. And whoever was hunting both Ezra and the artifacts may very well have had eyes on that battle. But there was nothing to be done about it now.

"We stay sharp," Mo said. "If we have to split up, we stay in pairs. Protect the Star Eater, and keep our heads low until we can move on."

The others echoed their agreement, so Mo considered that settled. They could figure the rest out when they got to Zerathia.

CHAPTER 35

The rest of the flight to Zerathia was uneventful, which Mo would gladly take. She'd forced Cass and Kynn to get some sleep, but Kynn had returned to the helm after only a few hours to do the same for Mo.

And she'd taken it. Something about Ezra's healing had made her so tired she could barely think. It was probably in everyone's best interest that Kynn had made her go back to bed.

Of course, Mo couldn't help but notice that her sheets smelled like Ezra, like evergreens. But she'd never admit that she liked it.

As they soared down toward the surface, Mo finished getting dressed. She thought her black tunic and leggings washed her out a little, especially with how pale she still looked after the attack on Mor'vex, but she wasn't going to get vain now. She just needed to gather some information, after all. Mo grabbed her silver hilt from off her bed and strapped it to her belt, then went to see if Kynn needed any help.

He must not have, because before Mo even made it halfway to the command room, the ship was touching down. She hated not knowing precisely where they were, so she joined Kynn anyway. Outside the cockpit, the first rays of sunrise were just starting to brighten the sky.

Zerathia was a small planet—some might barely consider it a planet at all—with dense forests, tall mountains, and mild weather. Mo had only been here a couple of times before, always a pit stop and never the real destination, just like now.

The main city—if it could be called that—was Titan's Gate. Apparently the original inhabitants of this world had thought some of the mountains framing the city were a portal to the Void, that mythical place people went after death.

Mo used to shake her head at such stories, but after talking to Krytix ...

Maybe this once really had been a place for the Eternal Ones to visit. Voxarus *was* the Eternal One of Mystery and Death. Maybe, if they were real, they did have portals like Titan's Gate.

She decided not to consider it more than that. It would just distract her, and besides, Krytix had said he and his siblings were too weak to return to Mo's "plane" of existence. It wasn't like Voxarus would come charging out of the mountains. She needed to focus on her problems, not hypotheticals.

Mo and Kynn worked in silence as they powered down *The Revenant*. Kynn had, apparently, found a Syndicate-approved shipyard on the edge of Titan's Gate, which was good enough for Mo. They'd get a better rate, and whoever worked here would be able to find whatever parts they needed to fix the shield generator.

As Cass and Ezra joined them in the cockpit, Mo tried not to look at Ezra. She wasn't angry with him, but things just felt ... different. Mo didn't like different.

"I was thinking," Mo said quickly, "that Cass and I could go to the Syndicate outpost here and look for any information about these treasure hunting contracts. You two"—she gestured to Kynn and Ezra—"can fix the ship."

"I'm really not a mechanic," Ezra said.

"So?" Mo asked. "Kynn can teach you." When Ezra didn't look convinced, she added, "Look, if this contract keeps dragging out, you're going to be on board for a while. Let him show you a few routine things."

The right side of Ezra's mouth curled up. "You're actually going to let me touch your ship?"

Something in the way he said it made Mo meet his gaze and hold it. "Yes."

Ezra turned to Kynn. "Hopefully I don't fuck anything up too much."

"I won't let you," Kynn said with a laugh.

She trusted Kynn with *The Revenant*, and as much as the whole "learn about the ship" thing was an excuse to not have to take Ezra with her to the Syndicate outpost, Mo actually did want him to learn. They all needed to be able to pitch in. She knew she'd have to let him fly the ship eventually, too, but she wasn't ready for that just yet.

"Shall we?" Cass asked, nodding at Mo.

"We'll be back," Mo called over her shoulder.

After Cass grabbed a couple of guns from the weapons locker, they headed out into the cool morning air. Mo relished the breeze on her face and the sun in her eyes. Zerathia wasn't quite the same as Miduna, but the towering trees and low-profile buildings made her feel more at ease.

She and Cass had spoken a bit more about the Mor'vex situation in private, but neither could come up with an answer more reasonable than Krytix being real. And now, what else was there to say? Rehashing it would do them no good, nor did talking about it out in public seem wise.

"You sleeping alright?" Mo asked.

"Getting enough," Cass said. "I can't say it's quality sleep, given ..." She gestured vaguely at the street in front of them.

"I get it," Mo said. "Believe me, I do." When Cass's stomach growled, Mo said, "We should pick up a few more things for the ship before we leave."

"I'm dying for some fire pepper rolls."

Mo smiled. Fire pepper rolls were one of Cass's favorites, a Luxinae dish cooked up at one of the best market stalls in Kalyndra. Mo liked them too; a meal based around roasted vegetables and fiery sauce was hardly ever *bad*, no matter what form it came in. Cass had learned how to almost perfectly recreate the thin, crispy wrappers a couple years back, and it was an easy dish to make on the ship.

"Whatever you want," Mo said. "We'll make time to get it."

This contract hadn't been easy on either of them, and Mo felt like she wasn't checking in with either of her friends enough. Sure, she was whenever she could steal a moment alone with them, but having Ezra around—and dodging empires—was making it increasingly difficult.

"Would Kynn want anything if we stop on the way back?" Mo asked.

Cass shrugged. "Oh, you know he's never picky. Maybe the stuff for gleamroot stew? He was complaining about his stomach earlier."

"Sure," Mo said. She also wondered if Ezra would want something in particular, but she had no idea what he liked.

The deeper they went into Titan's Gate, the more crowded the streets became. This was the heart of the small city, filled with street vendors, banks, and restaurants. People gathered around to buy their breakfast and head off to work, a mix of species from across the Federation. No matter where you went in the Federation, whether crowded city-planets or small outposts, people were just people. Yes, they all had their own traditions and histories, but they also all wanted mostly the same things: good food, a decent wage, and a peaceful life.

Mo didn't think that was too much to ask for, but life wasn't that simple. She knew that all too well.

Cass took half a step behind Mo as a large Ivari man with lavender skin brushed past her. She rolled her eyes. Mo snuck a peek over her shoulder. The man kept retreating, and more impatient pedestrians forced Mo to face forward again.

They turned down a few side streets, the layout of the city clear in Mo's mind. One more turn, and they exited onto a quiet pedestrian avenue. Several doors down was a familiar door and insignia, one Mo would be able to pick out anywhere across the Federation.

She and Cass approached the dark steel door. Cass knocked twice, then a third time. A slat opened near their eye level.

"Business?" came a worn, gravelly voice.

"The Phantom and The Demon, Miduna chapter," Cass said. "Looking for work."

A small camera popped out near the doorframe. It extended on a long, thin arm, and a blue light nearly made Mo squint. It had taken years of practice for her not to flinch whenever she encountered a light like that.

Whoever was on the other side of the door said, "Enter."

The slat closed, and the camera disappeared. The heavy door slid open, and cool air and darkness awaited inside. Mo relaxed a fraction as she and Cass entered the Syndicate base. It wasn't their home base, and Ril Staga wouldn't be there, but it felt less risky than any other place they might visit on the planet.

"Job board's up in the common room," said the bouncer, a tall Sorthian man with dark brown skin and a shaved head. "You know how it works."

Mo nodded. If they decided to take any jobs from the board, they'd have to clear it with the base's leadership. Not that they were there to actually take on any jobs. They just needed to poke around and see if there was anything about treasure hunts or ancient artifacts, and this was the best place to do it.

They wandered leisurely down a few halls, ignoring most of the other well-armed members they passed, from Humans to Ivari to Luxinae and more. Mo felt naked in just her casual clothes, but she'd had to leave her armor behind for repairs.

The dark corridor gave way to a warmly lit common room filled with tables and other sitting areas, a bar on the far wall, and a dormant fireplace. It was impersonal, with hardly any decoration, but that was how the Syndicate always was. Impersonal.

A crowd of members gathered around the large screens to the right of the fireplace. Those were the job postings, no doubt fresh with the early morning hour.

Cass and Mo moved that way, lingering near the back of the group for just a moment. Three Humans, two Ivari, one Sorthian, and three Luxinae. Mo didn't recognize any of them at first glance, which meant she likely hadn't ever had a run-in with them.

"Move!" Cass barked, shoving her way into the fray.

A few of the other members grumbled their frustration, but Cass was small, and she was able to easily maneuver in while letting the others still take their look at the board. Mo stayed near the back.

One Ivari and the Sorthian moved away at the same time, splitting off from the group and going to take a table near the middle of the room. Perhaps they were partners like Cass and Mo? One of the Humans muttered something under his breath as he turned on his heel and stomped out of the room, while another joined the three Luxinae in hushed conversation as they stepped away. That left just the one other Ivari up near Cass.

"Looking for something specific?" they asked her.

"Something interesting," Cass said, not deigning to look at the other bounty hunter. She tilted her nose slightly up into the air. "Everything's been boring lately."

The Ivari chuckled. It was a pleasant, friendly sound. "It has been, hasn't it?" they asked. They ran a hand over their four long braids, then focused back on the screen. "Both of you are bored?"

Mo stepped up to join them. "Not much challenges us these days."

"I expect not for The Demon and The Phantom," the Ivari said with a smile.

Mo raised an eyebrow.

"I'm Sen," they said. "Second-in-command here in Titan's Gate. It's my business to know who's coming in and out of the base."

Mo wouldn't have guessed. Sen was dressed casually in a simple white shirt and tight black pants. They only had one gun on them, and they wore no jewelry except for the small ruby earring piercing the point of one ear. Back home, Midunian Syndicate leadership liked to play up their role and wealth.

"Well, Sen, do you have anything that might interest us?" Mo asked.

"All that we have is posted here," Sen replied.

"Oh, now," Cass said, adding a distinct false sweetness to her voice, "we know *that's* not true. Higher-ups always keep the better listings private or delay them when they know the best hunters will be around."

Sen sniffed. "I don't know what you're talking about."

Mo clicked her tongue as she stepped in closer. "We've been in this game a long time, Sen. We know how the Syndicate operates."

"Perhaps I have some extra listings in my office. Again, what kind of challenge are you looking for?"

"Something"—Cass pretended to think, pursing her lips before tossing her purple-tipped hair over one shoulder—"adventurous. Something that sounds impossible."

"We like the impossible," Mo added. She wasn't about to dare ask specifically about treasure hunting jobs, but hopefully Sen would catch their drift—if there even were any such contracts.

"I'll see if anything's come across my desk in the last half hour," Sen said, then turned and strode out of the common room.

Mo wanted to relax, but she forced her posture to stay strong as she focused on the job board. Cass would've signaled to her if there had been anything like what they were looking for, but Mo double-checked anyway. There were contracts to hunt down murderers and thieves—nothing new there. Contracts for security details, especially on cargo vessels. Nothing about treasure or even anything to do with any universities, like the one they'd taken back on Miduna.

"Well?" Cass asked. "Ask around?"

Mo supposed it wouldn't hurt. That was how she'd heard about this in the first place, just speaking with Bax and Amane. But she had some rapport with those two, a decently friendly history. She knew no one in this room—probably this building—and she didn't care to. Besides, trust couldn't be built in one morning chat over coffee.

Still, Mo eased her way over to the bar, where a red-haired Human boy was drying cups. Mo remembered those days, as a young trainee and ward of the Syndicate, doing odd jobs and services around the base. She'd actually liked working the member bar, as it had given her a great chance to observe the full-fledged hunters. They'd seemed like such incredible heroes to her as a child, but now she understood the realities of the job all too well.

"Can I have two coffees?" Mo pulled a credit out of her belt and slid it to the boy. Drinks were free, but a little money went a long way in the Syndicate.

He grinned up at her but didn't say a word, just nodded and tucked the money into his pocket before getting to work. He set two clean mugs on the counter, then grabbed a nearby coffee pot. Steam curled up from the hot liquid.

"You know," Mo said, leaning across the bar and lowering her voice, "I used to be in your position, and now I'm one of the top hunters in the entire guild."

He tried to hide a smile as he set a bowl of sugar on the counter. "Really?"

"Really," she said. "I bet you hear a lot of talk when you're working, don't you?"

He nodded.

"Heard anything about treasure hunters?" Mo asked, then pulled out another credit and slid it to him as discreetly as she could. "Just between you and me."

The boy made quick work of putting that money away, too, before he set a bottle of cream next to the sugar. "Some," he whispered. "I heard a guy a few days ago talk about joining an expedition looking for treasure. Everyone else thought he'd lost his mind."

Mo dumped a few spoonfuls of sugar into both cups as she asked, "Do you know who he was?"

He shook his head. "No. I'm still learning. A lot of people come in and out."

Damn. Mo would've loved a name. "Did he have anyone else with him?"

"I don't know," the boy said sheepishly.

"That's alright," Mo said. What was she going to do, yell at a kid? "Thanks."

After pouring cream into both their mugs, Mo took them back to where Cass was chatting up the three Luxinae sitting at a round table.

"What in the Void is someone from Miduna doing on this side of the Federation?" one of them, a woman with silky white hair, asked as she stared up at Cass.

"Decided to cut our vacation short and get back to work," Cass said with a shrug. "You know how it is. Time is money."

One of the other Luxinae, a man with black hair and snowy skin, lifted his glass in a one-man toast. "Can't remember the last time I took a vacation."

"It's necessary sometimes, isn't it?" Mo asked.

"I wish," said the white-haired woman. The third in their group, another woman, signed something in quick, fast movements. The white-haired woman nodded. "She says it's not something we can afford."

"Maybe your next contract will be decent," Cass said with a sympathetic smile. "Though everything on the board was trash."

The man snorted. "You can say that again."

"We've heard about some—" the white-haired woman started, but the man glared at her.

"Didn't mean to intrude," Mo said. "We're not exactly looking for something too tough right now. Can't make our first job back from vacation too hard." She forced a laugh, and Cass smiled along with the lie.

"There's talk," the white-haired woman said. "Of big bounties coming from Mobos M67."

"Not familiar with it," Mo said, the truth this time.

Just as the woman was about to respond, Sen appeared in the doorway. They whistled, then jerked their head for Mo and Cass to join them in the hall.

"Nice talking with you," Mo said, setting her untouched coffee down on the table and ignoring the confused looks the Luxinae gave her and Cass. "Good luck with everything."

They strolled out into the corridor, where Sen was waiting in the shadows. With a huff, they passed a small data stick to Cass. "Here," they said. "Four of the biggest bounties up for grabs right now. Federation-wide too."

Mo's eyebrows furrowed. That was unusual. Clients often reserved their contracts for specific branches in just a few systems; the work was often local, so it just made sense. There were some deviations, of course, but rarely were contracts Federation-wide.

"I know for a fact you're not the only ones looking for something like this," Sen said. "All interested parties have been encouraged to try. After all, having some of our best on it is better for the guild in the long run."

Cass tucked the data stick into her belt. "Much appreciated for passing on the information."

Sen waved them off, grunting and mumbling something under their breath as they headed back into the common room. Mo really had no concern for them. They'd done their job, and now Mo had to do hers. She needed to figure out if one of these contracts had something to do with the Eternal Ones.

CHAPTER 36

Ezra groaned as Kynn continued explaining the way the shield generators on *The Revenant* worked. While he was admittedly flattered that Mo wanted him to learn about the ship, he'd always been bored in school. This was no different.

"For fuck's sake, man," he finally said, cutting Kynn off. "I don't need to know how it all works. What do we need to do to fix it?"

Kynn grinned at him. "Nothing. Mechanic's working on it."

"Mechanic?" Ezra groaned again. When had they hired a mechanic? He'd left the bounty hunter alone for all of ten minutes after Mo and Cass had headed out. "Then why'd you force me to listen to this for the last hour?"

"Because it's fun."

Ezra huffed. Of course. Kynn seemed to like everything to be fun despite the fact that life was sometimes just horrible.

"How long will the repairs take?" Ezra asked.

"Syndicate members get priority here, but they still said the better part of the day."

"Mo's going to hate that."

With a shrug, Kynn said, "What're we gonna do? Can't make them work faster."

"I don't like being stuck here with the Ascended *and* the government so close by," Ezra said. "Seems like we're just waiting for trouble to come to us."

"Better we're here than blown up in the middle of space because our shields failed, eh?" Kynn asked, slapping Ezra on the shoulder. "C'mon, let's get some lunch."

"It's barely nine in the morning," Ezra said as he followed Kynn out of the small engine room. "Isn't it time for breakfast?"

"I already had breakfast," Kynn said over his shoulder.

"When could you possibly have had time for that?"

"Before we landed."

Ezra had no interest in eating, but he wasn't going to deny Kynn whatever it was he wanted. He was obviously handling all this better than Ezra was. Someone needed to keep a cool head. It went far against his Vanguard training, but Ezra's mind kept wandering off, to the threat of them being tracked, to the idea of Mo and Cass out in Titan's Gate on their own, to that experience with Krytix, to so many things.

"If I remember from my few months in Vanguard training," Kynn said over his shoulder, "aren't you supposed to be more observant, Commander?"

As soon as they made it to the top deck, Ezra dropped into a seat at the kitchen table. "Yeah, just tired after everything. I'll pull myself together before we get back out there, if that's what you're worried about."

What he needed was a damn cup of coffee—and thankfully, Kynn started brewing some.

"Not worried, just pointing it out." Kynn rummaged through the kitchen drawers and cabinets, then sighed. "We need to do a supply run before we leave. Damn near out of anything good to eat."

"We can go once Cass and Mo are back," Ezra said. "I don't know if Mo told you, but she renegotiated the contract. I'll be covering everything."

Kynn turned around slowly, lips pursed and eyebrows raised. "She did what?"

"She—we—renegotiated the—"

"I heard you," Kynn said. "That's just not like Mo. To her, a deal's a deal. And she doesn't like accepting help."

Ezra shook his head. "Oh, believe me, I've noticed *that*."

Kynn smirked and turned back to the coffee pot. "How'd you get her to do it?"

"What?"

"I mean, I know it wasn't her idea," Kynn said over his shoulder. "And it seems like something you'd push for."

"She didn't seem to want to take all the soltherin I gave her, so I convinced her to renegotiate, that I'll cover all supply and medical expenses." Ezra scrubbed at his face and sighed. "I just wanted her to have what she needs. Why is she like that?"

Kynn chuckled. "Haven't we already had this conversation? Or one similar? That's Mo. It's hard for us to get her to accept help too. It's going to get her fucking killed one day if she's not careful."

Ezra swallowed thickly, his chest hollowing out as Kynn said it so matter-of-factly. He knew Kynn didn't mean it to be so casual; he was just telling the truth. Because being that stubborn certainly could get Mo killed. Ezra just hoped nothing like that came to pass.

Why did it bother him so much? He'd barely been able to stand the thought of working with bounty hunters a month ago, and now here he was, practically one of them and worried for their safety.

But they were decent people, and he liked them, all three of them. Of course he didn't want any of them to die.

"What was it like when Krytix spoke to you?" Kynn asked.

Ezra flinched, nearly slamming his knee into the bottom of the table. Shit, he really was on edge. This was not like him at all. He sat up straighter and ran his hands through his hair.

"Loud," Ezra said. "Loud and all-consuming, like a thunderstorm in my head."

Kynn carried two mugs to the table and set one down in front of Ezra. "You don't think it could've been fake?"

"I really don't," Ezra said.

"Why?" Kynn dropped into the chair across from him.

"I could feel it in my body, not just Krytix but even the way my magic reacted to that place," he said. "The way it consumed us, both of us. The way the voice sounded in my head. The images Krytix showed us of the past, the way he spoke of this Ikna and chaos magic."

"But that could all be fake," Kynn said.

"I guess we can't know for sure," Ezra conceded. "But it felt so real. My gut is telling me it's real."

"And you didn't believe in the Eternal Ones before?"

"No." Ezra had hardly given them much thought outside of whatever had been required learning in school when he was young. It had just never seemed possible to him, gods like that. "No, I really didn't."

Kynn nodded slowly.

"You're obviously skeptical," Ezra said.

"It's just hard to fathom." Kynn stared down at the coffee cup clutched between his hands. "Especially what Valtor's notes said about the Genesis Crystal having once been on Veronis. I can't help but think that's what got my home—our home—destroyed. Or that someone has not just a piece of Veronis with them but probably wants to use it for something bad."

"This whole 'underground ancient relics market' angle is starting to look implausible," Ezra said as Krytix's warning rang in his head again. *You must protect the Star Eater.*

"Don't I know it." Kynn took a long sip of his drink, then sighed. "I guess even if I'm skeptical, you and Mo think Krytix is real, so that holds some weight."

"Some?" Ezra asked with a forced laugh.

"More from Mo than you, honestly."

Ezra actually laughed that time, but it was tired. "Fair enough."

Loud footsteps sounded on the lower deck, and soon, Mo was climbing up the ramp. She stopped in the middle of the common area and crossed her arms over her chest. Cass slipped in behind her, dropped a bag on the counter, then waltzed into the command room.

"What are you two doing?" Mo asked. "Is the ship fixed?"

"*Damn*," Kynn said as he stood and turned toward her in one fluid motion. "You think I'd just slack off like that?"

"Actually, yes," she said. "And you roped Ezra into it."

"You're giving me more credit than I deserve," Ezra said lazily.

Mo's gaze flicked to him, then back to Kynn. "Seriously, though, is it fixed?"

"Mechanic's working on it," Kynn said. "Too complicated for me to do. They needed to source a couple of parts. Said it'd take the better part of today."

"Damn," Mo muttered.

"Learn anything?" Ezra asked.

"Maybe," Mo said. "Cass is going to check it out. Come on."

Even though Cass had only had a momentary head start, she already had the holo table up and running in the command room. "Obviously we couldn't ask directly about treasure hunting or anything we've discovered the last few weeks," she said as she typed furiously on a small keyboard. "But the base's second-in-command said a few such contracts are floating around. There were whispers of it, too, among some of the hunters."

That was really all the proof Ezra needed. "Where are the contracts based?" he asked as he came to a stop between Mo and Kynn.

"Several places, unfortunately for us," Cass said as she kept typing. "Four places, more specifically."

"Which four?" Kynn asked.

"Mobos M67, Andarix, Eryndor, and Trinias."

"How the fuck are we supposed to pick one to go to?" Kynn asked. "We have a one-in-four shot of getting it right. Should we—"

"We can't split up," Mo said quickly.

"I'm already pulling in Valtor's notes and setting the computer to cross-reference them for any of these planets, or descriptions similar to these planets based on the Syndicate database," Cass said.

"And how long will that take?" Ezra asked. On top-class Federation ships, an algorithm like that wouldn't take more than a few hours to run. But given *The Revenant*'s age ...

"Should have it sometime tonight," Cass said.

"And that's faster than doing it ourselves?" he asked.

"When you consider the computer can actually track every minute detail about these planets in the database and compare them to the professor's notes," Cass said, "yes, I think it's much faster."

Maybe she had a point.

"Can't leave until then anyway," Kynn said. "Mechanic's still working, remember?"

"Fuck," Ezra muttered.

Mo shifted uncomfortably. "Alright," she said. "We let the computer do what it needs to do while the mechanic works. We use the rest of the day to restock whatever we need, then we leave as soon as we have our answer and our shields."

Ezra hated being sitting ducks. It wasn't that they couldn't protect themselves if they were found, but he didn't like the thought that they were waiting amid a bunch of civilians.

But what choice did they have? At least if they could maximize their time and energy, they could leave as soon as they knew where they were going next. And in the meantime, he'd send a silent plea to Krytix to not let any violence fall on this quiet community.

Chapter 37

It had been a long day of shopping, certainly not Ezra's preferred way to spend time. It seemed neither Mo nor Kynn enjoyed it much either, but it had to be done.

Probably the worst part of it all was that Mo wouldn't let him pay, as previously agreed. She'd argued that with the FSC showing up on Mor'vex, it was likely they were tracking Ezra's accounts and movements. It made sense, unfortunately, and Ezra had insisted they keep a tally of what he owed her once everything settled down. There was still the risk of the FSC realizing Ezra had continued his contract with the bounty hunters, which could lead to Mo's accounts being tracked, but not every risk could be avoided.

Mo and Kynn had paid for as much in cash as they could. They'd gotten Mo's legguards repaired, followed by a visit to the local market for food—and a bottle of Ivari whiskey, at Ezra's request—then a hunt for a new water recycling system filter. When Mo had gone off to restock some of their medical supplies, Ezra had slipped away, just for a few minutes, to buy her a new set of sheets—paid for with the personal credits he had on hand, of course. Neither she nor Kynn had seemed to notice his absence or his additional bag.

They'd returned a couple hours before, and now, the sun had long since set. Ezra was lounging in bed, contemplating not just getting that bottle of whiskey but how to give Mo the new linens, when muffled shouts came from the hall outside his quarters.

He shoved to his feet and rushed out, only to find Mo muttering and cursing to herself as she stormed into *The Revenant*.

"Problem?" he asked.

"The mechanic says she won't have our parts for two days."

"Shit."

"Yes, shit." Mo rubbed at her knuckles, as if trying to soothe some ache. "It's all shit!"

"Hey." Ezra's soft words pulled her attention back toward him. "It's shit, but what else can we do? We need the parts."

"I know we do."

"Is there another shop we can get them from?" Ezra asked.

"I don't know Titan's Gate that well. Probably. But everything's closed for the night."

"Then we go out first thing in the morning."

"I don't like just sitting here."

"Then let's go for a walk," he said. "Because I don't either, and Cass is trying to get some sleep, so you yelling probably doesn't help her."

Frowning, Mo looked toward the ramp leading upstairs. She wilted, as if she couldn't believe she might've disturbed her friend. "Where's Kynn?" she asked.

"Watching the radar and waiting for the algorithm to tell us where to go."

"Why weren't you with him?"

"Because he said he wanted to be alone."

"Oh." Mo glanced at Ezra, then at the open doors behind her. "Fine, I guess we can go for a walk. Not far, though."

"No, not far."

When Mo nodded, Ezra went back into his quarters, shoved on his boots, and grabbed his saber too. Titan's Gate was quiet, but he wasn't taking any chances.

Mo double-checked that the weapons locker was secure before they headed out. None of them had touched the Star Eater since Krytix had let them take it, and Ezra wasn't sure that they should. Not when they knew so little about what it could do.

"We should've asked him," he said, mostly to himself.

Mo frowned. "Asked who what?"

As they reached the bottom of the ramp, the ground under Ezra's feet shifted from metal to tightly packed dirt. He shook his head. "Sorry. I meant we should've asked Krytix about the sword. What it does more specifically."

"I've been thinking about that too," Mo said. "I'd really like to know what the fuck is on my ship. Too bad we can't just contact him."

"Right," Ezra murmured. "Do you think it was only at that temple that we could? Do we need to go back?"

"How should I know?"

Mo's tone wasn't rude or biting; it sounded more like a joke. She stared straight ahead as they went out the shipyard's rear gate. With the yard being on the edge of town, that meant the gate emptied into the forest beyond the city walls. As they passed through, Mo breathed in deep the way some people would around a cup of coffee.

"You like the forest," Ezra said, more an observation than a question.

"It feels like home."

"Which home?"

"Both." She finally looked up at him. "Veronis was full of trees, just like this. Or, the part we lived in was, anyway. Cass, Kynn, and I all lived in the same town. All the kids would play in the woods together. But we three really bonded after ..." She toed the mossy ground with her boot. "You know where I'm going with that. Doesn't matter anyway."

"It matters if you want to talk about it."

She shrugged. "What's there to say that hasn't been said a thousand times already? I think a part of me will always feel like it's missing, but we've done alright for ourselves."

"I suppose you have."

They continued on, sticking close to the city wall and only walking its perimeter. Even just a hundred feet from that wall, the darkness of the forest ate up the light. Ezra wasn't afraid of the shadows, but he didn't trust that they wouldn't encounter more assassins—or worse—out there.

Mo sucked in an audible breath. "I'm sorry."

"What? Why are you sorry?"

"That you had to heal me the other day. I should've been watching our backs."

"We had to get the fuck out of there, Cevi," he said. "That's nothing to be sorry for. Speed was a priority."

"Maybe ..."

The way she trailed off left an uncomfortable pit in Ezra's stomach, but he didn't push. If he'd learned anything about Mora Cevi, it was that it was better to let her come to you.

"How's your leg?" he asked. He hadn't gotten to look at it since that initial bout of healing.

"Fine," she said quickly.

"Really?" He'd been watching her walk all day, and her gait seemed normal, no limps or anything out of the ordinary. "Because I can do more if you need more."

"The scar's a little unsightly," she said.

"Afraid I can't help with that. I've got the power, not the finesse. I wasn't trained in the subtleties of healing."

"I suppose a Vanguard wouldn't be," Mo said.

Ezra shrugged.

"I guess it's a good thing I've never been that vain anyway."

He laughed. "You, not vain? What's the deal with your ship, then? You're obsessed."

"Because that's the product of my work! There's nothing vain about taking care of your home *and* transportation."

"Maybe not," he said. "Admittedly, I was surprised you were going to let me help Kynn."

She stopped then and peered up at him. "Why?"

A few lightning bugs flashed around them and among the trees, creating a beautiful sparkle amid the shadows.

"Because you're very protective of that ship," he said quietly.

"You did save my life twice, Lyre. I can let you do repairs on my ship."

"That's how you repay me? Putting me to work?"

He'd meant it as a joke, but as soon as the word "repay" left his mouth, Mo flinched and started walking back toward the shipyard's gate.

"I'm sorry," he said as he hurried to catch up with her. The fireflies continued winking, as if saying hello to the trespassers. "You know you don't owe me anything, right?"

"Of course I do," Mo gritted out. "Like I said, you saved my life twice."

Ezra set a hand on her shoulder, making her stop. He circled around to her front. "And you've saved mine once and agreed to stick around to figure all this out," he said. "I think we're even." When she began to protest, he added, "But even if you hadn't done all that, I wouldn't say you owe me anything."

She crossed her arms over her chest. "A life debt is still a debt."

"Not to me. It's what I want, to help people." He swallowed thickly, then said, "To help you, alright?"

"I don't need your help," she snapped, shoulder-checking him as she pushed past.

She wouldn't get away, not that easily. Ezra didn't even know why this point was so important to him, why he had to *prove* to Mo that he meant no harm, that she could trust someone other than Cass and Kynn.

Ezra grabbed her shoulder again, whirling her around to face him. She glared up at him, eyebrows knitting together and forehead wrinkling.

"What?" She practically spat the word.

"Why won't you accept my help?" he asked. "Why do you think there are strings attached? You don't do this with Kynn or Cass."

"Because I trust them."

"You don't trust me?" Even in the darkness, Ezra could see Mo's chest heave as he said, "After I've saved your life?"

She pressed her lips together.

"Seriously?" he asked. "You don't trust me? After all this?"

He trusted her. He trusted all of them. He didn't want to take it personally, but how could she not see it? No, she hadn't known him as long as she'd known Cass and Kynn, but hadn't he proven himself?

"Fuck," he muttered when she still didn't say anything. "You really don't? How the fuck are we going to do what Krytix asked of us if you don't trust me? Why are you even still working with me?"

Mo averted her gaze to the forest, to the lightning bugs continuing their dance. Ezra didn't even know how they'd gotten onto this topic, but here they were. His heart sank with every second that passed and she remained quiet.

"Fine," he said. "Fine. Whatever. I'll see you back on the ship." As he began to brush past her, Mo's hand landed on his forearm. Glancing down, he found her focused on his face.

"Trust is ..." Her voice was tight. "Trust is hard for me, Lyre. It's not personal. It has nothing to do with you."

"Does it have to do with him?" Ezra didn't know where the question came from; it just slipped out.

Neither one of them needed to clarify who Ezra asked about.

Tallas Bara.

"Yes," Mo said. "Yes, it has everything to do with him. I wasn't always like this."

"What did he do?"

"Everything."

But what did that mean? Ezra didn't think he had a right to push, so he just set his hand on top of hers, where it still rested on his forearm. She didn't pull away, though she looked down again.

"He's a *bad* person," she said. "I don't mean bad as in questionable. He's also Veronian, and he's a talented fighter. He's a few years older than us and ended up becoming one of our trainers for a brief period. I fell in with him first. That shared connection ... he used it to get me—us—to trust him and work with him."

Ezra could read between the lines, especially with what Tallas had said that night on Aerilia, that he and Mo had been partners not just in bounty hunting but romantically.

"I was so young and new to all of this," she said. "So were Cass and Kynn. And I believed what Tallas told me, not just about Veronis but about bounty hunting, about how much he cared about the three of us and how he only cut us down—cut me down—to make us stronger."

Even in the darkness, the red creeping into Mo's cheeks was obvious.

"Tallas used us to make as much money as he could," she said. "He always split us up on contracts, taking me as his partner. That was how we went on for nearly two years. And when I finally stood up to him while in the middle of hunting an arms dealing gang on Aerilia, he shot me, then left me, Cass, and Kynn for dead."

Ezra's blood chilled. Kynn had hinted at the fact that Tallas had betrayed them, but even without the details, that was brutal.

"Doesn't the Syndicate have some rules about that or something?" he asked.

"Yes, but they didn't believe us," Mo said. "He lied. Told them he thought we were already dead after we 'all got separated.' Claimed it was a miracle we made it out. It was a small but dangerous arms dealer's operation we were breaking up. Stumbled into at least half his best fighters on Aerilia."

Ezra still didn't move his hand, and Mo didn't move a muscle.

"Do you know how I got my code name?" Mo asked. "The Demon?" He shook his head.

"I killed almost every last one of them myself, ripped half apart with my magic and killed the other half with my saber. Sixteen of them." Her voice trembled. "I didn't want to do it, but I had to. It was the only way I was going to survive and get Cass and Kynn out."

Ezra could almost picture it, a much younger Mo surrounded and unleashing herself. He didn't think that made her a demon. She'd done whatever she had to. A gang of arms dealers wasn't going to play nice.

"And they were only there because of me," Mo said. "Because I trusted Tallas. Because I let Tallas twist me around and manipulate me and use me."

"You didn't let him," Ezra corrected. "He abused you."

"Yes," she whispered, finally looking up at him again. "I hardly knew who I was anymore. I was young, and I was weak, and he didn't want me to be around Kynn or Cass if it wasn't for a job. And I wanted to please him so badly. I never thought he'd hurt me physically, no matter how loudly he yelled. But he tried to fucking kill me the second I stood up to him."

Ezra still had so many questions. So, so many. But understanding was starting to click into place in his mind. Why Mo was so defensive and prickly. Why she wouldn't let her guard down very easily, and why she was so adamant about protecting Kynn and Cass. Because she already carried around so much blame for something that wasn't her fault. The scars Tallas had left on her soul were still there years later, just like the scars the FSC and the Ascended had inflicted even earlier.

"You've saved my life twice," Mo whispered, tears falling down her cheeks. "You've saved me twice, and all I can do is be an asshole to you. I'm sorry."

Ezra pulled her into an embrace, wrapping his arms around her so tightly she could barely move. Mo went stiff, but after a few moments, she slipped her arms around his waist.

"You're not an asshole," Ezra whispered. "I haven't thought that about you in a long time."

"But you thought that about me once?" she asked with something between a sniffle and a hiccup.

"Yeah, but I'm pretty sure you thought the same about me," he said wryly. She laughed, and Ezra let her pull away as he added, "I'll kill him. If you want me to."

"Doesn't that go against FSC regulation or something?" she asked.

"When have I ever been a stickler for regulation?"

She laughed again, and it was like music to his ears. All he wanted to do was make her laugh now, make her forget about the past and all the pain it held. Even if just for a little while. Mo had continued on in the face of immense pain, more pain than any one person should have to suffer. But she was strong. She was a survivor.

He'd meant what he'd said about killing Tallas Bara. If the Syndicate wouldn't punish him or report him to the proper authorities, Ezra would take out the fucker himself. That was, if Mo didn't do it first, of course.

"We should get back," Mo whispered. "We need to be up early to find another mechanic."

"Right," Ezra said.

They walked back toward the gate in silence. Mo didn't seem open to talking more at all, and his head was spinning worse than it had been earlier. There was a lot for him to think about, maybe too much. Too much for one night, anyway.

"Lyre," Mo said, stopping just before she reached the shipyard gate.

The Revenant waited nearby, the lights in the cockpit still on. Kynn was probably up there working.

"Yeah?" Ezra asked, turning to face her.

"For what it's worth, I do trust you," she said. "As much as I can right now."

He gave her a tight smile. "I know."

"How could you possibly know that?"

Wasn't it obvious? She'd partnered up with him in fights. She'd trusted him to get them out of the battle on Mor'vex. She'd started letting him do more on the ship, and she'd just told him what was surely a closely guarded secret of hers.

He'd become so obsessed with hearing her say it, seeing her act more relaxed, that he hadn't realized she *was* starting to trust him. And given what he'd just learned, it would understandably be a while before she fully loosened up.

If she couldn't see that yet, she was just going to have to figure it out for herself.

His smile softened. "I just know."

"Asshole," she muttered.

"Come on, Cevi." He slung an arm around her shoulders and pulled her into his side. "Didn't you say it's past your bedtime or something?"

She shoved weakly against him, so he held tight. She didn't shove him again, and he felt her body relax as they approached *The Revenant*. As they stepped through the cargo doors, Mo slipped out from under his arm. Her pale skin was blotchy, and her eyes had reddened, almost like she was trying to hold back more tears. Maybe she was. And if she didn't want to share those tears, Ezra wouldn't make her. But he hoped she would. He wouldn't judge her. He hoped she knew that, but saying it out loud felt like he'd be drawing too much attention to it, and she'd probably hate that.

"So ..." She stopped at the bottom of the ramp. "Good night, I guess."

Ezra was about to ask if she needed anything, but ... "Hang on one second."

She gave him a strange look before he ducked into his quarters and grabbed the new bed linens he'd bought her. They were thin and crisp, like the ones already on her bed. He thought he'd done a decent job matching fabrics. The only difference was that these were light blue, not gray. In the hall again, he tossed them to her.

Her eyebrows furrowed. "What's this?"

"New sheets," he said.

She stared at him, lips slightly parted. "Right. Thanks."

As she headed to the top deck, Ezra ran both hands through his hair, tilted his head back, and sighed. Mora Cevi was getting under his skin—in the best way. He just hoped that tonight was a breakthrough rather than a setback, but he couldn't be sure until the new day.

He locked up the ship the way he'd seen Mo and the others do several times, then went to his quarters. He stripped his clothes off, left his saber on his bedside table, and collapsed into bed. He barely had a moment to wish he was in a different, bigger bed that smelled like cinnamon and vanilla before the night took him.

Chapter 38

Mo's life could not get any worse.

"What do you mean you don't have any parts?" Mo asked the Human man standing on the opposite side of the counter.

He scowled at her, his upper lip curling and revealing yellowed canines. "It's pretty simple, don't you think? I don't have *any* parts."

They were in a grungy old mechanic's shop on the outskirts of Titan's Gate, hardly the first place Mo wanted to be looking for a power relay regulator, but they were running out of options. She and Ezra had checked almost every shop on this side of town while Kynn checked the other side and Cass worked on getting her algorithm back up and running.

Because of course it wasn't just that they couldn't get their shield generators fixed in a timely manner. No, the computer had to go and take a shit, too, and Cass still hadn't fixed it by the time the sun rose.

Worst of all? Ezra was acting like the night before hadn't even happened. He was just being so ... casual. She'd *cried*. They'd *hugged*. And he hadn't said a damn word about any of it.

"What I think my friend is trying to say," Ezra said as he slowly moved toward the counter, "is that we can see your stock clearly from here, and you haven't even checked to see if you have what we need." He gestured toward the open door behind the counter, which led into a stock room filled with all manner of ship parts.

"Don't need to look," the man grumbled.

"You sure?" Mo asked.

"Positive."

"Why?" Ezra asked.

The man's thick eyebrows furrowed, and he folded his arms across his chest. "I don't serve Aerilians."

"You're not serving *him*," Mo said. "You're serving me. This is *my* ship we're talking about. I'm Midunian."

"Don't care," the shopkeeper said.

"Fuck me," Mo muttered, turning toward the exit and putting her hands on her hips. She had half a mind to pull her saber out and throw her weight around a little, but making a scene probably wasn't smart. They needed to keep lying low, until they could leave town.

"Not even if I pay extra?" Ezra asked.

"Nope." The man said it with such finality that Mo let out another low curse.

"You won't take perfectly good credits just because he's Aerilian?" she asked, but all he did was stare her down. "Fuck you," Mo snapped, then stomped back out into the open street.

She was so tired of dealing with people. She needed a long vacation in some far-off corner of the Federation where no one but Cass would bother her. Kynn would be allowed to join them. And Ezra ...

"We still have a couple places to check," Ezra said. "We'll find it."

"We needed it yesterday," Mo said, scanning the street. It was mostly empty at this time of morning, with most people either at work or school. Not that Titan's Gate was ever particularly crowded, but any time outside of rush hour was especially quiet.

When Ezra set a hand on Mo's shoulder, she tried not to flinch. "Come on, let's go. We'll be done soon." He steered her to their right, toward a shop with an open storefront and canopy extending out over a bunch of parts on the ground. "And who knows, if we don't have luck, maybe Kynn will have."

"Yeah, maybe," Mo muttered, though she didn't have much hope left. At this rate, they'd be stuck in Titan's Gate forever.

"Excuse me!" Ezra called as they entered the shop.

An Ivari woman was working behind the counter, her back turned to them as she reached up to the highest shelf for a part. She peeked over her shoulder, grabbed a small metal tube, and relaxed again. She straightened her gray tunic. "May I help you?"

Ezra finally dropped his hand from Mo's shoulder, and she almost missed his touch.

No. No, she did not.

"Yeah," Ezra said, "we're looking for a power relay regulator."

"How soon do you need it?"

"Now?" he asked with a lazy smile.

"What for?" the woman asked, grabbing a data pad off the counter and tapping it furiously with her long, thin fingers.

"Shield generator," Mo said, grateful to find her voice steady.

"Ship class?"

"It's an old FSC supply vessel, about thirty years old, but the shield generators are decently new, and it's outfitted with a Class 12 hyper-drive."

Frowning, the woman glanced up from her tablet. "Seriously?"

"Yes," Mo said. "Seriously."

Mo's upgrades to *The Revenant* had made it more than functional. Most ships were retired after a decade or two, partially due to the cost to upkeep older models and partially due to the changes in technology. Hyperdrives, reactors, and computers were getting stronger every few years.

The woman sighed a little and went back to whatever program she was rifling through. "Well," she said, drawing out the word, "I can get it for you."

"Outstanding," Ezra said. "Thank you."

"But," she continued, "it's in our shop over in Draxis Cove, about thirty klicks from here. My assistant can go get it, but you won't have it until this afternoon."

Damn. Mo had been hoping they could just walk out with it.

"That's fine," Mo said. "We'll take it. How much do we owe you?"

"Six thousand credits," the woman said.

Mo let out something between a groan and an unattractive choking sound. "What?"

"Six thousand," the woman repeated, glancing at Ezra. "Is that a problem?"

"It is when a fucking regulator is usually three thousand for a ship my size, no more," Mo said. "What kind of scam operation is this? Do you always rip people off?"

Ezra put his hand on Mo's shoulder again. She glared daggers up at him, but he didn't seem to notice.

"While my friend has a point about your price gouging," Ezra said smoothly, "we'll take it."

"What?" Mo hissed. That would nearly be the last of their cash.

"I can give you half now, then the other half when you deliver the part," Ezra said, holding the woman's pale gaze.

She studied Ezra for a long moment, then nodded. "Deal."

As Ezra began pulling credits from a pocket on his belt, the shop owner began tapping into her data pad. Once he'd laid out six small, silver bars, she nodded.

"And where should we bring the part?" she asked Ezra.

"The Syndicate shipyard."

She nodded again, and with that settled, Mo tried to walk out of the shop as calmly as she could. Spending large sums of credits on ship repairs never felt good, but this felt worse. It was like they were running against a stopwatch but couldn't see how much time was left until someone else got to the next Eternal artifact first. And if you wanted things done quickly, that usually came at a premium.

But double the cost? It just made Mo sick. The shopkeeper must have somehow sensed their desperation. Mo wasn't always great at keeping her expression neutral.

She wished the damn Syndicate shipyard could've sourced the part sooner. They always got a better price when using guild-approved vendors.

"We need to go to a bank," Mo said as soon as Ezra was within earshot.

"Why?" he asked.

"We're just about out of cash."

"So? We have everything we need right now."

"Because we don't know when we'll be able to get more. We might need it wherever we're going."

"I thought we weren't going to take out anything else to avoid being tracked?" he asked, lowering his voice as he closed the distance between them.

"Fuck," Mo muttered.

"You're really on a roll with that word today," he said.

"I don't like not having resources."

"We have them."

"Directly in our possession."

"I don't know what you want me to do," he said defensively. "We needed that part."

"I know." Chances were that Kynn probably hadn't found one. Mo supposed it wouldn't hurt to have a backup, even if he had found one. And at least if he didn't, he'd still have some extra cash.

Mo shook herself mentally. She was far too on edge for her liking. She needed to pull herself together. The money situation was bad enough; Ezra touching her and calling her his friend somehow only added fuel to the fire of confusion burning in her brain.

Maybe he'd just meant it casually in the shop, but something about it had felt … normal? Good, even?

Pull yourself together, Mo thought.

So what if he considered them friends? He wasn't entirely wrong. Mo wouldn't have told him about Tallas the night before if they weren't, on some level, friends. But she hadn't had any real friends aside from Cass and Kynn in a very long time.

"We should go see if Cass got everything up and running," Mo said. "Maybe she'll have had some luck too."

Ezra motioned for her to go first. "Lead the way."

As soon as they walked onto *The Revenant*'s upper deck, Cass rushed out of her room, a data pad in each hand.

"Good, you're back!" she called over her shoulder. "We've got a problem."

"Of course we do." Mo ran after Cass, calling, "Is the computer broken too?"

"Nope, got that up and running," Cass said as she rushed into the command room.

As Mo and Ezra followed her, Mo asked, "So what's the issue?"

"Two things." Cass circled around the holo table and began tapping all sorts of buttons, then strode to the comms station and pulled up two holographic screens. "First, it looks like someone has been fiddling with the Syndicate database."

"What?" Mo asked. "How is that possible?"

"Don't know, but as I was trying to get the algorithm set up again, I got an official alert from Syndicate leadership," Cass said.

"Why was it hacked?" Ezra asked.

"Don't know."

"Do they know who did it?" Mo asked.

"Nope, but I think it was someone from inside the Syndicate. You know the systems are locked down tight," she said to Mo. "Someone would have to know the system very well."

Mo *did* know, but she'd never really cared much for the intricate workings of computer security networks the way Cass had. If Cass wasn't such a talented sniper, she probably would've made an excellent digital architect or data mechanic. She probably would've enjoyed it too; she'd always liked those classes back on Miduna.

"Did the Syndicate say what the hacker was after?" Ezra asked.

"No," Cass said again, "but it doesn't seem unlikely to me that this has to do with what we're after. Nobody's hacked the Syndicate in over a decade, and they just happen to when all of this is going on?"

"I'm inclined to agree," Ezra said.

Who at the Syndicate would be trying to find one of these artifacts? It wasn't like the database even had that kind of information.

Cass tapped a few buttons, and one of the screens changed to a planet in the Syndicate's database, Andarix. "I think this is where we need to go. The computer has it matching up with the professor's notes and active treasure hunting contracts."

"None of the others matched?" Ezra asked.

"Not according to the algorithm," Cass said. "We can go through manually, but that's going to take a lot of time."

"Was that all of your bad news?" Ezra asked.

"No." Cass tapped a few more buttons, and the second screen changed to a view of a radar encircling the entire planet. A few ships were on the very edge and moving closer. "The FSC is here. They should land in about two hours."

Mo's heart jumped to her throat.

"Are they coming *here*?" Ezra asked.

"I don't know their exact trajectory, but given it's the only major trading hub on the planet and *we're* here, I'd say yes."

"Fuck," Ezra muttered, running his hands through his hair. "Shit."

"Did we find the parts we needed?" Cass asked.

"We did, but it won't be delivered for a few hours," Mo said. "And we got ripped off, so today's shaping up to be really shitty."

"There's a chance they aren't here for us," Ezra said. "I know Titan's Gate isn't huge, but they're probably going to the actual FSC base first. They almost always do. It's just the standard operating procedure."

"That buys us what, a couple extra hours?" Cass asked.

"If we work quickly, that should be enough," Ezra said. "We can leave before they find us."

Mo didn't know where Ezra's confidence came from, but it made her stand a little taller. She'd gotten out of worse situations before. They could figure this out.

"Right," she said. "Let's plan a course for Andarix, and as soon as Kynn's back, fill him in. Then we get to work."

Chapter 39

Not knowing the extent of the FSC's involvement in recent events had Ezra on edge. While their arrival wasn't a complete surprise, just knowing they were set to land on the planet at any moment had his skin crawling.

We'll deal with it, he told himself as he strode down the ramp after Kynn. While they went to deal with the mechanics, Mo and Cass were keeping an eye on the radar and skies, not just for the FSC but the Ascended. They might not be far behind.

The shipyard was quiet, at least, and there was no sign of any soldiers. He forced his shoulders to relax. Getting all tense and worked up was not going to help him.

They wove their way past a few quiet ships, then toward the stone and metal wall encasing the yard. There was an office and garage there, but they passed those too. Just outside the shipyard was a young Sorthian boy who couldn't have been older than seventeen. He looked small for his age, but Ezra had learned long ago to judge no one for their body. Everyone was capable of incredible things.

"Are you the Aerilian?" the boy asked, eyeing Ezra.

"Yeah," he said. "For the power relay regulator."

"Do you even know how to fix a shield generator?" the boy asked, eyebrows raised.

"Not really," he said, "but I've got friends who do." Friends like Kynn but also the original mechanic at the shipyard. Hopefully she'd be able to get things up and running quickly.

The boy harrumphed. "Boss said you owe another three thousand credits."

Kynn took the required amount out of his pocket, just six slim silver bars. Then he pulled out another. "For your trouble," he said. "We appreciate you getting this to us quickly."

The boy tucked the first six into one pocket on his belt, then the extra into a pocket on his dark green jacket. "Thanks." He handed them a metallic gray brick with both dark and neon blue accents.

Kynn inspected the part, focusing on the various input and output connections on the back before opening it up and peeking inside. Ezra had no idea what he was looking for, but Kynn nodded. "Looks good. Almost brand new."

Six thousand credits for a piece that wasn't even brand new? The FSC sometimes refurbished and recycled all manner of tech, but for shield generators? And at that cost?

As soon as the kid trotted off down the mostly empty street, Kynn tilted his head toward the yard behind them. "C'mon."

Ezra hurried after him. "Is that normal?" he asked. "To not get new parts?"

Kynn shrugged. "Often enough, yeah. Especially on worlds like this." Ezra frowned.

"You've got a lot to learn about our way of life," Kynn said with a laugh. His words weren't unkind, but Ezra sensed the hesitation beneath them. "Things are different out here."

"I'll say. But that part is good?"

"Oh, yeah. This'll do the job. Should hold up for a few years if we don't sustain heavy damage."

That made Ezra feel a little better at least.

Kynn made his way toward the yard's office. Its wide windows overlooked both the yard and street outside, but it was otherwise as worn in as everything else in Titan's Gate. The metal table being used as a desk was filled with scratches and dents, and even the computers and data pads had to be at least a decade old. This really wasn't like Aerilia at all. It wasn't even like Miduna.

"Arana?" Kynn called.

A steel gray door at the back of the room swung open, and a half-Human, half-Ivari woman stepped out. Her skin had a pinkish hue to it and her pointed ears were only half the length of a full Ivari's.

"Oh, good," she drawled as she stepped into the office. "You're back. I don't have the part."

"We do." Kynn held it up for her. "And we've already paid you for the work, so let's get on with it."

She rolled her eyes and began tying her dark hair back into a braid. Little pieces sprang free, but she evidently didn't care because she just grabbed the part from Kynn and pushed past both men. "Let's *get on with it*, then."

Ezra didn't see why she had an attitude about it, but Kynn took it in stride, so Ezra tried to shove down his frustration as they headed back toward *The Revenant*. Each ship they passed was dormant; he recognized most of them, but a couple were different than what had been there the night before. How many bounty hunters passed through this yard on a weekly basis? It didn't really matter, but Kynn had been right, that Ezra had really no concept of how this way of life worked.

The Revenant was just a few dozen yards away, but something in the sky drew Ezra's attention. Something dark.

The FSC ships had cleared the atmosphere, and though they were far in the distance, Ezra would recognize those small cruisers anywhere. He'd been on all manner of starships with the military, including ones like those. Luckily they were too far off and their trajectory too northward for them to be landing in Titan's Gate, just as he and Cass had predicted.

"Kynn!" Ezra called.

The mechanic, Arana, continued on and opened an access panel on the underside of the ship. She hoisted herself up inside, disappearing from sight.

Kynn fell back in line with Ezra. "What?"

The ships were already gone over the horizon. Lowering his voice, Ezra said, "FSC just headed north. How soon can we get this thing fixed?"

Kynn shook his head. "Soon enough, I hope. I'll help Arana." And then he ran off after the woman, disappearing through the same door as Arana.

Ezra would be no help trying to fix a shield generator, but he could help Mo and Cass. He'd been nervous about spending the day with Mo, but she seemed mostly comfortable around him despite her show of emotion the night before. He didn't judge her for it, of course, but he'd expected her to grow distant again. The fact that she hadn't was a pleasant surprise.

None of that mattered right now.

"FSC incoming!" he called as he ran into *The Revenant* and started up the ramp.

"We saw 'em!" Cass yelled. "I lost them once they landed."

"They were heading toward the base north of here," Ezra said as he stormed into the command room. Mo and Cass were both standing at the holographic screens at the comms panel on the far side of the space.

"You're sure they're going to take a while to get sorted out there?" Mo asked, not taking her eyes off the screen. It looked like she was busy checking their course to Andarix or running simulations of some kind, but it was hard to tell from this angle.

"Almost a hundred percent sure," Ezra said. "It's what they always do."

Mo grunted and continued tapping away on her keyboard. "I think I found us the fastest route to Andarix."

"Let me see." Ezra circled around behind her, forcing himself to focus on the simulated flight path rather than the way Mo smelled like vanilla and cinnamon.

Andarix was a good ways away, on the far outer edges of the Federation. Mo's simulation showed them getting there in a little more than three days, which wasn't ideal, but she had them taking less popular hyperspace lanes.

"I trust your judgment," Ezra said. "Looks good to me."

Mo nodded and punched a few more buttons. "Then we're set whenever the ship is fixed."

"Kynn's working on it with Arana," Ezra said. "He said he'd try to get it done as fast as possible. He knows the FSC is here."

"I'll go help them." Cass left her screen up and disappeared into the common room.

"Take over for her," Mo said, jerking her chin toward the other setup.

Ezra moved away from her, instantly missing the subtleties of her soap or shampoo or whatever the fuck made her smell so good, like fresh-baked cookies. He forced himself to read Cass's screen, which had not just a radar focused around Titan's Gate but logs about Andarix.

"She's really been studying," he said, mostly to himself.

"Cass is quick," Mo said. "She's gotten through a lot."

"Good, because I'm not exactly the fastest reader."

Mo laughed, but her smile faded quickly. "It's fine. Cass and I have it covered."

"What do I need to know?" Ezra asked. "Tell me and I'll watch the skies."

"Well"—Mo toggled her screen away from the flight path and to the notes on Andarix—"there are four major cities on its sole continent, located in its southern hemisphere. It's a cold, small planet with long days and nights."

"Great, but where's the artifact?"

"Don't know," Mo said. "Professor's notes didn't specify, just that he thought it would be on Andarix due to previous Ascended attempts to take the planet and some expeditions there many years ago, or something? There's a lot he *hadn't* finished fleshing out with all his theories. He literally would stop mid-sentence. A lot of what he wrote is just chaos."

"So what's the plan?" Ezra asked. "See about this treasure hunting bounty?"

"There's a Syndicate base in the second largest city, Drakara," Mo said. "We'll go there. The contract says we have to go there to accept it."

"I don't like that we have to go into town."

"Neither do I, but it's not like we've got a choice," Mo said. "Contracts don't usually require this kind of shit either, so we all need to be prepared."

Ezra really didn't like this, but saying that again wasn't useful. It didn't solve anything. He just had to sit with the discomfort, as he had before many times on missions over the years. There was something else he wanted to address, though.

"So ..." Ezra trailed off, but Mo didn't say anything. "About last night ..."

"Don't," Mo warned.

"But—"

"Don't." She turned and looked him dead in the eye. "Don't, Lyre."

"It's not a big deal," he said. "I just wanted to make sure you're feeling alright."

"Why?"

"Because that's what friends do."

Her expression shifted, a tiny furrow forming between her eyebrows and lips pulling into a thin line. She didn't look *entirely* displeased, perhaps more … contemplative?

They were colleagues, sure, but Ezra considered them friends, at least by most definitions. They'd shared meals, personal stories, and even saved each other's lives. But were friends attracted to each other? He couldn't speak for her, but Ezra certainly found Mo attractive. Which was unusual for him. He received plenty of attention thanks to his good looks and career, but he rarely found himself reciprocating. He just didn't have an interest most of the time, but Mo was different. Not that he could tell her that.

"Right," she finally said. "Because we're friends."

"You don't think we are?"

She sucked in an audible breath. "I guess—"

The radar beeped. Mo whirled back to her screen, her long silver hair flaring around her shoulders.

"Shit," Ezra said as he focused up too. "Ships incoming, low."

"FSC?"

"Gotta be."

Mo scrambled over to the cockpit, where she pushed a button before yelling, "Cass, Kynn, you better hurry the fuck up!"

No response came, but Mo was already moving on, fingers flying across the dashboard.

"We don't know that they're hostile to us," Ezra said.

"I'm not sticking around to find out," she said over her shoulder. "Help me get this thing ready to go."

He knew he shouldn't be smiling, but he couldn't help it. "You're actually letting me touch your ship *again*?" he asked as he dropped into the copilot's chair.

"Shut up and work," she said.

Ezra laughed. He couldn't help that either. "What do you want me to do?"

"Start powering up everything except the engines. I'll load in the flight path."

What Mo didn't know—what none of them knew—was that Ezra was actually a skilled pilot. Very skilled. But Mo's protectiveness over the ship and Cass and Kynn's tendency to go along with it meant they hadn't given him a chance to prove that yet. He didn't think he would get to, either, but just getting to sit there and help felt good.

Mo flipped a switch near the middle of the console, and another screen popped up with the radar. Four small ships were circling Titan's Gate, but that was all they were doing. Circling.

"Systems are on," Ezra said, watching as each little light triggered across the console to his right. Safety systems, life support backups, many others. No shields, no engines, but everything else. "And in the green."

"Flight path is in," Mo said, voice steady as she pushed one more button.

The Federation ships continued circling. Ezra rested his hand near the last two systems: shields and engines. He would be ready when Mo gave the go-ahead.

Something clinked and rattled outside. Then there was shouting, followed by footsteps downstairs and more shouts.

"Closing doors!" Kynn yelled.

"Engines, Lyre," Mo said. "Now."

He flipped the switch, and the light associated with it lit up red, then yellow, and finally green just as Cass reached the upper deck.

"Shields should be fixed," she said. "Load them in."

Ezra flipped that switch too, holding his breath as the light stayed red for five beats longer than he expected. "Are you sure?" he asked Cass.

"Positive. Give it a sec."

Ezra did. He waited, and waited, and waited.

Yellow.

"Ships are closing in around the city," Mo said. "Two east, two west."

Still yellow …

"Tell me when, Lyre," she said.

The light changed.

"Go," he said.

Mo grabbed the steering yoke, then engaged the engines. The ship lurched off the ground.

"Ships are moving in on us, Mo!" Cass called from her comms station back in the command room.

Shit. Were they really too late? Ezra couldn't see them outside the cockpit—

"One's moving off!" Cass yelled.

Mo frowned. "Really?"

"No, I'm lying. Yes, really!"

"Why would they do that?" Mo asked, glancing at Ezra.

Outside, the view changed from late afternoon sun to darker reds and oranges, and above that, dark blue and black. They were ascending quickly and would soon break through the atmosphere.

"I don't know," he said. "Maybe they were just doing routine sweeps, looking for Ascended after what happened on Mor'vex."

"They really wouldn't be looking for us?"

"I mean, they could try to track us?" he half asked, half stated. "We'll need to watch our backs. But if they were going to come after us, I think they would've by now."

"They aren't following us yet," Cass called.

They broke the atmosphere, millions of brilliant stars dotting the endless vacuum stretching out in front of them.

"Still nothing," Cass said as Mo put distance between them and Zerathia. "Jump as soon as you can."

"Is the hyperdrive up?" Mo asked Ezra.

"Ready," he said.

Mo shifted in her seat, then engaged the hyperdrive. The inevitable lag made Ezra's stomach drop slightly, and then they were off, speeding through the cosmos toward Andarix.

CHAPTER 40

Flying around so much meant Mo was finally finding some sort of routine: a set piloting schedule, consistent workouts, and even defined meal times, cooked by either Cass or Ezra. As it turned out, Ezra was an exceedingly good cook, almost as good as Cass. And while Mo usually liked having some kind of routine, she didn't love it now. All this travel just put more wear and tear on *The Revenant*, and it also meant the discomfort of being cooped up in a ship for days on end.

But finally, they were about to land on Andarix. Even from space, the planet's cold environment was clear, with much of the sole continent being covered in white snow or thick streams of clouds. The one good thing about the flight taking three days was that Mo had time to dig up some of her warmer gear, as had Cass. Kynn and Ezra hadn't packed any such things, but they swore they'd be fine.

Mo actually loved the cold, but it had a tendency to make her joints ache and protest. She'd preemptively wrapped them for compression, as that should help stave off the worst effects.

The other good news was that nobody had seemed to track them. If the FSC was looking for all of them specifically and not just Ezra, they would know to check the Syndicate base, and Mo could only hope that the Syndicate leaders back in Titan's Gate wouldn't say shit. The Syndicate liked to handle brushes with the law internally—not that Mo had broken any laws she knew of. Maybe stealing an artifact from an abandoned temple wasn't *technically* the right thing to do, but the sword belonged to Krytix, right? And he'd given it to them. He'd asked them to protect it.

Mo adjusted her cloak. Though many preferred jackets in the winter, many in the Federation still wore cloaks, especially those with jobs like Mo's. They were easier to remove in a fight, whereas even the most streamlined jackets could restrict movement. Hers was made of a lightweight but versatile thermal regulating fabric. It was expensive, but it had been well worth the money.

As she strode through the common room, she yelled, "Let's go!" It was already nearly twilight here in Drakara, and Mo wasn't keen on getting stuck in a snowstorm at night.

Cass emerged first in a dark gray cloak similar to Mo's. They walked downstairs together to find Ezra and Kynn emerging from their quarters at the same time, Kynn in layers and Ezra in a long-sleeved shirt and combat pants.

"You're going to freeze," she said to him.

Fire burst to life over his palm. "No, I won't."

Mo rolled her eyes but let it go. Either he was being sincere or she'd be right; it didn't matter either way.

All the shipyards had been full when they'd landed, so they'd had to touch down just outside of Drakara. Not ideal, but they'd been able to find an empty area of land not too far from the Syndicate base.

The second they stepped outside, Kynn cursed, and Mo pulled her cloak tighter around herself. The wind was no joke, especially with the sun being so far below the horizon already.

They sped up, making it through the city gates in no time thanks to the abandoned streets. It was just a few turns down equally empty roads and past low, dark buildings before they made it to the Syndicate base. Mo wasn't keen on bringing Ezra in with them, but they had little choice.

She supposed they could've left him back on the ship, but Mo thought they all needed to hear whatever it was this contract was really about. They needed to do this together if they were going to succeed.

"Name?" the bouncer behind the door asked.

"The Demon, Miduna branch," Mo said. "The Titan's Gate base gave us a lead on a contract, told us to come here." She gestured behind her. "This is my crew."

The narrow slider slammed shut, then the door opened. Mo strode in, forcing her shoulders back and head up high, like she owned the fucking place. This base was larger than the one back in Titan's Gate, its color scheme lighter and interior warmer overall. It felt more like a comfortable tavern rather than a place for bounty hunters to slink around.

"Where's the leader's office?" Mo asked the bouncer, a short, plump Luxinae woman with snowy skin.

"She has a wait list," the woman replied coolly.

"Like hell she does," Mo said. "This is time sensitive. We need to speak with her now."

The four of them, crammed near the front door with the bouncer, surely made for an imposing sight. Mo didn't need to turn around to know her team was backing her up, closing this bouncer in. She could feel them around her, behind her.

Mo curled her upper lip slightly as she leaned forward. "Now," she repeated.

The woman glared at them, and for a moment, Mo wasn't sure she'd give in. But finally, she nodded. "Upstairs. Last door on the right."

Mo spun on her heel, following Cass and Kynn as they led the way. Ezra, though, stepped aside for Mo to go in front of him. That didn't exactly give off the sense he belonged there in the Syndicate camp, but Mo couldn't admonish him for it either.

Down the hall from the wide stairs were voices, speaking mostly in the Federation's common tongue and with all manner of accents. It sounded like a crowded night, and Mo wanted to avoid entering the bar as much as possible. With any luck, they could talk to the leader and get out quickly. They'd need to stop and buy some clothes for Ezra and Kynn too. They looked unprepared and unprofessional.

Cass stopped at the last door on the right, as instructed by the bouncer. The branch leader's name was carved into a plaque mounted next to the door: Aria Zorrin. Cass knocked.

"Enter," called out a feminine voice with an accent Mo had never heard before.

As soon as the door slid open, Cass marched in. She was petite, but she knew how to hold herself. Kynn joined her, then Mo and Ezra. The office was large enough to fit a few more people, plus an antique wooden desk, an assortment of small accent furniture, and a weapons rack.

Aria Zorrin sat behind the desk, tapping away on a data pad. She didn't even look up, her forehead tattoos wrinkling as she frowned.

"May I help you?"

"The Phantom, Demon, and Silencer with the Miduna branch," Cass said, "here to claim a treasure hunting bounty. Tried to pick up the contract back in Titan's Gate, but they said we had to come here."

Aria squinted and frowned again. "Three call signs but four of you?"

"We're a crew," Mo said. Maybe they should've given Ezra a call sign too. "Is that a problem?"

"I don't give a shit," Aria said, but Mo didn't like the way she was looking at Ezra. "Yes, I know the contract. You're not the only ones after it. I've been warned to expect multiple interested parties."

"We first?" Kynn asked.

Aria nodded.

"How much does it pay?" Cass asked.

"Fifteen thousand credits." Aria looked pointedly at Ezra. "Each Syndicate member, that is."

Ezra didn't so much as blink.

"And what are we looking for?" Kynn asked.

"A relic for an anonymous collector." Aria tapped on her data pad again and began reading off the screen. "Any interested party must reach the High Sanctum located in the Embercrag Mountains by the sixteenth day of this month."

That was only in three days.

"What's the artifact?" Cass asked.

"A key." She frowned. "Seems like a pointless thing for someone to buy."

"Let clients waste their money however they want, right?" Cass asked, and Aria nodded. "Can you give us coordinates?"

"Sure," Aria said. "Be warned: it's not an easy trek."

"What else is at this Sanctum?" Kynn asked.

"Recluses and dust, mostly. Sometimes they come down to the city, but not often. It's a far journey for them."

Kynn crossed his arms over his chest. "And what do these recluses do out there?"

"Don't know, nor do I care to," Aria said. "They keep to themselves, which is the way I prefer things."

"And you're sure no one's headed out that way yet?" Mo asked.

"Not that I'm aware of. Embercrag Mountains," Aria repeated. "If you're successful in finding this relic, bring it back here to be connected with the client and receive your payment."

As much as it pained Mo to give up that many credits, she would definitely *not* be bringing the artifact back for the client. But Aria didn't need to know that. It wasn't lost on Mo that they were leaving traces of their Syndicate-associated movement. Eventually—if she even found this artifact—she'd have to lie to leadership and convince them she'd never found anything in the first place. She'd cross that bridge when she got to it.

Aria gave Kynn and Ezra another derisive look. "And do yourselves a favor and get yourself some warmer gear, for fuck's sake."

Taking that as a dismissal, Mo left Aria's office and headed back down the stairs. There wasn't much of a point in sticking around if she wouldn't give them any further information. But they knew they were on the right path, or what sounded like the right path.

"Clothes for you two," Mo said, jerking her chin at Kynn and Ezra as they stepped back out into the cold night. "Then back to the ship. I want to be there before morning."

Finding clothing for Kynn and Ezra on such short notice hadn't been ideal, especially with how big Ezra was. But they'd managed, and Mo hoped it would make whatever came next a little easier.

Cass was piloting now, taking them closer to the Embercrag Mountains. It was a mountain range hundreds of klicks north of Drakara, and the conditions outside were only growing worse the deeper they flew into the night.

"We're approaching," Cass said, flipping a few switches on her side of the dash. "You see it?"

"Oh, I see it," Mo said.

There was no way she couldn't see it. One particular peak rose up out of the darkness like a beacon, warm flames lighting up one side of the mountain. That had to be the High Sanctum. It was actually less of a mountain and more of a complex, with flat areas and buildings alike built into the landscape. There was nothing strange on their sensor readings, nothing to suggest spikes in peculiar energy or something related to the gods.

"Who the hell would live out here?" Cass asked absently as they circled around the highest peak and back around toward those lights.

The comms crackled, and then a calm, steady voice said, "Who is this?"

Cass and Mo exchanged a look.

"My name's Mo," she said. "I'm here looking for something."

"What is it you seek?"

Aria had said the contract was for a *key*, right?

"I'm here to learn more about Voxarus," Mo said. She didn't dare say the Void Key, as Krytix had called it. "Can we land?"

"We?" that voice asked.

"My friends and I," Mo said. "We're trying to learn more about Voxarus. May we land?"

Silence stretched on, and Mo and Cass had to circle the peak again. But finally, the voice returned.

"I've sent coordinates to your ship. You may land."

"Got 'em," Cass said as she looked at something on her left. "I'll take us in."

Mo sat back in her seat, letting Cass take over for this final landing. Instead, Mo began running scans of the mountain, trying to assess whatever it was that might be waiting for them down there. Aside from the heat signatures and obvious humanoid life, *The Revenant*'s sensors weren't giving them much. There weren't even the massive energy signatures common when landing in a city or town. So were these strangers hiding something, or were they just low tech? Mo had come across desolate outposts before, but the sheer number of lights down there suggested there had to be at least a couple hundred people.

Cass could always be counted on for a smooth landing. She set *The Revenant* down gently, and as soon as she called the all clear, Mo began helping her power down the engines and other systems.

"Anything?" Ezra asked as he poked his head into the cockpit. He was still in a short-sleeved shirt, showing off his tattoos and muscles.

"Why aren't you dressed?" Mo asked.

He frowned. "I can *get* dressed."

"Then go."

With a sigh, Ezra left.

"You could be nicer to him," Cass said as she engaged the cockpit shielding. It slammed into place with heavy metallic thunks.

"What're you doing that for?" Mo asked.

"Not taking any chances," Cass said. "And why are you ignoring me?"

"I'm not trying to be mean," Mo said as she pushed out of her seat. "I'm just also not trying to have him slow us down. We need to go."

She really wasn't trying to be mean to Ezra. But they'd *just* been over this, literally having to take time to get him and Kynn clothes suited for this environment. Not that he had to wear a heavy cloak inside or anything. It just seemed impractical for him to not even be prepared.

Mo grabbed her cloak from the back of her chair, then scrambled down to the lower deck. Kynn was coming out of his quarters, as was Ezra, who was trying to get dressed as he walked.

She headed straight for the weapons locker and unlocked it, then grabbed her saber and a blaster. She attached both to her belt, then began handing Cass her preferred weapons.

"We assuming friendly?" Cass asked, mostly directing the question to Mo.

"Didn't seem hostile," Mo replied.

"Want to fill us in?" Ezra asked as he worked to fasten on a cloak of his own. It was dark gray fabric, almost black, and cascaded down nearly to his ankles. It was nothing short of a miracle the store in town had something large enough for him. It even fit across his wide shoulders with room to spare. Underneath was a lighter, thinner version of his Vanguard armor, a breastplate and legguards, and underneath that, Mo could see a thermal turtleneck.

At least he'd gotten dressed quickly.

She thought about offering him an apology for her earlier shortness, but he just gave her an easy smile.

"Someone gave us clearance to land," Cass said. "Not entirely sure who. They only gave it when Mo told them we were here to learn about Voxarus."

"Voxarus—because of the Key?" Ezra asked.

"Figured it was our best bet," Mo said. "Didn't seem hostile, but I don't know who they are or what they're doing out in a place like this, especially not with this contract in effect. I'd rather be cautious and not fucking scare them in case they can help us."

"You think they'd help us?" Kynn asked, squeezing past her and Cass to grab a blaster and his own saber from the locker. He eyed a few of their larger guns. "You're sure we don't need to go in heavy?"

"The sensors showed nothing nefarious, and besides, my gut says no," Mo replied. "Now come on. Wrap this shit up."

"Bossy," Kynn quipped. "You're lucky I'm not into that shit." He glanced over his shoulder at Ezra, his full lips pulling up into a grin.

But before he could say anything, Ezra stalked forward and reached for the keypad to unlock the door. "I agree with Cevi," he said. "Let's assess the situation before we go in, guns blazing."

"Thank you," Mo said.

Kynn shot her a knowing look, which she chose to ignore. She didn't have time for whatever it was he was implying.

Ezra unlocked the cargo doors while Cass secured the weapons locker again, including the Star Eater. None of them had touched it in days, and Mo wasn't about to let some random civilian from the mountains steal it. Not if everything was real and that sword was highly powerful.

Cold air blasted through the doors, and Mo pulled her cloak up around her mouth and nose. Even her eyes hurt from the temperature and wind. Fuck, the *wind*. Snow whirled around outside; it hadn't looked so bad from up in the cockpit.

And in the distance, against the silhouette of the mountains, were flickering torches, massive columns, and a dome that had to belong to this new temple. Only this one had people living there. They couldn't just easily steal the next artifact and run, which meant their jobs just got that much harder.

Chapter 41

"What the fuck is this place?" Kynn asked, voice low, as they started down the ramp and into the freezing darkness.

"A temple to Voxarus," Ezra said, then jerked his chin at Mo and Cass. "You said they agreed to let you land when you mentioned the god?"

"Yeah," Cass said, almost in disbelief.

It was hard to make out any details in the darkness other than the vague shape of the temple and mountains. Ezra wished they'd gone the more aggressive route and worn their full armor out here. They had no idea if these were civilians or someone in on the bounty.

But, Ezra reminded himself, *Mo said her gut didn't think these people meant any harm.* The Ezra from a couple months ago wouldn't ever have believed in a bounty hunter's gut feeling, but Mo had a good sense of the world. She'd proven that time and again.

"No use standing here," Mo said, her voice muffled slightly by her cloak. "Let's go."

She made it to the bottom of the ramp first, every step steady and strong. He was a little surprised the cold didn't seem to be bothering her joints, but only because he'd known many soldiers whose wartime injuries had caused problems worsened by the weather. Or was she back to hiding her pain?

When they were halfway to the temple, three hooded figures emerged from between the tall columns. The warm light behind them cast a strange glow and even stranger shadows along the snowy ground.

Mo, still leading the way, stopped in her tracks. So did the rest of them.

"Welcome!" shouted one of the strangers.

Mo and Cass both straightened slightly, as if they recognized the voice. Maybe they did; they said they'd spoken to someone.

"You may enter."

The hooded people walked back inside, disappearing amid that warm light. Ezra frowned.

"This doesn't seem weird at all," he muttered, the howling wind carrying his voice away.

"This is where the contract leads," Mo said over her shoulder. "Are you coming in or not?"

"Of course I'm coming in," he said. "I'm just saying, it's weird."

Mo shrugged, almost to say she'd seen stranger things. Maybe she had. And if Ezra was being honest with himself, what happened back on Mor'vex had been more bizarre than this. At least there was no god in their heads this time.

They hurried ahead, only lowering their hoods once they crossed the threshold into the temple. Its layout was similar to that of the one on Mor'vex, with a singular long hallway running through the middle and various alcoves and staircases off to each side. Several stories towered above them, and people peered out at them through open windows. There were even statues here not unlike the ones in Krytix's temple, only these ones had neither swords nor flames but instead keys and shields.

"Welcome," that same voice said again.

Up ahead, the same three hooded figures from before stood with arms outstretched. Or, Ezra assumed they were the same three. Only now, their hoods were down, and the speaker in the middle was a short Human man with long black hair, shaved on one side.

"Are you the one we spoke to when we were trying to land?" Mo hooked her thumbs into her belt.

"Indeed," the stranger said. "I am Vizla, Keeper of the High Sanctum. Who are you?"

"I'm Mora Cevi, member of the Starlight Syndicate."

Vizla tilted his head to the side. "And your companions?" They all introduced themselves the way Mo had, and Vizla nodded. "Bounty hunters and soldiers at our door. This cannot be good."

"Why do you say that?" Mo asked.

"Nobody ever comes here, least of all to learn of Voxarus."

"We're new believers, converted after many years away from the old beliefs. We're hoping to learn."

That was her angle? Study?

Vizla's gaze roamed Mo's body in a way Ezra didn't like at all, then the rest of them. It was both contemplative and curious, concerned and awestruck. Why? Did they really get so few visitors here?

"What do you think, Keeper Tav'ri?" Vizla asked the woman standing to his right. She was short for an Ivari, and her skin was bluer than the sky back on Aerilia.

"Teaching is part of our duty," she said, her voice like a whisper of wind. "But only to those who are worthy."

"Keeper Idre?" Vizla asked as he turned to the person standing to his left. They were Luxinae, with a stocky build, pink-white skin, and dark geometric tattoos.

"It is as Tav'ri said," they replied. "We shall tell them what we can, should they prove worthy."

"Worthy how?" Kynn asked.

Vizla just nodded. "Please, follow us."

Mo glanced back at the rest of them and shrugged, then followed after the Keepers. Those peering out their windows began to retreat, hopefully to mind their own business.

They followed Vizla down the main corridor, and as they got to the end, that was where all similarities with Krytix's temple ended. Instead of a deep chasm with only one option—down—the main hall split off in three directions. Each was wide and brightly lit. The deeper they moved into the temple, the warmer it became.

Vizla and his companions led them down the hallway to the left. They passed several sets of closed double doors, then several single ones, before turning down two more corridors. The walls were all inscribed with symbols or covered in tapestries and artwork, depicting everything from war to the stars and Void.

Was this what Krytix's temple had once been like? More ... alive? Cozy, almost? How long had these Keepers been here, and what had happened to the Star Eater's Keepers? Krytix had said mortals were tasked with keeping the artifacts safe ...

Finally, they stopped at one more set of double doors. This pair were opened from the inside, revealing a large communal dining hall. The fireplace burning at the far end actually made Ezra so warm he was tempted to take off his cloak, but he decided better of it. He could handle a little discomfort.

"Please, let us sit." Vizla gestured for one of the round tables. It could seat eight and was made of a thick dark wood, sections of it clearly worn with time and use. "We shall have tea brought in."

"You'd bring us tea?" Cass asked.

As she asked, Idre rang the small bell sitting in the middle of the table.

"You haven't proven yourselves *unworthy*," said Tav'ri. "Unless you think you are not?"

"It's just not what we were expecting," Cass said.

"Then what was it you expected?" Tav'ri raised an eyebrow. Ezra had a feeling this was part of her test to judge if they were worthwhile students.

"We've yet to encounter any Keepers like yourselves," Ezra said. "We're grateful, but as I'm sure you can understand, cautious. The Federation's outer worlds are a dangerous place these days."

"Indeed, they are," said Vizla, his lips pressing together in a thin line. "Andarix is no different, but we have largely been forgotten out here. Nobody cares to learn about the Eternal Ones."

"When did you become interested in them?" asked Idre.

"Very recently," Kynn said.

"And what do you know of them?" they asked.

"Pretty much what they teach us in school," Mo said. "Krytix, Voxarus, Evlos. All of them granted humanoids their magic, but they disappeared, and now nobody really believes in them."

"A shame that our education system teaches so little," Vizla mused. "We have tried to lobby Andarix's representatives to introduce reform bills in the Commons and Senate, but to no avail."

It didn't seem to Ezra that these Keepers knew about the bounty at all, otherwise they likely wouldn't be welcoming three bounty hunters and a Vanguard into their sanctuary.

Another monk, this one an older Human dressed in plain boots, dark pants, and a light sweater, came from a door in the back of the room. She carried a tray laden with two copper teapots and small stone cups, plus cream and sugar.

The four of them waited in silence as the monks began serving the tea. Ezra was far more interested in wherever this magical key was, but upsetting and pushing the Keepers didn't seem like the best idea. Instead, he waited patiently and accepted one of the cups when Vizla handed it to him.

"Now," said Vizla with a content sigh. "Where to begin?"

"What would you like to know?" asked Tav'ri.

"We'd like to know why the Eternal Ones disappeared," Kynn said. "None of the texts we've read have explained, and none of the scholars we've spoken to seem to know."

"You've spoken to scholars?" Idre asked.

Tav'ri lifted her cup to her lips and took a long sip of the steaming tea. When she was done, she raised an eyebrow at Idre and Vizla. It seemed some silent message passed between the three of them, but Ezra had no idea what.

"Some," Cass said.

"Where were they working?" asked Vizla.

"Aerilia," Ezra said. When Vizla's eyebrows raised, he added, "I have some friends who work at the university, and they knew of my interest, so they introduced me to a few professors …"

"Friends of friends," Tav'ri replied with a small shake of her head.

"What's wrong with that?" Mo asked.

Tav'ri let out a long, heavy sigh. "We are Keepers of this temple," she said. "Keepers of the knowledge Voxarus left for us."

"What I believe Keeper Tav'ri is trying to say is that those in universities try their best, but they no longer see the full picture," Vizla said, offering the four of them a tight smile. He relaxed more into his seat than Tav'ri or Idre did. "They do not see that there is more to the Eternal Ones than what ruins and old stories can tell them."

"What are they missing?" Mo leaned forward, elbows on the table, as she took a sip of her tea. She looked so perfectly casual, a posture Ezra had never seen from her before. "I don't want to know what those in their ivory towers talk about. I want the real story. I feel there's more."

"And there is," Tav'ri said. "So much more."

Yes, Ezra wanted to scream. *We already know this!* But he forced himself to remain stone still.

"It's why we've sought you out." Mo set her tea down, then lifted her right hand. Lavender tendrils swirled out from her fingertips, delicate as they reached for her cup.

Vizla's breath hitched.

"I was gifted with Evlos's magic," Mo said, "but lost my family and my people before I could learn much about it. I want to know everything."

"It has been a long time since we saw anyone touched by Evlos," said Tav'ri.

Mo glanced at Ezra. It was a quick look, little more than a heartbeat of eye contact, but it said everything.

Ezra held his tea in one hand and summoned a small flame above the other. Vizla gasped again, a little louder this time.

"And one of Krytix," he whispered. His attention fixed on Cass and Kynn. "Are you—"

"Thankfully not," Kynn said with a wry smile.

Vizla nodded. "Few here are touched by Voxarus," he said.

"Where are they?" Mo asked.

"Secluded. It is a dangerous gift, like all magic."

Ezra didn't think magic was *dangerous*. Not inherently. It could be, but he'd met plenty of shadowbinders. They were no different than mindbenders or sunshapers. It all depended on the wielder.

She frowned. "I was hoping to meet more magic users."

"Perhaps soon," said Vizla.

Mo's frown deepened. "I see."

"It is for everyone's safety," said Tav'ri. "We mean no offense, Miss Cevi."

"I told you I lost my people before I could learn much. We all"—Mo gestured between herself, Cass, and Kynn—"are from Veronis."

"A tragedy," said Vizla, "on many levels."

"When we were children, we were told stories of crystals on our planet that gifted some with Evlos's magic," Mo said. "Do you know if that was true?"

At least Mo was getting to it. Ezra didn't think sitting around drinking tea all night was going to give them the answers they needed, but maybe she could get it out of these monks.

"Crystals …" Vizla pursed his lips.

"It's hard to believe crystals could control magic like that," Cass said. "We always assumed it was just a myth, but some of those professors …"

"Yes?" Tav'ri asked.

"Some of them suggested it was true," Cass said. "They said all the Eternal Ones left items here on our plane that spread their gift to mortals. Is that something you've heard of? Were our parents right?"

"Items?" Vizla asked.

"I've heard of no such things," Ezra said. "None that my family told me, anyway. But we've been on Aerilia for generations. Perhaps the truth was lost to time? Most people in my family have no magic anyway."

Vizla and Tav'ri shared another look, then he shook his head. "I've heard theories, yes, but never seen proof of such relics."

Mo's lips twitched.

"Do you know where the Eternal Ones went?" Cass asked. "It seems strange that they'd just disappear."

"There was a great war between them and a foe centuries ago," said Vizla. "A brutal war that not only weakened them but destroyed worlds. It was why they returned to their own plane, to recover their strength. But just as it takes mortals time to recover, so too do the Eternal Ones need rest."

"But gone for centuries?" Kynn asked.

Tav'ri held up a finger. "Not *gone*. Slumbering."

"Did they defeat their enemy?" Cass asked.

"They did, but only by working together."

Ezra wanted to scream. This was hardly any more information than what Krytix had given them.

"After all, it is only together that we will succeed," said Tav'ri. "All things—all life, all success and failure—are connected."

Mo sucked in a sharp breath, as if to ask a question, but a loud bell chimed through the sanctuary. Vizla frowned.

"It seems it is time for us to go," he said. "We can speak more in the morning, but in the meantime, you might find Keeper Cini in the library." As Mo perked up, he added, "Do not linger where you're un-invited. We have eyes everywhere."

"Where is the—" Mo tried, but he stood up as someone shouted for him.

"Apologies, Miss Cevi, but we must go."

Vizla, Tav'ri, and Idre left the four of them sitting alone in the large dining hall. Ezra couldn't really fathom the Keepers just leaving them alone, but the threat of "eyes everywhere" made him uneasy. He slumped into his chair and tilted his head back toward the ceiling. It towered near-ly two stories above them, and dark tapestries hung from old wooden beams. This place was like an ancient relic, not the shiny and polished life Aerilia offered most people.

"Now what?" Cass asked, voice low. "We don't have time to wait around."

"Right." Mo stared out across the room absently, as if deep in thought. "I don't think we have much of a choice, though. We have to play by their rules for now."

"Since when were you one for rules?" Kynn asked.

"I don't really want to hurt a bunch of monks. They weren't even armed. And besides," Mo continued, glancing again at Ezra, "they seem to have information. What Krytix told us—"

"Keepers," Ezra said. "I get it."

If they could take the time to learn anything else, they should. Perhaps they could even find a way to communicate with Voxarus the way they had with Krytix back on Mor'vex. Perhaps the Keepers would allow it, especially if they learned what Mo and Ezra had been able to do before.

But telling them was a risk. They might be giving away the fact that they had the Star Eater on board *The Revenant*. Ezra didn't get the sense these people would want it, but these days, he just didn't know.

Whatever they did now, they'd have to tread carefully, and they needed to do it quickly, an impossible task.

But Ezra was getting very used to the impossible. He swallowed the last of his tea, surveyed his team, and said, "Let's find this library."

<h1 style="text-align:center">Chapter 42</h1>

If Mo had thought Krytix's temple back on Mor'vex was creepy, this one was worse. Unexpected, really, given the warm firelight and monks moving around the building.

But the impossible darkness outside and knowledge they were on the edge of a mountain did nothing to calm Mo's nerves. She wasn't afraid of heights. She couldn't be with a job like hers. But the edge of a mountain with nothing but jagged cliffs and freezing cold temperatures? *That* bothered her.

They'd been circling around the main level of the temple for the last half hour in search of the library. It was a complete labyrinth, but the more they circled, the better she was beginning to see the layout. The few monks they'd encountered had scurried off out of sight, and Mo couldn't help but wonder if Vizla's warning about "eyes everywhere" had been hollow or even more subtle than she could detect. She also wondered if this was part of the test of their "worthiness" as newcomers.

A half hour of searching was long enough. As they passed a young Luxinae monk, a boy who couldn't have been older than nineteen, Mo stuck her hand out to get his attention.

"Excuse me," she said. "Keeper Vizla told us to speak with Keeper Cini in the library. Can you show us where that is?"

His white eyes widened.

Mo suppressed the curse on her lips. Had he never seen outsiders before or something? Were children born here and raised in the traditions of keeping Voxarus's secrets? Another thing Mo could find out if they could just get to the fucking library.

"We mean no harm," Ezra said with a kind and patient smile. "Truly, we want to learn about Voxarus's teachings. We're very new to all of this. Keeper Vizla invited us to learn."

The boy finally nodded. "Yes, sir. Right this way, sir."

That was a little surprising, but Ezra's easy smile was hard to resist. Even Mo found herself loosening up whenever he brought it out. It was a damn good weapon, better than his sword.

They followed the young monk through the halls, back the way they'd come earlier. The air chilled again the closer they got to the main entrance, and Mo pulled her cloak tighter around herself. The altitude and weather were beginning to make her joints ache, but she needed to ignore that and get the damn job done.

"Here we go," the boy said as they approached a door flanked by two statues. Nothing about it betrayed the idea that it might be a library. "Keeper Cini is somewhere in here. She works the night shift."

The boy scurried off before Mo could even yell her thanks, so she kept her mouth shut and reached for the door handle. Inside, the light was low and the air was warm. Mo's muscles relaxed. Bookshelves lined the long, narrow room. Several tables took up the middle of the space, each one modern enough to have holographic tops instead of stale wooden ones like everything else in the room. The bookshelves were filled with both ancient manuscripts and modern data pads and drives.

A short Human woman waddled about on the far end of the room. Like the other Keepers, she wore dark robes that fit this antiquated place.

"Keeper Cini?" Kynn called.

The woman's head popped up. She had gray hair and cool brown skin with deep wrinkles. "May I help you?" she asked, her voice rough but not unpleasant.

"Keeper Vizla invited us to look around," Mo said. "To learn. He recommended your library as the place to start."

The old woman eyed them skeptically. "He did?"

"Ask Keeper Tav'ri if you don't believe us," Mo said.

Cini stared at them for so long Mo wasn't sure if they should leave or not. But finally, Cini must've found what she was looking for, because she said, "Fine."

"Fine," Kynn whispered. "*Fine*. Great."

Mo would take whatever clipped answers this librarian wanted to give. It was better than no answers at all.

"What do you want to know?" Cini asked as she moved toward the table closest to her end of the room. Mo and the others headed that way, and it was only when they got closer that Mo was able to make out the cane in Cini's right hand. It was surprisingly quiet on the old stone floors.

"I don't even know where to begin," Ezra said. "Vizla mentioned something about the connection between all things before he was called away ... and a war the Eternal Ones fought in?"

"Indeed, everything is connected," said Cini. "All people, all things, all planes."

"But how do we know that?" Cass asked.

"The proof is all around us," Cini said with a grunt, almost as if to ask if they were fools for not seeing it with their own eyes. "The Eternal Ones connected planets and life to each other, to magic. Without them, we wouldn't have anything you see or experience today. We would be stuck on our home worlds."

Mo wasn't so sure about that. Surely mortal species would have eventually developed the technology to travel through the stars.

"We would have no magic," said Cini. "We would have no connection to the Void, through Voxarus or Evlos or Krytix."

"I thought only Voxarus was connected to the Void," said Kynn.

Cini clicked her tongue. "All are connected to the Void. It's where the Eternal Ones slumber now, waiting to return."

"I thought the Void was just the realm of the dead?" Kynn asked.

"No," said Cini. "A common misconception. The Void is where the Eternal Ones originated. And before you ask me, young man, *no*, it does not mean the Eternal Ones are dead. It is a higher plane, where life forces exist in different ways."

Mo did not like the sound of this.

"And you really think they'll come back to our plane?" Cass asked.

"Of course they will." Cini moved around the table and pushed a few buttons on a small panel. A hologram projected from the middle of the table and up into the air in front of them. It was of stars colliding and twining together amid a mix of red and black explosions. "They must prevent this."

"What exactly are we looking at?" Ezra asked.

"What will happen if they do not return," said Cini. "Chaos will reign."

Chaos. The back of Mo's neck prickled. That was what Krytix had spoken of, the fourth Eternal One, Ikna, agent of change and chaos. With the Chaos Shard. With all the artifacts.

Mo looked up at Ezra, who stood next to her. He held her gaze, his expression calm and neutral. "The stars are sundering," she whispered. He nodded.

"So you've heard," said Cini, tilting her head as she glanced at Mo. "Where?"

"A new friend," Mo said.

Cini pressed her lips together, but she didn't push the issue. Instead, she said, "Our plane is sick. So much war and chaos, and it will only get worse if the Eternal Ones and their Keepers do not stop it."

"What's causing so much turmoil?" asked Ezra.

"What isn't? Governments, divided factions, marauders. We're all responsible. We're all *connected*." Cini emphasized the last word so harshly it was like she was speaking to schoolchildren.

Not the answer Mo was hoping to get, but maybe Cini didn't know about Ikna.

"Do you think the Eternal Ones disappearing had something to do with the chaos growing to its current state?" Mo asked.

Cini shrugged. "It could be. The sickness began not very long after they left, only a generation. Which, to the Eternal Ones, is not very long at all."

Mo hardly thought that gods leaving this plane could be the cause of all humanoid greed and corruption, but this didn't seem like the time or place to argue philosophies.

"But they can fix the chaos?" Kynn asked.

"Indeed, they can," Cini said. "They must."

That still didn't give them any more information. Maybe collecting the different artifacts would be the key to bringing the Eternal Ones back? Krytix hadn't said that was the case, but it wasn't like they had anything else to go on. What Mo really wanted was to find the chamber with the Void Key and get out of here. Even if they didn't—or couldn't—use the artifacts to bring the Eternal Ones back, Mo really did not want any governments, warlords, or other selfish forces to get their hands on them.

"In fact," Cini continued as she disabled the hologram, "the chaos only worsens."

"How do you know?" Ezra asked.

"How do you not?"

"That doesn't answer my question."

"It's all around us, boy."

"I've seen war and chaos firsthand," Ezra said. "I know it's all around us. But how do you know that"—he gestured to where the hologram had been—"will come to pass? What even was it?"

Cini lifted her chin. "Voxarus speaks to me."

"They do?"

"Shows me things, in dreams."

"How do you know it's them and not just a dream?" Ezra asked. "People dream of many things."

The old librarian leaned forward, pursing her lips as she inspected him. "Has a god ever spoken to you, Vanguard?"

"How do you know I'm a Vanguard?"

"Answer my question and I'll answer yours."

"Yes." He said it so matter-of-factly that even Mo flinched a little. "Yes, a god has spoken to me before."

Cini's eyebrows raised. She probably hadn't been expecting that answer. "Well," she said, "then you know what it's like. You know that it couldn't be anything but them."

That was how it had been with Krytix. It had seemed so implausible and yet ... like nothing else would be the right answer. Mo still didn't quite know how to explain it, that sensation of a power that wasn't your own lingering in the back of your mind.

"And the answer to my question?" Ezra asked.

Cini tilted her chin up. "I heard you in the hall earlier when you met Keeper Vizla."

Mo rolled her eyes. Of course.

"Now, if you'll excuse me," Cini said, "I need to get back to work."

On a normal day, Mo would be frustrated by the circumstances, even more so at being dismissed. But she didn't have it in her to argue with this old monk, nor did she want to test Cini's patience. She didn't seem like a very patient woman.

Mo led the way out of the library in silence, eager to get back to *The Revenant* and call it a night. It was well past midnight on this planet, and it was even later for Mo's body. It always had trouble adjusting to so much space travel at once, followed by different planetary cycles. They could pick back up on trying to find the Key in the morning, after they all had a chat.

None of the monks had tried to stop them on their way out of the temple, though a few had bid them good night, which Mo had taken as a positive sign. Mo didn't mind throwing her weight around or flashing her saber when she needed to get a job done, but something told her that aggression was not the route to go here.

Especially not the way Keeper Cini had spoken of war and chaos. Keeping the peace was the best way to go about this, but they'd need to be quick. If they didn't have the Void Key tomorrow, they'd have to change tactics. They didn't have forever to stay here and try to win these people over, especially not with the contract having been issued to the entire Syndicate. Mo could only assume that smaller bounty hunting guilds had received a similar proposal. And with the contract having a deadline in just a few days, it meant other hunters would likely start showing up soon.

As soon as Kynn closed and locked the cargo doors behind them, Mo shivered and let out a yelp of frustration and relief as the ship's comparatively warm air made her skin ache. They all shook the snow from their cloaks, leaving it to melt near the door.

"How does anyone live out here?" she asked, mostly a rhetorical question.

"Your gear's not warm enough?" Ezra asked. She turned, ready to sass him, but he just gave her that easy smile and said, "I have an extra set of thermals if you need them."

Her whole body warmed. "Why?"

"Can't have you freezing to death, Cevi." Ezra skirted past her, his hand brushing her elbow as he said, "I'll start tea."

As Ezra headed up to the kitchen, Kynn circled around to Mo's front. He put his hands on his hips.

"What?" Mo asked.

Cass joined on the other side, effectively blocking Mo in.

"What?" she asked again. "What do you two want?" She did not like being cornered.

"What was that?" Kynn asked.

"What was what?"

"Ezra—"

Cass shushed him. "Don't be loud."

"Look, I don't know why he told Cini about hearing—" Mo started, but Cass shushed her too.

"Not that," she said. "Why'd your whole face turn red when he offered you his clothes?"

"It did not!" Mo hissed.

"It did so," Kynn said. "It's still red." He reached out to pinch one of her cheeks, but Mo batted him away.

"You're both making shit up," Mo said, forcing her way in between them. "That always happens to my face when I go from one temperature extreme to another. You know that."

She hurried into the kitchen, ignoring the weight of their stares. Of course, her face *had* turned red when Ezra had made the offer. But he was just being nice, a very Ezra thing to do. So what if she couldn't help but imagine that those "extra thermals" probably smelled like winter trees? So what if she didn't entirely hate the idea of borrowing them?

None of that was important. Kynn and Cass could pick apart whatever body language they wanted to on their own time, but right now, they needed to talk about what had just happened.

In the kitchen, Ezra was already setting out cups. A steaming kettle sat in the middle of the table. Kynn and Cass filed in after Mo, and she was happy to see them composed.

"So," Kynn said as he dropped into the seat across from Ezra, "why'd you tell Cini that you'd spoken to a god?"

Frowning, Ezra said, "Was I supposed to lie? It seemed like a good way to see what she had to say."

"Maybe that's not something we go around shouting about," Kynn drawled. "Just a thought."

"If we're going to tell anyone, shouldn't it be a reclusive group who worships one of the Eternal Ones?" Ezra asked.

"Out of anyone in the world, they may be the last ones we should tell. What if they become obsessed with you now?" Kynn shot a pointed look at Mo. "That'd be *bad*, right?"

She didn't like the implication under his words. That surely hadn't been about the gods.

Even though it would only add fuel to whatever fire Kynn was building, Mo said, "Look, Ezra's right. You know we have to take calculated risks sometimes. It got us information."

"Not the information we need," Cass said. "Where's the Key?"

"We'll see if we can't get it out of them tomorrow," Mo said. "It has to be here, especially if Keeper Cini is communicating with Voxarus. It only makes sense after what happened on Mor'vex."

The air grew tense as Ezra began slowly filling their cups with peppermint tea. Just as he went to reach for her cup, so did Mo. Their hands brushed, and Mo pulled away like she'd touched a live wire. The few times he'd made physical contact with her when they were alone, it hadn't been terrible. Mo didn't like to be touched, but it had somehow seemed natural with him.

It wasn't now. Not with Kynn and Cass watching them like hawks. It made everything feel heavy and awkward and loaded. Mo ducked her head and waited for Ezra to fill her cup, then carefully took it between both hands.

"What do you think the chaos was that Cini showed us in that hologram?" Kynn asked.

"Some metaphor for the destruction of the Federation?" Cass half stated, half asked. "Could the relics bring the Eternal Ones back? Stop all this?"

"Krytix said the stars are sundering," Mo said. "I'd thought he meant it in reference to Ikna's prison growing weaker, and part of what Cini said suggests the same."

"That chaos will continue spreading like a sickness," said Kynn.

Mo nodded. "Right. But what if it's not just Ikna brewing whatever chaos is doing this? People are greedy and violent. They have been since the dawn of time. I'm not saying Ikna isn't real or influencing events, but it can't all be her doing. I mean, what about the assassination attempts? There's no way a god is targeting Ezra from her prison among the stars."

"Targeting us, you mean," Ezra said. "Us."

The way he repeated that word made Mo's face warm again. She swallowed thickly, then said, "We should still focus on keeping these artifacts from the governments and militaries. If they somehow lead to us restoring the Eternal Ones to this plane, we'll deal with it. But right now, my concern is more practical than divine."

"Maybe we don't just trust disembodied voices," Kynn said. "Y'know, in case it really is someone messing with us."

"C'mon, Kynn," Cass said. "There's no way all of this is fake."

"Not fake, just ... unfathomable," he said.

Mo didn't exactly disagree, but the more distance she got from that experience on Mor'vex, the more convinced she was. That hadn't been a mere humanoid interfering. It just hadn't been.

"If we don't get the Void Key by tomorrow night, we'll have to try something else," she said. "Let's see what these Keepers know. Maybe it'll help us figure out what the fuck we're supposed to do with the artifacts."

"Fine." Kynn let out a heavy sigh. "One more night, but then I'm done with all the diplomacy. We need to get out of here."

"And we will," Mo said. "One more night, that's it."

It was a promise to herself as much as it was a promise to the others. They'd figure out what they could, and then they'd move on.

Chapter 43

Why was it that stretching never truly helped Mo's joints unlock?

She released the position and slowly rolled her torso back until it was straight again. She'd barely gotten any sleep, and the cold was wreaking havoc on her body. She was going to have to wrap her joints again.

She had more of the doses of soltherin Ezra had gifted her, but the pain wasn't so bad she felt she needed them, nor was anything inflamed. It was just aches and pains. *Just.* As if that made the constant, intense discomfort any better. It was a small lie she told herself, that they were *just* aches and pains. If she didn't, every day was going to be even more of a battle. This gave her some kind of passive acceptance of it all, or at least, she liked to think it did.

The speaker near her bed buzzed, the sign that someone was outside her door. She sighed.

"Come in!"

If it was Kynn or Cass coming to bother her about her cheeks turning red or her accidentally brushing hands with Ezra, she was going to—

Her bedroom door slid open, and Ezra filled the opening completely.

She was still sitting on the floor. In her lounge pants, a fleece sweater, and thick socks. Nothing else. She hadn't even bothered to put a bra on when she got up.

And there her cheeks went, flushing again.

Something tugged in her chest as she stared up at Ezra, trying to keep her focus on his face and not the way his thermal undershirt clung to his arms and chest. Evergreen filled her nose, like he'd doused himself in whatever soap it was that made him smell so good. Did he know she liked it?

"I was stretching," she said as silence roared in her ears.

"Do you"—he gestured vaguely toward her—"need some help getting up?"

"No." Mo shoved to her feet, ignoring the way her body protested. She forced her expression to stay neutral. "Thanks though." She brushed her palms against her thighs, then folded her arms tightly across her chest. "What do you need?"

"I wanted to go back to talk to Keeper Vizla," Ezra said.

"It's still early."

"So? Someone's got to be awake in there. I figured you'd want to bother them with me."

"I don't *want* to bother anyone."

"You know what I mean."

She shifted again. "What about Kynn and Cass?"

"Cass is running a diagnostic on the shield generators and Kynn's ready to go." Ezra turned to leave, but he looked back over his shoulder and tapped her doorframe twice. "You coming or what?"

She nodded.

"Then hurry."

He didn't say it with any malice, but Mo still didn't like feeling like she was doing something wrong. As soon as her door slid closed, she rushed to disrobe, wrap her knees, and get dressed again. It took longer than she wanted, but she was soon attaching her saber hilt to her belt, inserting her gun into its holster, and heading out into the corridor.

Ezra and Kynn were both there, arms crossed over their chests as they spoke in hushed voices. They both studied her for a beat too long when she joined them.

"What?" she asked.

"You're limping," Kynn said.

"I'm fine. Just need to loosen up." When he pinned her with a look that said he didn't believe her, she said, "Trust me."

"I can heal—" Ezra started.

Mo put her gloved hand up. "Trust me. I know my body." She'd surely be fine if she could just move around a little. She could take some soltherin again later, after they sorted this shit out.

They'd all opted for lighter versions of their full armor, plus their heavy cloaks. It didn't stop the wind from being devastatingly cold the second they stepped outside. The lack of sun didn't help either. Thick, dark clouds blocked out most of the light, casting a strange red hue over the mountain.

"Never seen that before," Kynn shouted above the next strong gale.

It wasn't like they could know every possible weather pattern in the Universe. It seemed to Mo like it was just some strange combination of clouds, sun, and the atmosphere.

As soon as they neared the temple, the doors swung open on terribly loud hinges. Mo cringed but hurried inside and shook the cold out of her limbs. Keeper Vizla stood not twenty feet away, his expression pinched.

"Just the man we wanted to see," Ezra said.

"Likewise, Mister Lyre," Vizla said. "All three of you, follow me. Now."

Mo didn't like the sound of that at all.

Keeper Vizla led them through the nearly empty hallways in silence. He didn't even spare them a second glance.

Eventually, deep within the temple's bowels, Vizla opened a plain door. Inside was a surprisingly plain office too. The furniture was simple, a mix of wood and steel, old and new. A few images of the mountains decorated the walls, though there were no windows. Vizla took a seat behind his desk. There were no chairs for the rest of them, and Mo silently cursed the man.

"What's this about?" Ezra asked. His posture remained relaxed, not at all the way Mo thought a Vanguard would stand when being questioned.

"Keeper Cini tells me you have spoken to an Eternal One, Mister Lyre."

"Commander Lyre," Ezra corrected.

Vizla's eyes narrowed. "You have spoken to a god? Why did you not disclose this sooner?"

"It sounds a little improbable, don't you think?" Ezra asked. "Speaking to an Eternal One?"

Vizla scoffed. "Not to a man like me. Especially not when some of our own have spoken to Voxarus."

"Surely you can understand why I was hesitant," Ezra said. "I wasn't sure even someone like you would believe me."

Vizla studied him for a few moments, then said, "Tell me, which Eternal One?"

"Krytix."

"What did he say? When did you speak to him? Was it all four of you?" Vizla frowned. "Where's—"

"She's busy right now," Mo said. "And no, it was just the commander and myself who spoke to Krytix, over a week ago."

"Just you and the commander," Vizla murmured to himself, eyes downcast. He snapped back to attention and spun around, searching for something on the sparse shelf behind him. "Mister Sathir, leave us."

"Excuse me?" Kynn asked.

"Leave us!" Vizla yelled.

Kynn started forward, but Mo set a hand on his forearm. He glared down at her.

"We'll be fine," she said. "Maybe you can see if Cass needs any help?"

"You're seriously going to have me do what he says?"

"We'll be fine," Mo said again.

They locked gazes for a heartbeat before Kynn shook his head. "Came all the way out here for nothing," he muttered, staring daggers at Vizla before turning to leave.

Mo's stomach sank as she watched him go, all tight shoulders and sullen face. She hated seeing him like that, but if Vizla wanted to actually talk to them, they couldn't pass this up. Kynn would understand. He had to. This could help them finish the contract.

"Well, he's gone," Ezra said when the door shut. "What is it, Keeper?"

Vizla set a data pad on his desk and tapped two buttons simultaneously. A small hologram projected up from the pad, revealing the same swirling mass of cosmic dust and energy that Keeper Cini had shown them the night before. Mo shifted again, trying to ignore the whispers of pain in her joints.

"The Void and the Universe are not as separate as people think," said Vizla. "All is connected, and we must protect those connections. Only a veil separates our planes."

What the fuck did that mean?

"Few have ever spoken to the Eternal Ones," said Vizla. "Few have been given such a gift. It's no accident that you're here, is it?"

"No, it's not," Ezra said. Mo held her breath, but he didn't elaborate.

"Voxarus and Krytix brought you here for a reason," said Vizla. "Do you know why?"

"No," Mo said. "Do you?" The way the keeper was looking at them—analyzing them—made her think he did.

"No," he echoed. "I do not."

"You're sure about that?" she pressed. Because she had a pretty good idea. This had to be about the damn artifacts. But how did they bring that up without tipping the keeper off? If they started saying they had to get the Void Key, he'd surely find them suspicious.

"Perhaps you are favored," Vizla said. "Perhaps you are Starborne."

"Starborne?" Mo and Ezra asked in unison.

"An ancient term once given to those chosen by the gods as their champions," Vizla said. "Perhaps Krytix has chosen you as his champions, the way Voxarus has chosen us."

Mo didn't think they'd been *chosen* exactly. It had seemed more convenient than anything, that they happened to be in Krytix's chamber when he needed their help. And being a convenient choice for the Eternal Ones didn't exactly settle any of the worries rattling around in Mo's brain.

"Did he say anything to you about this?" Vizla asked, leaning forward on the table.

"Nothing quite so specific as calling us Starborne or champions," Ezra said. "He just told us the stars are sundering."

Vizla nodded. "Yes, as you told Cini last night." He gestured to the hologram again, the black and red swirling around in a violent clash. "You saw the sky this morning, did you not?"

Black and red, almost like the shift in the world outside.

"What about it?" Mo asked, uneasiness prickling her skin.

"There is a belief among my people." Vizla circled around his desk and both Mo and Ezra, forcing them to turn to face him and the door. "That the sky would bleed when the Eternal Ones were preparing to make their return."

The sky had been similarly red on Mor'vex.

"Their champions would arrive first," Vizla said, "a warning of the conflict to come."

Ezra crossed his arms over his chest. "A prophecy?"

"A foretelling," Vizla corrected.

Mo didn't think there was much of a difference.

"The sky bleeds today," Vizla said, "and here you two are, Starborne, champions of Krytix."

"I wouldn't go so far as to call us that," Mo said. "We're not his champions." At least, he hadn't called them that, even if he'd asked them to protect the Star Eater. Wouldn't a champion of the gods—one of these Starborne—have to do more than that? Worship them? Proselytize and educate and fight?

"But you are, even if you do not see it yet," Vizla said. "All is connected."

Caution be damned; Mo was getting tired of whatever game Vizla was playing. They needed to get this done before—

The mountain trembled. A boom echoed in the distance.

Fuck.

They needed to get this done before *that*. Before that very thing.

Vizla's eyes widened as another explosion came. The floor shook.

"We're under attack," he whispered. "Nobody ever comes here—"

"Can any of you fight?" Ezra asked, reaching for his saber. "Can you evacuate? We need to get you out of here."

Ascended or Federation or bounty hunters—it didn't matter. Ezra was right. They needed to get the monks out of there, and they *really* needed to find this artifact.

"I must gather the others," Vizla said, mostly ignoring Ezra.

Ezra gave Mo an exasperated look, but she wasn't worried about that. They *needed* that Void Key.

"Vizla!" Mo called as she ran after the monk, who was sprinting down the hall. Her knees protested every step. "Vizla, wait! We need the Void—"

Another explosion cut Mo off. The ground fell out beneath her, and she toppled back against Ezra. He righted her. Somehow, Vizla kept going, disappearing from sight around a corner.

"What the fuck is his problem?" Mo muttered.

"Do you think it's other bounty hunters?"

"Does it matter?" she asked.

"It might," Ezra said. "Military's gonna have bigger weapons."

Mo actually laughed.

"What?" he asked.

"You haven't met enough bounty hunters." And with that, she took off again. "Make sure Cass and Kynn are powering up the ship!" Mo called over her shoulder. "I'm going to find Vizla!"

Ezra yelled something after her, but another explosion cut him off. Mo ignored him and willed herself to go faster. She had to find the Void Key. They couldn't have come all this way to let some other asshole get it first.

As Mo searched, she passed monks arming themselves with daggers, small guns, glaives, and spears, all of which came as a surprise. These hadn't seemed like people who could fight, but up here, she supposed, someone would need to know how to protect the temple. Especially if they were protecting Voxarus's artifact, if they were his champions, as Vizla claimed.

Finally, Mo found the head keeper striding out a large room. Gone were his dark, heavy robes. He wore just pants, boots, and a long-sleeved tunic. He had two blasters and a dagger strapped to his belt.

"Keeper Vizla," Mo said, cursing her joints as they throbbed. "Keeper Vizla, wait."

"There's no time to wait," he said. "We are under attack!"

"Yes, and my friends are going to help with that," Mo said, grabbing his arm.

He stopped and scowled at her. More monks moved past them, no doubt going to find their attackers.

"What is it?" he asked.

"You said all is connected," Mo said, voice low. "The sky was red on Mor'vex, where we found Krytix's temple. He tasked us with locating the Eternal Ones' artifacts and keeping them secure. There's an active bounty on the artifacts, and the Ascended and Federation both want them. Where's the Void Key?"

"You know about that?"

"We *have* the Star Eater on our ship," Mo said. "Where's the Key, Vizla?"

Another explosion rocked the temple. Vizla pulled away from her. "We need to go."

As he took off at a run again, Mo screamed in frustration. What did this man not understand? Hadn't he just been proclaiming her and Ezra to be there for a reason? Hadn't he said they were Krytix's champions? Starborne? She might not want that title, but damn it, she would use it if she had to.

She took off after him, cursing his bloodline and hers at the same time. Her gods damn joints. This gods damn monk and his fucking prophecy.

Mo trailed just a bit too far behind him to close the distance, but she at least didn't lose sight of him for more than a couple of seconds before she rounded each corner. The closer to those double doors they got, the more crowded it was, with monks and foreign fighters both.

It was just like the fight at Mor'vex, only this time, it wasn't Ascended or Federation soldiers.

It was bounty hunters.

Squads of them. More than sixteen, if Mo was counting right. None of them in matching gear, but the teams were clear enough as they moved together through the temple.

Monks shot at them through windows from the upper stories, and others attacked with blades of green and purple. And among the fray just outside the door was Ezra, with his golden saber, and Kynn with his blue.

"You said you're the chosen of Krytix," Vizla said as Mo came to a stop behind him. "Prove it."

This man wanted her to *prove* it?

She would.

Mo unhooked her saber from her belt and engaged the blade. She would not let these bounty hunters cash in on the contract, and she would not let Vizla keep that fucking Void Key.

This ended now.

Mo rushed the nearest bounty hunter, an Ivari woman. The hunter went in for the kill on an unarmed monk, blaster raised. Mo slid in front of the fallen monk, raising her blade with one hand and pulling on her magic with the other. The Ivari's shot ricocheted off Mo's sword in sparks of white and blue.

The Ivari woman sneered. "You protect those standing in our way?"

Lavender swirled around the other bounty hunter's legs. Mo pulled back, slamming her into the ground. The force of the impact knocked her unconscious.

"Bind her!" Mo called to the monk, who was trying to sit up. "Don't let her go!"

And then Mo was off again, throwing herself toward the next bounty hunter, a Sorthian man wearing dark red leathers and no formal armor. His axe glowed red, casting unsightly shadows on the walls as he moved in on Keeper Cini.

"Where is it, monk?" he asked, his weapon moving closer to the old librarian's throat. Cini trembled where she stood pinned against the wall. "Where's the Key?"

"Hey!" Mo shouted, ripping at the clasps on her cloak and throwing the damn thing on the ground. "Leave her alone!"

The man slowly turned toward her, his dark eyes alight with recognition.

That beard. His graying hair.

Mo knew him ... Jardan Illescas, formerly of the Midunian Syndicate chapter and frequent team member of—

"Hello, Momo."

CHAPTER 44

Cold rage worked its way down Mo's spine.

"Tallas," she growled, spinning around.

There he stood. Tallas fucking Bara, dressed much like her in a lightweight half-set of armor, all dark colors and fine material. He'd always had a taste for the finer things in life, from elegant fabrics to expensive wine. It didn't suit him.

"What the fuck are you doing here?" she asked.

"Same as you," he said. "I'm on a contract. I told you I had information about treasure hunters, but you didn't listen to me." He smiled viciously. "Just like you never did."

Fuck. He'd been serious about that? He was always trying to fuck with her. Nearly all the words that came out of Tallas's mouth were lies and false promises.

But fuck, she shouldn't have written him off.

Mo glanced over her shoulder. Jardan had let Cini go and was closing in on Mo's flank, trapping her.

She faced forward and raised her blade.

Tallas laughed, such a disgusting sound amid the battle. "You don't scare me, Momo."

"I should."

She grabbed her blaster with her free hand, shooting back at Jardan without even looking. He swore. Mo didn't check to see if she hit the mark. She spun out of range of Tallas as he ignited his glaive—green, his favorite color—and charged her.

He swung wildly. Mo blocked and parried, barely jumping out of the way as Jardan joined the assault. They attacked from both sides, from all angles, pushing Mo farther and farther away from the exit.

Mo threw her gun down the hall to her right and pulled on her magic with her free hand. It swirled around her fingers and pulsed under her skin. It was strong. It made her strong. It was how she'd survived far worse than Tallas Bara, and it was how she would survive again.

Mo flung her hand out in front of her. Purple tendrils shot at Jardan, engulfing him before he had a chance to flee. She slammed him against the wall. The ancient brick crumbled with the impact, and Mo slammed him against the wall again. Her chest heaved with the effort; magic had its price. Then she tossed him down into the worst of the fighting and didn't bother to see where he landed. The ground shook as an explosion echoed outside.

Tallas circled around her, that vicious smile still plastered on his face. "Come on, Momo," he said. "We can work together, like old times."

"Who issued this contract?" she asked between heavy breaths.

"Does it matter?"

Of course it mattered. Tallas was *here*. There was no way that was a coincidence. But she doubted he'd tell her anything.

Mo charged, gritting her teeth against the pain spreading from her knees up through her hips and down through her ankles. She kept going even as he pointed his glaive directly at her. She ducked low, sliding across the stone floor and swiping at his shins. He danced back—barely. The edge of her blade caught his boot, exposing angry skin underneath.

"Fuck!" he shouted, staggering back against the wall.

Rolling to her feet, Mo steadied her breathing and stalked forward. Tallas ran past her.

"Coward!" she yelled, forcing herself to chase him.

He wove in and out of the crowd of fighters. It was bigger now, an array of monks, bounty hunters, and Federation soldiers in a mix of black, white, and red armor. *Shit. Fuck.* How many were there?

Mo couldn't think about that. She focused on Tallas's green weapon and dark armor, following him through the fray and into one of the hallways near the front doors.

A few unconscious—maybe dead—bodies lay on the ground, but Tallas had disappeared. Mo slowed and raised her blade up in front of her. Its white glow sent light skittering down the empty corridor. A couple of doors were open.

Mo cursed silently. Backup would be ideal, but she'd completely lost track of Ezra and Kynn. Cass was hopefully on the ship, waiting for them and taking out whoever she could.

"Tallas!" Mo shouted, voice bouncing off the walls. "I'm not playing whatever fucking game this is!"

No answer.

"Tallas!"

Only silence and Mo's ragged breathing.

"Fine!" she yelled. "Be a coward. I don't give a shit."

Mo turned and started back out to the main part of the temple, but before she could cross the threshold, Jardan stepped into her path. He was bruised and beaten, bloodied, his armor torn. He snarled at her and raised his red axe.

Behind him came a short woman dressed in white, complete with a mask obscuring most of her face. All Mo could see were her blue eyes. She had no idea who that might be.

"Momo," said Tallas from behind her. "Let's just talk about this."

Mo's grip on her blade tightened. "There's nothing to talk about," she said, turning so she could keep an eye on all three of them. She cursed herself for throwing away her blaster earlier, but the other woman had one on her belt.

"Why not?" Tallas asked, head tilting to one side. "Or do you still have trouble communicating?"

Mo spat at his feet.

His upper lip curled. "Was that necessary?"

"Unless you're going to tell me who issued the contract and who you're working for, we're done here," Mo said.

"I work for the Syndicate, Momo," Tallas said. "Or have you forgotten how that works now that you're fucking a Vanguard and taking his money?"

"I'm not—" she started, but she didn't owe Tallas any explanation. But how'd he know about all of Ezra's payments? Mo hadn't logged any of it with the Syndicate.

Tallas laughed. "I have friends everywhere, Momo, or did you forget? There's nothing you can hide from me."

There's nothing you can hide from me. The words bounced around her skull, a warning and a promise from long ago. That's what Tallas had always said when she tried to take time for herself, or when she wanted to take jobs without him, or when she just wanted to spend time away from him. He'd always find her, admonish her, swear that nothing was her own, that partners didn't separate like that, that she wouldn't leave if she *really* loved him.

Her chest heaved.

He'd had power over her years ago, but he had no power now.

Mo was the one with power. She was the best bounty hunter on Miduna, one of the best in the entire guild. And if Keeper Vizla was right, she was a fucking champion of Krytix. Tallas certainly couldn't consider himself chosen by the gods.

"You gonna fucking say something, Cevi?" Jardan asked, voice gruff.

Magic only made Mo's body hurt worse. But she needed to get out of there and find that artifact.

Mo opened herself to the power in her core again. She felt it in every bone, every joint, on every inch of her skin. Her power burned, and Mo would burn with it if it meant stopping Tallas from finding her again.

She sucked in one deep breath, then another, as her magic smoldered and grew within her, around her. Lavender snaked up from the ground, ensnaring Tallas, Jardan, and whoever that woman was. It tightened around their legs and slithered up their bodies until they were forced to drop their weapons.

"What is she doing?" asked the woman, panic in her voice.

"Mora!" Tallas yelled. "Let me go!"

Mo stared at him, a satisfied smile pulling at her lips as he squirmed and writhed. *Good*, she thought. *Let him be afraid.*

Let him feel the way she'd felt years ago whenever he'd cornered her, threatened her, belittled her. Let *him* feel small and trapped for once.

Because that was all he was, a small man desperate for whatever shred of power he could claw out of the Universe.

Mo raised her free hand, forcing herself not to cringe as the power coursing through her veins threatened to bring her to her knees. The three bounty hunters lifted off the ground, still caught up in Mo's magic.

They shouted and yelled, but Mo took aim and threw them down the corridor. They traveled through the air like vessels, lavender trailing in their wake. They slammed into the far wall so hard it broke, sending them careening into the snow and battle outside.

Mo wanted to run out there and finish the job, but as her magic left her, every fiber of her being screamed at her to stop. She stumbled half a step forward. If she gave chase and tried to fight them on her own, she would fail. She knew her strength just as she knew her limits. She could only hope they'd either fall off the side of the mountain or get impaled by one of the fighters out there.

Besides, she still had work to do.

Mo gripped her saber tighter and ran back into the temple.

She needed to find Ezra and Kynn, and they needed to find the Void Key, fast.

Chapter 45

Ezra slashed at his opponent, an FSC soldier in white armor who kept aiming for his head. The Federation hardly ever wore white, the Ascended's color. They only did in environments like this, and even that was rare.

Focus. Ezra blocked the man's red blade, their weapons creating fiery sparks. He pushed back, overpowering the other man, and moved in with quick, sharp swipes. The edge of Ezra's blade caught the man's torso, leaving a burning trail of blood and skin in its wake. Screaming, the man dropped his weapon and toppled to the ground.

Ezra tried to ignore the feeling of wrongness creeping into his mind. These were his brethren, but there they were, attacking him. It didn't matter that he was one of them. It didn't matter when he told them he was one of them, and it didn't matter that he wore his Vanguard crest on his armor. They still attacked.

And so he fought back. He had no choice. He'd taken down half a dozen soldiers already.

He still couldn't see Mo anywhere. Last he'd seen her, she'd been fighting an Ivari, but that had been a while ago.

They needed to find her and leave.

"Where is she?" he shouted over his shoulder at Kynn.

Kynn raised his blade to block a blow and used his free hand to fire his blaster. The bounty hunter in front of him dropped to her knees, her shoulder smoldering and bleeding.

"I don't know," he said, desperation in his voice. "Maybe she went to find the—"

"There!"

Mo stumbled out of a hallway not more than a hundred feet away. Her sword and posture were sloppy, not the rigid and ruthless way Ezra knew she could fight. She swayed on her feet as she searched the crowd.

A soldier charged. Mo raised her blade half a second too late, barely stopping the attack. She somehow shoved back against the soldier, baring her teeth.

Ezra ran, and Kynn cursed as he followed suit. Mo's footwork was weak, like she could barely hold herself upright. Kynn sprinted past Ezra, throwing himself between Mo and the soldier. His blue blade clashed with their green, sending sparks dancing through the air.

"Mo!" Ezra wrapped one arm around her waist as she fell back into him. "Fuck, what happened?"

She swallowed hard, like she was trying to get her throat to work. "Tallas," she said. "His team. I used my magic to throw them outside."

Outside? Was there another entrance?

Mo must've seen the confusion on his face because she said, "Through a wall, Lyre. I tossed him through a wall."

Despite himself and the battle raging on around them, Ezra laughed. "Good."

"Should've made sure he was dead," she said. "Too tired."

"Better to be smart."

Kynn's blade glowed brighter. He cut through the soldier's torso, sending them sprawling to the ground. Dead. Ezra forced himself not to look too closely. *He's defending himself*, Ezra thought. *Defending us.*

"Do you know where the Void Key is?" Ezra asked Mo. "We need to go. The Ascended are probably nearby if the FSC's here."

Mo groaned. "Fuck me. No, I don't know where."

"Hey," Kynn said.

Ezra and Mo both looked up. Keeper Vizla was just a dozen feet away and closing that gap fast.

"What is the Federation doing here?" he asked Ezra. "Who are all these bounty hunters?"

"They're here for the Void Key," Kynn said.

Dawning flashed across the keeper's face, like he'd just connected some dots. "You have proven yourself," he said to Mo. "The sky still bleeds. I know what we must do."

What were these fucking riddles? Ezra just wanted the damn artifact and to get his people out of there in one piece.

Vizla whistled, the sound barely audible above the fighting. But all the monks—those still alive—stopped. Some were killed instantly, but others began fighting back, killing their attackers.

"Chosen of Krytix," Vizla said, his voice low as he leaned in toward the three of them, "it is now your sacred duty to protect Voxarus's power. Find what you seek on Pyralis, at the temple there in a region not unlike this. Do you promise to safeguard this power with your lives?"

"What—" Ezra started.

"Do you swear it?" Vizla asked, grabbing Ezra's free hand. "Will you protect Voxarus's power with your lives?"

"Yes, we swear it," Mo said, groaning. "We swear it."

"Good." Vizla turned to face inside the temple, his back to them. He unsheathed the dagger at his waist, brought it to his throat, and sliced deep.

"What the fuck?" Kynn cried out as Vizla dropped to the ground. "What are they—"

The monks around them all began turning their weapons on themselves, going so fast there was nothing Ezra could possibly do to stop it.

Mo's eyes widened in horror. "They ... they ..."

"Yeah," Ezra said. "Yeah, they did."

The Keepers had all just taken knowledge of the Void Key to the grave with them, so that nobody else could have it. Had entrusted that secret to the three of them. Keeper Vizla must have been a man of great faith to trust them after barely a day of knowing them.

The rest of the fighting between the remaining bounty hunters and the FSC hadn't slowed down. Outside, engines roared, and another explosion rocked the temple.

Ezra tightened his grip on Mo's waist. "Can you walk?"

"I can walk," she said.

"You better not be lying, Cevi."

"Shut up and let me go."

Something tugged in Ezra's chest, a realization. He didn't want to let her go. Getting his muscles to move took incredible effort.

He dropped his arm, then grabbed his blade and, with his other hand, summoned his shield. They took off through the fray, Ezra in front and Kynn bringing up the rear, sandwiching Mo in between them.

The faster Ezra ran, and the wider he made his shield, the more people moved out of his way. He slashed at anyone who didn't move fast enough. The three of them made it out the front doors and back into the freezing cold.

Bodies covered the ground, those of monks and soldiers alike. It made Ezra sick to his stomach, but worse was the Ascended ship disappearing around the mountain. This was already a brutal scene; it was about to turn into a bloodbath.

High above, smaller ships were circling and firing upon each other, but with the dark clouds, they were hard to see. They popped into view only momentarily, a flash of silver or white siding or a blast of blue weapons fire, then they were gone again.

Ezra pushed his legs faster. Ahead, *The Revenant* sat among several other nonmilitary vessels—the other bounty hunters. It was bright with lights and power, and the engines were already melting snow and kicking up dust. Cass was ready for them. He would just clear the way for Mo and Kynn, and—

"Hey!" someone yelled from behind. That single word was filled with rage, like whoever said it was barely holding it together.

Ezra turned. Stalking through the fighting and the bodies were just two people, one dressed in red and the other in damaged black armor. Kynn and Mo had stopped too.

Mo went rigid, then ignited her saber.

Tallas Bara. Ezra couldn't see much among the smoke and snow, but that had to be him. Mo had said he was there.

Ezra started forward, but a high-pitched whine pierced the air. Tallas fell to one knee and screamed. In a heartbeat, his companion was down too. Shot after shot came from behind them—from *The Revenant*—and hit their marks. Soldiers, bounty hunters, anyone left out here in the cold.

Mo wavered, like she wanted to go finish the job, but Kynn grabbed her by the arm and pulled her away. She turned and tried to keep up but was too slow. Ezra disengaged his blade, attached it to his belt, and scooped Mo into his arms.

"Hey!" she shouted, wriggling in his grasp.

"Relax," he said. "We gotta go."

To his great surprise, she actually stopped fighting him and just clung to his neck.

A dark shape moved back inside their ship—Cass. Kynn ran ahead, beating them to the ship by only a few seconds. Ezra hurried up the ramp, ignoring the thrum of another explosion as it echoed in his bones.

Cass's rifle was leaning against the open weapons locker. Kynn slammed his fist against the cargo door control panel, and the ship began to seal itself. "Cass!" he shouted, leaving Mo and Ezra downstairs as he scrambled up the ramp. "Tallas is here. Ascended incoming."

A muffled "fuck" drifted downstairs as the ship lurched into the air.

Ezra went to set Mo on her feet, but the ship rolled to the right. He steadied himself against the nearby wall and locked his knees, trying to shove down his misplaced satisfaction as Mo clung tighter to him.

Something on the ship's underside groaned and squealed. Mo perked up. Then the floor rocked and vibrated, like a weapon had just gone off.

Of course. Cass was firing on someone on the ground.

She fired again and again and again. Kynn's excited whoop drifted downstairs just as the ship swung around again. They began to climb higher.

"Put me down," Mo said.

"But—"

"Put me down. Please. You look like you're going to collapse."

"Am not," Ezra said, but he set Mo down as gently as he could.

As soon as her boots touched the floor, she staggered to the wall, then slid down it until she was sitting on the floor. Ezra dropped down next to her and sighed.

"Told you," she said.

Despite it all, Ezra laughed. He couldn't help it.

"You really have to rub it in?" he asked.

She smiled at him. "Of course."

That thing tugged in his chest again. He swallowed hard and turned away from her.

"What's wrong?" she asked.

"Nothing."

"Are you hurt?"

"No."

Ezra wasn't hurt in the way she was asking, but his head and heart hurt.

Mo's hand brushed his, but she pulled it away quickly. "You don't have to lie to me, you know."

"I know."

"Friends shouldn't lie to each other."

"Friends ..." He smiled a little. "Really?"

She shrugged. "I've come around to the idea."

Friends. Being Mora Cevi's friend was an honor few people held.

The problem was that Ezra didn't want to just be friends with her. He wanted something more—hoped there might be something more. But she probably didn't want to hear that, especially not now. Her white hair was covered in soot and half-melted snow, and her face was streaked with something dark. Ezra was sure he looked the same, a mess.

The ship rumbled again, and time seemed to lag for a heartbeat. Then they were off, barreling through hyperspace. Ezra had no idea how Cass had gotten them out of that with almost no fight, but he was glad. Hopefully Kynn had told her where they needed to go.

Mo's head lolled back against the wall, and her eyes closed.

"You couldn't run," Ezra said. "You're definitely hurt."

"Hardly," Mo whispered.

"What was it you just said?" he asked. "Oh, that's right. Friends shouldn't lie to each other."

She slapped his upper arm, but there was no power behind the blow. A few tears cleared paths down her round cheeks.

His heart clenched. "Mo—"

"Stop," she whispered, then wiped at her face. "We need to see what's going on."

"Why?" he asked.

"Because there might be more fucking FSC—"

"No, why should I stop?"

Bracing herself against the wall, Mo slowly pushed to her feet. Her joints were barely able to straighten; she could barely hold herself up. But she did. She lifted her chin, and despite her messy hair and bloodied face, she looked powerful.

"Because I'm never going to *not* hurt," she said. "There's no point in focusing on it. Now are you coming with me or not?"

Which part of her would always hurt? Her body or her heart? Ezra suspected she meant both. They'd both seen Tallas, heard that rage in his voice.

Ezra didn't want her to hurt in any way. But what could he do? She may have "come around" to the idea of being friends, but she didn't even seem to want to be near him half the time. At the very least, she didn't seem to want him to care.

Ezra pushed to his feet too. "Right behind you."

Chapter 46

As he climbed up the ramp behind Mo, Ezra tried everything he could think of to push his hurt feelings down.

His hurt not just about battling the FSC but his hurt about Mo trying to shut him out. Every time he thought they were on the same page, she went cold. He couldn't think about any of that. Not right now. Not with the Federation and Ascended on their trail.

"Thanks for your help out there," Mo said as she dropped into the seat behind the captain's chair, where Cass sat. Kynn was checking something on the screen on his side of the cockpit.

"Blew up Tallas's ship," Cass said, a hint of a smile in her voice.

"Shit, really?" Mo asked.

"It was the same as it used to be. Blew the other ones up for good measure too, just in case."

"Good," Mo said. "Though maybe luck will be on our side and the FSC or Ascended will have killed him by now. Nice shot, by the way."

"That was him?" Cass asked. "I didn't have my helmet on and couldn't tell. I should've killed him."

"It's fine," Mo said, but Ezra didn't miss the tightness in her voice. He wanted to embrace her, let her know she wasn't alone, but he didn't move. "Visibility was shit. We got away, at least."

"Where we headed now?" Ezra asked. "We shouldn't go straight to—"

"We're going to a system about half a day's travel to Pyralis," said Kynn. He was busy tapping away on his keyboard and didn't bother even looking at them. "We can restock and refuel if we need to; there's a trading outpost on one of the moons in the system, and it's generally not frequented by either bounty hunters or government officials."

"Which leaves criminals as its visitors," Ezra said.

Kynn shrugged. "Pretty much. Should be a safe place for us to hide for a day or two. I don't think they're going to be able to track us there, and they certainly don't know we're headed for Pyralis."

"Unless the monks kept records of the Key's location somewhere," Cass said.

"I don't think they did," Mo said quietly.

"I don't think so either," Ezra said. They wouldn't have sacrificed themselves like that if they had.

Mo's shoulders slumped forward, whether in relief or frustration, Ezra couldn't guess. Maybe both.

"Anything you need me to do?" Ezra asked.

"Yeah," Kynn said, "don't hog all the hot water when you shower. Go. We're taking turns."

Ezra didn't exactly appreciate being told to go take a bath, but the only one of them who wasn't a complete mess was Cass. He needed a minute to himself anyway to gather his thoughts.

"I'll be quick," Ezra said.

None of them replied as he headed back down to the lower deck. Maybe it was better that way.

The Revenant continued rattling its way through hyperspace. Its walls were closing in on Ezra, especially this tiny fucking room he spent most of his time in.

The FSC had spoiled him. Being a Vanguard had spoiled him, really. When he'd been a young recruit, he'd shared a room this size with another new soldier. But as he'd climbed up the ranks and eventually became a Vanguard, Ezra had grown accustomed to certain perks. A decently large bedroom on any ship had been one of them.

Just thinking about the FSC made him sick to his stomach.

Every run-in with the FSC was turning violent, his presence ignored. He was a fucking *Vanguard*, but that hadn't mattered to any of them. Were they compromised like Darius and the others had been, or were they being sent there by the government? Had the Federation turned on its own people in an effort to gain the power of the Eternal Ones? Ezra hadn't told them that the artifacts held power—hadn't known that was a possibility when he'd given his last official report—but maybe they'd figured it out somehow.

He didn't know what to think anymore. He used to believe in the mission, the idea that the FSC was there to do good across the Federation, for people from all walks of life. To protect them. To help them.

But how was the impossible power of the gods going to help anyone?

All it would do was escalate the war, and once that was over, there was the risk the government would turn it on civilians like the Separatists or anyone else they thought was standing in their way. There was no honor in that.

He just couldn't get the thought of those soldiers out of his mind, the ones killed by bounty hunters or the ones killing the monks.

The ones he'd killed to defend himself and Kynn. The one Kynn had killed to protect Mo.

Ezra had grown accustomed to the brutal reality of war ever since things escalated with the Ascended, but this was—

The speaker next to his bed buzzed.

Ezra pushed the button to engage his side. "Yeah?"

"Come to my room." That was Mo's voice crackling through the speaker.

Mo wanted him to go to her room?

"Please," she added.

Something in her voice was ... small.

"I'll be right there." Ezra rolled out of bed and went straight for the door. He hurried upstairs, to the quiet part of the ship where her quarters were. He opened her door with the push of a button.

Mo was sitting on the edge of her bed, gripping the sides so hard her knuckles were red. So were her knees, exposed in the small spandex shorts she was wearing.

"I need your help," she said.

"I don't even get a hello?"

"*Hello*, I need your help." She pressed her lips together. "Kynn's at the helm and Cass finally went to clean up."

"You don't have to explain it to me," Ezra said. "I'd help even if they weren't busy."

Mo's shoulders relaxed. "Can you get me a dose of soltherin? It's over there." She pointed toward the wall opposite her bed, the one closest to the door. "The panel with the scratch down the middle."

Just how much pain was Mo in that she was willing to ask him for help? Frowning, Ezra went over to the panel. It gave easily, and he set it on the ground. Inside the cubby was the black bag of medication he'd given Mo, as well as a small data pad with a purple case, a piece of what looked like a knitted blanket, a delicate silver necklace, and a miniature starship of some old class Ezra couldn't name.

She kept her medicine in with these things? They had to have sentimental value; Ezra didn't peg Mo as the kind to hang onto items for no good reason.

Careful not to disturb the other contents, Ezra eased the black bag out and brought it over to the bed. With careful hands, he unzipped the bag, pulled out one syringe and one of the little cleansing wipes, and closed it again. He set it next to Mo and knelt in front of her.

"What are you doing?" she asked.

"Where do you inject it?" He expected to find her glaring daggers at him, but she wasn't. Her expression was tight, guarded.

"Why?" she asked.

"Your hands are swollen and red," he said. "Let me do it for you."

Her shoulders fell even more. "It has to be in a big muscle. Abdomen, thigh, glute. You get the idea."

"Do you prefer one of those?"

"Anywhere's fine."

"Come on. Where do you prefer?"

She glanced away. "Hurts less in my glute."

"Then should I help you turn around?"

"No. Thigh's fine."

Ezra scoffed. "Would you let Cass or Kynn stab you in the ass?"

"Yes."

"Then why not me?"

Her cheeks reddened, and she still wouldn't look at him. "Because you're you."

"Bodies are just bodies," he said. "They beat modesty out of you very quickly in the FSC. It won't be weird."

"Says you."

Of course she was going to be stubborn about it. It was infuriating, but it was a little amusing too. He liked that side of her, even when it was a pain in his ass.

"Fine," he said. "Thigh it is."

Mo relaxed her legs, and Ezra took care choosing a spot that wasn't bruised or otherwise scarred. Her legs were covered in all kinds of marks, some bigger than others. A hazard of the job, he guessed, just like his. There was the place he'd healed for her, too, after Mor'vex. He ran his thumb over it, and her skin pebbled.

When he found a good spot, he put the syringe between his teeth, ripped open the cleansing pad, and gently wiped at her skin. He tossed it on the floor.

"Hey!" Mo frowned.

Ezra took the syringe out of his mouth and pulled the cap off. "I'll get it after. Ready?"

"Just do it. I'm not fragile."

Ezra angled the syringe, pinched Mo's thigh, and inserted the needle. She hissed as he pushed the plunger down, shooting the medicine in quickly. As soon as it was drained, he pulled it out, dropped it into the disposal bin she had underneath her bedside table, and pulled on his sunshaping.

His palms glowed with a warm light. His whole body grew hot, a pleasant side effect of his magic. Krytix's magic. Was the god watching now? Did he know when mortals used that power?

"What are you doing?" Mo whispered.

"That shit doesn't kick in instantaneously, does it?" he asked.

Mo shook her head.

Ezra set his hand on her thigh, right near where he'd injected the soltherin. Her skin was a little cold and impossibly soft. He used his free hand to take one of hers. This was not so soft, with callouses on her palms and a death grip that squeezed his fingers.

He pushed that warmth into her. She sighed, not in exasperation but relief and … pleasure? Her eyes grew sleepy. He let go of her palm, and his other hand slid down to her knee. Her white skin was no longer reddened, the joint no longer swollen. Her knuckles and fingers already looked better too.

"You didn't have to do that," she said.

"It was nothing."

"It was a lot. Nobody but—" She swallowed. "Nobody but Cass or Kynn ever helps me like that."

"Help shouldn't be hard to come by."

"But it is where I come from."

"It's what friends do," Ezra said. "They help each other."

Friend. Ezra had never hated a word so much, even if it was true.

Mo stared down at where his hand still rested on her knee. "I'm sorry about earlier."

"Why are you always apologizing to me, Cevi?" he asked, letting a smile tug at one corner of his mouth.

"Because I can be an asshole."

He squeezed her knee. "I already told you I don't think you're an asshole. I think you're stubborn."

"Is there a difference?"

"Of course there is."

"Well, I'm sorry I shut down our conversation earlier," she said. "But I know you were lying to me, and I don't like when people lie to me."

"I would never lie to you."

"You said you weren't hurt, but I know you were. By what happened. The FSC—"

"Of course I'm hurt by it."

"So you did lie."

Ezra pushed to his feet, then grabbed the discarded cleansing pad and the bag of medication and brought both to the storage cubby.

"Oh, don't leave just because I've finally decided I'm open to talking," Mo said.

He walked back to her bed. "I'm not leaving," he said as he toed off his boots. "Lie down."

Mo sputtered, then managed to say, "Excuse me?"

"Cevi, I'm exhausted. You gave me the worst bed on the ship, and you might need more healing, *and* you want to talk, so lie down and let me take the other side."

"First you wanted to stab me in the ass, and now you want to get in my bed?" she asked. Despite what was obviously supposed to be a joke, Ezra didn't miss the apprehension in her voice or face.

"What are we, sixteen? Two grown people can lie down and have a chat without it being weird."

"You're lucky I'm too tired to fight you," Mo said as she finally flopped over.

Ezra climbed into the empty side of the bed and tossed her blanket at her. "I have a feeling you don't actually do *anything* you don't want to do."

Her chest heaved. "Maybe."

As Ezra rolled over to face her, he was immediately swallowed up by the smell of her sheets, that light vanilla and cinnamon from the first time he'd slept in here. And her sheets. They were still gray, not the blue ones he'd bought her. Some tiny thrill sparked in his chest.

Her hair was a mess, falling across her face, and Ezra was tempted to reach out and brush it back behind her ears. But he didn't. He had to keep his hands to himself. Instead, he just watched Mo. Her eyes had fluttered shut, but he didn't think she was sleeping.

"What's with the purple data pad in your wall?" he asked.

Her eyes flew open. "Excuse me?"

"I wasn't snooping. It was in with your medicine."

Mo relaxed again. She was always *so* on edge, but he supposed she would be after all that had happened recently.

"Purple's my favorite color," she muttered.

"Oh? Mine's green."

"Shocking, considering your civilian wardrobe." She gestured vaguely toward his legs.

He was, in fact, wearing forest green cargo pants and a white shirt. "I like what I like. I've dressed like this since I enlisted."

"You're like a walking advertisement for paramilitary attire. Are all you Vanguards like that?"

Ezra laughed, but it left him quickly. "Most of them I knew," he said. "Other divisions aren't so uptight." Other divisions like the ones he'd killed. "I—"

Something tugged in his chest again as Mo's hand brushed his. "You had to do it today," she said.

"I'm basically a traitor." He hadn't wanted to admit it out loud, but there it was. The truth. "I've disobeyed direct orders, abandoned my post, and even killed some of my own."

"You're trying to identify a threat that may put the entire Federation at risk, and your superior officers wouldn't listen to you."

"I don't know what I'll do if they kick me out." Ezra willed his voice to stay steady as he said, "I've been part of many teams over the years, but I've never really found my people. Not like what you, Cass, and Kynn have. And despite the FSC just treating us like numbers, it was better than my blood family. It's really the only place that's ever felt anything like a home."

Mo was quiet for so long that Ezra didn't think she'd answer. There was just the subtle rattle of *The Revenant* and Ezra's heart pounding in his own ears.

"Back in that bar on Vonnoth," Mo said, "I told you I knew what it was like to be betrayed. I know what it's like to not be able to go home too. I've never cared for the FSC but ... I'm sorry. It's a terrible feeling."

"I got myself into this situation. It's not the same."

"Probably feels similar." She sighed. "It's sometimes like I feel lost. Miduna's been great, but I just ..."

"Feel like you don't belong," Ezra finished for her.

She nodded.

"That's how Aerilia feels to me."

"Then why do you keep that apartment there?"

"I have to be near headquarters any time I'm on Aerilia."

"Maybe ..." Mo swallowed hard. "As much as it hurts, maybe the FSC isn't your home either. It kept you tied to someplace that's hurt you."

"Maybe Miduna's not your home." Ezra shifted closer to her. "It's kept you tied to someone that's hurt you."

"Maybe," she whispered.

Ezra reached out, brushing her fallen hair out of her eyes. His fingers trailed down her cheekbone and jaw, resting there as he cupped her face. She watched him carefully, but it wasn't the same guarded look from before. She was relaxed under his touch, most of her periwinkle irises obscured by hooded lids. He ran his thumb over her bottom lip.

"How'd you know I was upset about all that?" he asked, voice low.

"You're an easy read."

He chuckled. "Am I?"

"So easy." The words were little more than a breeze against his skin.

Fuck.

Ezra wanted her.

He wanted to *be* hers, wanted to know what it would be like to wake up every morning like this, to stay up late into the night, whispering secrets and fears, hopes and dreams, with someone who understood him a little too well. They hadn't known each other all that long, yet it felt like a lifetime. He had the distinct feeling that if he went deeper now, he'd never get enough of her. He didn't know if that thought thrilled or terrified him.

Ezra's pulse quickened. She was so close to him now. Her face was warm under his touch, so warm he couldn't tell if she was blushing or had a fever.

"How do you feel?" he asked, stroking her cheek with his thumb.

"Tired. Need to sleep it off."

"Should I leave?"

"Stay. Please."

"Wow. Mora Cevi saying please."

"Smart-ass," she mumbled.

He smiled. "Go to sleep, Mo."

But it seemed she already had. She didn't respond, and her body relaxed deeper into the bed. So Ezra let himself relax too. He crawled under the blankets with her, leaving a few inches of space between them as he settled in and let his fatigue win.

Chapter 47

Something heavy and hot curled around Mo's body, holding her down.

She blinked rapidly, trying to clear the darkness from her vision and the sleep from her mind. She groaned and tried to move, only to realize it wasn't a something but a someone behind her. Ezra's strong arm was draped over her middle, tugging her close. His head was next to hers.

Stay. She'd asked him to stay. And he had.

She hadn't shared a bed with anyone other than Cass or Kynn in a very, very long time. She wanted to enjoy it, revel in that feeling of him being close. She didn't like very much physical contact, but this felt … right. She liked when he was close. And he'd been so kind to her, so helpful.

But her body wanted to run. Her muscles twitched. Her chest tightened.

He pulled her closer until her back was fully flush against his front, her ass against his crotch. It was possessive, somehow gentle but demanding. He snuggled into the bed and sighed happily.

"Mo?" came Ezra's raspy voice, still heavy with fatigue.

Shit.

As Mo opened her mouth, an alarm sounded, shrill and obnoxious in the quiet of her room. The ceiling lights flickered on, first warm white and then harsh red.

"Fuck," she said. "Fuck." They were under attack—or something equally bad—and here she was, tangled up in bed with Ezra.

What was she doing?

They should be focusing on this mission. They weren't out of danger. Three of them shouldn't have been sleeping.

"Fuck me," Ezra said, sitting up and helping Mo do the same. "How long were we out?"

"Don't know." She forced her stiff legs to move. Ezra's healing was helping, but she really needed the soltherin to start working soon. Or more healing. It didn't matter which. She couldn't go into another fight in pain. "I'll meet you out there," she said, tilting her chin toward the door.

Ezra rolled out of bed, tugged on his boots, and was about to move for the door but turned back to her. He looked like he wanted to say something. And despite that alarm, she *wanted* him to say something. About waking up like that. About the night before, when she'd been so sure he was going to kiss her.

But he just gave her a small smile. "See you out there."

Mo shoved away the disappointment curling in her belly. As soon as Ezra was gone, she pulled on her clothes as quickly as she could, opting for leggings and a plain tunic in case she needed to get into her gear quickly. She ran to the door.

Fuck. Fuck whoever or whatever had made that alarm go off. And fuck this mission. Mo could still feel Ezra's skin on hers, the warmth of his body behind her. She wanted more of that.

Yes, she'd been drawn to him for days now, but she hadn't even known she'd wanted *that.* Not until he'd been there, in her bed. She rarely reacted to anyone like that. It was just how she was. Tallas was the only man she'd ever been with, and no one had touched her since. But gods, Ezra was ... different.

Maybe they weren't quite under attack. No shots had come. Even if their shields were absorbing the worst, they'd *feel* the attack. But nothing came.

"What's happening?" Cass asked from behind Mo as they both stepped into the hallway and headed for the front of the ship.

"No clue."

"Kynn couldn't have filled us in?" Cass yelled as they neared the command room.

"Because I don't know what's going on!" he called back.

Mo reached the cockpit. Ezra was already there, his hand brushing between her shoulders as she skirted around him to look at the dashboard. There was nothing intimate about his touch now; he was all business.

"Nothing on sensors?" Mo asked. The warning lights continued flashing, and the alarm rang in her ears. She was trying to get her mind to focus again on the dashboard in front of her but just couldn't. "Nothing internally?"

"Nothing," Kynn said. "Nobody's even around us. This part of hyperspace is empty."

"That's not nothing," Ezra said, pointing at a swell of ... energy readings on the radar? Everything at its edge was shifting and warped. "Fuck."

"What?" Mo asked.

Kynn frowned. "I've never seen anything like that."

"I have, once," Ezra said. "It's a gravitational distortion. Saw it a couple years ago; the Ascended were trying out some new tech."

"So what do we do?" Mo cringed as the alarm kept blaring. It grated against her very soul. "Can we turn that fucking thing off?"

Cass hurried over to the comms station, and as soon as the screen turned on, she began typing in random sequences. The alarm ceased, but the red lights continued flashing. "We've got maybe sixty seconds before that thing pulls us out of hyperspace."

"Can it do that?" Mo asked. "Can we avoid it?"

"It's already affecting our engines," said Cass. "I don't think we can."

"Put all non-essential power to shields," Ezra said, then tapped Kynn on the shoulder. "Move."

"Move?" Kynn asked.

"I've escaped one of these before," he said. "I can do it again."

Kynn half stood, but he focused on Mo, a silent question passing between them.

"Do it," Mo said. "But if my ship gets so much as a scratch, Lyre, I'll kill you."

Ezra actually grinned at her, and despite the warning lights and impending disaster, her stomach flipped.

As soon as Kynn moved out of the pilot's seat, Ezra dropped into it and strapped himself in. "Brace yourselves," he warned. Kynn climbed into the copilot's chair. Ezra searched the dashboard, then asked, "Did you divert power to shields?"

"It's done," Cass said as she joined Mo in the cockpit. They strapped themselves into the second row of seats. On the view screen was nothing but darkness and streaks of light. "Controls are on Kynn's side."

"I'll keep 'em steady," Kynn said.

Mo really, really hated not being in that chair. But Kynn was a good pilot, and she hoped with every fiber of her being that Ezra was a good one too.

A drop out of hyperspace was always sudden, but the way their ship shook and trembled was too rough. Mo held onto her harness and braced her feet against the ground. Outside, the distant stars were distorted and bent, almost like Mo was looking at them through a lens. And whatever wasn't bent was blanketed by hazy darkness.

"What the fuck?" Cass whispered.

Mo had no idea. She just stared.

The ship banked left so suddenly that Mo toppled sideways, her restraints the only thing keeping her in her seat. The ship swerved right as Ezra fought to gain control. The alarm started again. The lights flashed faster. Mo didn't even know they could do that; she'd never run into anything like this. So many things could cause gravitational distortions—both natural and manmade—but she'd never actually come close to one.

"Shields are dropping," Kynn said.

Ezra's voice strained as he said, "Divert all non-life-support power to engines and shields."

Kynn's hands danced over his side of the controls. "Done."

"Short jump," Ezra said to Kynn. "On my mark."

"You want to jump back into hyperspace?" Mo yelled over the alarm. "Where?"

"Trust me!" he called over his shoulder.

Mo shut her mouth.

"And ..." Ezra drew the word out as he pulled the ship left, left, left. Cass gripped Mo's hand. "Now!"

The ship lurched, like they were being stretched. But then the speed hit, like a sharp jab to Mo's core. And again the ship dropped out of hyperspace, rough and sudden. Her head spun.

The Revenant was at a total standstill. It was like none of them were even breathing.

"Well?" Kynn asked.

"We're at the edge of the nearest system," Ezra said with a heavy sigh. "A few hundred million miles away from whatever that thing was."

The space outside was no longer distorted or obscured. It looked as it should, with clear stars and no strange haze bleeding out into space. Even the alarm and lights had stopped.

"What was that thing?" Cass asked. "Where'd it come from?"

"I don't know," Ezra said. "I didn't see any Ascended ships."

"Would they be testing their tech near random Federation systems?" Kynn asked.

"Probably not, even with everything else going on," Ezra said. "I don't see how they'd manage it. Someone in the system is probably going to detect it soon, whatever it is."

Mo had to agree with Ezra; it didn't seem like something the Ascended would be testing in open space. Not when they had other areas to choose from that were less likely to lead to a confrontation with the FSC.

"Well." Mo sucked in a deep breath. "Good job. At least we're not dead." When Ezra and Kynn turned around to look at her, she asked, "What?"

They both shook their heads.

"We need to run a system diagnostic," Cass said, already unbuckling herself and moving back toward the comms station. "That thing could've fucked us up."

"Looks fine from here," said Kynn.

"Looks fine isn't good enough," Cass said. "What system are we near, Ezra?"

"Uhm." He leaned toward a small screen on his left. "The Zistea System. Never heard of it."

"Shit," Cass muttered. "We're still nearly a full day away from Pyralis." She punched a few buttons on her station, then said, "There's a large mining colony on one of the moons here. A few towns, too, if we need to make any repairs."

"You want me to head that way?" Ezra asked.

"Let's just wait here until we know for sure if we're fucked or not," Mo said. "I'd rather have a quick exit."

Nodding, Ezra slumped back in his seat. Mo could hardly blame him. She hadn't even gotten up yet. Her legs didn't want to work. But this was her ship. It was her responsibility to ensure they were up and running.

"What do you want me to help with, Cass?" Mo asked, finally unbuckling her harness and forcing herself to stand. She was a little unsteady on her feet, like the gravitational distortion had altered her sense of balance. The whole room spun around her, and her knees slammed into the hard floor.

Screeching filled her ears, like rusty gears trying to turn. Only there were thousands of gears, so loud her eardrums might shatter. Mo curled in on herself, trying to block it out. The darkness behind her eyes exploded with red, shifting and warping, almost like she was watching a storm ravage a planet from space. It burned and bled, harsh against the shadows. Her head pounded in time with her heart, and Mo was sure she was going to die.

Until it stopped.

Stopped like it had never happened, and that red trickled away into black.

"Mo?" Kynn asked. He was on her right.

A large, warm hand pressed against her left shoulder. Far too big to be Cass.

Mo blinked against the cabin's low lights. Everything was as it should be, from Kynn and Ezra's worried expressions to Cass running back into the room. With Ezra and Kynn's help, Mo sat up.

"What happened?" Cass asked, squatting down in front of Mo and offering her a cold compress.

"I ... don't know," Mo said. She took the compress but didn't use it.

"You passed out," said Kynn.

"For how long?" she asked.

"Half a minute? You were completely unresponsive."

Ezra pulled his hand away, taking the heat with him. Mo caught a look at his palm and his solar magic as it died off.

"Whatever that was, it was incredibly painful," Mo said. "Could the distortion have done something to me?"

"Why you and not the rest of us?" Cass asked.

Mo had no idea. She wasn't a doctor or a scientist. She was a gods damn bounty hunter. "I don't know. I did just take soltherin, and I did overuse my magic on Mor'vex." She'd been pushing herself too hard for weeks. "It was almost like a migraine but ... louder."

"You should go lie down," Ezra said.

"I'm fine."

"Whatever caused it, you certainly aren't getting in that chair." Kynn gestured to the cockpit. "Either one of them."

Mo couldn't really argue with that. They didn't need her passing out at the helm. But what the fuck had that been? The colors reminded her of that hologram the Keepers had shown them, but was it connected or just her mind playing tricks on her?

"Fine," Mo said. "I won't fly. Do we know if the systems are clear? Is the ship good?"

"Nothing's amiss other than a few sensors, but we can fix those," Cass said. "A small miracle, honestly."

"So we're clear to keep going to Pyralis?" Mo asked.

"I don't see why not. Just give me a half hour to recalibrate things."

"What happened to going to that base or space station or whatever you said it was?" Ezra asked. "To hide out for a couple of days?"

"We should keep going," Mo said.

He pinned her with a look that said he clearly didn't agree.

"If we have everything we need, we should just go," Mo said. "We need to get there first."

His eyebrows furrowed and lips pressed into a thin line. "You're seriously not concerned about whatever just happened?"

"Of course I'm concerned, but we can figure it out on the way." She glanced at Cass. "It's safe to go?"

Cass gave a single nod. "It's safe."

Mo looked up at Ezra, at the concern in his forest green eyes. Her breath caught in her throat. "Then I'm trusting you to get us there," she said. "Just in case we run into any similar issues. Clearly you know what you're doing."

He nodded. "I won't even get a single scratch on the hull."

"Better not," Mo muttered.

Ezra laughed, and his gaze drifted to her mouth. Mo swallowed. But he didn't move, nor did she.

"C'mon, Mo," Kynn said, jostling her shoulder.

With Kynn and Ezra's help, Mo got back to her feet. She didn't stumble or sway this time. Her vision didn't change. Whatever that had been, at least it didn't seem to be leaving any lingering effects.

"Let's get to it," Mo said as she dusted her hands on her leggings. "We've got a long way to go."

Chapter 48

As much as Mo hated sitting around on the ship waiting for something to happen, the break from flying had actually given her a chance to look through both the Syndicate's database and Professor Valtor's notes for anything about gravitational distortions, migraines, or other bodily issues.

There was nothing. Mo didn't know if that made her feel better or worse. As she'd told Cass, she *had* also taken a dose of soltherin just a few hours before the incident. Maybe it was some freak side effect. Mo certainly wasn't going to go back near the damn distortion to test her theory, though. Maybe a pharmacist or doctor could tell her. She'd keep looking into it next time they got back to civilization.

Kynn, Ezra, and Cass had been switching off pilot duties over the last day. Mo felt bad about it, but she *was* feeling better physically. Not great, but better. The soltherin was working, and Ezra's healing the day before had helped. She actually felt able to go down to the surface despite everything.

The speakers near her bed crackled. "Just entered orbit around Pyralis, Mo," Kynn said.

"Anything on sensors?" she asked as she finished tugging on her boots.

"No. Place seems deserted. Computer's running more scans."

Mo headed out of her room and straight to the cockpit. Kynn was back in the captain's chair, his posture stiff as he read one of the monitors. He was alone. Outside, amid the darkness of space, was a planet covered mostly in blue and green. White clouds obscured a good chunk of the surface too.

"Did the computer find anything yet?" Mo asked as she dropped into the copilot's seat.

Footsteps echoed behind them. Ezra and Cass took their spots behind Kynn and Mo, respectively.

"Pinpointed a few likely locations," said Kynn. "Vizla said it was in a region not unlike where his temple was, right?"

Ezra nodded. "That's what he said."

"Planet's land mass is small," Kynn said. "The whole planet is small, barely bigger than either of Miduna's moons. And only two mountain chains on the whole thing."

"Where's the highest peak?" Cass asked.

"Several thousand miles north of the equator. Nothing on sensors says there's a settlement there."

"There wouldn't be," Mo said. "Not if the monks were willing to take themselves all out of the equation to protect their knowledge about this place. It's probably abandoned like Krytix's temple was."

"Then we should run flyovers," Ezra said. "Sensors can probably pick up more."

They all agreed, and so Mo buckled her restraints while Cass and Ezra strapped themselves into the back. Awareness prickled the back of Mo's neck, and she couldn't decide if it was Ezra or Cass watching her now. Maybe both. She hadn't gotten to speak with either of them much since the incident near the gravitational distortion.

Kynn and Mo began their descent into Pyralis's atmosphere. The whole cabin was quiet aside from the occasional beep of a sensor or the jostle of the ship as they descended. Mo didn't usually mind the silence, but now, she wanted to scream. She didn't even know why. It was just building up inside her chest. She forced it out as little more than a huff.

"You good?" Kynn asked, voice low. "Feeling okay?"

"Fine," Mo said. "Just ready for a break."

"Guess this thing really did become more than we bargained for," he said.

"Weren't you the one who insisted we'd be home in a week?"

"I suppose that was me. Sorry."

"I don't blame you."

"I know. Still can't help but feel a little guilty."

"We had the chance to walk away, and none of us did," Mo said, hopefully so quietly that Ezra couldn't hear her. "I'm tired, but I'm glad we stayed."

And she *was* glad. But she was tired. And annoyed. One didn't necessarily negate the other.

The ship leveled out as they neared the surface, Kynn keeping them at a high, steady altitude as they flew passes over the mountain range far below. It was still daytime on this side of the planet, but it likely wouldn't be for much longer. Judging by the sun's angle, they had only a few hours until sunset.

"Should be good if you want to start checking sensors, Cass," Kynn called.

Cass unbuckled her restraints and moved through the cabin with ease, not even fazed when they hit turbulence and the ship bumped.

"What about me?" Ezra asked.

"Hang out?" Kynn said with a shrug.

"Just what I wanted to do."

"Ship's not really built for a crew of four," Mo said.

"Maybe you need a bigger ship, then."

She shot a glare over her shoulder. "My ship's fine."

His easy smile faltered, and a twinge of guilt pulled in Mo's chest. Had he meant he wanted to stay on *The Revenant* with them? This wasn't Kynn's permanent place of residence, but he was there often enough. Assuming Kynn would just leave felt wrong, like she was kicking her brother out. Maybe Ezra didn't want to leave either.

Mo didn't want him to leave, surprising as that idea was to her. She really needed to watch her attitude. Ezra didn't deserve to be on the receiving end. She needed to work on her defensiveness. Not everything was a dig at her or her character, especially not with him.

"Sorry," she mouthed at him.

He smiled again, then unbuckled his restraints and scooted forward in his seat. He rested one hand on the back of her chair, leaned in, and said, "This place looks empty."

Far below, mountains stretched out in every direction. An unusually tall peak shot toward the sky off near the horizon. They were headed straight for it. That had to be the place if Vizla meant for them to literally look for someplace like the temple he'd overseen.

"What do you think happened to the other temple?" Mo asked. "Or Krytix's?"

"Would they have been destroyed?" Kynn asked.

"I sure as fuck hope not," Ezra said. "But I don't know. The Ascended rarely leave places untouched, and the FSC never backs down from a fight. It's a destructive combination."

"I'm surprised they didn't destroy each other on Mor'vex, then," Mo said.

Kynn looked out the view screen to his left. "Maybe they did and the ones on Andarix were just new fleets."

"I'm not getting anything on radar or sensors," Cass called from her station in the back. "Looks like there's nothing."

"Then we'll keep sweeping," Ezra said, "unless we see something without the tech."

Kynn took the ship down closer to the mountains, about a thousand feet above the tallest peak, for a better view. "This thing's massive," he said.

It was so tall that from Mo's angle, she couldn't even see the bottom of the valley clearly. Fog surrounded the lower half of the mountain. The entire range, actually. She frowned.

"Maybe we need to go down there," she said. "Krytix's temple wasn't up in the mountains, and the ground looks too rough. There's not even a flat spot to land." At least, there wasn't according to either her eyes or the ship's computer.

"Maybe ships aren't meant to land near the temple," said Kynn. "A precautionary measure for the artifact."

"I sure as all hell am *not* climbing a mountain," she said, and he laughed.

"We should go down," Ezra said. "Finish this pass, then fly as low as we can. It's got to be around here somewhere."

Following Ezra's suggestion, they finished circling the tallest peak, then went farther south. They doubled back at a lower altitude and slower speed. Mountain ranges like this caused all sorts of issues for pilots, from changes in airflow to the tighter spaces for navigation, but Kynn handled it like a pro.

Mo strained to pick out anything amid the growing fog. Everything was the same: flashes of black, gray, and brown between the clouds. Her jaw clenched as they neared the tallest peak again, this time far below the summit.

"Got something," Cass said. "Sending it to you, Kynn."

"Shit," Ezra said as he leaned forward between Mo and Kynn's seats again. "What is that?"

Based on Cass's sensor readings, there was a plateau another thousand feet below them and what appeared to be a massive spike in energy readings. Mo's sensors started going off, too, as that strange energy spiked again.

"It's like that day on Miduna," Ezra said.

And just like on Miduna, the energy dissipated, leaving empty sensors.

"Then I bet we found the Void Key," Kynn said. "Heading down."

They doubled back again, flying even lower this time. The more they descended, the clearer the plateau became. It was massive, almost unnatural, a perfectly flat cliff big enough to land four or five ships the size of *The Revenant*. Mo couldn't help but wonder if Voxarus or one of the other Eternal Ones had shaped the earth here specifically for the purpose of the temple, which was now visible outside.

Kynn landed the ship close to the tall pillars marking the entrance into the mountain. "Suit up," he said. "Be ready to leave in ten."

"Who put you in charge?" Cass asked.

He snorted. "Contrary to what you think, Cass, I'm always in charge."

"Tell yourself whatever you have to," she sassed. "See you down there."

As they all scattered, Mo headed back for her room and put on her gear. Boots, legguards, chest plate, spaulders. Everything but her gloves and helmet—and weaponry, which was locked away downstairs to charge. She hooked her gloves to her belt, grabbed her helmet, and went to the lower deck.

As she rounded the corner into the rear hold, she nearly slammed into Ezra. He grabbed her by her shoulders, steadying her.

"In a hurry?" he asked, eyebrows drawing together.

"Sort of." Her face burned. "Sorry."

"Why are you apologizing?" he asked as she skirted around him to one of the benches on the far wall.

Mo set her helmet down, unhooked her gloves from her belt, and scrubbed at her face. The awkwardness washing over her came out of nowhere. He felt too close yet too far away. And his black Vanguard gear was suddenly imposing, too serious.

"I'm ..." Mo swallowed hard as she turned to face him. "I'm just feeling out of sorts, I guess. After everything."

"It's a lot, isn't it?" he asked, one corner of his mouth quirking up as he closed the distance between them. "We've barely had a moment to settle."

"Yeah." She swallowed again. "Who knows when we will, either."

"After today," he said. "We'll go find a place to hide out for a bit until we can figure out what to do next."

"You sound so confident, like that's actually possible."

"We can't all be pessimists around here, you know," he said with another smile.

That gods damn smile.

"You look like you have something to say, Cevi."

Mo just had to say it. She had to say *something*, as difficult as it was for her.

"I'm sorry about what I said before, about the ship not being suited for a crew of four. I don't want you to think I don't like having you around."

He waited. Her chest heaved.

"I mean, it's a bit cramped when it's more than just me and Cass, but it's not so bad, having you here."

Ezra still watched her closely. She was making a fucking fool out of herself. But she liked Ezra. A lot more than she'd let herself acknowledge. He was kind and compassionate, an incredible fighter, and kept a cool head in dangerous situations.

"And I just want you to know I appreciate everything you've done for the three of us. For me. I know I don't always do a good job of saying thank you, but I'm trying."

He searched her face, almost like he was trying to discern if she was lying.

Mo's heart thrummed in her chest as she pushed up on her toes and brushed her lips against his jaw. The short hair of his beard tickled her cheek as she moved to pull away.

Ezra grabbed her forearm with one hand and her chin with the other, his touch light but firm as he held her in place and gazed down at her. He looked like he wanted to say something, but instead, he lowered his mouth to hers. Their lips met not in a crash but a caress, like whatever this was they were giving into was fragile, breakable. Maybe it was.

"Tell me to stop, Mo," he whispered.

"I can't." She couldn't. She wouldn't.

He kissed her again, this time with more force. His hand fell from her chin to the back of her neck, the other pressing against the small of her back. Mo's heart beat wildly in her chest as his mouth claimed hers. Even his kiss was powerful, steady, confident, like he was in a fight. When she moaned, his fingers dug into her hair.

And finally, he pulled away. She was left breathless, wanting more. She almost chased him, ready to pull him in again.

"Let's finish this in one piece," he whispered, one hand still near her waist. "You're good? Do you need healing?"

"I'm good," she said.

Footsteps sounded in the corridor and on the ramp. Both Mo and Ezra jumped away from each other, like teenagers getting caught by their parents. Cass caught Mo's eye as she strode into the rear hold, a silent question hanging between them.

"Later," Mo mouthed at her.

She would tell Cass everything later. In fact, getting Cass's perspective on things would be useful. Cass wasn't prone to romantic entanglements; she cared neither for romance nor sex personally. Mo hardly did. She'd been attracted to very few men in her nearly thirty years of life. Regardless, Cass was smart, empathetic, and observant. Surely she'd have something to say on the matter.

"Looks like everyone's on time, at least," Kynn said as he opened the weapons locker.

Ezra shot Mo a bemused smile, then leaned around Kynn. "Vanguards are good at following orders," he said, grabbing his saber and a gun. "Or did you miss that class?"

"Yeah, yeah," Kynn said with an easy laugh. "I get it, Commander."

Mo braided her hair and pulled on her gloves. She needed to focus. Whatever that was with Ezra, she would have to figure it out later. They needed to finish this, and quickly.

She was the last to grab her weapons. The Star Eater sat untouched in the locker, its hilt almost unremarkable among the other weapons. Nothing about it obviously screamed *sword of the gods*. Maybe it was better that way. Nobody complained when she locked it up again.

"Just like last time," Mo said. "We'll split up and search the place. If comms go down again, don't spend too much time apart. Ready?"

"Ready," they all echoed.

Mo strode forward, tapped in her code, and sucked in a deep breath as the cargo bay doors slid open. She put her helmet on, opened her comms channel, and stepped out into the Pyralian afternoon.

Chapter 49

As Ezra stepped out of *The Revenant,* he had to run through every grounding exercise he'd learned in his seventeen years in the FSC. Every single one. It was important for a Vanguard to be able to center themselves, especially in the middle of battle.

All he wanted to do was grab Mo, haul her back into the ship, and finish what he'd so desperately wanted to start. He wanted to rip that armor off her and show her exactly how he felt. But he couldn't. They had a mission to focus on, a mission he was growing weary of.

Ezra sighed as he took in the dusting of snow on the ground and the afternoon shadows. He was tired of searching ancient ruins and temples. Nothing good had come of these excursions yet, and the darkness looming before him did nothing to bolster his confidence that this time would be different.

Two statues of hooded figures flanked the entrance to Voxarus's temple, their spears crossing above the doorway. Both the statues and entrance carved into the mountainside were more than twenty feet tall, not so big that they felt like they'd swallow him whole but imposing enough to set him on edge. Again. Every fiber of his being screamed at him to run, but he forced one foot in front of the other as Mo led the way into the mountain.

They all switched on their helmet's external lights, sending strange shadows cascading down the walls. This was not like the other temples they'd been in.

"Fuck me," Mo said.

Staircases spiraled up and down, leading to platforms amid the never-ending darkness. Walkways crossed over chasms so wide Ezra couldn't yet see the other side. Was this some kind of maze? A puzzle?

"How do we figure out where to go?" Kynn asked.

"We might have to wait for the energy reading to come back," Cass said.

"That could take forever. Which we don't have."

The silence of the abandoned temple rang in Ezra's ears. "We should still split up," he said. "Start mapping out this place as best we can while we wait for the energy reading to come back. That should at least cut down on time trying to pinpoint the Void Key later."

"Krytix's sword was just in a small room at the end of a hallway," Mo said. "Lyre had to use his fire to open the door, almost like his magic was some kind of key."

"None of us are shadowbinders," said Cass.

"No, but if neither mine nor Lyre's works," Mo said, "we can try to rig it in some way. We'll figure it out."

It would have to do, even if Ezra didn't like it very much. He also didn't like what he was about to suggest.

"Kynn and I should go together, and then you two"—he gestured to Mo and Cass—"that way we aren't stacking magic. If you're right about the door."

He thought Mo hesitated for a second too long, but she said, "Good idea."

"Check-ins every twenty minutes," Kynn said. "Meet back here in an hour."

With that, Mo and Cass headed down the main wide corridor, eventually disappearing into the darkness. Ezra still hadn't moved. He knew he should, but he couldn't help the dread building in his bones. But was that his intuition, or was it whatever this thing was between him and Mo?

"Hey," Kynn said. He was already halfway up a staircase on the left side of the hall. "You coming?"

Ezra jogged over to him. "Sorry."

As they continued up, Kynn said, "You're distracted."

"Yeah, well, this place gives me the fucking creeps."

"Shouldn't a Vanguard be able to ignore that?"

"I'm usually pretty good at it," Ezra said as they reached a landing with a room off to one side.

Kynn headed in. Nothing in Ezra's visor sensory readings changed, not even the temperature. It was reading steadily cold. No energy spikes. No heat signatures or signs of life. The room had no windows or furniture, just dust and debris on the floors. An open doorway led into another room that ran parallel to the main corridor downstairs.

"I guess it's tough to focus on the mission when you're focusing on Mo," Kynn said.

"Yeah." But then it hit Ezra. "I mean, no," he added quickly. "No, I'm not focusing on her, this place is just—"

"Creepy. Yeah, I know," Kynn said with a laugh. "But they can take care of themselves."

"I know." Ezra had absolutely no doubt about Mo and Cass's ability to overcome whatever it was they found downstairs. "Believe me, I know."

"Then why were you just watching them?"

"Do we have to talk about this now?" Ezra asked.

The second room was just as barren as the first. There weren't even statues or carvings in the wall like back on Mor'vex. They moved into the third, where another staircase spiraled upward. That was the only thing different about this room, and Kynn started that way.

"No," Kynn said, "but I don't really want to walk around in complete silence."

Ezra grunted.

"She likes you, you know," Kynn said.

Ezra grunted again. After everything that had happened between them in the last day, he was fairly confident Mo liked him. She'd even kissed him first—if a kiss on the cheek counted. She'd asked him to stay in her bed with her. And before that, she'd trusted Ezra enough to tell him about her past. There were the brief glances, her blushing, the hard-to-come-by compliments.

All of that had to mean something.

"A lot," Kynn added. "Even if she doesn't see it."

Fine. Ezra would take the bait.

"How do you know?" he asked.

They reached the top of the stairs, revealing another empty room. This was just getting annoying now. A waste of time. But they continued back in the opposite direction, back toward the front of the temple. The rooms were smaller up here, but they otherwise followed the layout of the lower level.

"Because she never asks anyone for help," Kynn said. "She also never lets anyone besides me or Cass fly the ship."

"Our lives were in immediate danger."

"You think that'd make Mo change her mind?" Kynn asked with a laugh.

"Maybe not," Ezra conceded. She was stubborn, maybe stubborn enough to get them all killed. And yet, he liked that about her. "You think she doesn't want me to stick around? After my comment about the ship?"

That was his one big hesitation. *It's not built for a crew of four.*

"Nah," Kynn said. "It's her default. Give her some time to shift. She needs it."

Ezra could do that, and he would take her at her earlier words, that she was sorry for implying anything with that comment.

"Hey, look," Kynn said as they got to the final room. The first staircase they'd taken continued up to this level and another. There was also a narrow window on the far wall. Beyond that was a series of carvings in the brick.

They both moved closer, bringing their lights as close as they could. Whatever language the words had been carved in, it wasn't one Ezra could read, nor was it the same as what he'd seen on Mor'vex.

"Back up," he said to Kynn. Once they were both a couple of feet back, Ezra turned his forearm and pushed a button on his gauntlet. He moved down the wall, taking pictures of the carvings. If they could somehow get back to one of the universities, this shit might be useful. That was a big "if" though.

With nothing else to show for their efforts on this level, they ascended to the third. It was more of the same, with a few sporadic carvings but nothing they could read. Ezra took more photos just in case.

"Kynn?" came Cass's voice through their group comms channel.

"Yeah?" Kynn asked.

"Anything?"

"No. You?"

"No," Cass said. "There's a lot of room left to check, though."

"Heard," Kynn said. "Us too. Check in soon."

"Now what?" Ezra said only to Kynn. "Check the other side?" They'd run out of stairs to climb, and Ezra wasn't keen on blasting a hole through the ceiling unless absolutely necessary.

"After you, Commander."

They'd searched similar rooms on the opposite side of the main corridor, but those had yielded more of the same: currently useless information that didn't bring them any closer to finding the Void Key. And there hadn't been any more energy readings.

Which brought them all back to the temple's entrance. Relief flooded Ezra's body as Mo's dark armor and Cass's opal set emerged from the shadows. Neither looked worse than when he'd seen them an hour ago.

Outside, only a sliver of sunlight remained, long since blockaded by the mountains surrounding the temple's entrance. It was almost like this place was destined to be shrouded by darkness, which, Ezra supposed, could've been the point. Voxarus was the Eternal One of Mystery and Death, of the Void itself.

As soon as they were back outside, Mo took her helmet off and sighed. Ezra did the same, breathing in the fresh air. As much as he'd gotten used to the recycled air in his helmet over all his years in the FSC, there was no relief like taking it off.

"So?" Kynn asked. "Obviously you didn't find the Key."

"No, but I'm getting a better sense of the part of the temple we were in," Mo said. "It looks like there were once traps that have since been triggered. Even found a few bones."

"Fucking gruesome," Kynn said, scrunching his nose.

"To protect something like the Void Key? I get it," Mo said.

"We didn't find anything when we took the stairs down into the chasm," said Cass. "The stairs actually stopped completely midair, so we didn't go farther. Couldn't see the bottom."

"Sounds like another attempt at a trap," Ezra said.

"Maybe." Mo shrugged. "We went across the bridge, and there's a *lot* back there. It goes deep."

Ezra muttered a curse. Of course it went deep. They really needed that damn—

His suit pinged. Ezra shoved his helmet back on, and on his visor's screen was a warning of an energy surge. Readings said it was nearly a klick due north.

"Shit," Ezra said, then told them what he saw.

"That's the direction we'd been headed," said Mo.

Ezra pushed a few buttons on his gauntlet, then Mo's suit pinged too. "You get that?" he asked her.

She shoved her own helmet on. "Yeah, I see it. Or saw it, it's go—"

"We've got incoming," said Cass.

"What?" Mo and Ezra asked at the same time. Ezra didn't see anything in his other sensor readings. What could possibly—

"Look," Cass said, pointing skyward.

Ezra looked up. Sure enough, in a break in the fog, he caught a glimpse of a black ship flying past. The engines made no sound.

How could his suit not have picked up on that?

"Is that Ascended?" Kynn asked.

The ship passed by again, and still Ezra's suit didn't pick up on it. Vanguard suits were supposed to be the best of the best. "I don't know," he said.

Was it just the one? Ezra didn't see any others, but with the dense cloud coverage and lack of sensor data, it was hard to be sure. He didn't dare run over to *The Revenant* to check.

"Okay," he said, turning to face the team. "Mo, stick with the plan. We may need a magic user to get into the Void Key's vault, so you do that. I'll stay out here with Kynn and try to negotiate with whoever this is. Cass, I want you up in that window, covering us."

"Ezra—" Kynn started.

"He's right," Cass said. "It's the only way, unless we want to abandon this place to them."

"We're not doing that," Mo said.

The ship made another pass, lower this time.

"Watch out for each other," Mo said as she slid her helmet on. "I'll be back."

She turned on her heel and sprinted into the temple, Kynn yelling her name as she disappeared into the darkness. And when she ignored him, he turned to Cass. "Why would you agree to this?"

"Because it's the *only* way, Kynn," she said, lifting her chin even as he towered over her. "We protect the Star Eater and we buy Mo time to find that artifact." She glanced at Ezra. "I trust you, whatever it is you have planned."

"Thank you," Ezra said. He'd known that for a while, but hearing it out loud was nice.

"I didn't mean I don't trust you," Kynn said as he turned toward him. "I just don't like Mo going off alone."

"I know," Ezra said. "I don't either. But it's like you said earlier. She can take care of herself. Or are you already forgetting about that?"

"Not forgetting," Kynn said. "Remembering all the times this has bitten us in the ass before."

Ezra wanted to ask him to elaborate, but the ship finally broke through the clouds and came about, slowly dropping to land not far from *The Revenant*.

"Cass, go," Ezra said. She took off. "Kynn, you good?"

"I'm good," he said, coming to stand just to Ezra's right.

As the ship powered down, Ezra resisted the urge to reach for his weapons. He didn't need them yet.

Hopefully he wouldn't need them at all.

Chapter 50

The ship wasn't a class Ezra was familiar with. It was almost the same size and shape as a typical small starfighter, but the longer Ezra stared at it, the more unfamiliar it became. It looked almost like an FSC ship, but the curve of its wings lifted a fraction too high, and the black paint was darker than any he'd seen in their fleet.

Was this some Ascended trick? Experimental FSC tech? Hell, for all Ezra knew, it could belong to a group of space pirates who had been pulling all the strings. He didn't like any of those options.

"What's taking so long?" Kynn asked.

A whole ten minutes had ticked by, but the ship's doors hadn't opened yet. No ramp or stairs had descended. Whoever was in there was taking their sweet time. Maybe that was for the best, at least for Mo.

"Cass," Ezra said, "you seeing anything?"

"Movement inside the cockpit, but I can't tell who it is," she said. "They're wearing armor, but it's not quite like yours."

Just like the ship wasn't *quite* like a normal FSC ship.

"Mo?" Ezra asked.

"Heading toward the last energy reading," she said, a little out of breath. Her words crackled with interference as she said, "Send me any updates if you—"

The connection dropped just as a ramp began sliding out from the ship's exterior.

"Shit," Kynn said, but he didn't move a muscle.

Ezra did not like this one bit.

"Focus," Cass said, as if she knew they were both going to be distracted by this.

Ezra shook himself mentally. Cass was right. He needed to focus.

The ramp hit the ground with a metallic thunk. The doors at the top slid open, revealing three people dressed in dark armor not unlike Ezra's. Just as Cass had said.

They strode down the ramp, two armed with energy spears and the other with a large rifle. The indigo FSC shield was emblazoned above their hearts, but he couldn't see their faces behind their helmets.

"Commander Lyre," called the one in front. "It's good to see you alive and well."

"Why wouldn't I be?" Ezra asked.

"Reports said you'd gone missing."

"Not missing," Ezra said. "On sabbatical, but I already cleared that with Command."

"Yes," said that voice. It was so modulated Ezra couldn't place them at all, not even their accent. "But after the events on Vonnoth, Command feared something had happened to you."

Ezra wasn't sure he believed them. "Clearly not."

"We received a report about a Vanguard fleeing the battle on Mor'vex," the lead figure said.

Mor'vex, but not Andarix?

Ezra loosed a breath. "Yeah, I was there."

"Why?"

"Investigating why someone's got a hit out on me and why my team was assassinated in Federation custody," Ezra said.

"You were ordered to stand down on that front, Commander."

"I guess I just couldn't let it go."

The soldier tilted their head to the side as if asking a question.

"What unit are you with?" Ezra asked.

"We're with Federation Space Command Intelligence," they said.

Intelligence. Of course. The FSC was made up of many divisions, and Intelligence was the most elusive of them all. Ezra's teams had received information from Intelligence officers before, but he'd never met any of them. They actually fell under General San'ri's command, just like Vanguards did.

They nodded at Kynn. "Who is this?"

"I'm Kynn Sathir."

The lead soldier was silent for a long moment, then said, "Kynn Sathir, orphan of Veronis, previous Vanguard trainee, current member of the Midunian branch of the Starlight Syndicate. Late on last year's tax payment."

"Only by three days," Kynn said. "The government got its money, don't worry."

The soldier focused on Ezra again. "Why are you with a bounty hunter?"

"That's not illegal," Ezra said. If this person wanted to talk, he'd let them talk. All it did was buy Mo more time.

"No, it's not," they said. "But unusual."

"Look," Ezra said, "Command knew what I was doing. I told them back on Vonnoth that I'd been trying to figure out why my former team betrayed me and the FSC, and that's led me on a wild chase through the Federation, including being targeted by multiple Vanguards trying to assassinate me. If Intelligence knows anything about that, I'm all ears. If not, I'd like to continue with my work here."

"You were ordered to stand down, Commander," the lead soldier said. "You were ordered to let this go."

"It's hard to let it go when it only gets more personal with every day that passes," Ezra said. "Am I under arrest or something?"

"No, but there is an investigation into your actions as well as everything you told Command about," said the lead soldier. "Including the threat against your life. We need you to come with us, Commander. Please."

"I'll return to Aerilia when I've—"

The roar of shuttlecraft engines rocked the ground. It came about, revealing a simple white and gray paint job, nothing to betray whose shuttle it might be.

"Friends of yours?" Kynn asked the soldiers.

A sharp blast pierced the air as the new shuttle fired their weapons. The FSC ship exploded. Fiery debris launched high above them, and some of it slammed into *The Revenant*.

The three soldiers scrambled back toward Ezra, all of them now watching the sky as the shuttlecraft descended toward the plateau.

"Not friends," said the lead one, voice hard. "We were supposed to be the only ones here."

If not for their ship being blown to bits, Ezra may not have believed them. But whoever that was clearly wasn't friendly toward these soldiers.

"Ezra," Cass said through their comms. "I see two more shuttles approaching from the south. Identical to this one."

Fuck.

"Listen," Ezra said to the soldiers, "I don't know what Command's told you, but we've seen some shit the last month. Were you here to haul me in for a court-martial?"

"Some disciplinary action but mostly for your own safety," said the lead soldier. "Intelligence discovered encrypted messages from Aerilia that issued the hit on you. General San'ri is concerned for your well-being and wanted to bring you into protective custody until this could all be sorted out."

Was this it, then? Was this whoever wanted him dead?

"Do they know who put the hit out?" Ezra asked.

"No, sir. They were still working on that when we were deployed," said the lead soldier. "But it seems they've found you."

Fuck me. Ezra didn't see much of a choice. He could either try to disarm and incapacitate these three, then fight off the newcomers with very little backup, or he could hope for the best.

"You with us?" he asked. "You willing to fight with us?"

"Yes, Commander," the lead soldier said.

"You got names?"

"We go by Atom, Fang, and Shadow," they said, pointing first to themself, then the shorter member of the squad, then the tallest.

There were surely stories behind those names; Ezra wasn't going to ask now. "Wish we were meeting under better circumstances," he said. "Welcome to the team."

"They're with us, Cass," Kynn said over comms. "Not sure who owns those shuttles."

"Heard," she said.

Two more shuttles landed, both identical to the first in size and color. They landed behind the burning wreckage of the FSC ship. Luckily, *The Revenant* didn't seem to be too damaged, though Mo was going to hate the clearly visible dent in its side.

The shuttle doors lifted up, and between the three ships, a retinue of nearly thirty stepped out. *Thirty.* How many fucking assholes did they think it would take to finally fulfill the kill contract?

Ezra reached for his saber hilt but didn't engage the trigger. He wouldn't, not until he knew exactly what this threat was.

They were all dressed in white and red armor, not a color combination Ezra was familiar with. Maybe they really were pirates, or some private squad someone on Miduna had put together. They picked their way around the wreckage, then came to a stop a few hundred yards away from Ezra.

"There you are!" came a familiar voice.

That couldn't be right ...

The leader of this new group removed her helmet, revealing straight blonde hair and a slightly upturned nose. His cousin and Triumvirate member Livia Valtor.

"Ezra!" she called. "I'm so glad to see you."

"Liv?" Ezra yelled back. "What are you doing here?"

She smiled viciously. "You have something I want."

Chapter 51

Mo's breath came in ragged bursts as she sprinted through the dark, abandoned temple halls. No energy readings had changed, but her in-suit computer was guiding her toward the last ping.

She wished she could check in with the team, but her comms had already cut out.

She had another quarter of a klick to go. She was *so* close.

It had turned into just one long hallway in the bowels of the temple, its floor littered with debris. The light from her helmet did nothing to make this easier. It was just a faint glow amid the oppressive shadows. It was almost like she'd walked into the Void itself.

Focus, Cevi, she reminded herself. She needed to focus. She needed to do this.

Just a couple more minutes and she'd be there … wherever *there* was.

She pushed her tired legs faster. Her joints were already beginning to protest; sunshaper healing or soltherin usually lasted so much longer. She hadn't been giving herself the time to really rest, though. Hadn't had the chance.

After today, she promised herself. She'd give her body a break. If they made it out of this shit show in one piece, they'd find some godsforsaken planet or moon or space station to hide out on for a while, just until things calmed down. There had to be a way.

Her visor blinked at her as she closed in on the last known energy spike. Mo slowed, but there was—

The ground rocked, throwing Mo off balance. It rocked again, and she swore as she tumbled into the wall to her right. What the fuck was going on out there?

Muttering a few choice words to herself, Mo straightened and examined the hallway again. She was supposedly where the last energy spike had occurred, but there wasn't anything here. The walls were solid, no hint of doors or keys or even a fucking out-of-place rock to give her an idea.

She tilted her head up. Above was just the jagged stone of the mountain. Down, maybe? But how?

Mo ignited her saber, casting white light in a nearly twenty-foot radius. *Much better*. She hadn't wanted to drain its power pack, but she needed better visibility. She continued down the hall slowly, inspecting both sides for a door or stairs of some kind. She ran her free hand along the walls, probing every bump, divot, and crevice that seemed remotely out of place.

"There you are," she whispered, her steps slowing. The darkness here was so oppressive that she hadn't even been able to make out the break in black stone. She shone her lights toward the opening, revealing stairs. Exactly what she needed.

Mo started down. They spiraled around themselves, and some of the steps were just loose, crumbling stone. Mo picked her way down farther and farther into the darkness. It choked the air, and even the glow of her saber did little to light the way anymore.

Her feet hit flat ground, and the space ahead of her straightened into one long corridor. She couldn't even see how far it went or where it might end. There were no doors on either side of her.

Krytix's temple seemed like a walk in a nice, sunny park compared to this place. Mo far preferred it, and she wouldn't apologize to Voxarus for it. It was one thing to protect an artifact like the Void Key, but did it have to be dangerously impossible to find?

Mo continued until her visor pinged and flashed again. She was just a hundred feet from the last energy reading. Slowly, she continued forward, her sword held out to one side to stave off some of the shadows.

And finally, there was a door. A small door, barely big enough for Mo to fit through. A small keyhole was in the middle of it, and no matter how hard Mo pushed, it wouldn't budge.

She pulled on her magic, guiding the lavender tendrils into the hole. She pushed them farther and farther, but they did nothing. The door still wouldn't move.

"Fuck," she muttered. Now what? She slammed her fist on the door and yelled, "Fuck!"

"That's not very ladylike, Momo."

That voice slithered down Mo's spine like the snake it belonged to. She spun, finding Tallas there among the shadows, Jardan Illescas at his side and the woman too. The two behind Tallas had their weapons raised, two blasters and that fucking red axe. None of them were wearing helmets, exposing their hostile expressions.

"I thought Cass shot you," Mo said.

Tallas smiled and spread his arms out wide. "Didn't kill me."

"She destroyed your ship."

"And yet it seems we found another way here."

Leave it to Tallas to steal another hunter's ship. That, or he had help. "Who are you working for?" she asked.

"I work for myself, Momo." He took a step forward, and Mo raised her blade higher. Behind him, Jardan shifted, obscuring a flash of green.

Green. Mo was very glad she had her helmet on to hide her hint of a smile.

"You know that," Tallas continued. "You *love* to tell everyone that, how selfish and greedy I am."

"You think I even spare you a second thought?" she asked. "You're a fool if you think I even waste my breath talking about you."

"I know you do," he said, voice low. "How could you not, especially after all our … *fun* … together?"

Rage burned brightly under Mo's skin. She hated him, hated him, hated him.

"You're not getting into this room unless you brought explosives," she said. "And I was here first, so back off. Syndicate rules."

Tallas threw his head back and chuckled. It bounced off the walls, surrounding her. "Oh, Momo," he drawled, "you still think those rules matter?"

"Don't they?"

"They never mattered. You want to know why?"

She didn't answer. He was going to keep talking whether she invited it or not. She was convinced Tallas just liked the sound of his own voice.

"Because rules are for losers," Tallas said. "If you want to be a winner—if you want to come out on top—you have to break them. But you love your rules, don't you?"

As he stepped forward again, Mo pointed her blade straight at his heart. "Why don't you come closer and find out?"

And again, he chuckled. "You're not a killer, Momo. Stand down."

"Fuck you."

She lunged, feinting left as Tallas reached not for the glaive on his back but a saber. Mo opened herself up to her magic, loosening her tight control. Lavender spun out from her free hand, snaking up the other woman's legs in a deadly chokehold. With a flick of her wrist, the woman slammed into the stone wall so hard her skull crunched.

Pain flared behind Mo's right eye, a warning from her body not to push. But she didn't have a choice. She had to keep going. She had to get the Key.

Tallas roared. To her right, Jardan's hands began glowing green. Exactly what she needed.

Her magic abandoned the dead woman, snaking along the floor to grab hold of Jardan. His entire body began to glow. Mo clenched her fist, and her magic snapped up, engulfing him all the way to his chest. Her veins burned as she directed him toward the door. Tallas rolled out of the way.

Mo slammed Jardan against the door, right near the tiny keyhole. His magic seemed to be siphoned into it, not of his own volition but the door's doing. The ground rumbled and shook as the door slid open.

Mo gritted her teeth against the pain pounding in the back of her head and flicked her wrist again. Jardan reared back from the wall, carried by those same violet tendrils. Mo held tight to her control over him as she barreled past Tallas, slashing at him with her blade to force him back.

She squeezed through the door before it even fully opened, frantically searching the next chamber. The next door was already opening, too, revealing a dark room beyond.

Mo squeezed her fist tighter, letting out a pulse of magic that knocked Tallas and Jardan back down the hall. She bolted through the second door, and instead of a pedestal, there was a chest on the opposite side of the room.

She cut through the lock with her saber and threw the chest open. Inside, a dark disc sparkled with an unnatural green light. She grabbed it, and the whole world tilted. Her helmet's light shut off and saber disengaged—or Mo just couldn't see anymore.

Child, a booming voice thundered in her head. *My brother warned me you would come.*

That makes me sound like a threat, Mo said.

You are not a threat but a force. You are Starborne.

There was that word again. What Keeper Vizla had called them.

How does Krytix know that about me? Mo asked.

He saw what you did on Mor'vex, said that voice. *I saw what you did on Andarix. You fight for us.*

You're Voxarus? Mo asked.

I am, Child.

Why didn't you speak to me then?

It's not always possible, said Voxarus. *This takes much energy, which I do not have.*

Mo couldn't exactly blame the god for that, although it would be awfully nice if they could speak to her more often. *What do I need to know?* she asked.

Somewhere, beyond the darkness and the oppressive weight crushing Mo's chest, Tallas let out an angry, guttural roar.

Tell me, please, she said. *Quickly.*

Ikna gains power with every passing day, Voxarus said. *Do not let anyone control my Key, for if her champions get it, chaos shall be unleashed.*

Who are her champions? Mo asked. *What chaos—*

Something hard and heavy hit Mo from behind. She toppled over, and the oppressive weight crushing her chest was replaced by the light of a blade and familiar green magic.

Tallas hovered above her, pinning her to the ground with his full weight. He had a short dagger pointed at her, its blue eerily similar to the color of Kynn's sword. Some far-off part of her mind conjured a memory of Kynn losing that dagger to Tallas in a bet.

"Now," Tallas said, chest heaving, "I can finally finish the job. With you down, it's just three more to go."

Mo knew she needed to move. She knew she did. But …

But Tallas was working for whoever put out the hit on them. On all of them.

She needed information. And if she was going to get information, she had to survive.

Jardan stooped to pick something up off the ground. Mo flung her arm out to one side, shooting her magic his way. It wrapped around his throat. She clenched her fist, and he slammed into the wall, cracking his skull open just like his partner. Blood exploded across the stones, lit up by the glow of Tallas's blade and Mo's helmet.

Tallas screamed again. Mo's head pounded. Her mouth went dry, and the power that usually hummed within her waned. The edges of her vision darkened, and static filled her ears.

Fuck.

He pressed his dagger closer to Mo's armor. She angled her hilt toward his leg and engaged the blade. It shot through his knee. He roared and toppled off her.

Mo staggered to her feet, snatched the Void Key off the ground, and ran.

She gripped the relic tight, praying silently to Voxarus that her plan was going to work, that she'd last long enough to get Tallas back to the surface. That she'd last long enough to get help so her friends could question him and figure out who was hunting them and why.

Darkness crept in at the edges of her vision. It was too much like that day on Aerilia all those years ago. She didn't know how she'd been able to keep going after that, why her stamina was so comparatively weak now when she was stronger, older, faster. She loved her body for what it could do but hated that it sometimes betrayed her.

Mo scrambled up the spiral stairs, slipping several times as she went. A heavy hand yanked on her shoulder, sending her tumbling back down. She slammed into the stone ground so hard that even with her helmet on, her vision began to spin.

"I'll be taking that." Tallas groaned as he stooped to take the Void Key out of her hand. "When are you ever going to learn that you can't run from me, Momo?"

Mo pulled on whatever energy she had left in her core, but there was nothing. It fizzled out like a firework. She couldn't even push the button to engage her blade.

With his good leg, Tallas kicked Mo's helmet. Her visor flickered just before the image disappeared. The entire world went dark.

"And now ..." It sounded like Tallas smiled. "Now, we're going to go to the surface so you can watch your friends die before I finally put you out of your misery."

Chapter 52

"What do you mean I have something you want?" Ezra asked. "What are you doing here? Is it even safe for you to be out here?"

Livia clicked her tongue. "Good thing you never tried to follow in the family footsteps, Ezra." She stalked forward, her elegant red cloak fluttering in the breeze behind her. Her sleek white armor looked more ceremonial than functional, especially in a desolate place like this. "Always were a bit dense, weren't you?"

What Livia wanted.

What her father had been searching for …

"You," Ezra said. "You put the hit out on me."

"Oh!" She smiled. "That didn't take you as long as I expected."

"Why the fuck would you try to have me killed?" Ezra asked. "Did you have your father killed? For these artifacts?"

The ground underneath them rocked, but Livia didn't seem the least bit fazed by it. She continued walking, her guards at her back. It was then that Ezra's brain began to work again, began to actually take in the fact that many of those standing behind his cousin were Vanguards. Their armor wasn't standard Vanguard black, but rather an identical design in white.

White like what he'd seen in the High Sanctum on Andarix.

"Ezra?" Cass asked through the comms. "What do you want me to do? Take her out?"

"No," he whispered. "No, she's a chancellor, even if she's a piece of shit. It'll be viewed as an assassination, not self-defense."

Fuck, Ezra hated this. Why did she have to be a member of the Triumvirate? Why did everyone in his family have to be so terrible?

"Is this some kind of coup?" he asked Livia.

She laughed, smiling at him like he was just a foolish child asking silly questions. "Oh, Ezra," she said, almost as if she were endeared by him. "Don't try to use words you don't understand."

"I know what a fucking coup is, Liv," he said. "And I know damn well you're not the head of the FSC or commanding those Vanguards under any authorization."

"No authorization?" she asked with a chuckle. "I'm a member of the Triumvirate, Ezra. That *is* authorization."

"No, it's not," said one of the Intelligence officers behind Ezra. The shortest one—Fang—stepped forward. "By order of the Federation—"

Livia flicked her wrist. A rifle fired somewhere in the distance. The shot pierced the officer's helmet, and they slumped to the ground.

"Anyone else?" Livia asked.

Ezra reached for his saber.

"Think hard, Ezra," she said. "I'd hate to tell your parents you died because you were trying to assassinate me. You already betrayed the family professions; we don't need to turn you into a true traitor too, right?"

"Don't," Ezra warned as Kynn and the other two Intelligence officers stepped forward.

Ezra had no clue how deep this treachery ran, whether it was just Livia, the entire Triumvirate, how many the FSC was bleeding to the cause ... whatever the cause even *was*.

More ship engines roared above them, and based on the way Livia didn't move a muscle, they were likely more of her … army? Allies? Dammit, he really wished he knew how many she had on her side.

But the ones at her back—several dozen Vanguards and that sniper, wherever they were—would be too much. Even for him. Even for Kynn and Cass and Mo. There were no Ascended here this time to serve as a distraction, nothing to give them cover to flee.

"What do you want, Liv?" Ezra asked, his jaw tightening.

"I want the artifacts."

"I don't have them," Ezra said.

She tilted her head to one side. "No? But you were on Mor'vex."

"So?" Ezra asked. "I didn't find a damn thing there before all hell broke loose. Were those your people?"

"Not most of them, no." She gave him another condescending smile. "But I have people everywhere. I'm not stupid, Ezra."

"And you're giving me more credit than you should," he said. "I'm a soldier, not an archaeologist. All I wanted was to figure out who had a hit out on me, but I guess I have now."

"Not an archaeologist …" Livia trailed off, then pointed at Kynn. "Where're the others? There are supposed to be two more."

Ezra didn't know how to answer that.

"So *they're* the archaeologists?" Livia taunted. "No matter, I've already got people canvassing the temple. They'll find the others and the arti-fact."

How did Livia already have people in the temple? Where was the other entrance? Was that the rumble he'd felt before?

"I'm fine," Cass said. "Trust Mo. Tell me when you want me to shoot."

"Don't," Kynn said, so low even Ezra almost didn't hear him. "There's too many. Stay hidden."

Livia folded her arms loosely over her chest but quickly unfolded them, smiling widely at something—or likely someone—behind Ezra. "Oh, good!" she exclaimed. "You found one."

Ezra's heart dropped as the sound of a body hit the ground behind him.

"Alive and ready for whatever punishment you see fit."

Ezra ground his teeth together. Tallas Bara was here? Working for Livia?

The picture began piecing together in Ezra's mind. Livia probably had spies in the FSC aside from the forces she was siphoning off—like all these traitorous Vanguards—and had issued the treasure hunting contracts. It was how she'd known about him being on Mor'vex and explained Tallas's recent appearances. It didn't explain why Livia's soldiers had been fighting the bounty hunters on Andarix, but Ezra had bigger problems to sort right now.

"She doesn't look alive," said Livia, her upper lip curling.

"She is," Tallas said. "Barely."

Ezra turned. He knew he shouldn't turn his back on his cousin or all those Vanguards, but he had to. He had to see Mo.

She lay unmoving in a heap at the bottom of the stairs leading into the temple. Her armor was dirty, and her helmet had a crack in the side. Her blade hung from Tallas's belt like some kind of sick trophy.

"What did you do to her, Tallas?" Kynn yelled.

"She killed two of my people." Tallas favored his left side. His legguard was broken and burned, where Mo had clearly injured him. "She wouldn't go down without a fight, so I gave her one."

"Shame," said Livia absentmindedly. "Did you get it?"

Tallas lifted up an obsidian disc surrounded by a strange green aura. "She found it in a chest downstairs. I assume this is it."

"Bring it here!" Livia called.

Tallas limped past Mo without even a second glance, holding up the Void Key for them all to see. The Intelligence officers shifted uneasily, and Kynn was practically vibrating with rage.

"You gonna shoot me if I check on her?" Ezra asked Livia.

"Why do you want to check on her?" she asked as she took the Key from Tallas.

"Because she's my friend," Ezra said. Because she was more than that, but he didn't dare give Livia or Tallas ammunition.

"Fine." Livia pulled a small handheld scanner from her belt. "But one hint of weapons and I'll have my sniper take you out, Ezra. Don't test me."

Ezra didn't know that he trusted Livia not to kill him where he stood, but he bolted to where Mo was unmoving on the ground. Kynn stayed behind, but he swore quietly over comms.

"Mo," Ezra said, ripping her helmet off. A few contusions marred her face, and her lip was split, but there didn't seem to be any major damage to her head. He gently shook her shoulder. "Mo."

She still didn't stir.

What had she done down there to just go lifeless?

Ezra tugged on his magic, on that warm, low fire stirring around his heart. He took Mo's face in his hands and pushed that heat into her, willing it to fix whatever was broken. When he let go, her head lolled to the side.

That gentle warmth within him ignited, exploding into something bigger, something worse. Ezra shoved to his feet and stalked toward his cousin.

She was still inspecting that disc. The sensors in his suit spiked, setting off the warning alarm. Sparkling green light—magic, energy—pulsed out from the Key, twining with red. The colors were gone in a flash, but his cousin still smiled viciously and sucked in a deep, cleansing breath.

Ezra reached for her, but a warning shot exploded on the ground near his feet.

"Ezra," Livia said, drawing out the last syllable. "What do you think you're doing?"

"What am I doing?" he seethed. "This jackass almost killed her because you—"

"Because I what, Ezra?" Livia asked, and Ezra swore for a moment that her eyes flashed red. "There's more here at stake than you understand. If you did, you'd see I had no choice. She was but a tiny little bug getting in the way of everything that's to come."

Tallas smirked as his gaze drifted toward the temple again.

Livia pulled a gun from her belt and pointed it at Ezra. "Now, you can either come with me, back to Aerilia so you can help me find the rest of these artifacts, or you can die right here, right now."

"What about them?" Ezra asked. "What about my friends?"

"I'm feeling generous," Livia said. "You help me back on Aerilia, and I'll let your friends go."

Go with her and do what, exactly? Act as some kind of glorified soldier aiding in a coup? Ezra would never.

"Commander," said Atom, the lead Intelligence officer. "Don't, she—"

Livia pulled the trigger on her blaster at the same moment the sniper got another shot off. The officer dropped to the ground beside Fang.

"You think they'd learn after one warning kill," Livia said with a sigh. "Apparently they're stupider than you, Ezra."

His throat worked, but he could barely swallow.

"You and this other FSC ... whoever you are," Livia said, gesturing vaguely behind Ezra. "You two come with me, and I'll let the bounty hunters live. That's what you want, right, Ezra?" she asked. "To not have more of your friends die?"

Ezra couldn't lose Mo, Cass, and Kynn. They didn't deserve to die. Especially not like this. Not because they'd taken Ezra's contract and stayed on with him through all of this unfathomable bullshit. Not after the way they'd let him into their world and welcomed him to the team—even grudgingly, like Mo.

This was the only way any of them had a chance of making it out alive.

"We can fight—" Kynn started.

"Fine," Ezra said to Livia. "I'll go with you. But you have to let them go. No criminal charges. No arrests. They go, alive, innocent, and free. You leave them alone, forever."

"It only seems fair," Livia said. "They did get me what I needed, in a way." She tilted her head back toward the shuttlecraft. "Now hurry up. Ship's waiting."

"Come on, Shadow," he said to the Intelligence officer behind him. "Let's go. Assignment's changed. We're needed on Aerilia."

"Fuck you, Ezra," Kynn snapped. "Don't be a martyr."

Ezra tried to ignore the crack forming in his heart. He didn't dare look back over his shoulder as he followed Livia, Tallas, and the other Vanguards toward the shuttles. He didn't dare, lest Livia take it as an insult or an opportunity.

He would find a way to make this right. He'd get the three of them paid—everything he owed them and more—and then try to work this job from the inside. He'd try to get to the bottom of this back on Aerilia, if it just meant that Cass and Kynn were safe. That Mo was safe.

Tallas split off from their group to go to another shuttle. As they reached Livia's ship, Ezra let Shadow go first, then stepped inside. It was cramped, clearly meant for transport and not comfort. Once Livia and the last Vanguard were on board, the door closed.

"Cuff them," Livia ordered the nearest Vanguard.

"Wait—" Ezra said, but two Vanguards wrangled his arms back and slapped a pair of energy cuffs around his wrists. The pilot already had the ship lurching into the air. Ezra strained against the cuffs, ignoring the way their energy crackled and pulsed through his suit and his veins.

Livia approached the dashboard at the front of the shuttle and pushed the comms button. "Tallas?"

There was a slight crackle, followed by, "Yeah?"

Livia looked at Ezra over her shoulder and smiled as she pressed the button again. "Kill them all."

Blood roared in Ezra's ears as he thrashed against the two Vanguards still holding him tight. Even as big and strong as he was, it wasn't enough.

It hadn't been enough. He'd walked right into Livia's trap—the only play he thought he had—and now he could only hope that Cass and Kynn could fight off the rest of Livia's forces.

Chapter 53

You must awaken, Child.

Mo gritted her teeth. Her head pounded. Her vision swam.

You must stop them, that voice said. Voxarus. *Save him and the Key.*

Mo pushed up to one elbow. Kynn stood by himself—two bodies nearby—watching as Ezra walked away with a blonde woman in white armor.

That very same woman glanced over her shoulder at Mo. It wasn't just *some* woman. It was Chancellor Livia Valtor. Ezra's cousin. Federation leader. And next to her, Tallas, head held high in triumph.

What ...

It all started to piece together in Mo's mind. The Federation troops clashing with the Ascended on the hunt for the artifacts. The mysterious bounty put out for the Void Key, plus the one on Ezra's head. Tallas promising to bring her upstairs so she could watch her friends be killed ...

Livia Valtor must've set it up. She must've been behind all of this somehow.

And Ezra was walking away with her. No handcuffs. No gun pointed at his head. He didn't even look back.

No.

He couldn't be going with the Federation.

He couldn't be going with Tallas. He couldn't ...

She pushed up to her knees, willing her heart not to tear into two. If it did, she wasn't sure she'd get up again. She'd decided to trust him. She'd *believed* him, and this was what he did? Abandon them and go back to the Federation?

Mo reached for her hilt, but it wasn't on her belt. Right. Fucking Tallas had stolen both her sword and the Void Key from her. She'd failed.

She couldn't watch as Ezra boarded one of the shuttles with Valtor. She just couldn't. And she didn't have to; Kynn ran over to her, blocking her line of sight.

"Mo!" He dropped down next to her, pulled his helmet off, and grabbed her shoulders. "What happened?"

"How could you let him go with them?" she asked, voice cracking. "How could he do that to us?"

"What—"

"How could he lie to me like that?"

The shuttle Ezra had gone into powered up, then the rest of them.

"What? Who lied?" Kynn asked. But he must've noticed her looking over his shoulder at the shuttles, because he said, "Ezra? No! Shit, Mo, no, he didn't lie."

Mo stared at him. Kynn's usual bright smile was gone. There was no twinkle in his eye. His expression was grim.

"Ezra made a deal, Mo," he said. "He agreed to go with them as long as they let us live and go on with no criminal charges. Fucking asshole is a martyr, not a traitor."

"He ..." She wiped at her eyes, finding unwelcome tears there.

Mo wouldn't believe the story if it wasn't coming from Kynn. He would never lie to her. Had never lied to her in the past.

"We can't just let him go—"

In the distance, just one shuttle remained. Next to it was one figure dressed in dark armor, and a handful more in white and red, just like

Livia had been. Was it some kind of coup? A power grab? Maybe Livia had believed all of her father's theories and decided to put the relics to the test.

"Where's Cass?" Mo asked.

"I don't know. She was hiding up in the temple before trying to find a good angle, but Ezra told her not to shoot. Said we couldn't assassinate a Federation leader. Maybe we should've." He looked over his shoulder again. "Oh, fuck."

With Kynn's help, Mo got to her feet. Everything ached. "Tallas stole my saber."

"Here." Kynn gave her his sword and pulled his gun from his belt. Then he put his helmet back on. "Cass, you there? Cass?"

Silence.

"You see them too?" Kynn's voice was muffled. "And—oh, fuck me." He shook his head. "Cass says Tallas is still here."

"Scumbag," Mo muttered.

Tallas and the group of Federation soldiers—or whoever they were—started back toward the temple. Mo gripped the unfamiliar hilt of Kynn's saber tightly in her dominant hand. It was heavier than hers, but she would work with it.

"Tell Cass not to kill Tallas yet," Mo said. "I want to talk to him."

"Why?" Kynn asked.

"Because he might have answers." Even if her gamble had failed earlier, they had a chance now. "I'm not letting Ezra do this. We're getting him back."

Mo had wanted to walk away from this contract more than once. She'd sworn she'd do it at the first real chance she had. After all, bounty hunters sold their loyalty to the highest bidder. And now Ezra was gone. Most people would wash their hands of the situation.

But Mo wouldn't leave him. She wouldn't let him sacrifice himself, even if he thought it was somehow for the best. She wouldn't let him walk into the lion's den alone. She wouldn't let it end this way.

"Exactly what I was thinking," Kynn said, then he relayed the message to Cass. "She wants to know if she should take out the others."

"Everyone she can get except for Tallas," Mo said.

The group was now close enough that Mo could count six soldiers fanning out behind Tallas. Three against seven, without her magic and exhausted.

Not the best odds, but she'd faced worse on her own and come out the other side. And now, she wasn't alone. Cass was at her back, and Kynn was at her side. Together, they could do this.

The wind kicked up. Fog rolled in, cutting down on the shuttlecraft's obnoxiously bright headlights.

Mo tightened her fingers around the hilt, then engaged the blade. Blue light lit up the ground near her feet.

"Well, Momo," Tallas said with a sigh as he stopped a couple dozen feet away. "Not how I thought she'd play that, but here we are." He raised his saber, the green casting strange shadows across his face. "Who wants to go first?"

A screech echoed off the surrounding mountains, then another and another and another. The shots came in such quick succession the soldiers didn't even have time to react. All six of them dropped dead behind Tallas.

Mo was glad, if not surprised. It took a lot more power to pierce armor like that. Cass might be out of shots now, but only Tallas remained.

He glanced down at the fallen, his upper lip curling. "Show yourself, Farr!" he yelled. "Don't be a coward!"

Cass didn't respond. *Good.* Mo didn't want her to, needed her to stay out of sight. Needed her and Kynn to stay out of the way for now.

"You gonna talk?" Mo asked. "Or should I do us all a favor and get rid of you right now?"

"You wouldn't," Tallas said. "You *need* me, Momo. You've always needed me."

Mo spat on the ground at his feet. "Fuck you."

"You always had a smart mouth," he said, then raised his blade and lunged.

Mo danced out of his way. He stumbled, then straightened. Her silver hilt hung from his belt, calling to her. A trickle of power hummed in her core. She *needed* to get her sword back.

Tallas lunged again, favoring his left leg. Mo moved, slower this time as she called on her magic. It almost groaned at her, like it didn't want to move. Neither did she, but she had no choice.

She forced that droplet of power to the surface. Two lavender tendrils shot out from her left hand, wrapping around her saber on Tallas's belt. She pulled it free, back to her. Her muscles went slack as her magic dissipated and the weight of the hilt made her arm drop.

She really had done too much.

"Bitch," Tallas hissed, ramming his blade forward.

Mo engaged her saber and blocked with both swords, sparks of white, blue, and green skittering through the air. She dug her heels into the ground and pushed against Tallas with all her might.

He stumbled back, putting distance between them as he circled. Mo disengaged Kynn's blade and tossed it back to him. And together, they advanced on Tallas, as they should've done a long time ago.

The three of them met just feet from the temple steps in a dance of colors and energy, jabs and parries. Tallas's blade caught the edge of Kynn's legguard. Kynn swore and shook it off, then went in for another attack. Tallas blocked, leaving his right side open. Mo swung out in a sharp arc, but he staggered back at the last second.

"Cass!" Kynn's yell was muffled by his helmet.

Tallas charged in, swinging wildly. Kynn blocked his next attack. Tallas spun toward Mo. She barely lifted her blade in time, squinting against the harsh glow of white and green.

An ear-piercing whine broke through the trio's heavy breathing, and then Tallas screamed as he dropped to one knee, then collapsed entirely. Both of his legs were bleeding now. High above, in one of the temple windows, Mo caught a glimpse of opalescent armor.

Kynn kicked Tallas in the ribs, forcing him to double over and drop his blade. Kynn kicked that out of the way too, then grabbed Tallas with his free hand. "Tell us everything we want to know."

"Why should I?" Tallas growled, his reddened face contorting in pain. "You're going to kill me either way."

"True," Kynn said. "But we can either make it very painful or not so much."

"What'll it be?" Mo asked. "Your choice, asshole."

"Fine." Tallas's breath came in sharp gasps as he struggled against Kynn's hold. "But can you put me down?"

"Cuffs are on my belt, back pocket," Kynn said to Mo.

She attached her hilt to her belt, then circled behind Kynn and found the energy cuffs. As soon as she slapped them on Tallas's wrists, they engaged, purple energy crackling through the metal. One bad move on Tallas's part and he'd be shocked.

Kynn lowered him to the ground. Tallas fell on his ass, cringing and cursing as he tried to straighten both legs.

Cass strolled out of the temple, rifle propped up against her shoulder. As she walked by Tallas, she kicked him in the ass—literally.

"What the fuck?" he yelled.

"Oops," Cass said nonchalantly. "Didn't see you there."

Tallas sneered at the three of them. "I really should've made sure I finished the job years ago," he said. "Forever my greatest mistake."

Mo squatted down in front of him, getting a certain satisfaction out of watching him struggle to keep a straight face. "I told you I'd kill you if you ever touched me again," she said. "And now here we are, several offenses later. I'll show you the mercy you never showed me, so long as you tell me what I want to know."

"What?" he spat.

"What's Livia Valtor doing?"

"What someone should've done a long time ago," Tallas said. "Taking charge. She's going to beat the Ascended."

"By getting the artifacts," Mo finished for him.

He just glared at her.

"And where is she now?" Kynn asked.

"On her way to continue her mission."

Mo hoped not. She didn't even know if they still had the Star Eater or if someone had stolen it from their ship while she was unconscious.

"Where?" Mo asked. "Aerilia? Another planet?"

When Tallas didn't respond, Kynn stalked forward and planted his boot on top of Tallas's thigh. As soon as he applied pressure, Tallas roared. Kynn pressed harder.

"Fine!" Tallas screamed. "Fine, fine, fine!" As Kynn let up and set his foot back on the ground, Tallas said, "A space station in the Ulara System. She's bringing a contingent of soldiers there."

"How'd you get mixed up in this?" Mo asked.

"She hired me." He raised his chin. "She likes my work. And *me*."

Now that was an interesting development.

Mo raised an eyebrow. "Oh, so you're fucking her?"

"Jealous?" Tallas asked.

"No, I almost pity her, actually."

He scowled at her. Mo took that as an affirmative to her question, or that he at least wanted it to be true.

"Looks like she abandoned you to the wolves," Mo said as she stood. "Not sure how much she likes you or your work. She'll be mighty disappointed to learn you broke before we even applied any real pressure."

"So, this is it?" Tallas asked. "You're going to kill me now?"

Mo smiled viciously. "Oh, no. Not yet. I don't trust one word that comes out of your mouth, Tallas," she said. "You're coming with us. If it turns out you were honest, I'll shoot you right between the eyes. And if you lied to me, I'll use you for target practice, then throw you out the airlock."

Tallas's chest heaved.

"Kynn, throw him in the brig," Mo said. "Cass, we're checking that shuttle for any flight manifests, hyperspace routes, coordinates—anything." She stared up at the thick fog obscuring the sky. "And then we're going to get Ezra and the Key back."

Chapter 54

In all his time serving the Federation, Ezra had never actually been in a brig. He'd *seen* them in passing or in photos and videos, but he'd never been in one.

He wasn't a fan.

They were already in hyperspace, traveling on the *SD Triumph*, a massive star destroyer usually deployed when the Ascended were on the prowl. Ezra had been on many ships like this in his day, but never here, in a cramped cell. The name was a little too on the nose if you asked him, especially considering what Livia was trying to do.

He paced its length in just three steps, then turned and went the other direction. As he continued back and forth, he felt no better than a caged animal. He'd been stripped of his armor, his weapons, everything. He couldn't even use his magic; cells like this were rigged with alarms to alert the guards to such activity.

"Commander?" came Shadow's low voice from the other side of the wall to Ezra's right. It was less modulated than when they'd been at the temple, but it was still gravelly. "What's she going to do to us?"

"I don't know," Ezra said. Truly, he didn't. If Livia had put the hit out on him, then why was he alive at all? He stopped pacing and dropped onto the narrow cot. It was hard as a rock and nowhere near big enough for anyone but a child. Ezra put his head in his hands.

He'd given it all up, *everything*, just for a chance to save Mo, Cass, and Kynn. And now they might be dead. They were good, but up against so many soldiers? Against Tallas? When Mo was unconscious and beaten already?

Fuck. Fuck, he'd never messed up this badly. He'd taken a gamble and it hadn't paid off. He should've stayed and fought. Maybe they would've lost, but he'd rather be dead with his friends than stuck here in this cell, that was for sure.

"Do you think anyone knows it's her that's doing this?" Ezra asked.

"That was unclear when I was given orders to track you down," said Shadow. "But I was in contact with Aerilia until we got to Pyralis. Someone will know something's wrong. Not even a chancellor can just commandeer a star destroyer."

"I don't know," Ezra said again. He didn't know shit anymore. Maybe he never had.

Ezra scrubbed at his face and lay down on the cot as best he could. He was exhausted. He was a fool for ever complaining about the bed Mo and the others had offered him. That was a thousand times better than this.

A sharp knock came from outside Ezra's cell, then the door slid open. Livia waited on the other side, two guards at her back. Their spears crackled with energy, a silent warning for Ezra to behave.

"Ezra," Livia said as she stepped into the cell. She was no longer in armor but a stylish Aerilian suit of cream and pink. "How are you doing?"

"How the fuck do you think I'm doing?" Ezra shoved to his feet. "What are you doing here, Liv?"

Lifting her left sleeve, Livia pressed a button on the golden cuff around her wrist. Static wavered in the air, then Ezra's ears popped. A faint blue glow coated the walls—a sound barrier.

"I thought a little privacy would be good," she said, then yawned, clearly trying to clear her ears. Ezra did the same. "As I was asking, how *are* you doing?"

"Cut the bullshit," Ezra said. "What do you want?"

"Making sure my baby cousin is doing alright."

Ezra rolled his eyes. "Didn't you try to have me killed?"

"I did," she said. "Plans change."

"Why have the plan in the first place?" he asked.

Livia crossed her arms over her chest. "Do you really want to get into this?"

"I don't have anything better to do."

She let out a long, dramatic sigh. "Years ago, my father was cast out by his colleagues for his *incessant* beliefs in the Eternal Ones," she said. "For the longest time, I thought he was a fool, just like everyone else. I thought he had embarrassed the family, but I was wrong. It was his colleagues who should be embarrassed. My father understood that the Eternal Ones' artifacts hold the key to understanding the Universe and Void both and will unlock incredible power. Power that can stop the Ascended."

"We stop them just fine on our own," Ezra said. "Those artifacts are too—"

"Too what, Ezra?" Livia asked, taking a step forward. "Too elusive? Too powerful?" His face must have betrayed his thoughts, because she smiled. "So you know what they do."

"Barely," he said. "If you appreciated his research, why kill him?"

"He wanted the artifacts not for their true purpose but to study," Livia said. "He threatened to expose my plans. I had to clean up loose ends."

"Why were your people attacking the bounty hunters on Andarix? They were there for your contract, right?"

"Loose ends," she said again. "I no longer needed their help."

"And my team?"

She shrugged and just said, "Loose ends."

Ezra ground his teeth together. "Why have them try to kill me?"

"Because I knew you'd never agree to what I envisioned, always with your"—she waved vaguely at where he stood—"self-righteousness and sticking to the FSC's code."

"Why have me on that mission at all?" Ezra asked. "You couldn't have just let me stay out of this?"

"Pulling you, one of our top Vanguards, off your team, one of our top teams in the entire FSC, would have raised too many questions," she said.

"You couldn't have said someone in the family got sick?"

"Everyone knows you aren't close to the family, and then when you came home and found nobody was sick, you would've realized something was going on."

"So you were going to have me killed just to ensure all this went off without a hitch?"

"What's one life to pay to save trillions of others?" she asked. "Do you know how many lives we'll save if we get those artifacts and unleash hell on the Ascended?"

Ezra certainly didn't want Federation civilians to die, but he also didn't want Ascended civilians to die. He wanted to see the war stopped, maybe some kind of peace brokered—if possible. It had to be possible. At the very least, unleashing divine power on their enemy hardly seemed like a moral way to win a war—if there was such a thing at all.

"Do you know what those artifacts will do?" Ezra asked. "Do you know what they'll unlock?"

"Oh, you mean release Ikna from prison?" Livia smiled again. "So you spoke with one of them too."

Shit.

"No, I found carvings at—"

"You found no such thing, Ezra," Livia chided. "You and I both know you spoke to one of the Eternal Ones. So, which one? Evlos? Krytix? Voxarus?"

Ezra forced his expression to remain neutral, just as he had so many times on missions and in meetings with military leaders.

"Hm ..." Livia circled around him like a shark hunting prey. "You weren't down in that temple basement earlier with your friend, so I doubt it was Voxarus. Darius said you never touched the crystal on Miduna, so that only leaves Krytix. What did he tell you?"

Ezra didn't see the point in hiding anything now since she'd already figured it out. "He said that if his sister Ikna escapes her prison, she's going to destroy everything."

"Destroy?" Livia's face lit up as she stopped in front of him. "No, Ezra. She's going to *free* us from this cycle of destruction and war. She showed me."

"By bringing about more destruction and war?" he asked. "Doesn't sound like much of a way to break the cycle to me."

"And this is why I was going to have you killed," Livia said. "No matter. Once we get to our destination, you'll cooperate."

"No, I won't."

"Yes, you will."

As she turned and started for the door, Ezra said, "What about the bounty hunters? You already went back on our deal. I have no reason to cooperate."

"Ah, right. The bounty hunters. Tallas checked in; shame they had to die, really," Livia said. "And now? You either go on trial for treason and receive top punishment, or you support my regime. It's that simple. I'll let you think about it."

She pushed her golden cuff again, and the air popped as the sound barrier retracted. Livia didn't even so much as look back at him or say goodbye. She was just gone, and his cell door was locked again.

Ezra dropped back onto his cot and buried his face in his hands.

They were really dead?

Just like that, they were gone?

He'd failed some of the only people in the Universe who cared about him, who cared about stopping this mission and stopping Livia. He was confident in his assumption that his parents would *want* him to go along with Livia's plans; it would feed into the family's quest for greatness.

He'd lost them. He'd failed them.

And that hurt worse than whatever Livia might do to force him to cooperate.

A metallic *tap, tap, tap* made Ezra startle out of his restless sleep. He'd been plagued by dreams of gods, keys, and destruction, the faces of Mo, Cass, and Kynn. It was probably for the best that he didn't doze off again.

The tapping continued.

"Shadow?" Ezra croaked.

"You awake?" the Intelligence officer asked.

"I am now." Ezra didn't bother to sit up.

"What did Chancellor Valtor talk to you about?"

Ezra scrubbed at his face. "Why?"

"Just tell me what she said, Commander."

"What do you even know?" Ezra asked. "Wait. Are we alone?"

"There's no one else here," Shadow said.

"How can you know that?"

"I am touched by Evlos," they said. "I sense no one."

That sure was helpful to know. No guards? He supposed there didn't need to be any guards; this was one of the most secure ships in the entire FSC fleet.

"Alright, so what do you know?" Ezra asked.

"What I already explained," Shadow said. "That there was a hit on you, taken out by someone on Aerilia, which clearly seems to be Chancellor Valtor. My director gave me all the files they had on these artifacts and bounties for them, issued by someone through underground markets."

"She thinks ancient relics are the key to unlocking some kind of power to defeat the Ascended," Ezra said. He didn't want to give away *everything* he knew, but maybe Shadow would see something he couldn't.

"Meaning she'll do anything to get those artifacts," said Shadow.

"Right," Ezra said. Anything.

Go on trial for treason and receive top punishment, or support my regime. Ezra shuddered as Livia's words circled his mind. Treason—especially for a Vanguard—came with severe consequences. At best, he'd be stripped of his titles, accomplishments, and property before being sent to work in a mining colony, where he'd likely die in an Ascended attack. At worst, he'd probably be subjected to a mind wipe. It happened rarely—there was rarely treason like what Livia would surely frame him for—but it *did* happen. It would steal all his memories—his entire personhood—so the government could retrain him.

And Ezra had no doubt in his mind that Livia would go for a mind wipe. Hell, she probably wouldn't even need to stage a trial if she really was successful in this coup. She could get a highly skilled Vanguard with a clean slate. She could mold him into whatever she wanted.

Ezra couldn't let that happen. Not when he knew what she really wanted, what Ikna supposedly wanted. And he certainly couldn't let

Mo, Cass, and Kynn's deaths be in vain. He'd already failed them. He couldn't dishonor them too.

He had to do this. It didn't matter that this was going to be nearly impossible to pull off. It didn't matter that his heart hurt so bad he thought he might simply die right there in that cell.

He had to fight.

Ezra sat up and swung his legs over the side of the cot. "You're really on my side?" he asked Shadow.

"Yes, Commander," they said. "I was tasked with retrieving you for your safety, and on a personal note, I don't agree with what Chancellor Valtor is attempting."

"What about a professional note?" Ezra asked.

"That either. When I left Aerilia, they were working on decrypting those messages about putting the hit out on you. Someone besides us has to know what's going on by now."

"If we stay on this ship, we're fucked," Ezra said. "The Federation's fucked."

"No doubt," Shadow said.

"You think you can help me get us out of here? It's going to be hard, maybe impossible."

"I'd rather die trying than stay in the hands of the enemy," Shadow said.

Truly spoken like a soldier, Ezra thought ruefully.

"Then we're going to need a plan," Ezra said. "And that starts with you keeping watch. You up for it?"

"I'm at your disposal, Commander," Shadow said. "Let's get to work."

Chapter 55

Mo pinched the bridge of her nose. If she had to listen to Tallas continue prattling on about how she was going to "regret every decision she'd made up to this point in her life," she was going to kill him.

And she couldn't. Not yet, anyway.

She wouldn't even risk gagging him. Tallas talked—a lot—which meant he might reveal something without meaning to. Mo had to be smart about this.

After more than two days of travel, they were nearing the Ulara System, where Livia's ship was supposed to be going. They'd pushed the hyperdrive as fast as it could go in hopes of beating Livia there. That was, if she actually *was* going there.

Everything they'd found on the remaining shuttlecraft had indicated Tallas was telling the truth, which was why they'd brought it with them. *The Revenant* didn't have shuttles of its own—it was too small for a full bay—but it did have a docking station that could accommodate such small vessels. They'd attached the two ships together, just in case they needed more information or to separate.

And separate they likely would. They'd have to get onto Livia's ship somehow to rescue Ezra—if he was even on it. And they wouldn't know until they arrived. Arriving on one of the battleship's own shuttles seemed like the only logical way in. The only problem was explaining how they had beaten the ship to the system, assuming someone asked them.

"You know," Tallas said from his spot in the prison at the back of the cabin, "I still don't understand why you're holding such a grudge against me, Momo. You wouldn't be 'The Demon' if that day had never happened. In a way, I'm responsible for your success. You owe me."

That phrase triggered something deep within her. A hatred for Tallas, self-loathing for getting twisted around by him. He used to say that whenever he'd treated her with the bare minimum respect one might expect from a partner or friend. He always threw whatever small thing he did for her back in her face like undeniable proof that he was the good guy and she was asking for too much.

Her hands tightened around the controls. "I owe you nothing," she snapped, "and I never did."

"You all owe me," Tallas said. "You wouldn't be where you are without me."

Kynn and Cass were there, too, Kynn in the copilot's seat and Cass at the station in the back, helping search for Livia's battleship.

"Shut the fuck up," Kynn said, "or I'll say to hell with this mission and throw you in the airlock right now, you piece of shit."

"Touchy," Tallas said. "I didn't realize you were still so reactive, Kynn. You never grew out of that?"

"I'm only reactive when someone deserves it," Kynn said. "Prick."

Tallas clicked his tongue. "You aren't going to stop her. She almost has everything she needs to finish all this."

"And what does our esteemed Chancellor need, exactly?" Mo asked.

"Ikna's crystal."

Tallas knew about that? Mo supposed he had to, given Livia's mission and apparent trust in him.

Which meant Livia likely had *two* artifacts: the Genesis Crystal and the Void Key. At least they still had the Star Eater. But why didn't Tallas mention it? Maybe he didn't know about it. If Livia had half a brain, she wouldn't tell Tallas all her plans.

All the intelligence they'd found on that Federation shuttle had suggested that Livia Valtor was trying to pull off a coup, not that the rest of the government or FSC was on her side. It seemed she was part of a splinter group trying to centralize power into one person rather than the Triumvirate. She wanted to be a dictator, not a leader.

And despite what Mo thought about the Federation government, having the Triumvirate was far better than one despot. They needed to rescue Ezra and try to stop Livia, even if it just meant slowing her down until they could get more help.

An alarm sounded, not a warning of an attack but an alert that they were onto something.

"We're approaching the Ulara System," Cass called.

"Heard," Mo said. The ship dropped out of hyperspace, and the streaks of stars outside were replaced by never-ending darkness. "I thought there was a space station here that she wanted to go to?"

"It's farther into the system," Tallas said. "Near the fifth planet from the sun."

"Sensors are showing that station," Cass said. "Looks like a pretty empty system, though."

"That's because it is," said Tallas. "It was run down by an Ascended raid a few years back. The station was abandoned."

That explained how Livia was hiding away her soldiers, but according to what they'd found on the shuttle and what Tallas had proudly proclaimed over the last two days, she had some FSC defectors on her side. People like Darius Kane and the rest of Ezra's now-deceased team. How had nobody investigated that many deserters? Maybe it was just like

Darius again, with the military claiming they didn't have the resources to investigate. Maybe they truly didn't.

None of it mattered in the moment. They needed to rescue Ezra, and they needed to disable Livia's forces however they could.

And they were going to need a plan to do so.

Another half day passed with no sign of Livia. Mo was going to tear her hair out if they had to wait much longer.

She'd done everything she could think of to prepare: checked that all their weapons were charged, that the ship's systems were functioning at optimal levels, and even taken a nap when Kynn forced her to. Not that she'd really been able to sleep, but it had been worth a try.

Mo just couldn't stop thinking about Ezra and how he'd foolishly sacrificed himself to save them. Although, she had to admit she probably would've done the same if their positions were reversed. There wasn't anything she wouldn't do for Cass and Kynn. Hopefully Livia hadn't betrayed Ezra again.

As she sank deeper into the captain's chair, Mo stared out at the darkness of space, wishing sheer force of will would make Livia's ship appear. Then they could get Ezra back.

"So," Tallas drawled from where he was still locked in the brig, "what if I told you I needed another bathroom break?"

"Piss yourself for all I care," Mo snapped.

Next to her, Kynn laughed.

"Helm's yours," she said to him. "I'm going to make some coffee."

"Aye aye, captain," Kynn said.

They both stood, and Kynn took over as soon as Mo moved out of his way. As she passed Tallas's prison, Mo could feel his eyes on her. She ignored him and kept going, closing the command room doors behind her as she entered the kitchen.

After starting the coffee, she stood over the kitchen counter, head bent as she waited for her drink. Every piece of her was on edge. After days in close quarters with Tallas, days of not knowing if they'd see Ezra again or stop the chancellor, Mo felt like she was unraveling. The lights were too bright, every sound too loud. Her body and heart hurt.

Focus. She had to focus.

"Mo?" Cass asked as she came out of her quarters.

"Just taking a break."

"You don't have to explain yourself to me," Cass said. "Ever. You know that."

Mo rolled her neck and massaged the pressure points at the base of her skull. "Yeah. Sorry."

"Tallas getting to you?"

"Everything's getting to me."

She risked a glance back at Cass, who had dropped into an empty seat at the kitchen table. As much as she'd wanted to talk to Cass about everything going on with Ezra, Mo just hadn't been able to make herself. She hadn't wanted to distract either of them while searching Voxarus's temple, but now with everything else going on, it seemed trivial and unimportant.

But fuck, it was messing with her head. Badly.

Cass raised an eyebrow, an invitation to talk.

"I don't know what to do about this Eternal Ones shit or the coup," Mo said. "And I'm really worried about Ezra."

"I am too."

"What if ..." She couldn't bring herself to say it. What if they didn't stop Livia? What if he was already dead? What if she never got to see him again?

"Mo?"

Groaning, Mo turned to face her best friend. "Right before we went to search Voxarus's temple, Ezra and I ... kissed."

Cass tilted her head slightly. "Why are you acting like that's a bad thing?"

"I mean, he's with the enemy now."

"So? We'll get him back."

Everything Mo wanted to say settled in her chest like a boulder, the words impossible to move. Why was talking so hard for her? "It's just that—"

An alarm sounded in the cockpit, and Kynn's voice came over the ship's speakers. "Large ship entering the system."

"That has to be Livia," Mo said.

"Mo—" Cass started.

"Can you double-check everything downstairs?" Mo called over her shoulder as she headed for the cockpit. "We'll be down in a minute!" Mo didn't check to see if Cass went; she didn't need to. Cass always did her job, just like Mo.

She strode past the brig, ignoring the weight of Tallas's ever-watchful stare as she rushed in to meet Kynn.

"Seems like it's her," Kynn said. "We should leave."

"Cass is going to meet us down there."

Kynn vacated the captain's chair, then followed Mo toward the brig, where Tallas leaned against the door inside. His blond hair had grown greasy, and stubble coated his usually clean-shaven face. Kynn double-checked all the locks were engaged.

"Afraid I'll get out?" Tallas drawled.

"Never can be too cautious with a snake like you," Kynn said. "Behave."

Tallas snarled.

Mo slammed her palm against the door, making him flinch and shrink away. "Behave," Mo repeated. "Cass'll shoot you out the airlock if you don't."

He just narrowed his eyes at her.

Mo followed Kynn out of the command room and down to the lower deck. Cass was already suited up in her opalescent gear. She was going to stay behind on *The Revenant* as backup while Kynn and Mo boarded Livia's ship. With Tallas on board, Mo didn't see much of a choice but to split up. Someone had to monitor him. Besides, Cass was the best shot with the laser cannons. It was hardly the Universe's best plan, but they didn't have any other options.

Unfamiliar red and white armor they'd stolen from Tallas's dead soldiers waited for Mo and Kynn on the drop-down benches near the weapons locker. Putting on a dead person's armor—the armor of traitors—didn't feel good, but they needed to be as smart as possible about this whole thing. Besides, Mo's personal helmet was still only partially functional; all the sensors in the thing were broken, thanks to Tallas. That wouldn't do her any good on this mission.

Mo put on her stolen gear first, then the matching helmet, dreading its weight but appreciating its working sensors and crisp view through the dark visor. Despite already having her saber on her hip, Mo grabbed two blasters from the weapons locker as well. Kynn grabbed two more guns and checked that he had his saber attached to his belt.

The Star Eater sat untouched, its black and gold hilt almost beckoning Mo. As she reached for it, Kynn grabbed her wrist.

"What are you doing?" he asked.

"Taking it with us."

"But Valtor wants it. And we don't even know what it does."

"Kynn," Mo said, looking up at him. "Two of us are going into a ship inhabited by hundreds, maybe thousands, most of them soldiers. If we can use that thing and increase our odds, then I'm doing it."

Kynn sighed and dropped Mo's arm. "Fine. But if we die, I'm going to blame you for the rest of the afterlife."

"Fair enough." Mo grabbed the Star Eater. It was heavier than her own sword but comfortable in her grip. She attached it to her belt, then sucked in a deep breath. "Cass—"

Cass pulled her into a hug, then Kynn piled on from the other side. "Be safe," Cass said.

"You too," Mo said. "I love you. Both of you."

Even though Mo couldn't see their faces, nor could they see hers, she swore they smiled at her as they said in unison, "Love you too."

They didn't say it often, but maybe they should more. Yes, if they made it out of this alive, Mo was going to make sure Cass and Kynn knew how much she appreciated them. Not just with her actions but her words too.

"Stuff Tallas in the airlock," Mo said to Cass. "Jettison him if you need to."

"And if I don't need to?" she asked.

Mo wanted nothing more than to be rid of Tallas Bara forever, but she wasn't going to ask Cass to take revenge for her. Mo would either need to do that herself or somehow turn him over to the authorities.

"Keep him locked up," Mo said. "We'll deal with him after we get Ezra back."

Mo and Kynn said a final goodbye to Cass, then hurried over to the airlock. They crossed through and into the waiting FSC shuttle. Kynn dropped into the pilot's seat and began powering it up while Mo watched through the porthole. Cass was indeed stuffing Tallas into the airlock.

It sealed on both sides, trapping him in. He pounded on the seal, his face contorted in rage as he screamed. Mo flipped him off. Kynn disengaged the shuttlecraft, and then they lurched forward, heading for Livia Valtor's warship.

CHAPTER 56

As soon as they split off from *The Revenant*, Mo crossed the small cabin and joined Kynn at the helm.

"This thing's fucking impossible," she said, searching the crowded dashboard for the controls she'd need to help him.

He laughed. "Ships have come a long way since *The Revenant* was built, you know."

"Yeah, and there's nothing wrong with my ship." Other than the dents it had sustained at Voxarus's temple, but Mo was trying not to think about that. It really didn't matter.

"Just push those two buttons when I tell you to," Kynn said, pointing to one green and one red button near the middle of the dash. "I'll do the rest."

They left *The Revenant* hiding behind a moon of the fifth planet, as close to the space station as they could get without being visible. Another ship's sensors might pick it up, but it was just a risk they were going to have to take.

Kynn piloted them to the space station, a white structure with two rings attached to a central terminal. If it were still inhabited, it would be full of lights and ships, but it was dark, abandoned. It was large enough that it could probably house thousands.

"I'm sorry about Tallas," Kynn said. "About having him on the ship."

Mo shrugged. "It was our only option."

"I know, but still. It wasn't fair."

She almost replied that life wasn't fair, but Kynn already knew that. He meant well. Tallas being around—and being obnoxious the whole time—hadn't been easy on any of them. "We'll get rid of him soon," she said, a promise more to herself than him.

Heavy silence settled between them as Kynn brought them closer to the space station and planet. The shuttle's sensors beeped, and Mo glanced at the radar. That same large ship they'd seen on *The Revenant*'s sensors was approaching fast.

"They're coming into visual range," she said.

A warship loomed in the distance, creeping ever closer. A red aura obscured its edges. Mo squeezed her eyes shut, and when she opened them again, the haze was gone.

"Did you see that?" she asked.

"See what?" Kynn looked up from his screen. "Oh, shit, it's been a while since I saw one of those."

"No, the red that was surrounding it," Mo said. When Kynn shot her a confused look, she said, "Like that gravitational distortion."

"Don't like that," Kynn muttered.

Mo didn't either.

The closer the ship came, the tighter the knot in Mo's stomach grew. She almost couldn't believe something that big existed. She also couldn't believe she and Kynn were about to try to break Ezra out of the damn thing.

When they got close to the warship, the comms crackled to life. "*SC Canary*, this is *SD Triumph*. Status? What are you doing here?"

"Completed my task," Kynn said, his voice oddly modulated by the helmet. Mo didn't like it at all. "Returning for further assignments."

Silence for one beat, two, then, "Why didn't you check in earlier?"

"Comms weren't working," Kynn said. "We had no way to reach out. I just got them online a few hours ago."

That hardly seemed like a good explanation, but whoever was on the other end of the channel said, "Heard. You are clear to enter Shuttle Bay Two, starboard side."

"What kind of force you thinking we'll meet?" Mo asked.

"Hopefully they'll all be busy elsewhere."

"That doesn't answer my question."

"Not a small one, that's for sure."

As he flew them toward the *SD Triumph*, Mo rummaged around in the back of the shuttle. She found several extra guns, an energy glaive, and a pair of gloves, but the weapons only seemed mildly useful. She would have loved some grenades or something explosive, things she didn't usually keep on *The Revenant*. They weren't necessary on her day-to-day contracts. But this was war.

As Kynn guided the shuttle into the launch bay through the shimmering blue forcefield, Mo checked all of her weapons. Her saber, plus the Star Eater. Both of her guns. She left the glaive for Kynn.

As soon as their shuttle touched the bay floor, Kynn began powering everything down. Based on what Mo could see out the cockpit windows, the bay was empty except for a bunch of stationary shuttles and some technicians. A few soldiers in white and red armor milled about at the far side of the bay, near wide double doors that were probably exactly where they needed to go.

Kynn secured the glaive to his back, then took the spare gun when Mo handed it to him. "Just follow my lead," he said as he slid it into a holster on his thigh.

"You're the boss," Mo said.

"Can I get that in writing?"

"Shut up."

He laughed but sobered quickly as he pushed the shuttle door up and out. Other than the occasional pings and zaps from tools, the bay was quiet.

"Welcome back," a modulated voice said. Another soldier dressed in the same white and red gear as them approached, boots clicking on the metal floor. "Where's the rest of the contingent?"

"Dispatched by the bounty hunters," Kynn said, "but we were able to overcome them in the end, Lieutenant."

The soldier had a small golden bar melded into their chest plate, right above their heart. "Unfortunate," they said, "but the cause lives on."

"The cause lives on," Kynn echoed.

"Go clean up, then report to the colonel's office in a half hour to receive your next assignment."

Kynn saluted, and Mo followed suit. It was all wrong, foreign. The lieutenant saluted back, then strode off to where some of the mechanics were opening up nearly half the panels on one of the empty shuttlecraft.

Mo's heart thundered in her chest as she followed Kynn through the bay. It was massive, easily three stories tall and able to accommodate ships far larger than the shuttles currently taking it up. Metal boxes were stacked up along one wall, and there was even a tall platform in one corner, attached to what had to be some kind of office.

Just how many people did Livia have on her side? How long had she been working at this? Mo didn't love the Federation, but damn. This was something entirely outside of what she'd ever imagined would happen. Frankly, she'd always figured the Triumvirate and the rest of the Federation government would continue on until they were either taken down by the Ascended or outgrew the system. Maybe Livia saw her actions as a piece of that growth.

Two soldiers flanked the exit. They nodded at Kynn and Mo as they passed by and through the doors.

Once the doors closed, Mo whispered, "That was easy."

"Told you my brief Vanguard training would be good for something," Kynn said.

"Only took years."

Kynn led them down several empty corridors as they headed toward the port side of the ship. These halls were so wide that they were more like streets. The farther they got from the launch bay, the more anxious Mo grew.

"You know where we're going?" she whispered.

"Yeah, I was forced to study blueprints of ships just like this back in the day," Kynn said. "There's a secondary lift that should take us up one level to the brig."

At the next junction, they had to pause and wait for a large cart to drift by them. It looked like it was carrying supplies—food, maybe? Mo resisted the urge to reach for her saber. An Ivari man strolled behind the cargo. As he passed, he gave them a polite nod and continued on his way with his delivery.

Mo's fingers twitched. They needed to get this done and get it done fast.

"We should try to sabotage whatever we can," Mo said, voice low.

"We should wait until we have Ezra before we do," Kynn countered. "Otherwise we'll draw attention. Repair crews will come out."

Mo supposed he had a point. A ship like this would have a full complement, or mostly a full complement. Any damage to any systems—critical or not—would just sound the alarm. She needed to be patient. They could blow something up on their way out.

"We need to hurry," Mo said. "They gave us a half hour to report to the colonel. They'll know something's wrong when we don't show."

"We still have some time," Kynn said. "We're almost there."

A couple more minutes of walking brought them to the lift. Kynn punched a button, and they went up one floor. As they reached their destination and the doors slid open, Mo expected to find the place brimming with life, but again, it was empty. Maybe ships like this were just *so* big that you didn't run into other people very often? She had no idea; the largest ship she'd ever been on had been a Sorthian freighter, and that wasn't even a third of the size of this monstrosity.

Kynn navigated them down two more hallways before they stopped in front of a new door. He nodded, which meant he was decently confident this was the brig.

So why weren't there any armed guards out here? Even if it was a highly secure prison, Mo would never leave a major threat like Ezra Lyre unguarded. It was just foolish. Or pure hubris, which Chancellor Livia Valtor seemed to have in spades.

Still, something uneasy prickled down Mo's spine.

Kynn reached for the keypad near the door, but before he could even hazard a guess as to what the code was, the door lifted. A soldier dressed in white, red, and gold waited just inside.

"Traitors in our midst!" they cried. "Get them!"

More doors slid open. Boots pounded on the metal floor. Mo put her back to Kynn's, both of them turning to get a better look at the rush of activity. Several soldiers stepped out from a room just at the end of the corridor, and three more joined from the opposite direction, blocking them in.

"Fuck," Mo muttered.

Grabbing her saber, she engaged the blade and launched herself at the four coming out of that room. One of them raised their gun. Mo called on her magic. It was still a stubborn thing, resisting her in its fatigue, but she pulled hard. It rose to the surface, shooting out from her palm in aubergine tendrils and yanking the gun from the soldier.

The others took aim, but Mo's magic wrapped around the soldier at the front. She threw them into the others, who stumbled as they tried to catch their comrade. Behind her, one body hit the floor, then another.

An alarm shrieked so loud Mo thought her ears might bleed.

Shit.

Mo lunged, closing the distance between her and the quad. She brought her saber out wide, slamming the white blade into the nearest soldier. It ripped through their armor and torso, blood exploding out from the wound as they fell to the ground in a heap.

She pushed in toward the next, but as they brought their forearm up, an energy shield appeared. Mo ducked and spun out of the way, barely avoiding the damn thing. She cut up with her blade, slicing through their knee. The soldier screamed and dropped to the ground. Mo drove her blade into their heart.

The second to last soldier on her side of the hall lifted their blaster and took aim. Mo ripped her sword from the dead one's chest and blocked the shot, sending it right back through the shooter's helmet.

One more. Mo's chest heaved as exhaustion threatened to drown her again. She pulled a gun from her belt, kicked up the power, and fired right into the soldier's chest piece. They dropped to the ground.

Behind Mo, two more bodies crashed down. She turned to see Kynn standing among them, already putting his blade away. Mo forced her shaking hands to do the same.

"Obviously he's not here," Mo said as she ran after Kynn. "Where is he?"

"I don't know …" Kynn trailed off as they got to another empty junction. He looked left and right, then continued straight.

"Do you even know where you're going?" Mo asked.

"There should be an access panel right—" Kynn skidded to a stop, then backtracked a few steps. "Right here."

Kynn pulled a key card from his belt—she had no idea where he'd gotten it, maybe one of the soldiers they'd just killed?—and inserted it into the panel. Its screen lit up, and a small keyboard popped out underneath. Kynn began typing furiously, bringing up various menus before finally, a map.

"Here," he said, pointing. Mo couldn't make sense of the damn thing. "A secondary brig. Two floors up, starboard side. There's another access lift over there. We can get back to the shuttle bay."

"You really think we can?" Mo asked as the alarm kept blaring.

"We have to." Kynn navigated away from the map and hit a few more keys. The alarm stopped. As he pulled the card back out, he said, "We have to if you want to save Ezra. Now come on."

Of course Mo wanted to save Ezra. She couldn't leave him behind. She wouldn't.

And so she took off after Kynn, heading deeper into Chancellor Valtor's ship.

Chapter 57

This cell was going to be the death of Ezra. So was the fact that he was trying to jimmy one of the wall panels near the door without any real tools.

"Any luck?" Shadow called.

"No, you?" Ezra asked.

"No."

Ezra sat back on his haunches. He needed something sharp. He'd managed to hide the dull fork they'd given him with his dinner, but it wasn't very useful as either a screwdriver or a knife. The screws on this panel were *very* small.

He could melt the damn thing off, but he didn't want to risk setting off any alarms. *Dammit.* Ezra ran his hands through his hair. He was so sick of being caged and treated like some criminal just because he wouldn't go along with Livia's plans. He'd been counting the passing of time only by the meals delivered to the brig, and he guessed he'd been on the ship for three days by that point. They'd only dropped out of hyperspace a couple of hours before.

He and Shadow had known this was a feeble attempt at an escape plan, but it was the only one that didn't put them in immediate danger of dying. If they tried to jump the guards who brought them food, they'd be trying to fight in extremely close quarters with two heavily armed individuals. No, if they were going to jump the guards, it needed to be in the hall, where they at least sort of had the element of surprise.

An ear-piercing shriek echoed from the speakers in the ceiling, and yellow lights began flashing overhead. Ezra cringed, and when the door to the brig opened, he backed away from his cell door.

But the guard never barged in. Instead, the brig door slammed shut again. Ezra frowned. Obviously the guard had realized *they* weren't the cause of that alarm, but who or what was?

Maybe the FSC had arrived in force to stop Livia's nonsense. Ezra could dream. But he really needed a way out; he didn't dare wait to see if someone came to their rescue.

And if the alarm was already blaring ...

He pulled on the heat coursing through his veins and directed it at that damn wall panel. The ceiling lights turned to orange—either an issue on the ship or a result of Ezra's magic—but he kept going. The metal panel melted and bent. Ezra stopped his fire and kicked at the hot metal again and again until it burst free. The better half of the wall ruptured. Ezra pushed his way through, not caring about the excess heat from his earlier flame.

The guards still didn't seem to notice. Maybe they'd left to go deal with whatever the greater threat was. Ezra did not care.

"Stand back, Shadow!" he yelled.

When he thought he heard an affirmative from the other side of the wall, Ezra pulled on his fire again. He repeated the process as before, heating the metal until he was able to use his body weight to break through.

He peeked inside. Where he'd half expected to see the same armor from before, he instead found a short Ivari ... short by Ivari standards, anyway. They were still nearly Ezra's height. Their blue hair was several shades darker than their skin and ended in a blunt cut at their jaw, and their willowy build would make it easy for them to get through the narrow opening in the wall.

Ezra helped them step through, taking their hand as he guided them out. "Nice to meet you formally," Ezra said. "You got a name?"

"I'll stick with Shadow," they said.

Ezra nodded. "Well, Shadow, you know where those guards went?"

"They're out there," they said. "Just one."

"Any sense as to what's going on?" He gestured up at the lights just as the alarm stopped. "Oh, shit."

Maybe the FSC really had boarded. Whatever the case, Ezra needed to get them out of here, find that Void Key, and get to an escape pod. No one could get their hands on that relic.

"Stay behind me," Ezra said. "Let me handle this."

Shadow asked no questions as Ezra moved for the door. Just outside the narrow window, he caught a glimpse of familiar white armor.

Ezra shook out his arms, then hit the button to open the door. The guard outside turned, but they were too slow. Ezra had them in a choke-hold, squeezing their throat with his bicep as he grabbed their gun. Then he shoved down his misgivings, brought it to their temple, and pulled the trigger. They slumped to the floor.

He was about to call for Shadow to come out, but another guard rounded the corner to Ezra's left. He took aim and pulled the trig-ger again, hitting them square in the chest and breaking through their armor. It wasn't the strong, expensive stuff like what Ezra wore as a Vanguard. *And thank the gods for that*, he thought.

"Anyone else?" Ezra called over his shoulder.

"Incoming," Shadow said as they slid out into the hall behind him. "But we have a moment."

Ezra hustled over to the second guard and grabbed both the gun and energy spear off the body. "What do you prefer?" he asked Shadow.

"The bigger gun," they said, so Ezra handed it off to them.

The real question was where Livia would keep the Void Key. Probably on her person, or at least in her ready room or somewhere only trusted officers could access. That meant this was about to become very difficult. He didn't have an access key. He supposed he could try to take one of the officers hostage and force them to do his bidding, but that seemed messy.

He'd just have to figure it out.

The ship rumbled and rocked. Ezra steadied himself. He was used to that feeling, not just from the way Mo's ship had rattled at high speeds but the way it felt to be under attack. Someone was indeed firing on Livia's ship.

"We need to go," Shadow said.

"How many?"

"A dozen, maybe more."

Ezra swore under his breath, then said, "Which way are they coming from?"

"Starboard."

"Then we're going port," Ezra said, already moving. "Come on. Keep up."

They sprinted away from the brig. It was only a matter of time before someone found them; these starships were rigged with some of the best security equipment available. And it wouldn't be hard to spot an Ivari and a Human, in plain clothes, running through these corridors.

"Here." Ezra shoved Shadow toward an open service duct.

They both stooped and crawled inside, then Ezra shut the door behind him. These tunnels didn't have cameras, at least, though they could eventually be tracked.

"There should be a lift not far from here once we find the exit," Shadow said.

"You been on ships like this a lot?" Ezra asked as they picked their way through. The service duct was cramped, with heavy tubing crowding the walls and ceiling. He had to stay low to avoid slamming his head into anything.

"We were often on them before going on away missions, yes," Shadow said.

"How long you been with the FSC?"

"Nine years, Commander."

"Seventeen here," Ezra said. "You ever get tired of their bullshit?"

"Like?" Shadow asked.

"Like their politics and their rules." Ezra had never been terribly fond of either, but it wasn't until recently that he'd realized just how much he hated both. He'd thought he had the same values as the FSC, and maybe he did to an extent, but there were lines he wouldn't cross that leadership would. He just couldn't get over that.

"Both have their place," Shadow said diplomatically.

Ezra rolled his eyes.

"If we can get to one of the larger access panels, I should be able to get a message to my commander," Shadow said. "They might've even had a trail on us. My suit had a tracker in it."

"Livia probably destroyed the tracker," Ezra said. "Probably destroyed both our suits."

"Even if they only got a small signal before it cut off, it would be something for them to go on," Shadow said.

Ezra wasn't going to hold out hope, but he also wouldn't take it away from Shadow if they needed it.

That damn alarm sounded again. Ezra cringed but kept going. The end of the service duct was in sight. They just needed to get to both an access panel and a lift, and then they could try to get to Livia. They could try to get the Void Key back.

"Anyone?" Ezra asked as they approached the door.

"Two heading our way," they said. "Just them."

Ezra wanted to keep this as clean as possible, but if they needed to take two more out to get this done …

"Stay here," Ezra said. "If they capture me again, try to get word to your commander. We need help if we're going to stop Livia."

Shadow nodded. "Understood."

Ezra rolled his shoulders, then slammed his fist into the button to open the service duct door. Upon seeing an empty hall, he stepped out slowly. To his left was a dead end, and to his right was a junction. That had to be where those two were coming from.

He steadied his breathing and took aim with his gun. As soon as they—

Two figures in white and red armor rounded the corner. Ezra's finger tightened on the trigger.

"Stop!" one of them yelled.

Ezra fired his first shot, but it didn't land.

A white saber blocked it.

A white saber …

The two soldiers ripped their helmets off. Two faces he never thought he'd see again.

Kynn and Mo, looking a little panicked and worse for the wear, but alive.

Ezra stared at them for one heartbeat, then another, trying to take stock of what he was seeing. Was this some kind of trick? A hologram to get him to put his weapon down?

Mo put her saber away and threw herself into him. Ezra wrapped his arms around her, and though he couldn't feel her body under the rigid armor she wore, vanilla and cinnamon greeted his nose as he buried his face in her hair.

This was no hologram. This was no trick.

Mo was there.

Tallas hadn't killed her or Kynn—or Cass, hopefully.

Ezra could've cried. Would've had it not been for the situation and his years of Vanguard training forcing him to keep it together. He hugged Mo tighter.

They'd somehow tracked Livia's ship and boarded it. They'd come for him despite how dangerous and, frankly, reckless it was.

He'd never been so grateful. There was so much he wanted to say to her—to Kynn—but all he could do was hold Mo close and breathe her in.

"Commander?" Shadow called quietly.

"You can come out," Ezra said, forcing himself to pull away from Mo. And despite the alarm ringing through the corridors and the very real threat of Livia's army, he smiled down at her. She smiled back. "Friends of mine."

Shadow approached slowly, and Kynn nodded at them. "Good to see you both alive."

"Fucking shooting at us," Mo said, nudging Ezra's shoulder.

"I thought you were dead," he said. "Livia said Tallas and his forces killed you three."

"Tallas is in *The Revenant*'s airlock right now," Mo said. "Cass has her eye on him. Now come on, we need to get out of here."

"We need to get the Void Key," Ezra said. "Livia apparently spoke with Ikna. She wants to take over the entire Federation and use the artifacts to destroy the Ascended."

"And anyone else who stands in her way," Kynn half asked, half stated. Ezra nodded.

"Fuck me," Mo muttered. "Where's the Key, then?"

"She probably has it on her person," Ezra said. "It'll be on the bridge or in her ready room, especially if we're under attack."

"That's got to be Cass," Mo said.

"By herself? Has she lost her mind?"

"She's very good at what she does," Mo said, moving across the junction. The lift was just on the other side. "Now come on. How do we get to the bridge?"

Ezra was about to object when Kynn pulled a key card out of his pocket. He wasn't sure how far it'd get them, but they'd have to try.

Chapter 58

Despite the flashing lights and blaring alarm, and despite the continuous rumble of the ship as they were fired upon, the elevator didn't stop. Nobody even *tried* to stop it.

That did not sit right with Ezra.

He'd expected a fight. Someone to disrupt the lift. Literally *anything*.

"This isn't right," he said aloud.

"No, it's not," Shadow said.

Mo and Kynn shifted uneasily. There wasn't anything to be said. They'd just have to see what was waiting for them when the lift finally stopped.

And stop it did, at the bridge as ordered. The door slid up. Ezra stepped out, gun raised and finger hovering over the trigger. Other than the faint lights coming from the stations, it was dark.

"Shadow?" he asked.

"Nobody's here with us, sir," they said.

"What?"

"How is that possible?" Mo asked, drawing her saber as they moved deeper into the bridge.

But Shadow was right. The whole damn place was empty, stations abandoned and left to run on their own. Warning lights blinked all across the various dashboards and monitors. Even the view screens that would usually reveal space were offline. They couldn't see a damn thing.

"Ship's on autopilot," Kynn said as he dropped down at the helm station near the middle of the cabin. "It's set for a collision course with the nearest moon …"

"Can you override it?" Ezra asked.

Kynn's fingers flew over the dashboard, but he shook his head. "No. I'm locked out."

"Can you get those view screens back up?"

"Locked out," Kynn said again.

"How long until impact?" Ezra asked.

"Twenty minutes."

Shit. That wasn't much time to find Livia or the artifacts. She surely still had the Void Key, and it was likely she had the Genesis Crystal—or whatever was left of it—too.

"Commander," Shadow said from where they stood near the comms station. "There's an incoming transmission."

A transmission?

"Put it up," Ezra said. A large screen materialized at the front of the cabin, revealing a familiar face. "General San'ri?"

"Commander," she said. "What the fuck are you doing on the bridge? We're trying to reach Chancellor Valtor."

"So am I," he said. "She's been holding me hostage for days. The whole bridge has been abandoned."

San'ri's eyebrows pulled together. "Concerning."

That was an incredible understatement, but Ezra wasn't going to nitpick the details right now. After all, Shadow had mentioned being in contact with Aerilia before everything went wrong on Pyralis. Maybe they'd been right to hold out hope that someone at Command would figure all this out.

"What's going on, ma'am?" Ezra asked. "Are you in the system?"

"Approaching your position."

"Any escape pods or shuttles?"

"No, just a sole ship registered to a Mora—"

"That'd be my friend," Ezra said.

San'ri nodded. "Call your friend off. Prepare to be boarded. We need to find Chancellor Valtor and stop her from leaving the system."

Again, that seemed like an incredible understatement, but knowing the FSC was *not* fully under Livia's control bolstered Ezra's resolve. Finally, they weren't doing this alone. Finally, he had confirmation that the FSC wasn't entirely corrupt.

"Everything's locked on our end," Ezra said. "They did something to the ship, set it on a collision course with the closest moon."

San'ri frowned and looked off screen, then nodded. "We'll leave comms open. Can someone there work with one of my technicians? We'll work to unlock it from our end."

"Can do," Kynn said, and Shadow joined him.

"Ezra!" Mo called from where she was hunched over a station near the back of the bridge. She scrolled furiously through the tabs on the screen, so fast Ezra couldn't keep track.

"What is it?" he asked.

"There's a massive energy signature two floors above the starboard shuttle bay," she said.

"Ships?"

"No, it looks a lot like the others we've seen ..."

"Kynn!" Ezra shouted. "We might've found her! You two handle this. Contact Cass, and check the ready room just in case!"

Kynn gave him a thumbs-up. Ezra and Mo sprinted back for the lift, and as they began their descent, he cursed the damn thing for not going faster. Shouldn't there be some kind of emergency mode?

"Here." Mo offered Ezra a saber hilt, but it was—

"The Star Eater?" he asked, eyebrows furrowing.

"Didn't know who or what we'd be up against," Mo said. "Thought it was worth the risk."

Ezra's fingers closed around the hilt. It was heavy and solid, more so than his saber. Wherever that was. Livia had probably destroyed it.

"You got yours back," he said, nodding toward her right hand.

"Yeah."

"He's really in your airlock?"

"Yeah." Mo stared straight ahead. "Kept him alive to try to find this ship."

Ezra nodded. It was a damn shame that Tallas Bara hadn't perished in the mountains of Pyralis, but if Tallas living meant Ezra got to be reunited with Mo, it was a worthwhile trade-off. Besides, now they could hand him over into FSC custody. He could face justice.

The lift slowed, and the screen in the wall suggested they were at their destination. Ezra just hoped Livia was still around here somewhere. It had only been a couple of minutes.

They didn't need long. They just needed to outlast Livia and whatever forces she had with her until the FSC finished boarding. As soon as General San'ri's people arrived, it would be over.

"Don't kill her," Ezra warned as he and Mo started down one of the long hallways that cut through the ship. "We need to let the FSC deal with her."

"You still trust them after all this?" she asked.

"I don't think we have much of a choice right now," Ezra said. "Either they're here to help, or we're caught between two enemies. I'd rather take my chances."

Mo's grunt sounded an awful lot like an agreement.

"Livia!" Ezra shouted, his voice echoing through the empty corridors. "Come out here!"

Now that he was thinking about it, he should've brought Shadow with them, but Kynn needed help, and Shadow knew this ship's systems a hell of a lot better than Mo would. Their mindbender talents would've been nice right about now, though.

"Livia!" Ezra shouted again. "The FSC is outside. You have to surrender!"

Only the sound of their boots echoed around them. But then a speaker in Mo's suit crackled. It sounded like it was coming from her gauntlet.

"Energy reading still on your level, three junctions ahead of you and moving toward a service lift," came Shadow's voice. "Someone is preparing the escape pods for release."

Shit. Ezra broke into a sprint, and Mo trailed just behind him.

They passed one junction, then the next, and the final. Ezra's chest heaved with the effort. They skidded around the corner, and sure enough, nearing the elevator doors were Livia and a retinue of six guards.

"Hey!" Ezra shouted.

Livia glanced over her shoulder. One of the guards reached for the elevator controls, but Mo pulled out her blaster and fired. The shot hit the wall, just close enough to make the guard back off.

"Ezra," Livia cooed as she turned to face him. "This is a surprise."

"Bullshit," he snapped.

She smiled at him. "Go away, Ezra. This doesn't concern you anymore."

"Weren't you going to have my mind wiped when you finished with your little coup?" Ezra asked.

"I was, but having you go down with the ship was the easier option." Livia pulled a gun from her hip and pointed it at him. "Now, if you'll excuse me, I've got to go."

Livia pulled the trigger. Ezra raised the Star Eater and hit the engage button. Heat burst to life in front of his face as a golden blade materialized. A dark aura wavered around it, and just like at Krytix's temple, Ezra's magic begged to be let free. It was all-consuming, a deafening roar in his ears and fervor in his veins. He didn't know what would happen if he let his fire out now, so he held it at bay and focused on the sword.

Livia's eyes widened again as her shot bounced harmlessly off the saber. "I knew you had it!" she shouted.

"General San'ri's boarding parties are en route," Shadow said through Mo's suit again. "Arriving in ninety seconds."

Ezra launched himself at Livia, all too aware of the air on his skin. He had no armor. Nothing to protect him from the soldiers surrounding her.

He blocked another shot as Livia took off down the hall, away from her guards.

"Go!" Mo shouted. "Follow her!"

Ezra hated to leave her with six guards to fight. He turned back for just a heartbeat, and instead of finding the soldiers chasing him, they were wrapped in purple tendrils. Mo's face turned red with the effort, then threw them all the opposite direction of Livia.

He had to remember not to underestimate Mo.

Or Livia.

Ezra scrambled after his cousin, the Star Eater drawn and pulsing with every beat of his heart. Livia rounded a corner up ahead. Ezra followed, gritting his teeth as he almost lost his footing. But he recovered and lunged forward, grabbing Livia's red cloak. He yanked hard, forcing her to the ground.

She angled her gun up. Ezra's sword arm moved before he could even think. He sliced through muscle and bone like they were nothing.

Livia screamed.

Something hot and unwelcome washed through Ezra, a satisfaction he'd never had during battle before. He was usually relieved or numb or even disgusted, but now? His blood sang, and his heart sped up. The Star Eater flared, almost as if to say it was responsible.

His heart thundered in his ears. His vision sharpened, and an overwhelming urge to stab Livia through the heart stuck in Ezra's mind.

This wasn't him. He couldn't do that.

Yes, you could, his mind seemed to say, like it was separate from him.

He wouldn't.

Ezra's arms and hands shook as he tried to disengage the blade. It was like it didn't *want* to be shut off. His thumb barely moved to the proper button, but he managed to force it there. The gold and black disappeared, leaving just the hilt in his hand.

"Fucking hell!" Livia roared, writhing on the ground and clutching her bloody arm to her chest.

"Ezra?" Mo yelled. "Ezra!" She rounded the corner, her chest heaving as she finally came to a stop. "Oh, fuck."

Ezra quickly attached the Star Eater back to his belt, unwilling to risk using it again. He double-checked his gun was in his holster, then grabbed Livia's weapon. She was still screaming, both obscenities and in pain. She certainly wasn't going to escape now.

"Does she have the artifacts?" Mo asked. "Hey, stop screaming," she snapped at Livia. "Where the fuck are the artifacts?"

Livia spat on the ground, her cheeks bright red. "You won't find them."

Had Livia hidden them? Passed them on to someone else? How'd they get off the ship when Ezra, Mo, and Shadow had all seen the telltale energy spikes?

"FSC have boarded," Shadow said through Mo's suit. "The general is en route. So is your other friend ..."

"Where are the artifacts?" Ezra asked.

Livia just spat again. He wrinkled his nose.

Shouts filled the hallway behind them, and a familiar voice yelled, "Lyre?"

"Here!" he called to the general, voice hoarse.

"You're shaking," Mo said, grabbing hold of his forearm.

Ezra looked down at his hands. Indeed, they were both shaking violently. His chest was too tight, but he somehow managed to breathe.

"Hey," Mo said gently. "You good?"

He tilted his head toward his hip—toward the Star Eater—then caught Mo's eye. Understanding and concern flashed across her face.

"Commander Lyre," General San'ri said as she rounded the corner behind them. Mo and Ezra turned in unison. "And you must be Mora Cevi."

Mo nodded.

"Situation has been neutralized, ma'am," Ezra said, shifting slightly as San'ri approached so that his hip was blocked by Mo's body. He didn't know if the FSC knew the truth about the artifacts, but he didn't want the commander to see the sword.

Whatever the Star Eater had done to him and made him feel, even for less than a minute, Ezra was not willing to hand that power over to someone else. Not because he wanted it but because he didn't trust anyone else with it.

"Chancellor Valtor," San'ri said, crossing her arms over her chest. Two soldiers in black and purple knelt down beside Livia, and one of them placed their hand on her injured arm, pushing healing light into her. "You put up quite the chase."

Livia glared up at the general.

With a sigh, San'ri said, "Chancellor Livia Valtor, you are under arrest for an attempted coup, first degree murder, third degree murder, and taking illegal control of a military vessel."

"This isn't over," Livia said, though whether it was to the general or Ezra, he wasn't sure. Hatred burned in her eyes, and the Star Eater pulsed against Ezra's hip again. It was like it was alive, begging for his attention.

"Take her away," San'ri said to the healers and the retinue of soldiers filing into the hallway. "See that her injury is treated, but keep her locked up under tight security. The Senate and other Triumvirate members have asked us to return to Aerilia as fast as possible."

As the FSC contingent dragged Livia away, San'ri focused on Ezra and Mo again. "What happened?"

"That's a ... very long story," Ezra said.

"I expect a full debrief, Commander," San'ri said. "I'd also like to debrief the team you hired."

"Is that necessary?" Mo asked.

"Yes. Today."

Mo huffed.

"And then you need to get some rest," San'ri said. "You look like shit, Ezra. I expect you to be presentable at the hearing."

"The hearing?" he asked.

"Chancellor Valtor's hearing. You'll need to testify. And your disciplinary hearing, since you disobeyed orders."

"Right." Ezra swallowed hard.

"You helped stop a coup. They'll take that into consideration," San'ri said. "Go back to your ship. My bridge crew will instruct you when to enter the hangar bay."

As San'ri walked away, Mo said, "General, wait."

San'ri paused.

"We have a prisoner on our ship," Mo said. "Tallas Bara, another Syndicate member. He was working with Chancellor Valtor and tried to carry out a hit on our team, including Ezra, several times."

San'ri's eyebrows rose. "Thank you. We'll collect him shortly." And then she was leaving again.

Ezra sighed and tilted his head back. None of this should have come as a surprise to him. And maybe it didn't. What really surprised him was the urge he felt to run away from it all. His head spun, and his heart still hurt.

"Ezra?" Mo asked.

He glanced down at her. Her eyebrows were furrowed.

"Yeah?"

"We should go find Kynn."

"Right. Right, of course," he said. "We should go find Kynn."

After all, they needed to get off this ship. They weren't done quite yet.

CHAPTER 59

Six days. It was going to take six days for them to travel from the Ulara System all the way back to Aerilia, at least on slow battleships like the *SD Triumph* and General San'ri's ship, the *SD Tenacity*. Ezra already missed *The Revenant*'s smaller size and faster hyperdrive. It was sitting in the enormous hangar bay of the *Tenacity*, being transported back to Aerilia with the rest of them.

Ezra did not like that *The Revenant* was sitting there in an FSC battleship, with the Star Eater secured just under their noses, especially if General San'ri or anyone else in the government had an inkling of what those artifacts could do—or if they believed what Livia and her father claimed about them, anyway. If Ezra hadn't seen it for himself and hadn't used the Star Eater, he wouldn't believe it.

General San'ri needed to debrief them—and Ezra needed to talk to Livia to figure out what the fuck she'd done with the Genesis Crystal and the Void Key.

As Ezra escorted Mo, Cass, and Kynn through the ship, their restlessness rubbed off on him. He used to find corridors like this comforting and familiar. But now? He just didn't know what to do anymore. Part of him trusted San'ri, but what about the rest of the government? The military? He needed answers.

The four of them had only had an hour to clean up—and agree on some things—before the general called them to her ready room. They would not tell her about the Star Eater or their communications with the gods, not unless it seemed absolutely necessary or safe.

"I'm surprised we don't have a bunch of armed guards surrounding us," Mo muttered as they entered the lift that would take them straight to the bridge.

"We're not prisoners," Ezra said.

"Sure feels like it."

"What do you think she's going to say to us?" Kynn asked.

"No idea," Ezra murmured.

The lift continued up in silence. None of them moved a muscle. Mo was especially rigid, and it looked like she was trying to not obviously favor her right side. Ezra frowned. Had she gotten hurt and he hadn't noticed? Was her soltherin wearing off already? She needed to see a doctor if that was the case, to try to understand why. It usually lasted longer. He'd try to get her in with someone when they were back on Aerilia—if she was open to it, anyway.

As soon as the lift stopped, the doors slid open and revealed a familiarly busy bridge. Officers rushed around their respective stations, their black and indigo uniforms perfectly crisp despite the chaos of the day. Ezra led his friends past it, taking a sharp left down a short corridor that led to the general's ready room.

The door slid open as they approached, and Shadow walked out, their long ears pinned back. They stood to the side and motioned for the bounty hunters to enter first. And as Ezra passed Shadow, they pressed something into his palm. A data stick.

"Keep what you know to yourself," Shadow whispered. "Read between the lines once you're off the ship."

Ezra shot a quick glance at Mo, Cass, and Kynn. None of them seemed to have noticed, because they kept walking into the general's ready room. Shadow strode down the hall like nothing had happened. Ezra frowned, tucked the device into his pocket, and hurried after the others to face whatever it was San'ri was going to say to them.

The general sat behind a long silver and black table. Her back was to the viewing screen that showed hyperspace zipping past outside. She stared at the door, fingers steepled in front of her mouth. Although Ezra didn't answer directly to General San'ri—there were ranks of officers below her that oversaw day-to-day operations—this wasn't the first time he'd been on this ship or in her ready room. It was still sparsely decorated. There were no personal affects, just the FSC's logo and motto on the wall perpendicular to her desk.

In duty, we rise. With honor, we fight. Ezra squared his shoulders as he stopped next to Mo, Cass, and Kynn.

"Commander," San'ri said. Her gaze flicked to the others. "Bounty hunters."

"You wanted to debrief us, ma'am?" Ezra asked.

"Yes," she said. "I'm concerned, Ezra, not just about you disobeying a direct order but what's been uncovered about your cousin. What do you know? How did this come to unfold?"

"I can't speak to Chancellor Valtor's actions," Ezra said. "You'll have to talk to her."

"My interrogators will work with her as soon as she's out of surgery. What happened?"

"She was going to kill me. I did what I was trained to do: disarm the enemy but spare their life if possible."

At the word "disarm," Kynn smirked a little.

"Is something funny, Mister Sathir?" the general asked.

"No," he said, straightening.

Gods help us, Ezra thought. If they were out there, listening, maybe they'd spare him from having to go through all that lay ahead, including this conversation.

San'ri turned back to Ezra. "Start from the beginning."

And so, Ezra did. He explained what had happened on Miduna, the theory about underground markets for stolen artifacts, and Livia's belief that ancient relics could be the key to stopping the Ascended. He said they were just trying to figure out who had the hit out on him but had stumbled into what they thought was that underground operation, and that was how they'd ended up on Mor'vex and Andarix. Sticking as close to the truth as possible was the best way to lie, especially considering what he'd already told Command weeks ago. If he changed his story now, it would just be suspicious.

Lying to a commanding officer didn't feel good. All the lies he'd already told and orders he'd disobeyed hung heavy in the back of his mind. But he'd had to. It was the only way. And he'd stopped a coup.

The words on the wall near San'ri's desk caught Ezra's attention. *In duty, we rise. With honor, we fight.* Maybe the quest had started off for selfish reasons, but Ezra liked to think he'd done what was right in the end. He'd stuck to his principles and tried to protect the Federation.

San'ri continued with her questions, focused mainly on the bounty hunters. They explained their involvement, surprising Ezra with their ability to stick strictly to the sanitized version of events. He shouldn't have been.

"Thank you for your time," General San'ri said.

That would usually be a dismissal, but Ezra said, "What about Chancellor Valtor?"

"What about her?"

"How'd this get started? How deep does this go? How much support does—or did—she have?"

San'ri pursed her lips. Her ears pinned back slightly. "Deeper than we expected," she said, "but not as deep as we feared. She managed to siphon off money from her own reelection campaign coffers as well as other projects, and she convinced and bribed multiple lower-level officers and platoons to join her."

"And Vanguards," Ezra said.

San'ri dipped her head. "And Vanguards."

"Which shouldn't have happened."

"No, none of it should have."

"How'd she do it?"

"That's still unclear. Lots of back channels. We only caught on about the hit out on you because of what you told us on Vonnoth. We might have missed her transmissions otherwise. The Ascended attack on Mor'vex was strange enough. Then the *SD Triumph* stopped responding, she went missing, and we started piecing it together. There may still be more to uncover, but we've arrested all major players that we've been able to identify."

"She mentioned that she had some people at the battle on Mor'vex," Ezra said. "Soldiers turned spies, I guess? She said she has people everywhere."

"Most likely," San'ri said. "As I said, we've identified as many as we've been able to."

Ezra studied the general carefully. She was often hard to read, sometimes harsh but almost always fair in all the dealings he'd had with her over the years. He didn't *think* she was lying, but he still wasn't entirely sure. He couldn't be sure about much these days.

What he really wanted was to go talk to Livia, but she would be under heavy guard, especially once she woke up from surgery. Unfortunately, he couldn't risk someone overhearing what it was he wanted to ask her about, and she'd probably refuse to answer his questions anyway.

"Well, I appreciate you sending Shadow after me, ma'am," Ezra said. "Even if Livia intervened. And I'm sorry we lost Atom and Fang."

"You're a good Vanguard, Commander," San'ri said. Her gaze flicked to the bounty hunters. "Thank you for helping stop the Chancellor."

The three of them just nodded. They'd barely moved a muscle and hadn't said a word unless spoken to.

"We'll talk more on Aerilia," San'ri said. "Be prepared for questions, Commander. Your hearing won't be short, but I'll lobby for you to receive no punishment."

Great.

"Appreciated, ma'am," Ezra said.

"Dismissed."

General San'ri's sharp tone left little room for argument, and the bounty hunters didn't even try to stick around. Ezra hurried after them, leading them once again through the ship's winding halls and all the way back to *The Revenant*. They'd been offered sleeping quarters outside of their ship, but the bounty hunters had declined. So had Ezra. Even if the FSC had come to their rescue, Ezra felt safer being locked within *The Revenant*'s walls.

Especially with the knowledge that Intelligence didn't know exactly how deep the coup ran. Maybe someone would try to exact revenge on Ezra now that Livia was in custody. Maybe some of her soldiers would break out of the brig and try to come after him. He wanted to sleep easy for at least one night, and doing so in Mo's ship seemed like the only possible solution.

As soon as they were inside *The Revenant*, Ezra initiated the lock sequence. As the ramp retracted and cargo doors closed, he pulled the data stick Shadow had given him out of his pocket and held it up for the others to see. "We need to talk."

"Why don't I like the sound of this?" Cass asked as Ezra led the way upstairs.

The others started going into the command room, but Ezra said, "No, let's stay here. We're not going to load this thing in yet."

"Now I *really* don't like the sound of this," Kynn said, sliding into the middle of the booth behind the table. Cass joined him.

"Spill, Lyre," Mo said from where she leaned against the kitchen counter on the opposite side of the room. She crossed her arms tightly over her chest.

Maybe fifteen feet separated them, but Ezra had never felt farther away from her than in that moment. He wanted to go to her, take her in his arms, and share their second kiss. Thank her for coming after him, for helping him with Livia. But she looked so closed off now. Maybe it was just the conversation with the general that had her on edge.

Ezra pushed his shoulders back. "Shadow gave this to me as they left the general's office," Ezra said. "They told me not to open it until we were off the *SD Tenacity*."

"Why would that be important?" Cass asked.

He shrugged. "Probably classified information? Maybe they're afraid it would somehow set off a system alarm or something of the sort?" For all of Ezra's training, he didn't know that much about FSC information security measures. "I think it's something about Livia's coup."

"Why would they try to help us?" Mo asked.

"Because their team was working on uncovering what she was up to," Ezra said. "And I told them some of what Livia was up to after she imprisoned us. I can only assume Shadow knows something pertinent that Command doesn't want me—or us—finding out."

"The true nature of the artifacts?" Kynn asked.

Ezra shrugged again. "Maybe."

"I certainly don't like that," Cass said. "You think we're safe during transport?"

"Yes," he said. "Safe enough."

"Oh, good," Kynn drawled. "Safe *enough*."

"Don't go mingling among the crew," Ezra said. "I certainly won't. Best to keep our heads down and an eye on the Star Eater."

"What happened when you used it?" Mo asked. "I've never seen you look so scared."

"It felt like in Krytix's temple," Ezra said. "Like it was calling to me and my magic. Like it wanted me to use it more, like it was also influencing my mind. I could barely even turn the damn thing off again, and it made me …" He shook his head. "It was like being violent satisfied something in me. I feel normal now, but it definitely isn't *just* a blade."

"Maybe that's why Krytix warned us about the sword," Mo said. "Maybe it does something to the user."

"Or something to sunshapers," he said. "Whatever the fuck it was, I don't want to touch it again."

"Should we find out if it does the same to one of us?" Kynn asked. "Or should we destroy it?"

Ezra shook his head again. "I don't think either of those is a good idea."

"So how do we figure out what that was, exactly?" Cass asked.

"We should try to find another of Krytix's temples," Mo said. "I spoke to Voxarus, and they suggested that they'd been in conversation with Krytix. That Krytix saw us fighting on Mor'vex, and that Voxarus saw us fighting on Andarix and Pyralis both."

Ezra's eyebrows raised. He almost asked why she hadn't disclosed that sooner, but it wasn't exactly like they'd been reunited for all that long. "Did they say anything else?"

"They called me Starborne again," Mo said. When Cass and Kynn asked what that meant, she said, "Keeper Vizla said it was the ancient term used for champions of the gods. Voxarus said I am Starborne because I was fighting for them at all three temples. So I guess that makes all of us Starborne."

Ezra turned the word over in his mind. *Starborne*. Were they really champions of the Eternal Ones now?

"And they warned me that if Ikna's champions get ahold of the artifacts, chaos will be unleashed. Which I suppose we already knew," she said. "But we're not the only Starborne, it seems."

"So, who?" Kynn asked. "Livia?"

"She's got to have more people helping her," Ezra said. "I think it's got to expand beyond what the FSC has uncovered so far. Livia's many things, but she's neither foolish nor ill-prepared. A bit disorganized, maybe, but she wouldn't go into this fight with just one star destroyer."

Groaning, Cass scrubbed at her face. "Great. So where are the Genesis Crystal and Void Key?"

"I don't know," Ezra said. "Both were surrounded by what looked like magic before we left Pyralis. Livia definitely did something to them. Probably passed them off to someone working with her."

Mo frowned. "But we saw the energy spike within her ship."

"Maybe she got them off the ship somehow," Kynn said.

Cass groaned again.

"Maybe whatever Shadow gave me will point us in the right direction," Ezra said. "It's like I said before. We should lay low until we get back to Aerilia and the hearings begin. Rest. Recover. See if Doctor Valtor's notes can tell us anything else."

Ezra didn't actually know if Shadow had any information that would help them continue the search, but there had to be something. There just had to be, and he'd be damned if he didn't find it.

Chapter 60

Watching Tallas flail and scream while being dragged away in handcuffs had to be one of the most beautiful things Mo had ever seen.

There was something even poetic about the fact that they were on Aerilia, surrounded by the skyline Mo had once seen while barely crawling out of the warehouse where he'd left her to die. She'd never forget the sight of him being forcibly taken into FSC custody. The ache in her chest eased just a little. Even if it didn't erase the terrible things in her past, knowing that he was going into the government's custody for treason meant she wouldn't have to see him ever again.

"Mo?" Cass asked.

"Hey." Mo gave her best friend a tight smile. "You ready?"

"Hardly," Cass said, gesturing to the military headquarters looming before them.

It was a strange thing, landing *The Revenant* in an FSC shipyard and heading in for an official debriefing with some of the highest ranking leaders in the entire military. Mo certainly didn't care for it—she hated meetings, and she still didn't like the FSC—but if it meant finally getting justice for what Tallas had done *and* stopping Livia Valtor? Mo could handle the discomfort for a little while longer. She'd been sitting in discomfort for a very long time.

Ezra was far ahead of them, speaking with General San'ri and several other very official looking people. That ache in Mo's chest returned but for a different reason. They hadn't exactly had a chance to talk, or perhaps more accurately, Mo had been avoiding him. In the six days they'd been stuck on the *SD Tenacity*, Mo had taken Ezra's suggestions seriously: staying far away from the FSC crew and resting as much as possible. Her body had basically given out the moment she let herself lie in bed, and Ezra had been busy fielding meetings with the general anyway.

"Couldn't tell a guy you were leaving?" Kynn asked with a laugh as he jogged up behind them. "I thought we were doing this together!"

"Sorry," Cass said. "We figured you'd just catch up."

"Always leaving me to catch up," he said, throwing his arm around Cass's shoulders and jostling her lightly. "This has been one hell of a mission."

"And we're still not done," Cass said.

A little over two months prior, Mo and Cass had been hunting low-level criminals like Gideon Benre. But now? Now, they had something so much more important to do. They still didn't know where the Genesis Crystal or the Void Key were. Mo didn't understand how the items were just *gone*, considering they'd seen those familiar energy surges within the ship's systems. If Livia was Ikna's champion, maybe Ikna had somehow used her chaos magic to do something to the relics.

Mo shook her head. They'd have to figure that out later. There was nothing she could do about it at that moment. The important thing was that the Star Eater was locked away on their ship. They had to keep it safe.

As the three of them made their way deeper into FSC headquarters, Mo shoved her discomfort down again. The only thing that made this bearable were Cass and Kynn beside her and Ezra waiting for them just a hundred feet away.

He smiled at her, and she tried to smile back, but it was hard. Seeing him back in his uniform, here among all the other soldiers and officers, was just a reminder that they were different. The more time she'd spent with him on *The Revenant*, the easier it had been to pretend he was just part of their team. Now, she couldn't ignore reality. He looked like he belonged here. Mo didn't. She never would.

"You three ready?" Ezra asked as they neared.

"Ready," Mo lied.

Ezra led them through the base, past offices and meeting rooms, up an elevator, and down empty hallways. It was clear they were only seeing a fraction of the building, and Mo couldn't fathom how truly big this place was. Finally, Ezra stopped in front of two glass double doors. Inside, five officers waited at a long table.

"This might take a while," Ezra said. "But it won't be that bad."

"Says you," Cass mumbled.

Ezra chuckled. "Come on."

He led them inside, then made introductions as everyone sat down. Mo ignored most of it, focusing on General San'ri, who sat in the middle of the opposite side of the table.

"Well," San'ri said with a sigh, "shall we begin?"

By the time they were done answering the FSC's questions, Mo wanted to tear her hair out. The officers went round and round in their discussion, doubling back and rehashing the same events over and over. She couldn't decide if they were being thorough or just plain dense. Maybe both.

But the FSC seemed not to know about the artifacts actually containing the magic of the Eternal Ones. They certainly had more of the story than Mo wanted them to, but with their vast network of informants, and with what Ezra had told them all the way back on Vonnoth, it wasn't a surprise.

Whatever the case, Mo's head hurt. And her heart hurt, because during the meeting, the officers had asked Ezra when he was going to return to duty—assuming his hearing went the way they all thought it would. She didn't want him to leave, and he seemed to want to continue on this quest with them, but maybe she was reading the situation all wrong. He looked so at ease here at FSC Command. Maybe he wouldn't want to leave it again.

Ezra walked with them back to *The Revenant*. The four of them were quiet, surrounded by the sounds of Aerilia and FSC headquarters both. Ships taking off, soldiers running drills in the expansive courtyard, the hum of shuttle traffic high above. Mo tried to make her body relax, but she couldn't.

They unlocked the ship and went inside, and Mo was about to ask Ezra when he was leaving when he punched in the lock sequence for the cargo doors.

"We need to look at that data stick," he said to the three of them. "Let's get out of here."

"And go where?" Mo asked.

"The shipyard by my apartment. We can be there in less than an hour."

They filed into the cockpit one by one and dropped into the empty seats. Mo took the captain's chair while Cass joined her up at the helm. Air traffic was lighter than Mo expected for a late afternoon on the city-planet. They snagged the second to last spot in the shipyard, and as they powered down *The Revenant*, Mo sank deeper into her seat. At least they were away from the FSC for now.

Kynn said something about putting on a pot of coffee as he excused himself, and Ezra went into the command room to begin pulling up the files Shadow had provided. Mo and Cass stayed where they were.

"I'm proud of you," Cass said.

"What?" Mo frowned. "Why?"

"For not killing Tallas where he stood that day. I almost didn't have the strength."

"I didn't do it out of compassion," Mo said.

"I know. You were thinking several steps ahead. I wasn't. I wanted to see him drop dead."

Mo had wanted that too. To know he *truly* wouldn't ever show his face again. "I figured saving the Universe was more important than a personal vendetta," she said.

"And saving Ezra," Cass added quietly.

"And that." Mo wouldn't deny it. She just wished she knew how to talk to Ezra now. But she felt all over the place, like a scrambled mess.

"I'm glad we gave him a chance," Cass said.

Mo glanced over at her best friend. "Me too."

"Even if the rest of this blows," Cass added.

Mo laughed. She had never, in her wildest dreams, thought she would get caught up in stopping a coup among mortals and preventing a chaotic Eternal One from escaping her celestial prison. But here she was, stuck right in the gods damn middle of it.

Mo shoved out of her seat. "Let's go see what Ezra's found."

He was already at the holo table, pulling up files for them to look at.

"What's it say?" Cass asked as she circled to the opposite side of the table from Ezra. Kynn strode in behind her.

"Not much," Ezra said. "There are only three files. One is blank except for a set of coordinates here on Aerilia, along with a date and time nine days from today. It's just before Livia's pretrial hearing is set to begin.

The second is a series of decoded messages about the hits Livia put out on me and her father."

"Didn't we already know about that?" Kynn asked.

"Yes, but the third is something else." Ezra pushed a few controls, and a short document appeared. "It keeps noticing all in silent acts. What a keen eye. Seemingly outraged visitors are truly horrible. Please review it meticulously evermore."

"What the fuck does that mean?" Kynn asked.

Ezra's eyebrows furrowed. "Shadow told me to read between the lines." Before Mo even had a chance to put the letters together, he said, "Ikna is awake. Sorvath Prime."

Sorvath Prime? That was the capital planet of the Ascended. Mo frowned.

"Does that mean Ikna's out of prison and living with the Ascended?" Kynn asked.

"I don't think so," Cass said. "That doesn't match what Mo's encountered with the other gods."

"No, it certainly doesn't," Mo said.

"I think it means the Ascended know something," Ezra said slowly. "Or are planning something, maybe."

"And what about those coordinates?" Kynn asked.

Ezra toggled to a map of Aerilia and entered the coordinates. The hologram changed from a view of the entire city to a targeted location far southwest of the equator.

"What's there?" Mo asked. It didn't look like much of anything to her.

"Nothing important as far as I know," Ezra said. "That's in the middle of a public park. I guess Shadow wants to meet us there, or thinks there's something important we need to see."

"Are we sure we can trust them?" Mo hadn't gotten to meet the Intelligence officer except for one quick conversation after General San'ri's forces had arrived to stop Livia that day on the *SD Triumph*.

"I think we can," Ezra said.

"I don't see what choice we have," Cass said. "Unless we can figure out what's going on over on Sorvath Prime, but that seems unlikely on our own."

Silence filled the room. Discomfort settled in Mo's chest.

"Will you stay?" she asked Ezra, the words almost catching in her throat. "Here. With us." *With me*, she wanted to add, but didn't. Couldn't. "Are you going to keep working this with us?"

"It's not an official contract anymore ..." He trailed off, then sucked in a deep breath. "Are you sure you want to work it?"

"This is bigger than any contract," Mo said. "Are you in, Lyre? Will you stay and work it with us?"

Ezra smiled at her. "If you'll have me."

Kynn slapped him on the shoulder. "Consider this your official welcome to the team, Commander."

There was no turning back now. The four of them were in this together, for better or worse. They worked well together, but there was so much they still had to figure out. So much they had to unravel before any of them—before anyone—would be safe.

The artifacts.

The Eternal Ones.

The four of them, Starborne.

Whatever lay ahead, Mo knew she couldn't afford to hesitate. None of them could. Not when the artifacts were out there in the wrong hands.

They had to find them, no matter the cost.

To be continued

Books by H.E. Bauman

The Starborne Saga

The Sundered Stars (Book 1)

The Darkened Skies series

Forged by Flames: A Darkened Skies Prequel

Under Darkened Skies (Book 1)

Into Whispering Shadows (Book 2)

Amid Twisted Chaos (Book 3)

Beyond Veiled Destinies (Book 4)

Toward Dawning Light (Book 5)

ACKNOWLEDGMENTS

This book kicks off my second series as a published author, and I couldn't have done it without so many people helping me, supporting me, and cheering me on.

To my husband and family: As strange as it may seem even after seven books, I still appreciate the silent support. It's probably going to be one of my quirks forever, but not having to talk at length about my creative process is a welcome reprieve and safe space. Love you all.

To my friends: Your excitement for my books will never not make me want to cry. You continue to be pillars to me, both in my publishing journey and outside of it, and I can't thank you enough for that.

To Sarah, Kayla, Laura, Michelle, and Kïrsten: Your feedback as alpha and beta readers helped shape *The Sundered Stars* into what it was always meant to be. You're all amazing!

To Jeanine: Look at us, another book done together! Your editor's eye remains invaluable, and I'm so grateful to have you on my team.

And finally, to all my readers, thank you for being here, whether you've been here since the Darkened Skies series or are new to my work.

About Author

H.E. Bauman writes romantic fantasy stories with epic worlds, defiant heroines, and sizzling slow burns. She is the author of the Darkened Skies series and Starborne Saga, with more books planned for the future. When she's not writing, you can find her playing tennis, immersed in a video game, or spending time with her family.

If you want to get in touch, visit H.E.'s website or follow her on social media.